MORE THAN YOU KNOW

BOOK YOUR PLACE ON OUR WEBSITE AND MAKE THE READING CONNECTION!

We've created a customized website just for our very special readers, where you can get the inside scoop on everything that's going on with Zebra, Pinnacle and Kensington books.

When you come online, you'll have the exciting opportunity to:

- View covers of upcoming books
- Read sample chapters
- Learn about our future publishing schedule (listed by publication month and author)
- Find out when your favorite authors will be visiting a city near you
- Search for and order backlist books from our online catalog
- Check out author bios and background information
- Send e-mail to your favorite authors
- Meet the Kensington staff online
- Join us in weekly chats with authors, readers and other guests
- Get writing guidelines
- AND MUCH MORE!

**Visit our website at
http://www.kensingtonbooks.com**

MORE THAN YOU KNOW

Jennifer Gracen

ZEBRA BOOKS
KENSINGTON PUBLISHING CORP.
http://www.kensingtonbooks.com

ZEBRA BOOKS are published by

Kensington Publishing Corp.
119 West 40th Street
New York, NY 10018

All Kensington titles, imprints, and distributed lines are available at special quantity discounts for bulk purchases for sales promotion, premiums, fund-raising, educational, or institutional use.

Special book excerpts or customized printings can also be created to fit specific needs. For details, write or phone the office of the Kensington Sales Manager: Attn.: Sales Department. Kensington Publishing Corp., 119 West 40th Street, New York, NY 10018. Phone: 1-800-221-2647.

Zebra and the Z logo Reg. U.S. Pat. & TM Off.

First Printing: January 2016
ISBN-13: 978-1-4201-3914-3
ISBN-10: 1-4201-3914-2

eISBN-13: 978-1-4201-3915-0
eISBN-10: 1-4201-3915-0

10 9 8 7 6 5 4 3 2 1

Printed in the United States of America

*I dedicate this book to my dear friend, Jeannie Moon,
with more gratitude and love than I can express.*

*You're the one who told me, "You wrote the wrong book
first." And I started this one. You beta read and critiqued
every chapter of this manuscript.
You helped me make this book as good
as it could be before I sent it out.
Then you helped me find who might be a good fit
as an editor for this series, and your hunch was right.
Then you introduced me to an agent,
who now represents me. Not to mention your constant
friendship over the past few years,
sharing of knowledge, guidance, unflagging support,
and all I've learned from you about the
romance writing industry in general. Simply put,
you were instrumental in getting this
particular book published.
I don't know if it would have been without all of your help.*

*"Thank you" doesn't seem like enough, so yes, Jeannie,
this one is for you.*

Acknowledgments

There are so many to thank for this book being published. I'm so grateful to and appreciative of everyone who had a part in this journey. But most of all, I must mention:

Huge thanks to my wonderful, lovely editor, the talented Esi Sogah, who believed in this story, and in me, and brought me into the fold. My gratitude to you is boundless.

Thank you to my copy editor, the art department, publicity, marketing—everyone at Kensington/Zebra Shout who has been involved with this book. Your efforts are appreciated!

Thanks to my literary agent, Stephany Evans of FinePrint, who initially took me on in good faith. Your help, insight, and support have been so appreciated and valued.

Thanks to the first beta readers of this story: Jeannie Moon, Patty Blount, Lisa Jo Brennan, Gordon Bonnet, and Karla Nellenbach. Your feedback, cheers, and suggestions helped me make this a better book.

To my core family—my lioness mom, Linda; my artist dad, Rob; my creative brother, Jamie; and Natasha, Kyle, Teri, and Stevie—thank you for everything and I love you all so much. Short and sweet, but by now I think you know how I cherish you.

To my sons, Josh and Danny, the most important people in my life—I am honored to be your mom. You're my greatest gift. You're my brightest light, my inspiration, my motivation, and my reason. I love you both more than I can ever express.

To my friends, both local and online, writers and non-writers—your daily encouragement, support, caring, and enthusiasm has been such a lifeline for me, especially in the past three years. I can't name you all, because I'm blessed that there's so many of you . . . thank you for your friendship.

This round, I must send special hugs to Karen DeLabar, Amy Weaver, Janelle Jensen, Claudine Kiffer, Jolyse Barnett, Maggie Van Well, Lisa Guilfoil, KD McCrite, February Grace, Randi Pellett, Joann Centrone, Christie Latorre, Robyn Reitano, Jenny Beal, Tobi Printz Platnick, Maryann Judge, and my writing sister Jeannie Moon. Your unwavering caring and support lifts and sustains me.

Thanks to LIRW, CTRWA, and Team Gracen on Facebook for your support.

Thank you, most of all, to the readers. Without you, the ride wouldn't happen or matter. That you took some time to read my book means the world to me, and I'm beyond grateful.

Chapter One

Long Island, New York—May

Looking for a beautiful and talented woman was a tough job, but someone had to do it. Dane Harrison had such specifics in mind, he trusted no one else to find what he needed. So he'd chosen to do it himself.

And going to different bars and clubs throughout Manhattan three or four nights a week wasn't one of the toughest jobs he'd ever had. In fact, it'd been a blast.

He'd seen more singers than he could count at this point. Some mildly attractive, some a bit trashy, some sweet and pretty, some of them downright hot. Dane loved women in every size, shape, and color. That wasn't the issue. The voice and presence; those were the important things. He wanted star quality.

Some were better singers than others. Some had charisma, but not a good enough voice to match. Out of all the singers he'd seen perform, so far only three had a combination of a quality voice, stage presence, beauty, and yes, even the right personality for what he had in mind. He wanted the woman to be likable.

Whoever he chose would be the headlining act at the lounge in his brand-new hotel. To say he had high standards for this job was an understatement. But he was determined. And if anyone could find an amazing woman, even in a city as big as New York City, Dane Harrison could.

He hadn't been nicknamed "Golden Boy" for nothing—he had natural charm. The kind that wasn't sleazy, or smarmy, or an act. His charm was endearing, contagious, and drew people to him wherever he went. Especially female people. They flocked to him, had since he was a boy. As his brothers always said—with a touch of admiration from his older brother and a touch of disdain from his younger one—he was "born with the touch." So how hard could it be to find a gorgeous female singer to work for him?

Harder than he'd realized, actually.

Something that should have been an easy task had turned into a major pain in the ass. He'd been so convinced that he'd find the right woman easily, and now time was running out. The new hotel was opening in only five weeks, and he hadn't secured the entertainment yet. Dane slumped a bit in the back of the hired town car that was taking him from his spacious loft apartment in Tribeca to the north shore of Long Island. His sister had suggested a club with a female singer that she'd heard about, and he'd decided to meet her there. Being with Tess would be relaxing; she always grounded him. He needed that, because this week, he'd started to do something he very rarely did: worry.

Maybe his standards were *too* high. Maybe the kind of woman he envisioned finding for the gig didn't really exist. Most of them had been fine, and some of them, more than fine. Possible contenders. But his gut just didn't . . . he hadn't *felt* it. And he always went with his gut.

The sleek car had already pulled onto the Cross Island Parkway when his cell phone rang. He pulled it out of his pocket, glanced at the caller ID, and answered with a smile. "Hey, Tess. Almost at the restaurant, maybe another twenty minutes or so."

"Damn," Tess sighed. "I hoped you'd be running late, or I wouldn't be. I'm still at the office."

"Oh." Dane let out a chuckle. Tess worked in midtown Manhattan. "Well, that puts a crimp in our plans, huh?"

"Yeah. I'm so sorry. But listen, I can make it up to you, and you'll thank me later," Tess wheedled. "You'll still stay over tonight, right? I should be home by the time you get back after the club. I'll see you in the morning?"

"Yes, you will."

"Good. Because I really don't know what time I'll get out of here. Gotta finish this proposal."

"Don't work too hard," Dane said with affection. "And hey, don't forget to eat something."

"I won't, Mother Hen," she joked. "My assistant already ordered me dinner, it's on its way."

"Good." Dane looked out the window at the passing scenery as the driver maneuvered the car from the Cross Island to the Long Island Expressway. It was late spring, and the trees were finally budding, a sea of yellow-green and white and pink. The sky was a deep blue above the branches as the sun had just set, but since they were heading east, the changing colors of the sky were behind him.

Tess had called him the day before to tell him about the club on Long Island, and its singer. "It's a martini bar, over in Glen Bay. On Friday nights, they have a regular singer who does everything from standards to Adele. Jeannie and her husband went there with friends two weeks ago and according to Jeannie, this woman's got a knockout voice, and is something of a knockout herself. So, since you haven't found your chanteuse yet, want to go check it out? I'll come with you."

"Sure," he'd said. "Your best friend is a good enough reference for me. Why not? I've been looking all over Manhattan; maybe I just didn't look far enough east. Frankly, I never considered looking on Long Island." He hadn't. And was getting desperate . . .

Now, Tess sighed. "I wish I could go with you tonight! Damn. Sounds like it'd be a good evening. I always have fun with you."

"That's what I'm here for, Tesstastic: a good time. Rain check. We'll do it again," Dane assured his younger sister. Only two years apart, they were more than siblings, they were truly friends, and he adored her. "Everything else okay with you?"

"Nothing new and earthshaking since yesterday morning," she said with dry amusement.

"Get back to work, then, so you get home before midnight. And eat, Missy!"

"I will, I will! Stop nagging me. Go have a good time for both of us."

"Not a problem," Dane said assuredly.

Tess chuckled. "Of course it isn't. Who am I talking to? Wherever you go, you have a good time. It's just a given. I think fun finds *you*."

"Yes, I do," Dane agreed with a grin. "And yes, it does."

* * *

By the time Dane strolled into the martini lounge, it was close to ten-thirty. It was a nice enough place; not as worn as some of the bars he'd gone to in the city, but not as upscale as some of the others he'd frequented. And to him, there was a distinctly different vibe in a Manhattan bar or club compared to a Long Island one—or anywhere else, really. New York City had a feel and energy all its own. Nothing and nowhere matched it.

He'd grown up on Long Island, not far from where he was now. The second son of a multigenerational, multimillionaire family, Dane had been born and raised in one of the most affluent communities on the Gold Coast of the North Shore. He had led a charmed life, despite his family's dramas, explosions, and scandals. When it was time to go to college, he got out of that mega-mansion of misery and went out of state. But neither his lively years as an undergrad at Duke nor his time at the Wharton School of Business could keep him from returning to New York by his midtwenties. He was a true New Yorker, it was in his blood. He loved living in the city, he loved the business he'd started and grown there, and he loved the vitality. He thrived on it. Long Island, though nice, just felt . . . muted. Smaller. Quieter. And that wasn't for him. Dane was all about color and sound, living large, taking life for a ride.

He smirked as he remembered Tess joking that a good time always found him. It was true. He loved life, so it loved him back. He never dwelled on negative things. There was no reason to. He was an upbeat, satisfied man, living a charmed life, so he just went with the flow.

The bar was dimly lit as he found a small table for two in the middle of the room. The waitress he'd passed on the way in brought his drink to him as he sat down. He'd heard the last bars of a song as he'd entered the midsize room, but now it was all applause. The audience obviously liked the singer, or the song, a lot—plenty of the gigs he'd gone to recently didn't get such an enthusiastic response. In fact, some of the patrons were too cool or sophisticated to acknowledge the entertainment, much less applaud like this audience was. This, to Dane, was a good sign. He sipped his dirty martini and glanced around to gauge the crowd before he looked at the singer.

But when he looked up and saw the woman onstage, everything just . . . shimmered. Maybe it was the air around her, maybe it was the woman herself, maybe there was something in his drink? Dane experienced something akin to when he'd done mushrooms back in college. The air seemed to actually twinkle and glow. It was the damnedest thing. Dane sat very still as he stared at her. Dark red hair that fell to her shoulders, big dark eyes, delicate pale skin, and an hourglass figure made for debauchery, encased in a navy blue sheath dress and matching stilettos. Beautiful and sultry, her presence was powerful, tangible. Time seemed to hang for a few seconds, spin out and slow . . . then everything was normal again as the singer spoke.

"Thank you so much," she murmured into the microphone, and Dane snapped out of his moment of . . . whatever the hell that was. He scrubbed his hands over his face as if it would help break whatever spell he'd been under for a few seconds.

"Kelvin here . . ." The vocalist gestured to the thin African-American man who tinkled the keys of the piano lightly behind her, a knowing grin on her face.

"He and I have done gigs together since our college days. That was a long, long time ago, in a galaxy far, far away. . . ." The audience laughed at the *Star Wars* reference. "This was one of the first songs he taught me, and it's one of my favorites. Hope you like it."

In a rich, smooth alto, she began to sing an old standard, "A Nightingale Sang in Berkeley Square". And looking at her, listening to her, taking in her polished presentation and charisma . . . Dane felt it in his gut. Her. *Her.* He just knew. Dane drew in a long breath, exhaled it slowly, and took a deep swallow of his drink. The search was over. He'd found whom he'd been looking for to headline at his new hotel.

Now all he had to do, after a talk with the bar owner and a quick background check, was convince her of that.

Julia Shay smiled at her audience as they showered her with applause. "Thanks so much," she said with genuine appreciation. "Thank you. Kelvin and I are going to take a little break, then we'll be back for the third and final set. Stick around." She replaced the microphone in its stand and made her way off the tiny riser that served as a stage. As she passed the piano to head toward the back hallway, her accompanist, Kelvin Jones, rose and followed her.

"Damn good set, sister," he said as they entered what served as a small dressing room. It had a table and chair in front of a mirror on the wall, and one leather couch that had seen better days. Kelvin flopped onto it at the same time Julia did, and they both exhaled. She put her feet up on his lap, careful not to let the bottoms of her shoes dirty his black suit. "I hate heels," she muttered. "My feet are killing me."

"I know, Princess," Kelvin said. He took off her four-inch navy stilettos, dropped them to the floor, and began to massage her left foot.

She threw her head back, closed her eyes, and moaned a guttural moan. "Ohhh, thank you. Damn. Your fingers really are magical." A smirk twisted her mouth. "Talented fingers, my man. Between the piano, your gift for massage . . . too bad you play for the wrong team."

"Excuse me, but I do *not*," Kelvin told her with a dismissive flip. He shook his head, making the short dreadlocks sway. "I like my team just fine, thank you. You may be pretty, but the men I date are prettier than you."

"God, it's sad but true," she said ruefully, and they laughed.

Julia and Kelvin had met during their freshman year at the Berklee College of Music in Boston. During the first week, he sat down next to her in a Composition class and they'd hit it off immediately. They'd been close friends ever since. Sometimes, more like family. Which was good, since Julia barely had any family of her own. After her life had fallen apart, she'd moved back to Long Island because she'd grown up there, and Kelvin had gone to New York with her. He and Randi, her best friend since childhood, were all the family she had.

She lay still, letting her limbs relax after standing onstage for almost an hour, and trying not to wrinkle her navy silk dress. "Speaking of pretty boys, can I ask you something?"

"About pretty boys? One of my favorite subjects," Kelvin said. "Ask away."

"Did you see that guy sitting alone, midway back, really handsome—"

"Yesss," Kelvin almost purred. "He's more than pretty, honey. He's smokin' hot. I'm proud of you for noticing."

"Well, yeah, I noticed him." She was underplaying it; the guy was seriously gorgeous. Dark curly hair, a full, sexy mouth on a square jaw that seemed to be carved from marble, broad shoulders, and blazing blue eyes that hadn't left her throughout two sets. "But it's not that. I felt like he was . . . *watching* us, intently. Or, actually, me. I don't know."

"Honey, everyone watches you when you sing." Kelvin smiled as he moved to her other foot, yielding another moan from her. "It's called magnetism. Style. Appeal. And double D boobs comin' out of your dress when you breathe."

"Oh shut up." She let out one chuckle, but shook her head in mild frustration. "No, it was more than that. It was like he was . . . I don't know, sizing me up?"

Kelvin laughed. "Baby, I'm sure he was."

"Nooo, I don't mean like that. I mean like . . . in an . . . analytical way. Not in a sexual way." She let her head drop back onto the padded arm of the couch. "Maybe I'm just paranoid."

"You're not paranoid," Kelvin said, working the arch of her foot and bringing more sighs of pleasure from her. "You're mistrustful, jaded, cynical, and bitter, but you're not paranoid. Of that much, I can assure you."

She chuckled wryly. "Thanks."

"You know I love ya, honey. But it's all true."

She scowled. "I know it is. But to hear it out loud makes me sound like a . . . a shrew."

His eyes and voice softened. "You're not a shrew. You've been hurt. A *lot*."

A wave of images flooded her and she shook her head, as if that would shake them out. She sat up abruptly, swinging her feet to the floor. "I'm going to the bar. One drink before the next set. You coming?"

"No, you go ahead." Kelvin pulled his cell phone from the inside pocket of his blazer. "I'm going to say a quick hi to Manuel."

She stood and shoved her feet back into her stilettos. "The new boyfriend?"

"Yessss." Kelvin started texting, his eyes now on his phone. "The man is dreamy."

"I'm living vicariously through you, Kel. You're a rock star."

He laughed. "You could be too, if you wanted to. Men swarm to you. But you don't want it." He scowled briefly. "Damn autocorrect. I know what I mean to type, and 'ducking' ain't it." His dark eyes lifted to her again as he asked, "Jules? When's the last time you got some, honey? You're a little cranky lately."

"Not in six months," she said, scowling.

His eyebrows shot up, a look of exaggerated horror on his face. "Has it been that long?"

"Last guy I slept with was Joe. That ended at Thanksgiving."

"Well, that explains a lot. No sex for my sweetheart equals *cranky*." Kelvin clucked his tongue and shook his head slowly. "Joe was nice. And *hot*. That man fell for you, and you jettisoned him into space the minute you realized that."

"It was supposed to be no strings," she said in a flat tone. "You know my deal. He broke the rules." She headed for the door.

"You're gonna have to break those rules of yours one day," he said softly. Something in his voice stopped her and made her turn back to look at him. He added with a pointed stare, "And if you do, you might let yourself find love again. Or at least, find something good."

"Nope. Not interested." She ignored the sad flutter in her stomach that her friend's concern created. Whenever he brought this up, she fought against the tug in her heart. By now, she always won. "My rules work for me just fine. See you back here in what, fifteen?"

He sighed, giving up. "Sounds good. And bring me back a Coke, would you?"

"You got it." Julia smoothed her dress over her hips and made her way toward the bar. Her longtime friend's words echoed in her head, but the noise of the bar helped drown them out. It was pretty full, and that pleased her. If she and Kelvin kept filling the place regularly, Everett would keep them on as a regular gig. And she loved singing here.

When Everett Bailey had opened the martini bar, she'd gone there a few times for drinks with Randi. Even for the north shore, it was high-class without being pretentious, a posh little jewel of a place. When Everett had brought in a piano and started having singers on Friday nights, she asked for an audition. She'd done a bunch of random gigs with Kelvin all over the tristate area; having a regular gig, much less close to home, would be great. Two years later, she and Kelvin were still here every Friday night, making music together and enjoying themselves.

The bar only had space for about a hundred people, but that was a good crowd when it filled up. And tonight, it was filled, even though it was after midnight and they'd already done two one-hour sets. Maybe it was the nice weather; spring in the air made people want to get out and do things after a long winter cooped up inside. Whatever it was, the bar was crowded, and it took her a good minute to get to the bar. There were no available stools to sit on, and she sighed inwardly.

A man in his fifties noticed her and rose from his barstool. "You need a seat?" he offered.

"That's kind, but not necessary," she said, smiling.

"No, please. I've enjoyed your singing tonight," he said. She recognized the flare in his eyes. He was attracted to her. Great. "Please, I insist."

"Okay, thank you." She sat on the barstool, flashing him an appreciative grin, but nothing flirtatious to encourage him.

But sure enough, she saw his eyes linger on her breasts before he looked back up into her face and asked, "Can I buy you a drink?"

Before Julia could decline, a Botoxed woman was there at his side. "You just offered to buy her a drink?" She glared at Julia, who shrugged carelessly in response.

He flushed, looking guilty. "I, uh . . . she's such a good singer. I was just trying to—"

"Yeah, we both know what you were trying to do," the woman snarled. Julia imagined if the woman could move her facial features, she'd be scowling. "Whaddaya think, women are stupid?" She stormed away.

"Susie, wait!" The man followed her without hesitation.

Julia just shook her head. It was so strange to her; she didn't do anything to invite the attention of men. At least, she didn't *think* she did. But she still got hit on all the same. It had to be the job. Just like girls flocked to musicians, men seemed to be equally entranced by female singers. They saw a figure on the stage and spun their own fantasies about what she was like, putting her on an impossible pedestal. God knew that had happened to her, more than once, with disastrous results.

She glanced down to readjust the neckline of her dress. Okay, so the dresses she wore, while never lewd and always elegant, usually gave a peek of her generous cleavage. That also came with the job. Men liked boobs. She had 'em in spades. So yeah, she played the girls up a bit at her singing engagements. But by now, she thought her quiet frost would keep men away.

She *wanted* her quiet frost to keep men away. At the very least, it would weed out the weaker ones. The ones who were intimidated by a strong woman, a smart and mature woman—and unfortunately, there were many of those men.

Why did they still hit on her? Other than a fun romp once in a while, she didn't want anything more. She wanted to be left alone. No emotional ties, ever again.

She shook her head and raised her arm to catch the bartender's attention. Hallie was working the bar tonight, which was good. She made strong drinks.

After watching two sets, and having a long, friendly chat with the owner/manager, Dane had come to a definite decision. He wanted to hire Julia Shay. Her voice was pure gold, she had genuine stage presence, she was polished and poised, he liked how she carried herself, and she was stunning to look at. He'd definitely enjoyed the view as he'd sat and listened for almost two hours.

She had a beautiful face—big dark eyes to drown

in, a sultry mouth, and smooth pale skin that he just knew would be soft and warm to the touch. And unlike the too-skinny women who ruled fashion pages these days, Julia was built like a *woman*. She was voluptuous. Her unbelievable breasts were to die for, and he'd bet they were real, because nothing about her seemed plastic or fake. Her slim waist led to curvy hips that were lush and inviting. She had the figure of a Greek goddess, the kind that was made for a man to lose himself in. But her physical appeal alone wasn't what made her attractive. The woman radiated confidence and sex appeal. Nothing sleazy, nothing like that—she carried herself with class. Her allure was subtle but powerful. She was hot and she knew it. She was a siren. A temptress. *Please, God,* he thought, *let her not be dumb.* That would break his damn heart. But he'd still offer her the job.

Offering her the job also had a challenge he almost wasn't up to taking—because he wanted to sleep with her, no doubt about it. In a different scenario, he'd be approaching her to spend a few nights, or even weeks, in his bed. Somehow he knew she'd be incredible. Just thinking about stripping her out of that dress sent a warm tug right to his belly, low and simmering. Dammit, he wanted her.

Which was more important?

Obviously, having her sing in his hotel . . . he'd been close to choosing between a few of the other singers he'd seen, though none had been . . . enough. This woman was. He was drawn to her, but he'd have to ignore the pull he felt; he wouldn't be able to pursue her, much less have her. Sleeping with one of his employees was a huge no-no. He didn't cross that line, ever. He sighed and swore under his breath. Well, that was it. There would be other women. There always were. Julia Shay would be off-limits.

He saw her emerge from the back and make her way through the small crowd toward the bar. She smiled at something someone said as she passed, and he sucked in a breath. Her natural smile—not the measured one she used onstage during her act, though that was stunning too—was like a flash of pure light.

Dane knocked back the last of his drink. In the future, just looking at her, possibly forming a cordial relationship with her over time, and having dirty, hot fantasies about her would have to suffice. All right, then. He rose from his table, his gaze focused on the flame-haired woman who'd just taken a seat at the bar. Time to make her an offer she couldn't refuse.

Dane moved in quietly, making sure to place himself right next to Julia at the bar. It was crowded, so he was close to her, enough for his arm to brush against her shoulder. Her head turned and she glanced at him in brief appraisal. Apparently, it only took her two seconds to decide she didn't like him. She looked away with what he took to be an expression of disdain, back down into her half-empty glass. The corner of his mouth quirked in a combination of amusement and surprised indignation. That wasn't usually the reaction he garnered from women. Especially ones he'd been picturing in a steamy position beneath him, naked and writhing, only minutes before.

"What'll it be?" the bartender, a pretty brunette, asked him. She smiled engagingly, a flirtatious sparkle in her eyes. Now *that* was the reaction he was used to.

He smiled back at her. "Dirty martini for me. And

a refill of whatever she's having." He gestured beside him with his chin.

That caught Julia's attention. Her dark eyes darted up at him as the bartender walked away. "Thanks, but you don't have to do that."

Damn. Her speaking voice was as sultry as her singing voice. He was a sucker for a woman with an appealing speaking voice. It did things to him. His blood started to simmer and surge throughout his body. Goddammit. He grinned softly and said, "But I *want* to do that."

She considered him for a moment. Her face gave nothing away; she was hard to read. Then she simply picked up her dark pink drink and sipped. He watched her lips curl around the rim of the glass and a rush of lust seared him. He never thought he'd be jealous of a glass.

"What are you drinking, anyway?" he asked. "Sex on the Beach?"

A chuckle escaped her. "No. Simple old vodka and cranberry."

He nodded and shot her a friendly grin.

Her gaze lingered on him for a second, then she looked away. Glanced at her watch. Took another sip. Looked back up at him. "Is there something you want?" she asked, a trace of annoyance in her tone. "Buying me a drink, making small talk . . . so?"

Whoa. Direct, and to the point. A bit defensive. Feisty. *Game on.* "Yes, actually," he said, keeping his tone amiable. "There *is* something I want." He smiled, but she didn't smile back. He continued, unfazed. "My name's Dane Harrison. I'm about to open a new hotel on the Upper East Side. I'm looking for a singer to work in the lounge I'm opening within it. It's an upscale lounge, glamorous, high-class. It'll bring in an exclusive clientele, so I need someone fantastic. And after what I've seen here tonight, I think you'd be perfect. So the 'something I want' is to hire you. Interested?"

There was a long beat as she gaped at him. God, she was gorgeous. He let his eyes wander over that thick red mane, her high cheekbones, her creamy, luminous skin, and those dark eyes that radiated intelligence . . . and mistrust. Now that they were so close, and she was sitting under one of the few lights in the dimly lit room, he realized her eyes weren't brown, but hazel. Gold flecks shone in the dark depths, reminding him of the tiger eye stones his sister used to collect as a kid.

"Is this a joke?" she asked in a suspicious tone.

"Not at all," Dane replied.

She studied him for another few seconds. There was so much going on in her eyes, but all she said was "Oh." And bit down softly on her bottom lip.

Dane's mouth went dry as an almost primal desire ravaged him mercilessly, like a flash flood. He couldn't remember the last time a woman had brought on such an intense, immediate physical reaction in him. He marveled at it, even as all of his senses started to pulse faster. *Focus, asshole. The job. You want her for the job. Stop thinking about what that gorgeous mouth is capable of. About pinning her against the bar and running your hands over every inch of her. About what her skin would feel like, what her mouth would taste like . . .*

The bartender came and set their drinks down before them. Dane turned for a moment to hand her a fifty-dollar bill, took a very deep breath, then turned back to Julia. Yes, he loved looking at her, he'd established that the minute he'd laid eyes on her. But talking to her was beginning to feel like a carefully orchestrated chess match. She was tough, edgy. His somewhat legendary powers of persuasion would obviously be needed to secure this deal. "It's a pleasure to meet you, Ms. Shay. Or can I call you Julia? It's a beautiful name."

"Julia's fine," she said.

Dane extended his arm for a handshake. Slowly she slipped her hand into his, her somber eyes scanning his features warily. Her skin was warm and soft, as he'd thought it would be, and something in his belly stirred at her light touch. Yup, he thought. Instant chemistry.

At least, for him. It seemed like for her, not so much. Again, not what he was used to when it came to women. He made himself focus, get back to the business at hand.

"I spoke to the manager here about you," he said as she pulled her hand back.

Her brows furrowed as her gaze sharpened. "What? Why?"

"To ask him about you. To get an idea of your professionalism—what you're like when you're off the stage." Dane lifted his drink to his lips and took a swallow. "I mean, I know how you handle yourself up there. You're seasoned, in the good way; I can tell the difference between a newbie and a pro within a few bars of a song. I've seen enough to know you're the real deal. I wanted to know some other things."

"Checking up on me?" she said with an edge, clearly put off.

"Yeah, I was," he said without apology. "I'm not going to make an offer of employment to someone I'm asking to represent my hotel, my *name*, who doesn't take her work seriously."

"And? What'd Everett tell you?"

"That you're a pleasure." Dane smiled softly. "That you've been doing gigs here—with your accompanist—regularly for the past two years. That you've only cancelled on him once, and that's because you had the flu. That you're always on time, have never had a problem with a member of the audience, that there are times you have them downright eating from the palm of your hand, and that you sing as well as any of the pros." Dane smirked as he added, "He said he tried more than once to get you to audition for *American Idol,* but you wouldn't hear of it."

"I'm too old for that show," she sniffed. "I'd never get past the first round."

"Bullshit. You're gorgeous and you have a killer voice." He stared at her, studying. "How old are you that you think you're too old? I never ask a woman her age, but you brought it up and now I have to know. You can't be more than thirty-three, thirty-four tops."

Her eyes lit up, and she couldn't hold back the delighted smile. "Yeah? Wow. Thanks." She was genuinely pleased, and that pleased him way more than it should have. "Well, I hate to burst your bubble, but you're wrong. In fact, I bet I'm older than you."

"No you're not," he scoffed. "I'll be thirty-six at the end of July."

She smirked, a triumphant sparkle in her eyes. "Yup. Told ya so."

Dane's eyes went wide as he sputtered, "No way."

"Way. Just turned forty-one in April." Her lips curved seductively and her dark eyes danced. "Forties and fabulous, that's me. Go ask Everett if you don't believe me."

He let out a puff of air, genuine surprise clobbering him. "Whoa. You look *great.* I mean . . . I didn't think that at all, and I'm usually dead on with guessing a woman's age."

One of Julia's thin red brows arched. "Yes, I'd bet you've been around *lots* of women."

"What?" He felt a flare of irritation, but played it coy. "Hey now. Did you just insult me, Julia?"

"Nah. Just an observation." Her mouth went from a judgmental twist to a barely concealed smirk. "Don't play modest, or dumb. It doesn't suit you. You're pretty gorgeous yourself, and you know it. You have that way about you . . . like you don't have a care in the world. So something tells me you don't lack for female companionship."

"I'm going to let that slide." He swallowed another gulp of his drink. She was sexy as hell, but her attitude toward him was unfounded—and really, it kind of pissed him off. Yet he pressed on. Something told him she was worth it. "So. I take it that you don't believe me," he said. "That I want you to come sing in my hotel."

"No, I don't," she said plainly. "Sounds like a line if I ever heard one."

Jesus, honey, who hurt you? he thought. Wariness came off her in palpable waves. "Well, it's not." He pulled out his wallet, and a business card from the leather. She took it from him with small, slender fingers. "You can call and check anytime to see I am who I say I am. My assistant will gladly tell you how I've been combing New York for two months, looking for the type of singer I had in mind for this job."

Julia placed the card down beside her fresh drink with barely a glance at it. "Mm-hmm."

His eyebrows shot up. Now he was getting a little agitated. The other women he'd considered had all jumped at the chance when he'd mentioned it, and he hadn't really wanted any of them. He hadn't felt that certainty in his gut. With Julia, he had. This woman was the one he wanted, he'd finally found what he'd visualized, he was even drawn to her himself—and apparently, she couldn't give a shit about the job, much less be interested in him.

He wanted her in his bed, sure. But even more than that, he wanted her to headline in his hotel. And he almost always got what he wanted. *Especially* when it came to women. So with a new resolve, he cleared his throat, speared her with his gaze, and smiled. "Julia. Do you want to hear about the job before you dismiss me so readily? Or should I just leave you alone, since that seems to be what you want? I can walk away right now." He moved as if to leave.

"No, I—wait." Her features softened, and she huffed out a breath. "I . . . I'm sorry. I didn't mean to be rude. I apologize. But cut me some slack—how do I know you're really who you say you are, or what you want from me is legit? I don't. You know?"

"Yes, I know." God, that voice. He could've listened to her talk all day. She could probably read the phone book and make it sound sensual. "You're obviously an intelligent woman, not easily snowed. But listen. It's a solid job, it's real. I'm a legitimate businessman, not a pimp. You can google me if you like." He grinned to break the tension, and she grinned back. *Okay. Better.* He lifted his drink and sipped before continuing, drawing out the moment to make her wait. A sideways glance told him she was willing to listen now.

"So here's the deal," Dane began. "I own a few hotels around the country. My first one was in midtown New York, a block away from Radio City. That one caters mainly to a business clientele, tourists, etcetera. Now, in June, I'm opening a new hotel. This one's sweeter. A little more glamorous. Elegant, top-notch." He smiled; just thinking of it excited him. "Luxury suites, a few upscale brand-name boutiques, full day spa and salon, all of that. Every amenity think-able. And the highlight, to me? What will set it apart? A swanky lounge and bar that'll have a piano and a small stage. That's where you come in."

He paused to make sure he had her attention. Her big, gorgeous eyes were glued to his. "I want a kickass singer who'll pull in my high-end clientele and keep them there, make them want to stay all night and buy lots of drinks. Make it a hot spot for the hotel. I envisioned having a singer who's gorgeous, sharp, professional, has charisma and stage presence, and is heaven to listen to. A musical seductress, if you will." His eyes locked with hers and held. "I've been can-vassing New York for over two months now. I've seen a lot of singers, a lot of performances. None of them have held a candle to you, Julia."

She blinked and her breath caught.

"You have a fantastic voice. And frankly, I really like looking at you. But you probably hear that a lot." He caught the split-second flash of surprise in her eyes at that, but she recovered immediately. She was like steel. He grinned as he went in for the hard sell. "You're very talented, you're gorgeous, you're sexy as hell, and I like the way you carry yourself. You hold an audience spellbound when you perform—I saw that here myself, so I know that firsthand. You cer-tainly captivated me." He leaned his hip against the bar, crossing his long legs at the ankle as he gazed down at her. "Maybe it's *because* you're 'forty-one and fabulous.' Maybe it's because you're fucking beautiful and obviously don't have rocks in your head, thank God. Maybe it's because you can sing your ass off. But what I know is: all combined, you're the whole package, Julia. You're what I've been looking for."

Still and silent, Julia's eyes went wide and her lips parted slightly. He imagined it was her cool, collected way of her mouth dropping open in surprise. He smiled again and reached for his drink. Finally, she murmured, "I . . . wow. That's all very flattering. Thank you."

"You're welcome, but I wasn't flattering you. I was listing what I consider your assets, why you're qualified for the job, and why I want you to be the headliner at my hotel. Would you consider a job like this?" he pressed, his gaze spearing her.

"I might," she hedged, still frozen. "Tell me more."

He nodded, both irritated and intrigued that she wasn't jumping at it. She was really making him work for this. "Okay. You'd work from ten to one on Thursday night, Friday night, and Saturday night, and do the occasional event if someone requests it. The rest of your time, all week long, is yours." He took another quick sip, watching her face. "You'll have an accompanist, who I'll hire as soon as I've hired you, and you can rehearse during the week anytime that works for you both. The two of you can select your song list, but I get final approval." He grinned to try to lighten the moment, to offset the tone of all his demands. "You seem to be responsible, a professional. The manager here gave you a glowing review. For now, that's good enough for me.

"But know I'd expect you to show up on time, if not early, and to give it your all every single night. And I'll

ask for permission to do a basic background check.
Just your employment history, that kind of thing,
nothing personal. Like I said before, you'd be repre-
senting my hotel, my name. So I expect nothing short
of the best." He stared more intently. She was listening
now, that was for sure. And damn, he couldn't take his
eyes off her. "Do you have a day job too, or is this it?"

She blinked. "I, uh . . . yes, I have a day job. And I
hate it." Blushing, her eyes fell away. That intrigued
him. She obviously hadn't meant to blurt that out. It
was the first time she'd been anything but controlled.
Fidgeting with the rim of her glass, she added, "It's
just that it's boring. But it pays the bills. My singing
gigs don't."

"Then why do you sing?"

"Because I'm good at it, and because I love it. Music
is my passion." Her gaze and her tone were unflinch-
ing. "I've been singing all my life. I wasn't going to
give it up altogether, and I haven't had to. I do weekend gigs, that sort of thing."

"Did you ever pursue it as your only career?" Dane
asked, truly interested.

Something shuttered in her eyes. "I wanted to. . . ."
Her voice went soft and flat. "Things happened. Life
happened. Didn't work out."

"Okay." His casual tone belied his sudden burning
curiosity. He wanted to know her story. Something
about this woman compelled him, made him want
to dig and find out all her secrets, her stories, what
made her tick. He also wanted to back her up against
a wall and have his way with her, but at least *that*
part made sense to him. The rest didn't. He was
drawn to her like a magnet, and while his brain didn't

understand it, his body was painfully aware of it. "What's your day job?"

"I'm a secretary at a construction company," she said evenly.

He surveyed her face. He didn't mean to be elitist, honest work was honest work, but something told him instinctively she wasn't cut out for that—that she was capable of much more. There was another story there. "How long have you worked there?"

"Six years."

"What do you make in salary?"

Her eyes narrowed and her mouth tightened. "How is that your business?"

"Because whatever you're making, I'll match it, and then some."

Her big dark eyes got bigger. "Bullshit."

"Try me." His mouth quirked as he took in her surprise. "Tell me what you're making."

"What if I said a hundred thousand?" she challenged.

"Then I'll pay you that much and more," he said without hesitation. He leaned in and said in a firm but quiet voice, "Julia, I really want you to work in my hotel. I'm prepared to do whatever's necessary to make that happen."

Now her mouth did drop open in shock. "Really."

"Really."

"And do you always get what you want?"

"Um . . . no." He smiled slowly. "But *almost* always."

She smirked back. "You've got big money to throw around to make sure you do, huh?"

His smile faded only a bit, and his eyes intensified on hers. He leaned in closer to murmur smoothly, "Yes, actually, I do. But it's usually my dashing looks and dazzling charm that win people over, not my bank account."

"I'm not like most people," she said, not dropping the locked gaze. "You're smooth and you're handsome, and you're rich. That's lovely. And oh yes, you're charming. You *ooze* charm." Pure steel flashed in her eyes. "But big-time charm, to me, usually reeks of insincerity. So, you know, that doesn't do it for me."

"I'm getting that." He edged closer, close enough now to feel the heat radiating from her skin and catch the light scent of her perfume. Musky, with a hint of vanilla. He wanted to bury his face in the curve of her pale neck and inhale her. Skim his mouth along her skin. "But, good news, Julia. Even though I'd be your boss, you don't have to like me. You just have to like the job." The air seemed to crackle around them, pure electricity. He took in the gleam in her eyes, the stubborn set of her jaw, her sweet little mouth, her luscious cleavage, and had a flash of ravaging her until that mouth opened to gasp and scream his name. His eyes lingered on hers . . . and he eased back. Stood up straight. "Hey, it's fine. If you don't want the job, I'm not gonna—"

"I make forty thousand a year," she said, and reached for her drink for a hard gulp.

He grinned softly. "Quit that job, Julia Shay. Sing at my hotel. I want you well rested and focused when you walk into my lounge. I'll pay you eighty grand a year. Hell, let's make it an even hundred grand. Why not? I think you'll be worth it. Deal?"

She choked on her drink and started to cough.

He couldn't help but laugh, even as he patted her back.

Chapter Two

Julia sputtered, her throat burning a little from where her vodka and cranberry had gone down the wrong pipe. Dane's big, warm hand on her back was gentle, even as he whacked her to help clear her lungs.

She didn't believe in fairy tales, and hadn't for a long time. But if she could have thought one up, this scenario would come close. A breathtakingly handsome man with lots of money walks into her gig and offers her the job of a lifetime? She would have laughed out loud if she weren't choking so embarrassingly.

Over her coughing fit, she heard Dane ask Hallie for a glass of water, which was placed before her seconds later.

"Drink that," Dane commanded, watching her. The look on his face was a combination of amusement, concern, and a hint of smugness. It made her want to growl.

She took a few deep breaths, then drank slowly. She downed half the glass. "Dammit," she muttered. She swallowed hard, trying to soothe the scratchy tickle in the back of her throat. "I still have to sing my last set. What are you trying to do, see how I perform under less-than-ideal conditions?"

He laughed, which made her temper burn. "No, Julia. I'm not trying to sabotage you. I'm trying to get you to work for me."

She took a few more sips of water, a stalling tactic as her mind raced. Quit her job? Be able to sing for a living? Only work three nights a week for double what she was making now? Jesus H. Christmas, that was some offer.

If only she trusted it.

She didn't trust this smooth, charming, smoking-hot man any further than she could throw him. "I can't just say yes right away. I want to google you, check you out too. See you're who you say you are, that this hotel really exists, do my homework."

He nodded slowly, a flicker of something in his amazingly blue eyes. Respect. "I'd expect nothing less. And know that of course, a legal written contract will be drawn up once you agree. You can have your attorney look it over before you sign anything. But a verbal agreement would be a great start. Is that a yes?"

"Not yet, Prince Charming," she said staunchly. She wished as fast as her brain was spinning, it would actually *work*. She was too shocked to think clearly, couldn't put things together at the moment, and hoped she didn't appear as flustered as she felt.

A movement near the front of the room caught her eye. Kelvin had poked his head out from the back hallway to wave to her. A *c'mon, let's go, back to work* wave. She lifted her arm and waved for him to come to the bar. Kelvin's brows furrowed, but he started heading toward her.

She turned back to Dane. He leaned against the bar casually, like he'd just offered her a drink instead of a possibly six-figure job opportunity that was a dream come true. *Cool,* she snapped at herself. *Play it cool. Do this right.*

"Let me ask you something," she said. "The accompanist. A professional musician with credentials, yes?"

"Yes."

"Have you actually hired one yet?"

"I have three candidates. I was waiting to find the singer, then let her meet with each of them and see who she felt most comfortable working with."

Julia gave him a silent gold star. That was a smart way to go. "Great idea, really. But here's the thing. I've worked with Kelvin for over twenty years, more or less. You won't find someone much better than him. I want him to come with me."

At that moment, Kelvin appeared at her side. "Where we goin', honey?"

"Hopefully, to my hotel." Dane flashed a smile and extended his hand. "Dane Harrison. Nice to meet you, Kelvin."

"Likewise." Kelvin shook his hand, but turned back to his friend. "Julia? What's going on? Fill me in here."

"I've offered Julia a job," Dane said before she could answer. "I want her to sing in the lounge of the hotel I'm opening in June. Seems she wants you to come with her, as her accompanist. I've seen and heard enough here tonight to know you're damn good, so I'm game. Want to hear about it?"

Julia had to bite her lip to keep from laughing. Kelvin was trying not to appear shocked, but failing miserably. He looked from Dane to her and back to Dane again. "Yeah, I wanna hear about it. I'm all ears."

As Dane filled in Kelvin on the details, Julia sipped her water and let her eyes feast on Dane. He was, without question, one of the best-looking men she'd ever seen. His dark curly hair was just shy of being unruly, and they were such deep, perfect curls that she had the urge to poke her finger through each one, slowly and deliciously. He had to be over six feet tall, probably six-one. A tight, lean body that looked damn fine in his deceivingly simple light blue button-down shirt and tan slacks.

And that *face*. She couldn't help but stare. Strong, square jaw, full lips she could nibble on for hours . . . and his eyes were truly beautiful. She'd rarely seen eyes that shade of blue, a brilliant blue that seemed to glow. They were lit with good humor, as if he had a secret he was dying to let you in on. This was a man who viewed the world as his playground, she could just tell. And for all she knew, it probably was.

She and Dane reached for their drinks at the same time and their hands brushed. The contact made a shiver run through her. Did he have to be so damn hot? She gulped more water.

So, she thought, *let's list all the bullet points.* Movie-star handsome, and just as charismatic. He was also bright, articulate, and so charming that she bet he wrapped people around his finger wherever he went. And, apparently, filthy rich and successful. Definitely rich enough to offer her a hundred thousand dollars to sing at his hotel without blinking an eye. That helped explain the air of power and self-assurance that surrounded him like a cloak. The whole combination was as sexy as sexy got. She wanted to climb him like a mountain.

In short, Dane Harrison was dangerous.

Every fiber in her body warned her to steer clear

of him, even as those same fibers were filled with lust at just being near him. Yup. Danger of the worst kind.

And he'd be her *boss*? Holy crap. Dirty thoughts involving your boss were an instant recipe for disaster. Any dumbass knew that. But . . .

Should she do it? Should she quit her job and give this crazy idea a try?

"Julia." Kelvin's insistent tone broke her from her thoughts. "Can I talk with you for a few minutes before we get back on? We do have to finish up."

"Of course," she murmured, still feeling like she was in a bit of a trance. She blinked a few times and finished the glass of water.

"I'll stay for your last set," Dane said to her. "Afterward, can we talk some more about this? I'll wait. I'm not leaving here tonight without an answer, one way or the other."

"Demanding, aren't you. I'll keep that in mind as I think this over." She rose to her feet, her large breasts accidentally brushing against his arm. A stab of heat seared through her, her nipples peaking instantly. Color flooded her cheeks as her eyes flew to his. He was already staring at her, the intensity in his blue, blue eyes almost startling. "Sorry," she murmured. "Tight quarters here."

"Nothing to be sorry for," he said. His eyes held hers for an intense second, pure electricity, before he moved back to let her pass easily. "It's been a pleasure talking with you, Julia. I'll be interested in hearing what you have to say when you're done singing. I'll wait for you at my table." He shook her hand again and the feel of his skin against hers brought another lick of desire. All of her girly parts were doing a little dance. He smiled genially, then shook Kelvin's hand before they walked back toward the dressing room.

Kelvin was silent until they reached the room and he'd locked the door. Then he spun around and exclaimed, "Is he fucking for real?!?"

She laughed nervously. "He claims he is. But Kel . . . anything that seems too good to be true? Usually is."

"Shut up and sit down, woman," Kelvin sputtered. He pulled his cell phone from his pocket as he pulled her down to sit with him on the couch. "Let's give our foxy Mister Harrison a quick Google, shall we? The audience can wait five more minutes." His eyes were wild as they swept over her. "He is *beautiful.* Good Lord, did you see his eyes? Are those not the bluest eyes you've ever seen? I almost swooned. No, I am swooning. I am in midswoon."

Julia giggled and shook her head. "You're shameless."

"And that hair! He's got curls so sweet, I could . . . oh, honey, *I could.*"

"I don't think you're his type, sweetie," Julia said, glad to be laughing. She hadn't realized how tense and wired she'd been until now. "Sorry."

"No, I'm not. He wants *you.*" Kelvin waggled his dark brows. "The heat between you two could've caused third-degree burns in spectators."

Startled at her friend's observation, she sat up straighter. "Well, even if you were right, which you're not, it's not going to happen. If I take him up on his offer, he'll be my boss. So end of story."

"Famous last words," Kelvin said dismissively as he scrolled on his phone. "Harrison . . . Harrison . . . if he's the real deal, you just stepped into the best offer of your life!" He stopped, and his eyes flew wide. "Oh. Mah. Gah. Look at this, honey."

She leaned against his arm to look at his phone. There were many pictures of Dane Harrison. At various hotel openings and celebrity events, in news articles on business Web sites, and even a few paparazzi shots of him with a few gorgeous models and society darlings, women who lived in the same stratosphere he did.

Kelvin tapped one of the links and began reading out loud. "Harrison Enterprises is a multimillion dollar international conglomerate . . . four generations . . . and . . ." Kelvin's eyes went as wide as they could go, practically popping out of his head. "*Holy shit.* He is big-time, honey. Big. Time. His family is worth millions. Millions of millions. That sizzling piece of man candy was born into old-school money. And grew up right here, over in Kingston Point."

Julia had driven past Kingston Point, but never actually through the small community. Why would she? It was home to some of the wealthiest, most powerful people in all of New York—in all of the United States. "Gatsby country," Randi called it. Kingston Point was the jewel of Long Island's famous Gold Coast.

Kelvin kept skimming and talking. "Went to top schools . . . yada yada . . . then he went out and founded his own company and made his *own* million dollar empire . . . sweet Jesus." Kelvin let out a puff of air that resembled a yelp. "According to this article, Dane Harrison owns *seventeen* hotels across the U.S., and three in Canada. This new hotel he's opening? His 'labor of love', the one he's always wanted to open. The hotel is real. The job offer is real. *He's* for real." Kelvin and Julia stared at each other for a minute.

"And he wants to hire *me?*" she finally said.

"Damn right," Kelvin said firmly. "Shows that man

is more than pretty, he's smart, too. Knows a diamond when he sees one."

"Shut up," she mumbled, trying to absorb everything that was happening. Her heartbeat started roaring in her ears.

"Holy shit, Jules. Holy fucking shit!" Kelvin whooped loudly, his short dreads swinging as he threw his hands in the air. "Um, Miss Thang? Tell me something. Why am I more excited than you are?"

"Because I don't trust anything that seems this amazing," she said.

He blew out a disdainful snort and went back to scrolling furiously on his phone. "Honey, you don't trust anything, period."

"Well, more specifically, I don't trust *men*," she corrected him. She put her hand on his knee. "But I trust you."

He stopped cold and looked up at her. With great affection, he slid his arm around her shoulders and pulled her close. "I know you do. And I love you too. But listen to me. You're going to take that job, even if he decides he doesn't want me in the deal. You hear me?" His smile warmed. "You're an angel for wanting me to do this with you, and it would be a ball. But if he only wants to hire you, baby, you have to do it. Come on, Jules. There's no thought process here. Let's see what else we can find out about him, shall we?" He leaned in to smack a loud kiss on her forehead and she couldn't help but giggle.

Julia exhaled the breath she'd been holding and tried to organize her thoughts. All her worst mistakes had been things she'd done on instinct, giving in to her feelings rather than facts that were right there had she opened her eyes wide enough to see them. She didn't want to repeat her past mistakes. She got to her feet. "I drank a lot. I have to pee. You keep looking."

As she slipped into the tiny bathroom, she realized her breaths were coming in short puffs of excitement and her heart was pounding against her ribs. The possibilities of a job like this . . . it was all so overwhelming. Yet something in her knew she'd be a fool not to go for it. She was forty-one now, with no one to answer to and nothing to stop her. She'd made sure of that.

She also had no life.

She'd turned self-isolation into an art form. If it wasn't for Randi and Kelvin pulling her back out into the world on a regular basis, and her singing job at the bar, she'd probably go home from work every night, hole up, and not leave her apartment. She'd have turned into a lonely old cat lady. Without the cats, of course. She was highly allergic.

So why not? The timing was right. The setting of the job, if Dane's description was accurate, was a dream. And making a hundred grand a year, or even the initially offered eighty, if he went back to that? She'd never made money like that in her life. She could bank enough to finally have a tiny but solid cushion for the first time ever.

Dane Harrison thought she was all that? It both surprised and thrilled her. She certainly thought *he* was all that, though she'd be damned if she'd ever let him know it. He and his offer were certainly tempting. If she could just stay away from him . . . which would be a challenge, considering the inexplicable, rousing draw she'd felt toward him almost the instant they met, and the unavoidable fact that he'd be her boss. But to sing in a new, glamorous Manhattan hotel a few nights a week, and be paid well, was a job most singers would kill for.

Maybe her luck was changing at long last. Maybe it was all another bomb waiting to explode in her face. But she'd survived bomb blasts before, much worse than a job not working out. How bad could it be?

Only one way to find out.

She caught her reflection in the bathroom mirror and smiled widely.

Chapter Three

"Dane?" Tess asked. "Do you ever want to get married?"

He blinked in surprise at his sister. "What? Where did *that* come from?"

"I want to know too," said Charles Harrison III, staring at her through his black-rimmed glasses. "That's an interesting question, especially for *this* guy." He gestured toward Dane with his chin.

Laughter bubbled out of Tess's mouth. "You two! You'd think I asked, 'Hey, wanna go get our kidneys pulled out?' Jeez." She shot a look at Dane and added, "Don't look so terrified. I'm not trying to set you up with anyone, nothing like that. I was just thinking about some things, and that led to other things, and long story short, I realized I honestly have no idea if you ever give serious thought to getting married."

Dane shrugged, sat back in his chair, and lazily crossed one long leg over the other. "Not really. I don't give it any thought at all, actually."

He grinned, enjoying the sensation of being truly relaxed. Spending some down time with his siblings always made him feel that way, feel more grounded. They weren't just his older brother and younger sister; they were truly his two best friends. He was glad Tess had asked him to come out and spend the day with her, and even more so when Charles had decided to join them for dinner—without his three surly kids in tow. Time alone, just the three of them, was more and more rare lately.

Sipping his Cabernet, Dane let his gaze wander along his family's majestically landscaped property. Up on a slight hill, a hundred or so yards across the expansive emerald lawn, was the Main House—which had always struck him as a funny title, considering it was a twenty-seven-room Georgian mansion. It stood proudly, a testament to four generations of Harrison work and rewards. His father still lived there, but only with a small household staff. The mighty Charles Harrison II had lived there alone since throwing their mother out almost two decades earlier.

Tess had moved back from Manhattan and into the guest cottage two years before, a picturesque four-bedroom house that shared the back property before dipping to the small cliff that overlooked the Long Island Sound. Dane had always loved that vista, one of the very best things about the magnificent estate. Now, the three of them sat outside on her back patio after a delicious dinner Tess had made, enjoying some wine as the sound of the water just beyond lulled them into a state of serenity. The late May sun glowed orange as it dipped slowly into the horizon, turning the sky over the Long Island Sound into streaky shades of purple, hot pink, and deep blue. The briny scent of the Sound carried up on the warm breeze that blew across the estate's tremendous backyard—all ten acres of it.

"You're evading the question, Golden Boy," Charles teased.

"He's never quiet. I think I scared him witless," Tess taunted.

Dane chuckled. "I ain't a-skeered of you two. I ain't a-skeered o' nothin'."

"Still avoiding," Tess singsonged.

"I guess I'm not morally opposed to getting married, if I genuinely thought I'd found the right woman," Dane hedged. "But hey. All three of us are single, and with good reasons." He kept his tone jaunty. "Besides, wouldn't it be bordering on cruelty to drag someone into our clan? Who in their right mind would want to become a part of the Harrison family dramas?"

"He makes an excellent point," Charles conceded, and took a swallow of his wine.

"And, well, my standards are too high. And I work a lot. And I travel . . . Hell, I've met so many amazing women, why should I have to choose just one?" Dane grinned as his brother and sister laughed at that. "Not to mention: after our parents' debacle of a marriage and shitstorm of a divorce, and then you doing the same thing, Charles, I don't need to follow along that path, you know? And then you, Tess, your broken engagement, all that ugliness after . . . I've seen enough."

"More excellent points," Tess allowed with a sigh. Charles nodded in agreement.

"So, yeah, I'm thinking it's unlikely I'll dive into that." Dane shrugged. "But never say never, right? Like I said, I don't think about it, to be honest. It's not on my to-do list. I'm too busy living my life."

"Fair enough," Charles said. He glanced at their

sister who sat between them and added, "I think he more than answered your out-of-nowhere question."

"He did indeed." Tess raised her glass in a toast. "To the Harrison legacy of shitty marriages: may it now be over." Her brothers both clinked their glasses to hers before they all drank.

"So Tess . . ." Dane eyed her, choosing his words carefully. "It's been two years since that broken engagement. What about you? Have you recovered from that disaster enough to consider ever getting married?"

"Touché, my dear." Her usually warm voice turned cold and her face tightened. "But no. I don't think I'll be getting married, for most of the same reasons as you. Except for all the women, of course. I live a monk's life compared to you."

Charles let out a guffaw. "We *all* do, are you kidding?"

"Shut up," Dane said. "I'm not that bad."

Both siblings started laughing.

"Shut up!" Dane said, half amused, half annoyed.

Charles laughed even harder and dabbed at the corner of his eye. Dane glanced over at his brother. Charles rarely laughed like that anymore. He was so stressed all the time, his mind filled with all the things that went along with being the COO of a multimillion-dollar conglomerate and the heir to a family dynasty. Charles never had fun unless Dane was around. If Dane had to be the butt of a joke to get Charles to laugh like that once in a while, he had no problem with that.

After finally composing himself, Charles let out a deep, cleansing exhale and asked, "Can we talk about something else now?"

"When's the last time either of you spoke to Mom?" Dane asked.

"Last week," Tess said. "I called her to say Happy Mother's Day. We spoke for about ten minutes. You?"

"Same," Dane said.

"That's three for three, then," Charles said. "We're all wonderful children."

"I got an e-mail from her today," Dane went on. "I'd invited her to the hotel opening. She wanted to let me know she won't be able to make it."

"What a shock," Charles remarked dryly, and finished the last of his wine.

Dane smirked. "Yeah. She and Rick will be on a cruise of the Greek islands for the last two weeks of June—*so sorry, darling.*"

Tess sighed. "She has her own life."

"She does indeed," Dane said. He'd given up hoping his mother would come around years ago. Laura Dunham Harrison Evans Bainsley was all about one thing: Laura.

"Speaking of living their own life and ignoring the rest of the family," Charles quipped, "anyone hear from Pierce recently?"

Dane laughed at the mention of their estranged youngest brother. "Nice segue, Chuckles."

"I hate when you call me that," Charles said with a good-humored scowl.

"I know you do," Dane said. "That's the bonus."

"I text with him regularly," Tess said, referring to Pierce. "You guys could too, if you wanted to."

"He and I have very little to say to each other," Charles said flatly.

Tess frowned at him. "There are *four* of us. You should try to reach out more than you do."

"Stop," Charles said. "Pierce is a grown man now.

He's capable of checking in too, Tess. He doesn't contact us because he doesn't want to. The only one in the family he gives a shit about is you. This isn't news."

Dane reached for the bottle of wine and refilled his glass. "Either of you want more?"

"No more for me, thanks," Tess said. "You know one glass is my limit."

"Top me off, old boy," Charles said, imitating their father's voice precisely, bringing smirks from Dane and Tess.

Dane filled his brother's glass, then placed the bottle back on the small table beside him. "I sent him an e-mail last week inviting him to the hotel opening. He also declined."

"Really?" Tess looked genuinely surprised. "I'm . . . I'm sorry. It's a big deal for you. I hoped maybe Pierce would—"

"Apparently not." Dane shrugged. "He's playing that week, can't get off. It's cool." He wasn't going to let on that he'd actually suffered a twinge of disappointment when he'd gotten Pierce's response. He was proud of his younger brother. Pierce was a wild child, but he was also a semifamous soccer star in Europe, for Chrissake. That was a major achievement, which almost offset the bad-boy behavior. But he kept Dane at arm's length, like he did everyone, except for Tess.

Pierce had left home at eighteen and never looked back. Dane didn't blame him. After the divorce, their mother had been driven out of their lives, and the relationship between Pierce and their father was horrendous. If it weren't for Tess, whom Pierce practically worshipped, he'd probably never come back to the States—as it was, he only returned home for Christmas, and that was it.

But Dane had always tried to stay in contact with his younger brother. Things like texting and e-mail made it easier; they could keep in touch without having to actually talk. And Dane tried. Hell, when Tess had asked Dane to come with her to London for the 2012 Olympics, he'd gone gladly, looking to have a good time. But Pierce had shocked him; he'd gone with them to at least one sporting event every day, and had dinner with them almost every night. It had been an amazing two weeks, and the most time the brothers had spent together as adults. Dane hoped they'd maybe turned a corner, where Pierce would be more open to him . . . but apparently not.

"It bothers you," Tess murmured, her gaze on Dane unrelenting. "You were hoping he'd come, weren't you?"

"I didn't think he would," Dane said earnestly. "I just wanted him to know he was invited. That he was welcome."

"And as usual, he tossed your olive branch back at you," Charles said. "Why are you surprised? Pierce has an attitude problem, always has. He doesn't care if—"

"Knock it off, Charles," Tess warned. "I can call him, Dane. I can tell him—"

"Nope. Not necessary, Tesstastic. Like Charles said, Pierce is a big boy. And so am I. It's fine." Dane stretched his long legs out in front of him and eased back in his seat. "Come on, we're enjoying a beautiful sunset here. Breathe in that salty air. Look at the trees. Drink more wine. It's all good."

The three of them sat in silence for a minute, taking

in the late spring evening. The quiet was interrupted by a series of sharp barks from inside the house.

"She probably needs to go," Tess said, rising from her chair. "I'll be right back."

When she disappeared through the sliding glass doors into the house, Dane turned to Charles and said, "Opinion."

"Shoot," Charles said.

"The woman I hired to sing in my lounge." Julia Shay appeared in Dane's mind, sultry and gorgeous. "I did a basic background check, employment history, she has no police record, all that. But not a personal check. Think I need to?"

"Do *you* think you need to?"

"No. My gut says she's fine. But it also says she's got a history of serious personal shit."

"Who doesn't?" Charles said with a humorless chuckle.

"True. The way I see it," Dane continued, "her record's clean. Her personal life is none of my business if it never affects her while she's working. Leave it alone. Agree?"

"Agree," Charles said. "If you want to have a good working relationship with her, and you're letting a lot ride on her, you want her happy. Personal background checks often make people very *un*happy." He shrugged and removed his glasses to clean them on the edge of his polo shirt. "Besides, you have the resources. You ever feel like you need to, you can."

"That was exactly my line of thinking," Dane said. He nodded to himself and relaxed once more. "Thanks."

Charles put his glasses back on and slanted a look

at his brother. "You're interested in this woman, aren't you?"

Dane's brows furrowed. "Of course I am. She's head-lining in my hotel. Like you said, I've got a lot riding on her. I could've hired a proven star, but I wanted someone unknown. Someone fresh, so she'd have an air of mystery."

"Then let her have that mystery," Charles said. "Leave well enough alone." The corner of his mouth curved. "And don't take her to bed."

Dane sputtered out a laugh. "Nice! What the hell do you take me for?"

"Don't make me answer that," Charles said dryly. "You're my best friend. I'd like to keep it that way." He winked.

Dane opened his mouth to shoot back, but the back door slid open and a burst of white fur shot past them. The dog ran out to the grass and disappeared behind one of Tess's rosebushes.

"Bubbles really needed to go," she said, retaking her seat.

"Apparently," Dane remarked.

Within seconds, the tiny white Maltese ran back to her owner, yipping happily. Tess smiled with delight and picked up her dog, cooing at her with affection.

"What kind of contract did you offer her?" Charles asked Dane. "Timewise?"

"Who?" Tess asked as she rubbed Bubbles behind her ears.

"Julia Shay, the woman I hired to sing," Dane said. "It's more than fair. In her favor, if you ask me. I wanted a show of good faith. For her, and her accompanist who she insisted come with her. Good thing he's fantastic, I had no problem hiring him, too. So for them both, I'm starting with a six-month stint. Brings us to the end of the year. If they like it there, and I like them there, I exercise my option to renew and renegotiate."

"Sounds reasonable," Charles nodded. "I look forward to hearing her."

"You also look forward to *seeing* her," Tess chimed in with a mischievous grin. "My friend Jeannie said she's absolutely gorgeous."

"Oh yeah?" Charles's eyebrows lifted, intrigued as he looked his brother's way. "Got a picture?"

"Of course." Dane reached for his phone, trying to seem casual as he scrolled through. His siblings knew him too well. He didn't want his lust for Julia to show all over his face. He located her photo and handed his phone to his brother.

Charles looked, and his eyes widened a drop. He let out a low whistle. "*Damn.*" Looking up, he met Dane's eyes. "A beautiful redhead. Your Achilles' heel. Good luck with that."

"Shut up, Chuckles." Dane snatched his phone back as his siblings laughed knowingly.

"Redheads are your weakness, huh?" Tess needled. She smiled as she stroked her dog's fur, cradling her in her lap. "I just learned something."

"Every day's a school day, Tess," Dane said.

Bubbles yipped and Tess shushed her as she said, "And here I thought you loved all women equally."

"Oh, he does," Charles said. "But redheads . . . oof. He's putty. Especially a beautiful and *smart* redhead." He glanced back to Dane. "Is she smart?"

"As a whip," Dane muttered. "She's tough, too. She takes no shit."

"Ha!" Charles crowed with a smug smile. "Forget it. If you're not careful, she'll have you lapping at her feet in no time at all."

"Just shut up," Dane ordered. "There's not going to be any of that going on."

Charles snorted. "Yeah. Sure."

"I'm serious," Dane insisted, an edge in his voice. "She works for me. I'm her boss now. I don't cross those lines. Our relations will be strictly professional. End of story."

"Famous last words," Tess murmured with a grin. Bubbles barked, seeming to agree.

Chapter Four

Julia made her way up the two flights of steep stairs to her apartment, straining from the weight of the four bags of groceries she carried along with her pocketbook. This was one of the times she hated living on the middle floor of an old house.

She dropped the bags with a thud in front of her door, searched her pocketbook, found her keys, and unlocked her door. After kicking the door shut behind her with her foot, she dragged the bags into the kitchen and started unpacking the items into the refrigerator and tiny closet she used as a pantry.

She'd lived there for a decade already. It had been twelve years since she'd left Boston and moved back to Long Island. At first, she'd shared an apartment with Kelvin over in Edgewater. He'd moved to New York with her, unwilling to leave her when she was so alone and at rock bottom. Between her emotional devastation at the hands of her ex, breaking away from her unsympathetic family, and her small income, having a roommate helped her slowly get back on her feet. He worked several gigs on Long Island and in Manhattan, piecing together enough to be able to live on his earnings. She found a quiet office job and a good therapist. For two years, they lived together, until she'd healed enough for him to feel she was fine on her own. He moved to Astoria, and she moved to Blue Harbor.

She loved Blue Harbor, with its seaside New England–type charm. A sleepy town dotted with tiny shops, restaurants, boutiques, and charming old houses, she'd dreamed of living there as a kid. Now, completely on her own, she could. Her landlords, a kind couple twenty years her senior, owned the tremendous old house and lived on the bottom floor. She rented the second floor, and another tenant lived on the top floor. She felt safe there. It was quiet, and although she was alone, there were people nearby.

When the last of the groceries were stashed away, she washed her hands and looked around. She'd given notice at her job the day before, and in a show of petulant anger, her shortsighted boss had told her to just leave. It had been sad to say such a rushed good-bye to her coworkers, but as she'd left the gray, stifling office, she'd done so with a smile and a rush of elation. The new chapter of her life was going to be exciting. Getting paid to do what she loved most, and getting paid handsomely. But she wouldn't be starting the job at the hotel for another two weeks. Her errands all completed, she found herself with nothing to do. It was a strange, almost unsettling feeling.

Leaning against the small table that was shoved against the wall, she drank down a glass of water and looked to the window. It was a beautiful afternoon. Golden sunlight poured in through the gauzy white curtain, splashing on the three pots of African violets on the windowsill and bouncing off the pale yellow

walls. She moved to the living room and turned on
the air conditioner wedged into one of the two windows. It started to hum and she sank down onto her
couch. A glance at the answering machine showed no
messages. She reached for her Kindle, curled up into
the cushions, and played a few rounds of Words With
Friends with the random strangers she'd challenged.

After the games were finished, she sighed. At this
time tomorrow, she'd be in the city, getting a personal
tour of the new hotel from its debonair, charming,
and gorgeous owner. Thoughts of Dane Harrison
floated into her mind, but she swatted them away.
It was a shame, because she would have loved a few
rounds of sheet gymnastics with him. But no, that
would never happen.

What to do? Randi was at work, and Kelvin was
spending the day at the beach with his new boyfriend.
Though she was a voracious reader, she didn't feel
like reading. She didn't mind being alone, she'd
gotten used to it over the years. But sometimes she
longed for company. Restlessness, laced with threads
of anxiety, stirred inside her. She looked around aim-
lessly at the periwinkle walls, the framed artwork, her
bookshelf, her few precious framed photos on the
top shelf. She'd done her best to make her home feel
cozy and warm. But there were times she couldn't
escape the quiet emptiness there, the loneliness of
her life. And suddenly, this was one of them.

With new determination, she rose from the couch
and went to her bedroom. She stripped out of her
sundress and changed into a tank top and loose
shorts. The SPF 70 sunblock was in her small bathroom, and she slathered it all over her arms, legs,
chest, face, every inch of pale skin that was exposed.
She grabbed her big floppy sun hat, her iPod, and

her keys, and left to go for a walk down by the water. The sight and sounds of the Long Island Sound always had a way of soothing her soul. She'd just make sure to stay away from the park; the sound of happy children playing would break her heart when she was in a melancholy mood like this.

The next day, as Julia emerged from the cab, her heart began to beat a little faster. Excitement and anticipation fired up all her senses. It was a gorgeous early June day in New York City, warm but not too hot yet, with the sun shining from a clear, bright blue sky. A few trees dotted the length of the sidewalk, and a soft breeze made the emerald leaves flutter and sway. The cacophony of city sounds—traffic, horns blowing, human voices—seemed to fade around her as she looked up at the entrance to the impressive soon-to-open Hotel Alexandra.

This was really happening.

She removed her wide sunglasses and tucked them into her large shoulder bag, shuffling around inside it for a mint. As she chewed it up quickly, she tried to calm her suddenly rapid breathing and swept her hair back from her face. The contracts had been signed and delivered two weeks before, her photo shoot and press kit arranged and completed the week before. In two short weeks, she'd be the headlining singer at this sleek Manhattan hotspot. It was surreal. Her head hadn't stopped spinning. And now, between the warm weather, her meager breakfast, and her nerves, she wondered if she'd even make it through the tour of the hotel Dane had invited her for—maybe she'd pass out instead.

She pushed her way through the glass revolving

door and into the lobby. Thankfully, it was cool, the welcome air conditioning flowing over her skin. She crossed the lushly carpeted floor to the main desk, smiling at the woman behind it. "Hi. I'm looking for Dane Harrison. I'm supposed to meet him here."

"Ms. Shay?" the woman asked.

"That's me."

"He was here five minutes ago, but had to take a call. He asked if you'd be kind enough to wait and he'd be right back."

"Sure. Could you just point me toward a ladies' room while I wait?"

Julia took the opportunity to survey her surroundings as she headed to the restroom. This would be her workplace, after all. From what she could see, the hotel was striking. Modern but not trendy, everything from the luxurious furnishings to the décor spoke of crisp elegance, style, taste, and big-time bucks. Dane Harrison had obviously spared no expense in the design and decorating of his newest hotel.

She washed her hands, fixed her hair, and touched up her makeup. The slight humidity in the summer air had made the waves in her hair more pronounced, but at least the expensive product she'd used had tamed the deadly frizz she'd suffered from as a kid. Her clothes had barely wrinkled, for which she was grateful. The sleeveless royal blue silk top and white pencil skirt still looked fresh. Her open-toe white wedge sandals were comfortable but attractive. She took a deep breath, released it, and stared into the mirror.

Forty-one, Jules. Took forty-one years to get to this place. You survived. It's your turn.

Her eyes took on an energized sparkle and her

chin lifted a notch as she popped another mint into her mouth. *Let's do this.*

She left the restroom to return to the lobby. Halfway across, she stopped in her tracks. Dane was standing by the large wall of windows that looked out to the street beyond. Sunlight shone through the glass, backlighting him dramatically. His dark curls were just a bit too long for business standards, and she had a feeling he liked it that way. His square jaw was covered with light stubble, another poke at the business world, letting everyone know that he was a man who did as he pleased. It also made him even sexier, damn him. Standing tall and sure, his trim frame dressed in a crisp white button-down shirt and dark gray slacks, he was even more handsome than she'd remembered. He was breathtaking, actually. Just looking at him made all her body parts jump to life, made her blood sing in her veins and her skin tingle. Ohhh, this was not good. She couldn't have such visceral reactions every time she saw this man. He was her *boss* now.

He spotted her across the lobby and flashed a grin. She swallowed hard as a wallop of heat spread through her. A grin like that should be registered as a lethal weapon. With all of her senses heightened and her head screaming red alert, she pulled out her most professional smile and crossed the rest of the way to meet him.

"Great to see you again, Julia," Dane said. "Glad you could come." His brilliant blue eyes swept over her briefly. There was both quick approval and the ever-present spark of light amusement there, like he had a joke or a secret to share. She wanted to be let in on that secret. She wanted a lot of things where this man was concerned, and all of them were naughty, if not downright wicked. He stretched out a welcoming hand.

She slipped her hand into his to shake it and felt a jolt of desire as she touched his warm skin, like she'd read about in books. Her hormones raged like a teen's, and that jarred her. But with measured cool, she said, "Likewise. Thanks for asking me. I really wanted to get a feel for the setup of the lounge. I appreciate your taking the time to show me around. I'm sure you're very busy."

"I am, but not too busy for this. It'll be a pleasure." His grin widened into a proud smile as his eyes flickered around the lobby, then back to her. "So? What do you think so far?"

"Your lobby and ladies' room are both magnificent," she teased.

He laughed and touched a hand to the small of her back. "Wait 'til you see the rest of it."

His tiny but intimate gesture kindled flames of lust in her, sending heat to all her most sensitive spots. Oh, what she could do with this man under different circumstances. Five years plus of an age difference didn't make her a cougar, did it? So what if it did. She didn't care. Being near him was excruciating, making every nerve ending alert and alive, and the growing, tingling tension building low in her belly was making its way to between her legs. The effect he had on her was both thrilling and nerve-wracking. Kelvin had been right: pure chemistry. She ignored the way her heart was pounding in heavy thumps as they walked side by side down a long hallway.

"So," she said, desperate to get her mind off her

wayward thoughts. "Why'd you name this hotel the Alexandra?"

His smile was tinged with affection as he said, "It's my sister's middle name."

Something tugged at Julia's heart. She smiled back. "That's . . . sweet. You're close with her, then?"

"Very. Tess is the best. I'll introduce you to her at the hotel opening." Dane turned and led her down another hallway. She took the moment to quickly check out his ass, which was a very nice one indeed.

The Alexandra Bar & Lounge had wide glass doors, hinting at the darker lair beyond. She stopped in her tracks. Beside the entrance was a blown-up photo on a stand, one of her publicity shots, announcing her as the main act inside. She stared at it. It was so . . . professional. Glitzy. Polished. For a second, she felt like a star. And dammit, it felt good.

"You approve?" Dane asked from behind her.

"Yes." She could feel him watching her, taking in her reactions. Nodding, she said, "It's nice. I like the shot you chose."

"It was hard to choose," he said, his deep voice warm, just above her ear. Even in her three-inch wedge sandals, he towered over her. "All the shots were good. Seriously. The camera loves you." She looked up at him, and though he wore an easy grin, his eyes glittered at her with a hint of sin. "And that's more than a 'nice' shot, Julia. It's gorgeous. Just like you."

"Thank you," she said demurely. He stood close enough that the faintest scent of his cologne teased her, sparking new fires in her body. Slightly spicy, it wasn't overpowering, it was just a hint—just enough to make everything tingle with desire.

"Come on inside." He opened one of the doors and ushered her in.

Her breath caught. This place was fabulous. Modern, stylish, and cool. Little round tables with curved-back chairs dotted the front of the room, the lounge area. Then there was more open floor space by the bar, and along the back wall, six deep, cozy booths, with seats covered in dark brown leather. Julia followed Dane farther into the room. Low lighting from funky fixtures above illuminated the room, except for the bar itself—eight or ten shelves held every kind of top liquor there was, backlit against mirrors. And at the front of the lounge area was what would be her domain: a small rectangular stage, not too highly elevated, to promote some intimacy with the audience. It was mostly filled by a black Steinway piano.

"You like it?" Dane asked casually, peering at her.

"Yes, I do," she said, understating it by a mile. It was amazing. She already loved it. She could imagine what it would be like when filled, crackling with lively late-night energy. A respectable, upscale place, a place to be proud to sing in, with Kelvin at her back . . . it was going to be very enjoyable indeed to work here. "How many does the lounge hold?"

"A hundred. And room for over a hundred more in the bar."

She nodded and stepped up to the stage, turned to face the room, and took in the view from her vantage point. She felt like she'd just stepped up on an Olympic podium to accept a gold medal. "Nice." Her eyes flickered to Dane. "The aesthetics are great, but how are the acoustics?"

He frowned. "Not sure what you mean."

"You don't have a mic here, do you?"

"It's somewhere in the back. I can go look for it if you like," he offered.

"Not necessary." She swallowed to clear and wet her throat, drew a deep breath, closed her eyes, and started to sing.

Dane stood mesmerized as Julia belted out two lines from a song he didn't know. Her voice was full, rich, and dazzling. He'd heard her sing before, of course. But watching her up onstage alone, singing without accompaniment and hitting every note right on target, with ease and passion . . . he felt like someone had punched him in the gut.

He'd never been the groupie type, but suddenly he understood the phenomenon. Julia's natural talent made her even more attractive to him. He wanted her to sing to *him*, seduce him personally with that voice. What a gift.

She stopped as she'd started, quickly and without warning. "It'll work," she said simply, and stepped down from the stage.

"Yes. It. Will." Dane felt a bit hazy. "What was that song? I don't know it."

"Annie Lennox. 'Dark Road.' One of my favorites." She passed him to head back toward the bar.

"Add it to your set list," he commanded.

"Already on it, Boss."

He watched her stroll around the space, examining details and taking it all in. His eyes greedily rolled over her curves. "Think Kelvin will like it here too?" He didn't really care, but had to keep the conversation flowing before he did something stupid with his newest, red-hot employee.

"Absolutely," Julia said. "He's very easygoing. He only comes off like a diva."

Dane laughed. "So who's the diva, then? You?"

"Nooo," she said, unable to hold back a grin. "I'm no diva. You don't have to worry." She took a seat on one of the barstools, covered in the same dark brown leather as the booths.

"Good to know," Dane said, taking a seat beside her. He leaned an elbow on the bar, mirroring her. "Okay, so you're not a diva. You're tough as hell, though. How come?"

"How come?" she echoed, looking at him strangely. "Um . . . life?"

"Okay." Dane let that go. For now. "I meant to ask you last week, forgive me—is there anyone you want to invite to the grand opening?"

"I'll be working, won't I?" Julia asked, confused.

"Yes, you will. Doesn't mean you can't enjoy some of the party before you start. You don't go on until ten. You should mingle, work the room." He kept his grin easy as his gaze sharpened. "So no one you want to invite? Family? Friends? A boyfriend?"

Julia snorted out a laugh. "Really?" She shook her head and said, somewhat bemused, "*That's* your idea of a fishing expedition? Jeez."

He stared at her in mild disbelief. "Excuse me?"

"If you want to ask about my personal life, just freakin' ask."

Her way of cutting right to the point threw him, and he wasn't a man who was easily thrown. He'd have to get used to being on his toes around her. Which wasn't necessarily a bad thing. "Fine. Do you have a boyfriend?"

"No."

"Are you married?"

"No," she said, with more of an edge.

"Do you have any family locally that you'd like to invite?"

"Nope." She met his eyes. "You've got money and means. You've probably checked out my entire life history already. What are you looking for?"

Affronted, he frowned. "You're right, I could have done that if I'd wanted to. I didn't. I only checked what was necessary for your professional life, not your personal life. That's your business, not mine. I'm not like that. Okay?"

She pressed her lips together and nodded.

His head cocked to the side as he studied her. "Do you believe me?"

She regarded him in silence for a long moment before saying, "I don't trust anyone until they've proven to me that I can. Don't take it personally. It's not you."

Watching her keenly, he only nodded, filing that away.

"I'd like to invite my best friend, Randi, and her husband," Julia said, closing the tense gap. "Is that all right?"

"Of course. Give me the names and address, consider it done. Anyone else?"

"Nope." She slid off the barstool. "Do I have a dressing room?"

"Absolutely." Dane stood and escorted her behind the stage, down a short hallway to the room at the end. He opened the door for her and stepped aside. "Ladies first."

She moved past him into the small but elegant room. Dane had ensured that the mirror on the wall was well lit, the counter attached to it wide enough to hold makeup, a drink, whatever she wanted, and the chair was comfortable. The walls had been painted taupe and the carpet was a rich brown, adding warmth to the room. Two chocolate-colored leather sofas lined opposite walls; a large vase of freshly cut flowers sat on the long glass coffee table between them.

He watched her face as she took it in. "You like it?"

"I do," she answered simply. She offered a smile. And that was it.

He'd been hoping for a more enthusiastic response, but swatted away the flicker of annoyance. Julia wasn't the type of woman to squeal like a fangirl over a nice room, even though he'd made sure it was nice solely for her enjoyment. He wondered what *would* get her to drop her guard around him, to express more emotion than cool respect, quiet gratitude, or wary mistrust.

On the back wall, opposite the vanity, was a closet door. Dane went and opened it to show her what was inside. "These are yours."

Julia had an odd look on her face that he couldn't read. Was she happy? Unhappy? Pissed off? She kept her cards so goddamn close to the vest.

"What's in there?" she asked.

"Your wardrobe," he said, opening the door as wide as it could go. "Dresses." He grinned at her. "They don't bite. Come take a look."

She approached the closet slowly. He could see the curiosity in her eyes that she was trying so damn hard to hide from him. That . . . and a hint of wonder. A flicker of vulnerability. Ah, hell. His heart twinged in his chest.

He moved to give her room. "This is a good start, I think. You don't need to do any wardrobe changes each night, this isn't Vegas. One dress per night is fine. You gave my assistant, Elise Cannon, your measurements, and then she did the heavy lifting. But between you and me, I think she had fun doing it."

"I'm glad," Julia murmured. Focused on the dresses now, she reached out to touch them. There were about a dozen hanging there. Black, midnight blue, royal blue, deep purple, emerald green, hunter green. Silk, cotton, beads, sequins. All of them stunning. "You had all of these made for me?"

"Yes." He couldn't take his eyes off her. "I hired you. I need to make sure you look your best."

"That must've been pricey."

"Not your concern. Just wear them well."

She glanced at him, then back to the dresses. "I've never had a wardrobe purchased for me for a job before. Much less anything like this. I . . . wow. Thank you."

Her eyes met his again for a long beat, and he saw there what her quietly spoken words had given away. She was genuinely moved. Possibly even a bit overwhelmed. It was a moment of softness he hadn't seen in her before now, and something in his heart pinged again. He smiled and said warmly, "You're welcome. My pleasure."

She broke the intense gaze and looked back at the dresses.

"I'm sure you'll look gorgeous in all of them." He let his eyes glide over her hourglass figure. The word *goddess* flashed in his head. "But if you don't like any of them, tell me, we'll send them back and get different ones. Don't be shy about that." He moved closer and lifted her chin with a fingertip, looking down at her. She stilled beneath his touch.

"Julia, I want you to feel beautiful up there. If you *feel* like a gorgeous queen, it'll come across. That's what I want."

Her hazel eyes shone and glimmered as she met his gaze. "Is that all you want?" she murmured provocatively.

Heat flooded his body, lust ruled him without mercy. *Goddamn.* "No, that's not all I want," he murmured back. Their eyes locked and held. Her softness was gone, replaced by a flirty sensuality. He took another step closer. "You are a vile temptress."

She smirked and purred, "I bet you say that to all the girls."

Her husky voice sent shimmers of desire through him. He let his finger trail along her smooth jaw. His eyes fell to her mouth, those lush, inviting lips so close. "We can't do this, you know."

"Of course not," she said. Her voice didn't waver, but she didn't step back from him. "You're my boss. I'm not stupid. I plan to keep my job."

"And you will." His heart started pounding against his ribs. He dragged his finger down her soft, pale neck . . . slowly, teasing. He let that fingertip wander back up the side of her throat. Her breath hitched, but she didn't break their gaze. "You . . . are incredibly sexy, Julia. You drive men wild. And you know it."

"Maybe a little." Something flamed in her eyes. "Is that why you hired me? I thought it was because of my voice."

"It was both," he said flatly. "You have an amazing voice. And you're unbelievably hot."

Her mouth curved up. "Thank you. But I've gotta tell ya . . ." She moved in a drop closer, their faces now only inches apart. He could feel her warm breath against his mouth, see the gold flecks shining in her striking hazel eyes. Her voluptuous breasts brushed against his chest and his heart almost stopped. She looked deep into his eyes, smiled, and whispered with carnal boldness, "You couldn't handle me."

Lust slammed him, almost made his knees weak. With all the women he'd known, all the women he'd been with—and yeah, there were more than he cared to admit to—not one of them had been this direct. This forward. This *hot*. Who was seducing whom here? Jesus Christ. "Oh, I could handle you," he assured her in a rough whisper, even as adrenaline and hunger surged through his body.

"Mmm. Maybe you could." Her eyes danced, teasing as she took a step back. "Too bad we won't find out, huh?"

His blood sizzled through his veins. He hoped she couldn't tell he had a raging hard-on. "No, unfortunately, we won't. We can't."

She nodded and turned her back to him. He stared at her hair, the cascading fiery waves, and his hands fisted at his sides. Everything in him longed to grab her, whirl her around, and kiss her senseless. But he couldn't. *I'm her boss,* he reminded himself, willing his heart to slow. *I'm her fucking boss.*

Before he could blink, she turned back to him, took his face with both hands, and pulled him down to bring his mouth crashing onto hers.

A second of shock blurred into instant passion as he kissed her back. Her mouth was as warm and soft as he'd imagined it would be. His hands grasped her waist and pulled her closer. Her kiss was demanding; she *wanted.* Goddammit, so did he. She touched her tongue to his and he tasted mint and fire and sensuality . . . *More.* He wanted more.

She broke the kiss, gasping for air. Her hands went

to his chest to push back from him, but he didn't release her.

They stared at each other for a moment. The air around them crackled and pulsed.

"Well, okay then," she gasped. She drew a shaky breath. "Okay. Had to just get that out of my system. I'll be fine from here on in."

"Really?" Dane said, his voice thick. "Okay. But I didn't get my turn." He gripped her face and crushed his mouth to hers. No mercy. Pure animal lust. He wanted her boneless when he was done kissing her. He wanted her so bad it ached, and he took it out on her luscious mouth.

His kisses were greedy, ravenous. He wanted to own her, and his mouth was relentless. Kissing, nipping, tasting, he consumed her. She whimpered softly into his mouth as the kisses deepened; as she surrendered with a tiny moan, her arms slid around his neck and held.

That tiny moan nearly undid him. He tangled his fingers in her soft, thick hair, holding her head as he took what he wanted. But she matched him, taking and giving, the heat between them rising. Their tongues tangled in an erotic dance. His hands slid down her sides, around to her back, over those lush hips to hold her tighter. She pressed her body against his and he grabbed her ass, holding her hips to his. His erection strained against her and a groan came from deep in his throat, vibrating into her mouth.

She pushed him away. Hard. "*Whoa.* Okay. That's . . ." Her eyes were dazed, dark with passion. Gasping, wide-eyed, she gaped at him.

His head spinning, he fought to catch his breath too. "Holy shit," he panted.

A quick laugh escaped her now-swollen mouth.

"Yeah." She stared a moment longer, then took a step back, recomposing herself in a flash. "But that can't happen again."

Annoyance flashed through him and he squelched it. He was ready to throw her down on the couch and totally ravage her. But she was right. He took a deeper breath and raked his hands through his hair. "I know." He couldn't help but smirk as he added teasingly, "You started it."

Her face flushed and she pointed an accusatory finger at him. "Okay. Yes, I kissed you first. But I don't care how hot you are, or how hot you think I am," she said staunchly. "This will *not* happen. This is a great job. A dream job. I want to *keep* this job."

"You will," he assured her. His mind had cleared, his heart rate was slowing, and as much as she was putting on a damn strong front, he'd caught a glimpse of something in her eyes before she'd shuttered it: fear. "Julia. Your contract is ironclad. You're safe. Don't show up drunk, don't be inappropriate in the hotel, don't get your name in the papers for anything negative, and your job is secure. Whether anything ever happens between us or not. Okay?"

She stared for another few seconds, then turned away. She went to the mirror and dropped her shoulder bag onto the counter. Her hair fell around her face as she rummaged through her bag, like a shield of fiery waves. She pulled out a lip-liner pencil and fixed her mouth, not meeting his eyes in the mirror as she worked.

Dane stared at her back. She'd brushed him off. She'd all but fucking dismissed him. He sat slowly on one of the sofas, trying to maintain an air of casual ease, but his insides were still throbbing and his mind was in a tailspin. To say she'd surprised him was the understatement of the year. She'd kissed him, *she'd* made the first move. He'd been, as Pierce would say, gobsmacked. He wasn't used to a woman taking what she wanted from him so boldly. She'd wanted it so she'd taken it, without apology and without restraint. It turned him on more than he wanted to admit.

He licked his lips, still tasting her. The sound of her soft moan of surrender still echoed in his head. Goddammit, he wanted her. She was fire and power and heat, and he wanted all of it. She could brush him off all she liked—the chemistry between them was undeniable. Those scorching kisses had proved it.

He drew in a deep breath and exhaled it slowly.

Maintaining a professional relationship with Julia Shay was going to be even harder than he'd thought.

Chapter Five

Dane made another pass through the lobby, shaking hands as he worked his way through the crowd. The party was in full swing and going smoothly. Food disappeared off the trays almost as fast as the waitstaff brought them out. Drinks were plentiful, music played, laughter sounded among the low rumble of conversation . . . the bash to celebrate the opening of the Hotel Alexandra was a success.

Dane had expected nothing less, but he always felt that click of relief and satisfaction once he was firmly in the game.

He heard a familiar voice call his name and looked over. His father, beside his older brother and sister in the corner he'd reserved for them, waved Dane over insistently. Dane held up a finger, telling him to wait, as he finished the chat he was having with the mayor's wife. When he was able to excuse himself politely, he crossed to where his family stood.

"How goes it, Harrisons?" he said amiably, and leaned in to drop a quick kiss on Tess's cheek. "You look fantastic," he told her. His sister was a beautiful woman on her worst day, but all decked out in a hot pink halter gown, over six feet tall with the added height from her four-inch heels, she stood out even in a room of glamorous, beautiful people.

"Thank you," she said with a pleased smile. She reached up to straighten his tie. "Having fun? Everything's going well?"

"All is well," Dane said proudly. "I'm even going to have a drink soon. Think I can relax and enjoy now."

"Hell of a party," Charles Harrison II boomed at his son. "Another Harrison success."

"Dad," Tess said in a soft reprimand. "This is Dane's *own* success."

"That too." Charles II clapped his free hand on his son's shoulder. "Another notch on your *own* belt. Good for you." He raised his glass of scotch in a toast and took a sip.

"Thanks, Dad," Dane said, smiling, then turned to his sister and winked.

"So when does your singer start?" Charles III asked.

"Ten o'clock. She'll do two short sets: forty-five minutes each, with a fifteen-minute break in between. You won't be disappointed," Dane promised. "She's really good."

"And very easy on the eyes, from what your brother tells me," Charles II said.

Dane chuckled. "Yup. She's sexy as hell, but with class and grit. You'll approve."

Charles II nodded firmly at his son. "Good. Sex sells. Men will want her, and women will want to be like her. Smart move."

"The only kind of move I make, Dad." Thinking of his fiery vocalist, Dane grinned and checked his watch. "Well, it's almost nine-thirty. Grab a table soon if you want to. I'll meet you in there, save me a seat. Got a few more hands to shake."

Dane slipped into the bar and lounge at five minutes to ten. To his satisfaction, the place was packed. Patrons filled the bar area, almost to overflowing, the sounds of the lively crowd music to his ears. Every table in the lounge was taken. Craning his neck, he spotted the backs of his family's heads at a table front and center. Of course his father would want the best seat in the house. Charles Harrison II always wanted nothing but the best, and usually got it.

Tess sat between both Charles Harrisons; Dane slid into the empty chair next to his brother. "Hello, kids."

"Hey, there you are. I love it in here!" Tess said enthusiastically. "This is fantastic."

"What she said," Charles III agreed. "Great atmosphere."

"Glad you like it," Dane said. Pride warmed him and he smiled.

"What kind of stuff does this woman sing?" Charles II asked.

Dane caught the eyes of a waitress and he waved her over. "One set will be your type of stuff—standards, classics," he added for his father's benefit. "The other set will be contemporary songs. But ballads, mainly."

"She's a torch singer," Charles II proclaimed. "Good. I like torch singers."

The waitress got to Dane's side and he ordered a round of the house's best scotch for the table. "Wait, only three, actually," he amended, knowing Tess wouldn't touch the stuff. "Just more sparkling water for her."

The lights dimmed slowly until the large room was

bathed in near darkness. The rumble of the crowd lowered to murmurs, then hushed altogether. The air crackled with excitement. Dane felt a tingle of anticipation run through him. This was it, what he'd been looking forward to for months: having a singer wow his clientele, and perhaps starting a new enterprise as a nightclub owner. Julia had to show her stuff. Thank God, she had the stuff.

Julia and Kelvin were both dedicated professionals. He knew they took their trade seriously, and it was important to them. But tonight, it was even more important to him. With this, his reputation was on the line. Whether she bombed or soared, either way, it would reflect on him.

He thought he saw something sparkle on the stage, only six feet away. And then, cutting through the dark, came Julia's voice. Smooth and sultry, without accompaniment, she sang the opening lines to the standard "Fever". Her compelling voice reached out and caressed the crowd with velvet fingers.

The spotlight came on, focused only on Julia as Kelvin started to play along behind her. And Dane's heart stuck in his chest. Beautiful. Captivating. Absolutely electric. She was the very picture of tasteful glamour and sensual self-assurance—the musical seductress he'd wanted. Exactly what he'd envisioned all along . . . and damn, so much more.

He didn't recognize the silver sequined gown that hugged her every luscious curve until the hem poured onto the floor around her stilettoed feet. It wasn't one of the dresses he'd bought for her; he would've remembered that knockout of a dress. Her fiery hair flowed loose, sleek, and silky. Curled at the ends, her locks stopped just above her glorious cleavage, which was definitely showcased, but not in a vulgar way. Those big hazel eyes stood out even more with her dramatic, smoky makeup, and her red, glossy mouth was a beckoning tease. As her lips moved, he remembered what it was like to taste her. . . .

Dane could only stare, completely mesmerized.

Julia cradled the microphone with one hand, her body swaying sinuously as she sang. The spotlight danced off her dress, making it twinkle and glimmer as she moved. He watched her hook her audience and reel them in with her enticing vocals like a pro. By the middle of the song, he could tell she'd relaxed enough to start enjoying it. She had them already, and she knew it. The look on her face was one of confidence, triumph . . . and even a hint of seduction. Dane felt his mouth curve up in a satisfied grin. He'd taken a huge risk with an unknown singer . . . and hit the jackpot.

The waitress discreetly placed his scotch before him, jolting him out of his trance. Feeling a little sheepish and slightly stunned by his visceral, almost primitive reaction to Julia, he knocked back a few hearty gulps of his drink, welcoming the warm burn as he sat back to enjoy the rest of the song. Julia and Kelvin were completely in sync, making it look effortless as only a well-polished team could.

When the song ended, the audience erupted in thunderous applause and approving shouts. Julia acknowledged the accolades with a poised nod and broad smile. She graciously waved her open palm back to Kelvin, making sure he was acknowledged too. Sitting so close, Dane could see the hint of pink in her cheeks and a sparkle in her eyes he hadn't seen until now—she was happy. Relieved. She knew she'd killed it up there, and she was thrilled. Dane clapped as loudly as he could. He was thrilled *for* her.

Charles III leaned in and said to Dane, "She's phenomenal. And man, can she sing. You sure know how to pick 'em."

Dane grinned softly, but gently tapped his glass to his brother's and they drank.

"What a voice!" Tess exclaimed. "Such presence. I'm so impressed. Jeannie was right about her!"

"Yes, she was, Tess," Dane agreed. "I owe her, and you, a big one."

"I'll remember that," Tess trilled with delight.

"You've got yourself a future star there," their father said. "Keep an eye on her."

"Believe me, I will," Dane replied, feeling elated and strangely proud. He stared at Julia, mentally willing her to look at him. She did almost immediately. He tossed her a wink and an admiring grin, nodding as if to say, "Well done." Their eyes held and the corner of her mouth turned up in a hint of a pleased smile. Then her gaze flickered back out to the crowd before she launched into her next song.

"That woman is an old-fashioned bombshell," Charles II proclaimed.

Dane snorted, but thought to himself, *She sure as hell is.*

Julia glanced back at Kelvin, and he started playing the opening bars of "Nice Work If You Can Get It." Smooth and cool, Kelvin's long fingers moved along the keys with mastery, his dreads swaying as his head bobbed in time. Julia cocked her curvaceous hip and smiled as she launched into the song, having fun with it.

Throughout the set, Dane sat back to enjoy the music and bathe in her sexy, powerful glow. She had more than delivered. He was grateful, he was relieved . . . and he wanted her even more now. He wanted to lift her up, lay her across the top of the piano, hike up that sparkling silver dress, and take her right there.

But as the set went on, and her patter with the audience gave glimpses into her sharp wit and personality, he enjoyed seeing aspects of her he hadn't before. That she hadn't *allowed* him to see. She was outgoing, smiling, and open—which she rarely was to him. Whenever he'd poked his head in at a rehearsal over the past two weeks—which was almost every day; he couldn't help himself, he wanted to see her— she'd held him at bay. He watched her joke around with Kelvin, be friendly to everyone she met. But for Dane, she was cool, all business, an employee talking to her boss. He'd banter with her anyway, as he did with everyone, and sometimes she bantered back. But her unspoken message was loud and clear: the kiss wouldn't be repeated. The chemistry between them was to be ignored. Their interactions would be strictly professional. She kept her distance from him physically and emotionally; her manner and body language around him were guarded.

Or, most of her was. Not her eyes. Those expressive dark gold eyes sometimes betrayed her. If he stepped closer to her, wanting to push a little to see how she'd react . . . her eyes flamed for a second when they met his, and he knew she was remembering that off-the-charts kiss as much as he was. The melding and crashing of mouths, the wandering hands, the feel of their bodies pressed together . . .

He thought of it now, watching her body sway under the lights, sparkles coming off her dress like glittery diamonds. He gazed at her eyes, heavy-lidded as she beautifully sang a song of yearning, as if she were making love to the notes. . . .

Damn. Damn, damn, damn.

He sat back in his chair, crossed one long leg over the other, and made sure he caught her gaze when he lifted his glass in a toast to her before he sipped.

It was after 1:30 A.M. by the time Dane made it back to the lounge. The grand opening party had been a success, most of the guests had dispersed, and as of six o'clock the following morning—now only hours away—the Hotel Alexandra would officially be open for business.

He'd pressed the flesh with members of the media, society mavens, politicians, and other movers and shakers in the hotel industry. Except for when he'd sat to watch Julia's first set, he'd been on his feet the entire night. He had laughed with friends and colleagues, sampled some of his new chef's fantastic cuisine, and seen his family into the limo that would take them back to Long Island. He should've been exhausted. But he wasn't. He was still pumped with adrenaline, not nearly ready to call it a night, and headed to the bar for a drink.

Ah, who was he kidding? That wasn't all of it. He was looking to see if the redhead was still around. He couldn't keep away from her if he knew she was in the building. The last two weeks had proven that. He'd found an excuse to see her almost every day. Just like he was now.

To his delight, the bar was still filled with patrons. *Ah, New Yorkers,* he thought, *you wonderful night owls, you never let me down.* He strolled toward the lounge area; no one was there. Maybe she was back in her dressing room?

"Everything okay, Mr. Harrison?" came a man's voice from behind him.

Dane turned and grinned up at his head bartender. "Better than okay, Tonio. It's been a great night. How's business in here? Looks good."

"Hasn't let up since we opened the doors," Tonio Ramos said. He gestured with his chin toward the four bartenders working behind the bar. "They're good. Smooth. Gonna be fine."

"Glad to hear it." Dane clapped a hand on Tonio's shoulder and noted it was like slapping concrete. Tonio was built like a linebacker—which he had been, back in his college days. After a five-year bartending and bouncing stint at one of Dane's favorite bars in Tribeca, Dane had hired him as head bartender for his midtown hotel three years ago. Then he'd moved Tonio to the Alexandra, wanting someone he knew he could count on, and given him a generous raise. "I trust your judgment, you know that."

"Thanks, Boss."

Dane scoured the area once more before saying, "Hey, any chance you've seen Julia Shay around? Or did she leave already?"

"No, they're back over there." Tonio nodded toward the high-walled booths at the back, on the other side of the bar. "Her, the piano player, and another couple. I made sure they got fed and had a round of drinks on the house. Hope that's okay."

"More than okay. I would've done the same. See they get that every night they perform, all right?" Dane shook Tonio's hand and started to leave, but turned back. "Question."

Tonio's thick brows lifted. "Answer?"

"What do you think of them?" Dane asked quietly. "Julia and Kelvin. Speaking as a colleague. Just between us."

"They're solid," Tonio said without hesitation. "They showed up early, did their jobs well, and were nice to everybody. All they asked for before the show were bottles of water, and a Coke for him. No attitudes. She ain't a diva, and he's funny as hell. He's already charmed half the staff."

"Thanks." Dane clapped Tonio's broad shoulder again. "Keep up the good work. See ya soon." And strode with purpose toward the booths.

"Um, look out, y'all," Kelvin said to his three friends. "Incoming. Heat seeking missile headed our way."

"What?" Randi laughed. She glanced at her husband's face; Stephen looked just as confused by Kelvin's secret language.

Julia stretched her neck to see whom Kelvin was talking about.

"Don't look!" Kelvin snapped at her. "Just be cool. Boss man's coming."

Julia eased back against the luxurious cushions and took a sip of her drink.

"I get to meet the famous boss?" Randi whispered. "I get to check him out for myself?"

"What does that mean?" Stephen asked, also in a whisper.

"Jules said he's hot," Randi whispered quickly. "I wanna see."

"Then look up, girl," Kelvin murmured, then plastered a wide, welcoming smile on his face. "Well hello there!" He got to his feet to shake Dane's hand.

"Hello yourself," Dane grinned. "Hell of a job tonight, Kelvin. Really. You're the goods. I couldn't be happier with you."

"Thanks!" Kelvin's dark eyes shone with appreciation. "That's great to hear."

Dane looked down at Julia and smiled. "You were amazing. Absolutely delivered tonight. You knocked it out of the park."

"Thank you," she said. Her eyes captured his and held for a long beat before she broke the spell. She held an open palm across the table. "Dane, these are my close friends, Randi and Stephen Jensen."

"Pleasure to meet you," Dane said, shaking each of their hands with a smile. "Dane Harrison. Hope you had a good time tonight?"

"Absolutely," Stephen said.

"The hotel is beautiful. Really impressive," Randi added. "Everything was wonderful. Congratulations."

"Thank you," Dane beamed. "Glad you enjoyed the evening." He shoved his hands in his pockets, and asked, "How long have you been friends?"

"Since grade school," Randi said. "Jules and I grew up together."

"Wow, that's a long time," Dane said. He glanced at Julia and his smile turned wicked as he said to Randi, "Bet you could tell me some stories, huh?"

"She's a vault," Julia said flatly. "Don't even try it."

Dane's smile didn't waver as his gaze sharpened. "What's the matter, Red? Got something to hide?"

She could feel the telltale hot pink bloom on her cheeks. But she kept her voice steady as she said, "No. And please don't call me that."

"Sorry. It's a habit of mine. I give people nicknames." Dane kept the calm, cool look on his face, seemingly unfazed. He always looked so at ease, so nonchalant.

Had the world on a string. Julia rarely felt at ease, much less nonchalant, so his laid-back manner sometimes frustrated her.

And he liked to bait her. The more she held him at arm's length, the more he tried to engage her. Clearly, he was a man who liked a challenge, and had apparently decided Julia was one. Okay, she'd kissed him. Her mistake. It wouldn't happen again, no matter how mind-blowing that kiss had been or how attractive she found him. She knew his type. Handsome as sin, loaded with money, naturally charming, and the world seemingly at his fingertips . . . she'd been there before and barely survived to tell the tale. She picked up her vodka and cranberry and took a hearty swallow. For her, Dane might as well have been wrapped in yellow police tape, with the word CAUTION blazing in neon instead of plain black letters.

He looked back to Randi and asked amiably, "Can I borrow your lifelong friend for a few minutes? Just need to discuss something with her."

"You don't need our permission," Kelvin said, standing so Julia could slide out of the booth. "Go on, sweetie. We'll be here."

She got to her feet and grabbed her small red clutch from the tabletop. "Back in a few."

"Nice to meet you," Dane said to the Jensens. "Hope you'll come back."

"We will," Randi said, smiling. "My best friend is your new star."

"That she is," Dane said, and looked down at Julia. In her four-inch stilettos, she still only reached his chin. He held out a hand toward the side door that led outside. "After you."

She walked ahead of him to the exit, recomposing herself as she went. What did he want? He'd seemed more than pleased with her performance, but was this a reprimand of some kind, that he didn't want to tell her in front of others? Taking a deep breath, she pushed through the glass doors, strode out to the sidewalk, and turned to face him. *Damn.* Did he have to look so damn good in that tux? She wanted to slide the tie out of his collar and wrap it around his neck to pull him down to her. . . .

Warm June breezes caressed her bare arms, but she shook off a shiver. She cleared her throat and said with a smile, "Everything okay, Boss?"

He snorted out a laugh. "If you're going to keep calling me Boss, I get to keep calling you Red."

Her eyes narrowed. "I really don't like it when people call me that."

"I'm not 'people'," he said with a sly grin. "I'm your boss. As you keep reminding me."

She huffed a breath of exasperation. "Fine. So. *Boss.* What's up? You wanted to talk?"

His features softened. "Julia . . . you were really incredible tonight. Seriously. I couldn't be happier with your performance. I wanted to thank you."

She hadn't expected that. That, or the earnest tone he used to speak. Her throat felt thick. "You're welcome," she managed to murmur.

"I took a big chance on you," he continued. "I wanted an unknown. That had its risks. But you're as talented, as professional, and as charismatic as any proven star I've seen." His blue eyes gleamed as he admitted, "You struck me flat tonight. I mean, I saw you perform the night I met you. I've caught bits of your rehearsals. But tonight . . . you *owned* that room, and everyone in it. I'm beyond impressed. And I don't impress easily." He grinned, almost sheepishly, and shoved his hands in his pockets. "I just thought you should know that. And that I think you're going to have a great run here."

Pleasure shimmered over her, but she couldn't show him how much his praise meant to her. He'd use it to his advantage if he knew his words affected her. Or how adorable he looked just then. So she did what she usually did: went on the offensive to deflect. "Thank you. But why are you buttering me up? You just opened a hotel tonight. You must be incredibly busy; you didn't have to seek me out personally to tell me that. So what's the catch here?"

He stared at her for a long beat, searching. She didn't flinch under his scrutiny, but wondered if she'd been too harsh.

"No catch," he finally said. "No buttering up. No false flattery to try to win you over. Just telling you, as your boss, that you did a fantastic job tonight. I believe in praising people when they do well. It's called positive reinforcement."

She winced on the inside, but didn't say a word. *Yup, too harsh. Idiot.*

His eyes roamed over her, intense in his quick scrutiny. "Where the hell did you get that dress? I didn't buy it. I'd remember a dress like that."

"No, you didn't buy it," she said. "I did. I wanted something really special for my opening night. I got this for myself." She paused. "Was it acceptable? It's not vulgar."

"Was it acceptable?" he echoed, a touch of disbelief in his deep voice. The corner of his mouth quirked up sideways and her heart fluttered; she found him unbearably hot whenever he grinned like that. He took a step closer, those blues blazing as they swept over her figure again before meeting her gaze.

"It's amazing. You knocked me out tonight in that dress. You knocked me out, period."

"Oh. Thank you." The way he was looking at her . . . there was more than appreciation in that stare. She saw hunger. Desire. And her heart started picking up speed. "I'm glad you approve."

"Oh, I more than approve," he murmured. A light breeze lifted some strands of her hair and he reached out to brush them back from her face. He tucked the wavy lock behind her ear with deliberate slowness, a feather's touch. A feather's touch that ignited a surge of desire throughout her whole body.

Up close, he was only better looking—the incredibly blue eyes, the Roman nose, the high cheekbones and square jaw. For once, it wasn't covered in day-old scruff, he was clean-shaven. She wanted to lick and nibble her way along that strong jaw, straight to those full, pouty lips of his. God, what she would do to him. . . .

She licked her suddenly dry lips and watched his eyes shoot to her mouth, glued. The pull between them was electric, a tangible thing. Unable to stop herself, she smirked as she purred, "You're thinking about kissing me, aren't you."

"Hell yes I am." His voice was husky, pitched low.

"Don't," she said, even as her stomach filled with butterflies and her heart thumped.

"I won't." He edged even closer. She could feel the heat from his body, he stood so close. The corner of his full, sensual mouth curved up again as he stared her down and added, "You want me to, though."

He wanted to flirt, to play? Oh, game on. She was still wired, on an adrenaline high from performing and the whole incredible night. After a good gig, she felt invincible. She sure did tonight. And she loved to flirt. And she sure knew how to play. She lifted her face to his, let her warm breath tickle his lips for a drawn out second, and murmured, "What makes you so sure?"

"I'm sure," he said. He lifted a finger to her neck, let it trail down the side of her throat with slow heat, and found her traitorous pulse, pounding away. He pressed his fingertip there for a few seconds before grinning victoriously. "Yeah, I'm pretty sure you want me to kiss you."

She moved in closer, letting her breasts brush against his chest as she leaned against him ever so lightly. His intake of breath was soft, but she caught it. Tipping up her chin, she whispered in his ear, "When—*if*—I want you to kiss me again, you'll know it." And she moved away, taking two steps back. If she didn't, she would've pounced on him right there on the sidewalk. "Anything else, Boss?"

His eyes blazed, that searing blue capturing her and sending heat straight down her spine. A muscle jumped in his jaw. She'd gotten to him. But he was cool and collected as always, damn him, reining it in and flashing that killer grin. "One other thing." He slanted a look at her. "You finish up pretty late here when you work. I know you have to go all the way back to Long Island, by yourself. And Kelvin lives in Astoria, right?"

"Yes. So?"

"So he's a six-foot-tall man who can obviously fend for himself. He goes home alone on the subway at two in the morning, I don't have to worry about him. You, it's a little different."

She quirked a brow at him. "Do you worry about all your female employees this way?"

"No. You're special," he said, then added, "I've got a lot riding on you."

Julia tried to ignore the flutter of disappointment. He wasn't worried about *her*, he was worried about his new hot commodity. She said nothing. She'd learned a long time ago that in business—hell, life in general—whoever speaks first, loses. She'd gotten quite good at letting her stony silence do the hard work. Not knowing what to say, she kept quiet.

Dane gazed at her, then seemed to realize she wasn't giving him an inch. He shoved his hands into his pockets. "I wanted to offer you something. An employee perk, if you will."

She still said nothing, just waited, meeting his gaze directly.

He shifted from one foot to the other. "On nights that go late, if there's bad weather, if you're too tired, if you just don't feel like going home, whatever—you can stay here. At the hotel. Have a room for the night, just to crash, and go home in the morning. At no cost, of course. It's on me."

Her brows shot up. She hated how he kept surprising her, especially with a kind word, nice things, or a thoughtful gesture. She hated surprises in general. "Why?" she sputtered.

"Because I want you safe. Because you work in a hotel; if you're really tired at the end of the night, why shouldn't you be able to get some sleep right here?" He pinned her with his gaze. "And because I *can*. It's my hotel, for Chrissake."

She pressed her lips together to smother a giggle. The tension suddenly broken, he smiled back at her.

"So, look—you ever want a room, it's yours. I'll leave notice with the front desk. Standing offer. No strings." He scrubbed a hand through his curly hair, tousling it a bit and making something ping low in Julia's belly. She wanted to rake through those gorgeous curls with both hands. . . .

Crap, snap out of it, Jules. She realized he was staring at her expectantly.

"That's very thoughtful," she said, shifting into neutral. "Thank you."

"You're welcome." He shrugged. "Even if you don't take me up on it, the offer stands for as long as you work here. You never have to ask. Okay?"

"Yes. Thank you," she repeated. "That's generous of you. Really."

"Again, you're welcome. It's nothing." He loosened his tie at the neck, unbuttoned the top button, and sighed with relief. "Ahhh. Been waiting to do this all night."

It was all she could do not to grab the tie and yank him to her. Damn him for being so smoking hot.

He flashed a killer grin. "Well, that's all, then. Good job tonight, Red. Damn good job. You made me proud."

She swallowed down her buzzing desires and straightened, forcing levity into her voice. "Thanks, Boss."

"See you tomorrow night. I'll come by the lounge at some point."

"Just to check on me?" she said with a coy smile.

His eyes flared wickedly as he said, "Nooo . . . to check on my new hotel." He winked. "I'm the owner. Whenever I open a new hotel, I'm there day and night for the first few weeks. Gotta make sure everything's running smoothly." His grin turned devilish as his eyes held hers. "But yeah . . . getting to hear you sing is a definite perk. Just getting to look at you, even better." He moved around her, gently brushing her arm with his as he passed. "Good night, Julia."

"Good night." She viewed his back as his long legs took purposeful strides up the sidewalk, watching him until he disappeared around the corner. Only then did she start to breathe normally again.

Blinking off the haze of lust, she glanced up at the sky. She couldn't see any stars with all the bright city lights. But she knew they were up there. She exhaled slowly, the adrenaline still racing through her. She was overwhelmed, as she had been for the past few weeks—still stunned by her good fortune, and more than a little thrown by her attraction to Dane. Things were so good right now, she was afraid to trust it. But they *were* good. Really good. So she'd enjoy the ride for as long as it lasted.

Grateful, she took a deep, centering breath, then went back inside to her friends.

Chapter Six

For Dane, the weeks passed in a blur. The new hotel was in full swing and doing well, filled with bookings and getting great write-ups. He went over there every day to see how things were going, along with checking in at his office to catch up on other business. With twenty-one hotels now in his possession, he was busier than ever.

He liked to pop in on his hotels without warning, see for himself how daily operations were without the staff knowing he'd be there. Once or twice a month, he was away from New York, traveling to one of his properties for a few days to check things out.

But he hadn't planned any trips for the next few weeks. He told himself, and his assistant, Elise Cannon, that he needed to be in New York for now. By the end of the second week of business, he knew damn well he was lying to himself. He'd handpicked the best people he could find to fill every position. The hotel was doing phenomenally well. He could've gone to check in on one of his other hotels. In fact, he *should* have. But he was hanging around because of Julia Shay.

He couldn't explain the power she had over him. He was drawn to her, by an almost tangible pull. So on Thursday, Friday, and Saturday nights, he'd pop into the lounge and take in one of her sets. Listening to her sing was such a pleasure. A drink at the end of the day to unwind, listening to her and Kelvin do their thing, and sitting back to just savor the view of the beautiful redhead . . . he was enjoying it. And he'd been right about her—the lounge filled up when she performed. Some fantastic online reviews had spread the word quickly; it was Julia Shay that was packing the house each night, no doubt about it.

Afterward, he'd linger to talk with her a little. She'd finally allowed him close enough to have some general conversation. Sometimes he flirted with her, partly because he couldn't help himself and partly to see how she'd react. Sometimes she shot him down, and he'd take the hit. But sometimes she'd flirt back. Like him, she was a natural flirt, loved to tease and play. And when she *did* flirt back, or ensnare him with one of her provocative stares? He was a fucking puddle. He played it cool, but he knew he was putty in her hands.

That boggled his mind. *He* was the one whose stares turned women into puddles, not the other way around. But Julia would slide him a frisky look, or lick her lips, and his blood would start to heat in his veins and fry his damn mind.

This had been going on for three weeks now. The sexual tension between them was ridiculous . . . and he kept coming back for more. Frustration over his limitations gnawed at him. If he was smart, he'd stop going to the lounge to see her, cease his flirtations, keep his distance. He was her boss. End of story.

But he didn't *want* to stop. He wanted *her*—in his

bed, against the wall, over the damn piano, wherever he could have her. And he'd never been very good at denying himself something he really wanted.

It was a hot mid-July Thursday, with brutal humidity and ninety-degree heat, the kind of steamy day that made the Manhattan streets bake and sizzle. Dane put in his time at the office, then went for his daily workout at the gym within his office building. He returned home, showered and dressed, checked some e-mails, then prepared to get to the Hotel Alexandra in time for a late dinner.

He should've been on a beach somewhere, not going from his Tribeca apartment back up to the Hotel Alexandra. He should've been heading out east, enjoying a leisurely weekend at the Harrison family compound in the Hamptons. Tess had called that morning to tell him she'd be there for the weekend and invited him to join her. But he'd turned his sister down, saying he'd come out on Sunday and stay for two or three days at the beginning of next week. Julia was performing tonight, and he wanted to see her. He was a glutton for punishment.

"Oh, thank God," Julia sighed the minute she entered the Alexandra Bar & Lounge. There were patrons inside, but she didn't think any of them would recognize her in her current disheveled state. Wearing big dark sunglasses and no makeup except for tinted lip balm, her thick mane pulled up in a high ponytail, she had almost sweated through her pistachio-colored T-shirt. She dropped her heavy duffel bag to the floor and straightened her black shorts, rolling her head around to stretch the muscles.

Her first set wasn't until ten, and she usually didn't

get to the lounge until eight-thirty. The commute from Long Island was fairly easy, the whole trip taking about an hour. She always liked to be early to a gig, but she was way early tonight and looked around, not having been in the bar for Happy Hour before. Justin Timberlake was singing about his suit and tie over the sound system, and the bar was fairly crowded for six o'clock on a Thursday. Business was booming here. Dane Harrison's golden touch had done it again.

She stood in place under the vent by the door, lifted her ponytail off her neck, tipped back her face, and closed her eyes. The blast of cool air on her flushed, sweaty face felt like a miracle.

"Hi, Julia." Tonio Ramos, the head bartender, came over to stand beside her. "You okay? You're a little flushed."

"I almost melted on the way here," she joked. "God bless air conditioning. It's disgusting out there today."

"I know." Tonio folded his thick arms over his broad chest, glanced at his watch, and added, "You're early."

"Yeah. I knew I'd be a sweaty mess by the time I got here," Julia explained. "So I wanted to take a shower and cool down before I got ready."

"I hear ya. Good idea." Tonio looked out over the small crowd, watching the three bartenders behind the bar as they worked. Julia let her eyes slip closed again for a minute as the cool air washed over her skin. She drew a deep, cleansing breath and exhaled it nice and slow.

"You want some water?" Tonio's deep voice startled her. "Hey, you hungry? Did you have dinner?"

Her eyes snapped open to look up at him. "Um, no, actually. I haven't yet."

"I was about to order something from the kitchen,"

Tonio said. "You want something too? You can eat out here, or in your dressing room, whatever ya want. Then you can go get ready. Ya got plenty o'time."

She smiled. "Thanks for asking. Yes, that'd be great. Especially if you'll join me."

His brows shot up. "Okay. Yeah. Whaddaya want?"

Twenty minutes later, Julia and Tonio were having dinner at one of the high-backed booths in the bar. She dug into her pasta primavera with gusto, not realizing that she'd been starving until the waiter had set down the appetizing meal before her. The cubes of grilled chicken on top were juicy and flavorful, and she ate a few as she finally felt herself relax. Tonio plowed through his bacon cheeseburger, finishing half of it by the time she'd taken only a few bites of her supper.

"So where's your friend Kelvin?" Tonio asked amiably.

"He'll be here by nine, as usual," she said. "So. Tell me about you. You married, Tonio?"

He almost choked on a French fry. "Ha! You don't beat around the bush, do you?"

"Nope." She shot him a wide grin, then speared another forkful of rotini and chicken into her mouth.

"I like you." His eyes narrowed a bit as the side of his mouth curved up mischievously. "No, I'm not married. Why, you hittin' on me?"

"No, sorry, I'm not," she said with a chuckle. "I was just curious."

"Ah, that's too bad," he teased, his dark eyes sparkling with humor. "I'm divorced. Two kids. They live with her, over in Park Slope." He downed a gulp of ginger ale. "You?"

"Also divorced," she said. "Long time ago." She took a few swallows of her mineral water and cursed herself inwardly. Knowing she'd opened herself up for more questions, she quickly changed tactics. "I bet women throw themselves at you all the time, working in a place like this."

He guffawed and shook his head. "I don't really pay attention if they do. I have a girlfriend now, and she's great."

"Good for you," Julia smiled. "What's her name?"

"Evie. She's a nurse. Home care stuff, per diem."

"That's admirable work," Julia said earnestly.

"Yeah, it is. She works hard. She's a good person." He ate a few more fries before smirking at her. "You get checked out every time you step in here," he said. "I've seen it. But I guess that comes with the job, you being onstage and all."

"I guess," she said, shrugging. "But . . . look at me now. Not exactly a glamour queen. This is the normal me. This me doesn't get hit on much. Men like the mirage, you know?"

"Well, I think the 'normal you' is gorgeous too, but I get what you're sayin'." Tonio nodded and wiped his mouth with a paper napkin. "Julia . . . if anyone ever bothers you, makes you uncomfortable, ya know . . . you just tell me, all right? I did my bouncing days. I'll take care of anyone who bothers ya."

She felt her face warm with gratitude. "Thank you. That's very kind of you."

"I mean it," he said. "I know Kelvin's got your back and all. But he don't have my brawn. And we wouldn't want him to take a chance on hurting those hands of his, right?"

They laughed together. Julia breathed a sigh of relief deep inside. She hoped she'd never have to take Tonio up on his offer. But with her past experiences, she knew better. It had happened before, and could happen again. Knowing this six-foot-three bruiser had her back made her feel a little more secure. Damn, she liked this job.

"Tell me a little about our boss," she said, striving for casual nonchalance.

Tonio gave her a sideways look. "Dane? What about him?"

"I don't know," Julia said. "You've worked for him for a while. Tell me something I don't know. Something interesting."

"Uh . . ." Tonio chewed a few more fries while he thought. Then a big, wicked grin spread across his face. "He likes gorgeous redheads."

Julia burst out laughing. "Shut up!"

"It's true!"

"He goes through women like I go through bottles of water, doesn't he?"

"I dunno," Tonio said with a heavy shrug of his huge shoulders. "And I don't care. I don't keep up with his social life."

"Come on," Julia scoffed. "His ladies' man status is kind of legendary."

Tonio's gaze narrowed. "How do you know? Done some homework?"

Julia felt color bloom on her cheeks, but said quickly, "Maybe a little. I wanted to know about who I'm working for. That's what seems to come up a lot where he's concerned."

Tonio leaned in on his meaty forearms and lowered his voice. "Who you're working for is a good man. Dane Harrison isn't your typical rich boy. Money like his, you'd think he'd be a dick, but he's not. He's cool. He likes to have fun, he's generous, and he's fair. He works hard. He keeps his word." His eyes held hers as he added, "Dane doesn't treat me like some lower-class guy, or just a bartender, none of that. He treats me like an equal. He treats *everyone* well, no matter if they're the mayor or one of his busboys. You'll never hear anyone who knows him say a bad word about him. *That's* who you're working for."

Julia took in the sober look on Tonio's face as she absorbed the information. She pushed around the food on her plate with her fork and nodded. "Good to know. Thanks."

"How's it going?" Dane asked with a grin. He slid onto a seat at the bar.

"Going great," Tonio answered. "Busy tonight. What can I get ya?"

"Uh . . . dark beer, whatever's on tap."

"Got Sam Adams, Beck's Dark, or Guinness."

"Beck's."

As Tonio turned away to get the beer, the crowd in the lounge started applauding. Dane craned his head to see, and caught Julia walking onto the small stage. Her red hair was down in loose, sexy waves, and her charcoal gray beaded gown hugged her curvy body like a glove. Kelvin, in his usual black Armani suit, was already seated at the piano. He started right in with a rousing romp on the keys, playing a few bars of true old-time jazz. Julia took a sip of water and set the bottle aside on a stool before getting back to the mic. When she did, Kelvin changed the tune, morphing from ragtime into the sweeter opening bars of an Alicia Keys song. Julia's eyes slipped closed as she hummed a few measures, then cradled the mic with one hand, opened her eyes to look out at the audience, and began to sing. Her rich voice suited the yearning song well. The song was almost over when

Dane realized Tonio had placed an open beer in front of him at some point. He must've gone to help another customer, because he returned to Dane now.

"You want anything to eat?" Tonio asked.

"No, I'm good, thanks." Dane took a long swig of beer. "She's something else, isn't she?"

"Who, Julia?" Tonio nodded. "Yup. That girl sure can sing."

Dane shot him a grin before turning his gaze back to her. He could stare at her easily from farther back in the room, and he was enjoying the view. "She's fucking beautiful."

"That she is," Tonio agreed. "She had dinner with me tonight. It was interesting."

Dane felt a tiny flare of jealousy burn in his chest, but ignored it. "Really."

"Yeah. She got here early, I was about to eat, so we ate together." Tonio leaned against the bar, glancing at Julia before adding to Dane, "Aww, don't get jealous. We're just two friendly coworkers. Actually, she asked me about you."

Dane's head swerved back to him. "She did?"

"Yeah." Tonio grinned at the look on Dane's face.

"What?" Dane asked with a touch of defensiveness.

Tonio shook his head, trying to hide his grin. "Nothin'. Nothin' at all." He straightened and said, "For what it's worth? I think she's cool. She's good people."

Dane only nodded.

"And the chemistry between you two is crazy," Tonio added. "So good luck."

Shooting him a stunned glance, Dane reached for his beer and took a hard gulp.

* * *

Julia stretched out on one couch, Kelvin stretched out on the other, and they both sighed.

"You rocked it, baby," Kelvin said.

"*You* rocked it, my dear," Julia replied.

"We both rocked," Kelvin pronounced. "And now, I. Am. Tired."

"I'm not tired," she said, surprised to realize it was true. "I just needed to lie down for a few minutes. I'm actually kind of wired."

"You always are after a gig," he said, loosening his black-and-gray striped tie. "Me, I'm always ready to collapse and sleep for a week."

"That's because you're old," she teased.

"Oooh, beeyotch!" he huffed. "You're only three months younger than me, you just watch yourself."

They grinned at each other over their long-running joke.

"You're going home, then?" she asked.

"Yup." Kelvin yawned and sat up. "What about you?"

"I think I'm going to have a drink at the bar, then head home," she said. She'd seen Dane at the bar tonight, watching her. He'd stayed for both sets, but hadn't tried to talk to her on the break in between. At the end of the second set, he'd been staring at her so intently she could feel the heat in those blazing blues from across the room. It had set her heart racing against her will. She wanted to see if he was out there, at the bar. She wanted to have a drink, and nurse her secret, dirty fantasies about him. . . .

Someone knocked on the door. Julia and Kelvin looked at each other.

"You expecting someone?" he asked.

She shook her head.

Kelvin rose from his sofa to open the door. Standing there was Dane Harrison.

Julia watched the men shake hands in greeting and exchange a few words as she looked her boss over. Damn, he looked especially good tonight. He wore a navy suit, white shirt, and a tie with several hues of blue that brought out his already amazing eyes. A day's worth of scruff covered his jaw, it was after one in the morning, and the man still looked like he'd just stepped freshly out of a *GQ* photo shoot.

Someone that handsome shouldn't be allowed out at night, she thought to herself. He's too dangerous. Sexy, handsome, and dangerous.

She realized her mouth had gone dry and grabbed her nearby water bottle for a few sips.

"I came to see you, Red," Dane said, moving farther into the room. "Got a few minutes?"

The air crackled with sudden electricity and their eyes locked as she murmured, "Sure."

"I'm gonna get going," Kelvin said, heading toward the closet to retrieve his messenger bag. He undid his tie, shoved it into the bag, and slung the wide strap over his shoulder.

"You don't have to leave on my account," Dane said, flicking a friendly glance his way.

"Oh, I'm not," Kelvin lied. "I was heading out anyway." He leaned down to kiss Julia's cheek and whispered in her ear, "Careful, girl."

She smiled up at him from where she sat. "See you tomorrow, babe."

"You bet." Kelvin shook Dane's hand and they exchanged good-byes.

When they were alone, Dane sat on the sofa Kelvin had vacated, directly across from her.

"So . . ." Suddenly edgy, her heart rate picking up speed, Julia fidgeted with the cap of her water bottle. Even as she did, she tried to be cool, calm, and collected. "Why'd you want to see me? Everything okay, Boss?"

"Not exactly." Dane leaned in, his elbows on his knees, and pinned her with his stare. "Thing is . . . I can't get you out of my mind lately. This . . . there's a draw between us. Something. Chemistry, just lust, I don't know. But it's not going away. It's only getting stronger." His eyes dropped briefly to her mouth. "So I thought . . ." His gaze raised to hold hers again. ". . . maybe it was time I do something about that."

She felt her eyes widen and her heart rate skyrocket, but carefully schooled her features into neutrality. Her chin lifted just a notch as she stared back at him. She said nothing. She didn't know what to say, so she waited for him to play out his hand.

A slow smile of intent spread across Dane's face. His eyes seemed to blaze fire as he said in a low, seductive tone, "I'll bet I can shatter that prized self-control of yours with one hot kiss. I'm here to find out."

Chapter Seven

"I told you," Julia said, trying to catch her breath and sound flip, "that when I wanted you to kiss me again, I'd let you know."

"You've been letting me know," Dane murmured. "You just won't own up to it."

She swallowed hard, but locked her gaze with his. Her mouth went dry and her heart dropped to her stomach before taking off like a racehorse. Before she could respond, a knock came on the door, and he rose to answer it. She watched him, wondering what he was up to. *Keep cool,* she warned herself, even as her blood pulsed and need tugged at her.

One of the busboys handed Dane a bottle and two short glasses. Dane thanked him, closed the door, and strode back to Julia with a cavalier smile. "You always drink vodka. Thought maybe you'd like this." He didn't sit on the opposite sofa this time, but planted himself beside her as he set the bottle of Armadale and glasses on the table.

"Never had this brand. I'll try it," she said, shifting over slightly to make more room for him.

"Atta girl." He opened the bottle and poured a shot's worth into each glass.

"You trying to get me drunk, Boss?"

He smirked. "No. But am I trying to get you to loosen up a bit? Yes." He handed her a glass and angled himself to face her. "I don't need to get a woman drunk to get her into my arms." And clinked his glass to hers before swallowing his vodka in one gulp.

Danger, Will Robinson, Danger! flashed in her head like a neon sign. She sipped her shot slowly to taste it. "Mmm." She took another sip.

"You like it?" He grinned. "I hoped you would."

She finished her shot, feeling it burn through her. "Strong stuff."

"Of course it is. You're drinking straight vodka." He poured another shot into her glass, then his own.

"You are so trying to get me drunk!" She couldn't help but laugh.

His grin widened into a smile. "I'm not! Don't want you sloppy, Red." He eased back into the cushions and let his eyes wander over her. "You're so beautiful, Julia. You're sexy, and sharp, and you're interesting. But I really enjoy looking at you. That's why I do it whenever I can."

Surprised by his brazen statements, she murmured thanks and took another sip of her drink. Between the vodka, his close proximity, his words, and the intent she saw in his eyes, her head was floating. She felt warmth flood her body and her senses, a heady sensation, both thrilling and fearsome. She liked to stay in control. *Needed* to. *Nurse this drink, dummy,* she chided herself.

"Tell me again," he said, swirling the clear alcohol

around in his glass. "No boyfriend, right? No one to come barreling in, looking to kick my ass?"

She laughed. "Nope. Just Kelvin, and he won't kick your ass because you're his boss."

"Even if he came in here and found me kissing you within an inch of your life?"

A shiver skittered over her. "Maybe then. He's very protective of me."

"I've noticed. It's . . . endearing."

"It is that," she said, and sipped her drink. "No girl-friend for a catch like you?"

His eyes lit up. "Am I a catch?" he asked coyly.

"To most women, I'm sure you are."

"But not to you, though." His gaze narrowed on her, scrutinizing.

"Don't take it personally," she said. "I don't do relationships. Especially with billionaire playboys. I'm not the notch-on-a-sterling-silver-bedpost type."

Dane felt his blood heat, but now it wasn't from the vodka, lust, or the gorgeous woman next to him. It was from irritation. "My bedposts aren't sterling, sweetheart. And while I also am not the relationship type, I'm not *that* sleazy stereotype either."

She pressed her lips together and nodded, but said nothing.

Her silences infuriated him. They were meant to incite a reaction. And dammit, they worked on him exactly as she intended. "You don't believe me." He stared at her, his jaw tightening. "I've never treated you with anything less than respect. Have I dated a lot? Yes. Nothing to apologize for. Do I have a string of endless women coming in and out of my bedroom? Hell no." He scowled and sat up, spearing her with a look. "If you think that about me, it's because you believe stupid gossip pages and trashy Web sites. I thought you were smarter than that."

Her eyes flared. "You don't have to insult me."

"Oh, but what you said wasn't insulting to me?" he retorted.

Color bloomed on her pale cheeks. "You're right. I'm sorry."

"It's easier for you to write me off as a douche-bag than to admit you're attracted to me," he said, knowing he was pushing now and not caring.

"I don't think you're a douchebag," she said, unable to hide the hint of a grin.

He stared at her and said quietly, "Admit you want me."

"Fine. I want you," she said, almost flip. "I want to grab you and do all sorts of wild things to you. I don't know what this is between us either, but it's there. Just crazy chemistry, probably. But none of that matters. You're my boss. I love this job. That's what matters most."

Stunned by her honesty, he knocked back the rest of his vodka in one swallow before conceding, "I know."

They sat in silence for a minute. Different scenarios went through his mind. He wanted her so bad it ached sometimes. Physically, they were definitely walking the same path to oblivion. But she didn't trust him . . . and yeah, he was her boss. *He* knew he'd never fire her over the demise of any relations between them, but *she* didn't know that. She was right to be wary; he understood it and respected it.

So how could he convince her that a purely physical relationship would work for both of them if they kept it light? And it'd be hot, and maybe even *fun*? "All sorts of wild things, huh? Can you give me a hint? Sounds really hot."

She laughed, and they both relaxed. He felt the negative tension leave his shoulders, but the sexual tension was thick as could be.

"You want me bad," she finally drawled in a teasing tone.

A surprised laugh burst from him. "Yeah. You're right. I do."

Smiling, she took a small sip of her drink.

"You want me too," he said.

She shrugged. "Covered that."

"So . . . what do we do about it?"

"I have a few ideas. . . ."

Dane leaned in closer, intoxicated by her, lured by her face. The curve of her lips was a seductive smirk. Her bedroom eyes . . . those gorgeous hazel eyes reflected confidence, power, and a hint of outright wickedness. She was playing with him now. Toying. At the moment, she held the cards. She knew she had the upper hand. And man, she was relishing it.

"You know why I'm a dream girl for a guy like you?" she asked, her brows lifting. Her eyes sparkled as she teased him.

"Because you're fucking beautiful?" He didn't ask it, he offered it. Their eyes locked and his heart started to pound in heavy, thick beats.

She smiled softly and said, "Thank you, but no. It's because I don't want a thing from you." She raised her glass to her mouth and took a longer sip of her vodka, making him wait as she finished it. When she lowered the glass back to the table, her tongue flicked out and dragged sensually along her lips.

Dane's cock swelled. But he kept it cool on the outside. "Sure about that?" His grin was slow and wolfish. "That there's not . . . *anything* you want from me?"

"Heh. Maybe *one* thing . . ." she admitted coyly, raking her eyes down his body.

He could barely breathe. Holy crap, what this woman did to him.

His gaze roamed over her features, searching. So much going on behind those gorgeous hazel eyes.

But right now, he was just concentrating on not grabbing her, pushing her onto her back, and kissing her until they were both breathless. Until they couldn't remember their names, until he had her dress hiked up to her waist and beneath him, until he was inside her to the damn hilt and she was screaming for more. Just the thought of it had him rock hard.

"So . . . what *are* you looking for, Julia?" His voice pitched low and his eyes stayed on hers. "What *do* you believe in?"

Her smirk changed to a provocative smile. "I'm not looking for anything. But if I was? It'd be sex." His heart stuttered in his chest, and she continued, "Just sex. I have needs, like anyone else." She'd cast a spell, she must have. He felt hypnotized and frozen in place. She leaned in close enough for him to feel her warm breath against his mouth. "But with no ties. That's my rule." She licked her lips slowly, then added in a husky purr, "What I believe in . . . is great sex. Really hot, passionate sex. With no strings."

Dane's heart almost stopped in his damn chest and his mouth went dry. For maybe the first time in his life, he was speechless. He had no smooth comeback, no words at all. And at that moment, he wanted her more than he'd ever wanted any woman in his entire life.

He'd never been with a woman quite so open about her wants. She was unapologetic in her sexuality, in the no-holds-barred way she discussed her desires.

He *loved* that.

He bet she likely intimidated most men; weaker men. But to Dane, her unrepentant hunger, combined with her beauty, brains, and confidence . . . all those things made her, easily, the sexiest, most desirable woman he'd ever met in his life.

But he'd be damned if he'd show it. She may have held the cards at that moment—and he wasn't going to lie to himself, she had him tied up in knots right then—but he wasn't ready to tip his hand just yet. How far would she take this? He intended to find out.

He liked this game. High stakes. His favorite kind.

Leaning back toward the table, he poured himself another shot, took a sip, then set it down and moved in closer to Julia. Their faces were only inches apart. He could smell a hint of her perfume, that musky vanilla scent, and even the sweet alcohol on her breath. His body surged with lust and adrenaline, making his heart pound in heavy thumps against his ribs. Christ, he'd never had such a powerfully visceral reaction to a woman before. He'd had a few drinks tonight, but that wasn't it. It might have helped, but no. It was all her. Julia Shay fascinated and mesmerized him. He had to have her.

He gazed deeply into her eyes, and she didn't look away. She didn't even flinch.

"Come with me," he murmured.

She didn't move. "Where?"

"Out of here." Quick as lightning, he leaned in and nipped her bottom lip. "I think I can give you what you . . . believe in."

"Do you," she whispered. Her eyes sparkled with challenge.

"You know I will," he whispered back.

Her lips quirked. "Mm-hmm. But we can't. Boss."

"We *shouldn't*," he corrected her. "But we *can*. And we both want to." He reached out to brush a lock of her thick hair behind her ear, then let his fingers trail ever so softly along the side of her neck. Her skin was warm and velvety. He heard her breath hitch and felt a flash of victory. She wasn't impervious to him. Far from it. "The attraction here, the pull . . . it's insane. We both feel it. We've been dancing around this for weeks."

"For good reasons," she said, but her voice was thick and her eyes had darkened with lust, giving her away.

"Yes. That's true." He traced her jawline next, dragging his fingertips slowly, never dropping his eyes from hers. "And I've never crossed this line before. I hold to that rule as firmly as you do. . . ." He moved his hand up and swept her thick hair back over her shoulder. "But you know what? We need to have this one night. Like you said, no strings, no ties. Just some crazy hot, throw-each-other-around-the-room sex. One night only. Get it out of our systems. Sound good?"

Her eyes were almost black with passion. "Hell yes. If you can stick to the no-strings rule." She paused before saying, "Dane . . . I do want you. But I want to keep my job more."

His fingers stopped at her chin. Tipping it up, he looked into her eyes and said solemnly, "Julia, one thing has nothing to do with the other. I swear I wouldn't do that to you." He saw the flicker of doubt in her eyes and continued, "You have a strong contract. I can't fire you without cause. And come on, why would I want to?" He caressed her cheek, her neck, and used his most persuasive tone. "We're adults.

We're professionals. I can keep these things separate if you can."

Uncertainty loomed in her gaze, battling the haze of lust he'd seen blazing there.

He leaned in, gently cupped her face in his hands, and brushed his lips against hers slowly, testing. Her mouth was warm, soft, and willing, so he kissed her. Gently at first, he sipped from her lips, coaxing her. She opened to him, kissing him back, touching her tongue to his, lingering. Need and desire clawed inside him, and he took her mouth with hungrier kisses. Her fingers slid into his curls and she pressed against him, matching his demanding kisses with heat of her own. She gave as good as she got as they grasped at each other, curling into each other's arms. As the kisses deepened, the claws of need in his belly sharpened. He was so hard he had to shift his position, bringing a lusty whimper from her that made his cock throb.

He pulled back and whispered against her lips, "Come with me. Now. I swear you won't regret it. You can trust me on this."

She pulled back and regarded him for what felt like the longest seconds of his life. Then she reached over, took her handbag off the coffee table, rose off the couch, and headed for the door. Not sure what was happening, he stayed still, his whole body pulsating with an animal-like desire.

With a cheeky glance over her shoulder, she said in a low dare, "Aren't you coming?"

Hell yes. He got to his feet and followed her out of the dressing room. They walked side by side in electric silence, down the short hall, through the lounge, through the bar, to the elevator. He could feel his heartbeat, thudding inside his chest as the adrenaline raged through him. She pushed the button and turned to him. "So where are we going, Boss?"

He slanted her a look. "You call me that in bed and I'll spank you," he growled.

She gaped at him, obviously thrown. He smirked. Score one for Team Harrison.

"When we're in bed," he told her, "I'm not your boss, you're not my employee. We're just two people, and we're equals. This"—he waved at the bar and lounge—"has no place in the bedroom. All right?"

She nodded, but he caught a flash of something in her eyes: assurance, relief. His nerves were buzzing now, making him edgy, wanting to touch her, but he reined it all in. Once he had her upstairs, in the privacy of his suite . . .

The elevator bell pealed softly and the doors opened. With a hand at the small of her back, he ushered her inside, then pressed a button. "I have a suite on the top floor," he said. "Nice and private up there. Okay with you?"

The doors closed. In a flash, she grabbed the lapels of his jacket, pushed him back against the wall with a hard thud, and kissed him passionately—a solid blast of scorching heat.

His brain shut off and his body fired to life. One hand held her head and the other grabbed her at the waist, yanking her voluptuous body against his as they kissed. Greedy, ravenous kisses that had their tongues tangling, tasting, taking . . . his blood rushed through his body like liquid fire, searing through his limbs and into his groin, making his heart pound. He groaned into her mouth and fisted his hands in her hair.

She pressed herself harder against him, her hands gripping his shoulders as she ground against his erection with her lush, curvy hips. He groaned again and pulled her head back by her hair to devour her throat, kissing and nibbling his way down. Her breath caught and a soft, aching moan floated out of her. He scraped his teeth into the curve of her neck, biting down gently, then not so gently. With a gasp, she swayed in his arms.

The elevator bell pealed, and Dane had to all but hurl himself back and off of her. They stood on opposite sides of the small compartment, panting as if they'd run a race and staring at each other with unmasked desire. When the doors slid open, he grabbed her hand and pulled her along. She went willingly, her eyes dancing and her mouth swollen from his kisses. He found it hard to catch his breath, and his heartbeat pounded in his ears.

His suite was at the end of the long hallway. He punched in the code, the signal beeped, and he flung the door open, pulling her inside eagerly.

As soon as they were inside, she did it again—she slammed him back against the wall and kissed him with the blazing passion of a woman who *wanted* this. She wanted him just as much as he wanted her. His mind spiraled as he let her take the lead, curious to see what she'd do. She kissed him hungrily, her warm hands sliding through his hair, down his neck, beneath his jacket. She pushed it off over his shoulders and it fell to the floor. Kissing him still, nipping and licking, she went for his tie, wrapped it around her hand, and pulled.

He groaned into her mouth and his fingers clutched at her soft hips. She pressed her breasts against his chest and her hips to his. Her dark eyes glittered lasciviously, staring into his for a few seconds before she pressed her warm mouth back to his. She was on fire, greedy, insatiable. And right then, *she* was in control. She'd turned the tables on him like no woman ever had. He couldn't think clearly. He didn't care. He was having too much fun being lost, flooded with sensation, ruled by animal lust. And dying to see what else she would do.

Still kissing, she unknotted his tie and pulled it out of his collar, flinging it blindly behind her with another carnal smile. He dipped his head to skim his mouth along her neck, her passion engulfing him. His hands slid up her arms, down her back, over her fantastic curves, to stop on her ass and squeeze as he nibbled along her throat. Her breath hitched and she let out the tiniest whimper, but her nimble fingers started unbuttoning his shirt. She spread it wide, caressing his chest, kissing down his neck, licking at his chest, taking what she wanted. He let her, leaning his head back against the wall and closing his eyes. Her warm, hot mouth and eager hands glided over him, and he savored every wild sensation. "God, Julia . . ."

She bit his nipple and he sucked in a sharp intake of breath, the jolt shooting straight to his groin. Then, as she kissed his chest, she brushed her hand against the front of his pants. He groaned and his cock twitched as his fingers dug into her waist. She pressed her palm against him and slowly rubbed the hard length of him. He opened his eyes to see she was watching his face as she touched him. Instinctively his hips moved with her rhythm, grinding against her hand. Their eyes locked as his breathing got choppy and his heart rate took off.

She licked her lips, stroked him with more pressure, and said in a throaty voice, "*That*. I want that."

"Christ . . ." he gasped. He tangled his hands in her hair and crushed her mouth to his. They kissed desperately, clinging to each other, hands roaming, mouths clashing. He dropped his head to her neck again, seeking that sweet spot that had made her sigh before. He knew he'd found it when she let out a low moan, her head falling back to give him better access. With a soft growl, his hands lifted, filling them with her sizable breasts. Her fingers plowed through his hair and she ground her body against his with sinful purpose.

Quick as a flash, he took her by the waist, spun her around, and pushed her against the wall, her back to his chest. To his surprise and pleasure, she moaned lustfully. Even in the dim light, he saw her smile with anticipation. His blood rushed through him, sending his senses spinning. With one hand, he grasped her wrists and held them up over her head, pinning them to the wall. With his other hand, he reached down in front to sweep his hand between her legs, trailing up her thigh, making her wiggle and whimper and grind her ass against him. His knees nearly went out, watching her catch fire this way. She held nothing back, she just went for it. What was that saying—a lady in the front room, a tigress in the bedroom? Her unabashed passion rocked him to the core.

He swept her thick mane aside, flicking her ear with his tongue, listening to her ragged breathing. Christ, her heavy breathing alone was such a turn-on. With teasing slowness, he pulled down the zipper on the back of her dress. Then he moved in, kissing and nibbling her smooth, pale back, pushing the dress aside with both hands, opening the clasp of her strapless bra with deft precision. His hands went around to cup her round, heavy breasts and they both groaned. He ground his erection against her ass and again she rocked back against him, welcoming his advances.

His entire body throbbed with need; he could barely see straight, and his blood roared in his ears.

With a low grunt, he whipped her around to face him. The dress and bra dropped and pooled around her feet. As they kissed urgently, she stepped out of them and kicked them aside. He stared and ran his hands over those glorious breasts.

"My God," he whispered in husky reverence. His hands caressed her, thumbs stroking her already pebbled nipples, and she sighed softly. "You're gorgeous . . . so gorgeous." His head dipped to suckle her breast, closing over her nipple with his teeth. She cried out and tangled her fingers in his hair, holding him to her. Her back arched as he suckled one, than the other, while his hands worshipped her incredible figure. All her curves revealed to him, he greedily reveled in them, touching her everywhere. Her breath came in short, hard puffs now, her lips parted, head thrown back with abandon. His eyes had fully adjusted to the dark room, and he could make out her pale body in the dim light. She was magnificent. Fucking beautiful. And he told her so.

"Then take me already," she demanded, her eyes glazed with passion. "Come on, Dane. Take me."

Pure animal lust slammed him, making his heart seize and his blood race. Gripping her face with his hands, he crushed his mouth to hers. The air around them seemed to crackle with electricity. She reached out and quickly undid his belt buckle, her gaze holding his as she unzipped his pants. She jerked them down over his hips along with his boxer briefs, then lifted her foot to push them down to his ankles.

"Nice," he grinned, diving back to her lips. Their mouths sealed once more and their tongues tangled, hot and demanding. For the first time, he pressed the length of his naked body against hers. She whimpered into his mouth. The only thing between them were her black lace panties, and he made short work of those as she ran her fingernails over his back, his ass, holding him against her as they kissed. All she wore now were her stilettos.

It flashed through his mind that they were like animals, driven by a primal urge. The feel of his hands on her skin . . . of her hands on his skin . . . their hungry mouths . . . he was mindless, gone. His world was white noise and heat as the air pulsed around them.

She reached down in between them and curled her fingers around his erection. A jagged moan ripped from his throat.

"Ohh Dane . . ." Her voice was a low, sultry purr of approval that sent a deep shiver through him. As he met her eyes, her thumb ran over the head of his cock, smoothing out the drop of moisture there before lifting her thumb to her own mouth and sucking on the pad of it. "Mmmm."

His heart almost stopped in his chest.

She began to stroke him in a torturously slow rhythm, watching his face as she did. He held on to her breasts, caressing her as her gorgeous fingers lavished lazy strokes up and down the length of him, and his head fell back as another groan rumbled out of him. It was the most erotic thing he'd ever experienced—the clear look of desire in her eyes as she watched him succumb to her, gauging what her touch was doing to him. Panting hard, his hips moved as he rocked into her hand. He cupped one hand around the back of her neck and brought her mouth to his, kissing her urgently, delirious with pleasure. Her hand moved faster, picking up the pace, and the need kept building in waves—nothing but incredible feeling, both of them grabbing at each other like savages, taking what they wanted, what they needed.

"Stop," he panted. "Can't take much more . . ."

"Sure you can," she said, nipping at his neck.

But he moved her hand away and slid his between her legs. "My turn." Running his fingertips slowly up her velvety thigh, he listened to her breathing catch and turn jagged. His whole body was throbbing with need, but he wanted to torment her as she'd done to him. He wanted her to go boneless with building desire, wanted to hear her sigh and moan again, wanted to watch her melt in his arms.

"Tell me you want me," he said in a hot whisper against her lips. He explored her skin as he watched the color rise and flush her face.

"God, I want you," she breathed. "I want you so much. Touch me, Dane."

Another rush of lust flooded him. He crushed his lips to hers, thrusting his tongue into her mouth as he ran his finger along her warm wetness. He pulled back just enough to look into her eyes as he brushed his thumb lightly across her clit and was rewarded with a deep, wonderful moan.

"Ah, Julia," he whispered against her ear, "I want you, too." With ease, he slid two fingers inside her. She cried out, her whole body shuddered, and her legs almost buckled. He held her up against the wall to steady her. "God, you're so wet." Setting a new rhythm, he worked her as his mouth plundered hers, hot and hard.

She was so reactive to his touch; her fiery passion fanned the flames of his own. He rubbed her clit with his thumb in lazy circles as his fingers moved inside her. The sounds she made, staccato gasps and moans of pure abandon, made his body flare with fresh waves of need. She grasped his cock again, stroking his shaft in a rhythm that matched his. His forehead dropped to hers as his body responded to her wicked fingers, breathing heavily against her mouth as the waves of sensation built, overtaking and submerging him. The pressure built to spiking.

"Now," he growled against her mouth, nipping at her as his fingers moved inside her. She was so warm, so slick. "I have to have you *now*."

"Yes, yes," she groaned, releasing his cock. "Do it."

Panting, feverish, he managed to stop for a second. "Protection," he huffed.

"You have any?" she asked breathlessly. "God, please say yes."

He nodded and kissed her again before he bent to grab his jacket. Finding his wallet, he pulled a condom out of it and got it on in record time. She went to kick off her stilettos and he growled, "Don't you dare."

She grinned and again locked her hands behind his neck. "Shoe fetish?"

"Yeah, for tonight. Those stay *on*."

She laughed and he swallowed it with another ravenous kiss, grasping her breasts with both hands. Then he looked deeply into her eyes, hitched her leg up with one hand, grasped her hip with the other, and plunged into her, slamming her back against the wall. She cried out and clutched his shoulders as he sank into her. With a hoarse groan, he eased deeper inside, almost to the hilt.

"God, *yes*," she breathed. He watched her eyes slip closed as she released a guttural moan of sheer pleasure that vibrated through him, sending shivers along his skin. He stole a kiss, then gently bit her bottom lip, sucking on it as he rolled his hips.

"You feel so good," he whispered. "So, so good . . ."

He moved slowly, withdrawing almost completely, then drove back in hard, bringing another low moan from her. "You keep moaning like that," he warned in a low growl, "and I'm gonna be done in about two seconds."

"It's too good," she rasped. "Not—*ohhh*—my fault."

His lips sought hers, kissing her as he moved with her. Exerting every ounce of self-control he had, he teased her with another slow, deep thrust, then another, and she moaned again and swore. Her passion stunned him. She was so openly wanting, so raw, and Christ, he loved how she loved it.

She grabbed his ass and pushed him even deeper inside her. A groan erupted from his chest, raw and low. The feel of being that deep inside her, warm and slick and wonderful, enveloped and drowned him. "Oh, Julia . . ." He pressed his forehead to hers as he moved. "Christ, that's so good."

"Too good," she panted.

"No such thing," he grinned, nipping at her mouth.

She grinned. "Won't last much longer," she warned, gasping.

"Me neither," he admitted, and kissed her again as his hips moved faster. As his breathing grew labored and his tongue tangled with hers, his free hand caressed her breast and pinched her nipple. She moaned helplessly into his mouth.

"Dane . . ." Her head fell back against the wall as he thrust into her, harder, again. And again. And again. Her nails raked down his back, over his ass, leaving trails of fire in their wake. "Oh God, I'm close already," she gasped. Her nails bit into his skin. "Don't stop, Dane. Don't stop . . ."

"Not 'til you scream my name," he rasped against her ear, swiveling his hips to grind against her, going as deep as he could, bringing another hot-blooded moan from her. She bit at his neck, licking him, grabbing at him everywhere she could, and he felt the last threads of his self-control fray and split apart. He wanted to possess her like no other man had. Bracing his free hand on the wall near her head, he picked up speed, driving into her faster, harder.

"*Yes,*" she groaned. She clutched his shoulders with both hands as her hips met his, matching him thrust for powerful thrust. Her nails dug in as their moans mingled and their breathing became panting. He lifted his head to look at her face. Her eyes were closed, lips parted, skin flushed, head thrown back in ecstasy. The sounds . . . Christ, the sounds she made lit him on fire. She was as lost to their passion as he was, completely carried away. She mesmerized him.

More. He wanted more. Wanted all of her. He pounded her with hard, quick thrusts, relentless as her breath caught, her back arched, and she cried out his name. He watched her come—felt her body spasm and shudder around him, listened to the erotic sounds of her release, and thought she'd never been more beautiful. Then his body tightened, his blood rushed, and the sensations swept him over the edge right along with her. He buried his face into the curve of her neck, grunting hard and low as he climaxed, holding her tight in his embrace.

Chapter Eight

They stood there for a minute, clinging, shuddering, their sweat-coated bodies sticking to each other. Julia couldn't catch her breath. Her head was spinning, and the heavy thuds of her pounding heart filled her ears. Dane was panting as hard as she was, but sealed his mouth to hers for long, slow kisses as he pulled out of her and gently lowered her leg to the ground.

"Jesus," he finally managed. He gave her a look of pure astonishment. "That was . . . oh my *God*." He kissed her again, and again, raising his hands to brush back the strands of hair that were plastered to her dewy forehead and cheeks. Kissing her mouth with aching sweetness, he held her face in his hands. "You're amazing."

She looked back into his eyes and smiled with hazy, carnal satisfaction. "You did all right," she teased in a sultry murmur.

He snorted and pinched her ass. She squeaked, making them both laugh.

"You're a moaner," he remarked, teasing her back. "Hot damn, porn star."

"I am," she said, chuckling ruefully. "Sorry if that bothered you."

"*Bothered* me?" He huffed out a disbelieving breath. "You kidding? That made it a thousand times hotter."

She rolled her eyes, but he caught the smile on her face. She slipped out of the stilettos at last, bringing her height down a good few inches.

"See, you needed the shoes," he grinned. "The added height helped with . . . the angle."

She snorted but was still smiling. "You're right, I'll give you that one."

He leaned into her for another kiss and felt her body quiver, but it wasn't from desire. "You're trembling," he noted. "Hey, your legs are shaking. You okay?" He rubbed her quivering thigh, the one he'd had hoisted over his arm the whole time.

She let out a soft laugh. "Yeah. My muscles got worked, that's all."

"Oh, you got worked, all right." He smiled and gave her a smack of a kiss. "Tell you what. I have to clean up, you need to lie down. You go on, I'll meet you in bed."

She looked into his eyes. "Um . . ." She didn't know how to say what she wanted to without sounding crass. *I don't need to stay. I can go now. That was some of the best sex I've ever had, but there'll be no cuddling here. Check, please.*

By his slight frown, she knew he sensed her hesitation. His eyes narrowed and he commanded, "You're not leaving so soon." And before she could open her mouth to disagree, he took her hand and pulled her farther into the dark suite. They walked together, naked and sweaty, through what she imagined was a large sitting room, around a sofa, into an adjoining bedroom.

He nudged her toward the bed. "Let me clean up." He gave her a soft poke in the shoulder, enough to make her fall onto the edge of the bed into a sitting position. "Get. In. The bed. Relax, lie down."

"Back to being the boss," she muttered, but with good humor.

He chuckled. "Damn right. Be right back." He kissed her lips and walked away. She glanced at his broad back and very fine ass as he went into the bathroom, then heard the sound of running water as she sat still, deciding what to do. Leave? Stay a little while? The truth was she wanted to stay, and that bothered her. In the darkened room, she could make out where the arch of the bedroom door was. Her dress was on the floor by the front door. . . .

But she crawled up the mattress and burrowed in under the covers. His king-size bed was soft and welcoming, and she sank in with a contented sigh. All her muscles relaxed.

Well, there goes that, she thought. Nothing like putting your dream job in jeopardy for a hot romp. An unbelievably hot romp, but still. *Dammit!*

"I can feel your brain churning from here," Dane called from the bathroom. "Knock it off, Julia. Everything's cool."

A shiver ran over her skin. How the hell had he known what she'd been thinking right then? It was more than uncanny, it was unnerving. It made her want to jump out of bed, find her clothes in the dark, and get out of there.

But Dane came back into the room and slid under the covers. He reached for her in the dark, pulling her close, encircling her in his strong arms. His mouth found hers to steal slow, luxurious kisses as his big, warm hand caressed her back. He smelled of sweat, sex, and a trace of soap, a heady, masculine combination that made her senses swim. Despite her instinct to flee only a minute before, she felt herself melt into his embrace, reeling from his tenderness.

"So," he murmured jovially against her lips, nipping, kissing. "You okay, Red?"

"I'm fine, Boss," she replied. "You?"

"I'm more than fine." His other hand reached up to brush her hair back from her face. "I'm pretty great right now. But I told you if you called me 'Boss' in bed, I'd have to spank you." His eyes sparkled with mischief as the hand on her back moved down to squeeze her ass. "Final warning, Ms. Shay."

She laughed and kissed him to shut him up. He held her head in his hands, pushing his fingers through her hair as he deepened the kiss. He explored her now, taking his time, slow and sensual. It made her body start to tingle all over again. Her fingers plowed through his tousled curls and she edged in closer, instinctively pressing the length of her body against his.

He groaned and shifted, rolling so they lay side by side and he could hold her close. They kissed for what felt like hours, and she realized he *liked* the kissing part. It wasn't just a means to an end for him, he genuinely reveled in it. She loved kissing, but had met very few men who did. Most saw it as a necessary part of foreplay to get to the good part. Dane's enthusiasm for it surprised and delighted her. The luscious waves of delicious passion took her under, and she went willingly.

Time seemed to get fuzzy. How long had they been kissing now? Ten minutes? Half an hour? Two hours? Who knew. She felt too good to care. They luxuriated in the feel of each other, taking their time to explore and discover. Even though the initial flames of passion had been quenched, they still craved each other. She let his greedy hands and mouth do what they wanted, and took the same pleasures herself.

She'd suspected he had a good body, but he'd been hiding a taut, powerful physique under his expensively tailored clothes. His body was even hotter than she'd imagined. He wasn't overly muscular, but muscled enough that she knew he put in time at the gym. Her hands roamed with slow delight, learning him—his broad, strong shoulders . . . his deliciously defined arms and legs . . . his solid chest, not covered in hair, but enough to let her fingers play through . . . and good Lord, a tight ass so fine it made her a bit self-conscious.

But he seemed to like her lush, womanly figure; he hadn't done anything but revere it. She was all soft-ness and curves; he was hard muscles and defined lines. The contrast was delectable. And that mouth of his . . . good Lord, what his mouth could do. What it did to her now as he kissed and sucked and licked his way down her neck, her throat, to close over her breast . . . his teeth grazed her nipple and liquid heat seared through her. Soon she was breathing harder, wanting more, and her hips rolled sinuously beneath his, nudging his growing erection.

"Wanna go another round?" she purred.

A low chuckle rumbled out of him. "You're insatiable, aren't you."

"Yup. You complaining?"

"Hell no." Eyes sparkling, he grasped her hips and ground his pelvis against hers, showing her just how much he wanted her. "Does that feel like I'm unhappy?"

"Nope," she said, grinning, and tangled her fingers in his soft, curly hair to pull his head back down to hers.

Dane lay sprawled on his bed, exhausted, floating in a satisfied postcoital haze. He let his fingers trail lazily up and down Julia's smooth back. She lay quietly beside him, her fingers playing softly with the sparse hair on his chest. Their skin glistened with sweat, the air felt thick. The only sounds in the dark room were the low hum of the air conditioning and the muffled noises of street traffic from far below.

"You're an animal," he drawled with a grin, turning his head to look at her. "In the best way, of course," he added quickly.

"I guess I *am* a cougar, then," she joked, and they both laughed.

"More like a wildcat," he said. "Jesus. You're amazing."

"Back atcha." She smiled and dropped a kiss on his shoulder.

"And you said I couldn't handle you. Ha!" He shot her a victorious look.

"Well, with all the practice you've had," she taunted, "I guess it readied you for me."

"Wow. Talk about a backhanded compliment." He rolled onto his side to face her. "Look. I haven't been with as many women as you seem to think I—"

"Dane. Stop." Julia's voice was firm. "It doesn't matter. I was teasing you."

"It does matter," he insisted, realizing with surprise that it did. "It matters to me. I'm not a sleaze. I know you may have . . . heard things . . . but I haven't slept with half the world's women. So even if you're joking? I just need to know you know that."

She exhaled softly and nodded. "Fine. Now I know that. I didn't mean to upset you."

"You're all but calling me a whore," he quipped. "Why wouldn't that upset me?"

"Because I'm lying next to you after we fucked each other's brains out all night," she said. "Even if I thought that, which I don't, it obviously didn't keep me away from you, or out of your bed."

Tension hung in the air. She scooted closer, cupped his chin, and kissed him.

He pulled back and stared at her, unhappy with the turn in the conversation.

"Dane. Hey . . ." Her brows furrowed and she frowned. He saw the remorse in her eyes. She kissed him again, softly, with something akin to tenderness. "I'm sorry," she murmured. "I really was just teasing, I didn't mean to offend you. Let's forget it, okay?"

He nodded and decided to do just that. His arms wrapped around her to pull her in and he brushed his lips against hers, soft and slow, nipping, then kissing, to show her he'd accepted her apology. They kissed for a while, letting the melding of their mouths and bodies take down the friction. He lost himself in her mouth, in the feel of her soft, naked curves against him, and felt the tension leave both of them.

"Julia . . ." Relaxed again, he wanted to talk. "Can I ask you something?"

"Sure." She rested her head on his arm and laced her fingers through his hair, playing absently with his curls.

"Can you give me a clue . . ." He paused, wanting to choose his words carefully. "I know you think I have this reputation, and I get that you don't trust me yet, but like you told me, you don't trust anyone. Which means some time, something . . . went really bad for you. Clue me in. I want to know."

He felt her stiffen in his arms, her hand stop cold in his hair. Her eyes shuttered. It was kind of fascinating, watching her pull away from him without moving a muscle. With a sigh, he tried to continue. "I just don't—"

"I've had some bad things happen," she bit out.

"Who hasn't?"

"Everyone has. I'm just curious about your story."

"Why?"

"Why? Because I like you. Because you interest me."

"This is just supposed to be fun sex," she said, rolling away.

"It is," he said, holding her in place. "But the advantage of sleeping with a smart woman is you can actually talk to her afterward."

"My being smart has nothing to do with my past."

"I know. I didn't mean . . ." He huffed out an exasperated sigh. "Sorry. I shouldn't have asked. Forget I did."

She went silent. They stared at each other for a long beat. He wondered if she was going to leave right then.

But she said quietly, "No, Dane. Look . . ." She leaned up on her elbow to look at him. "Yes, I've been hurt, okay?" she said, almost in a whisper. "It was really bad. I've lost things . . . that no one should ever have to lose. It made me harder. I survived." She swallowed and drew a deep breath. He stared into her eyes. Searching, he caught a flash of something there he'd rarely seen in her: stark vulnerability. In a sullen tone, she added, "Is that what you wanted to hear?"

"No." His heart softened. He reached up and

caressed her cheek, murmuring, "I'm sorry to hear all that."

"Don't you dare feel sorry for me," she said, even as her voice cracked.

"I don't." He kissed her mouth gently. "I said I'm sorry to hear you had hard times, not that I feel sorry for you. Different things. Okay?"

She nodded in stubborn silence. The haunted look in her gorgeous hazel eyes made him want to hold her tight, soothe her. It was a strange feeling, this wave of . . . protectiveness.

"Dane." Her voice didn't waver now, it was back to steel. "You're a powerful, extremely wealthy and well-connected man. I *know* you did a background check on me before you hired me. So why are you asking questions that you likely already know the answers to? I feel like you're . . . I don't know, setting me up or something. I don't like it. That's why I got defensive."

Just when he thought all she'd ever offer him were cutting comebacks, she knocked him flat with her open, honest admission. He stared at her for a few seconds before saying, "I told you I didn't run a personal background check. I wouldn't do that, to you or to anyone. Your life before here, away from here, isn't my business. I don't know anything about you other than you live in a one-bedroom apartment in Blue Harbor, you don't have a criminal record, and you were a secretary until you quit your job a few weeks ago to take on this job. I don't know anything else about you that you haven't told me yourself. I swear."

He saw the fight in her eyes; she wanted to believe him, but was afraid to. Whoever had hurt her in the past had done a sadly thorough job. He dipped his head to kiss her mouth with all the tenderness he possessed. She responded slowly, kissing him back timidly at first, then easing into it. Her arms snaked around his neck and she pressed herself closer. He held her face in his hands, kissing her until he felt the tension leave her body, until she was melting into him and responding as she had before. Only then did he pull back, look into her eyes, and whisper, "I really hope you believe me. For your own sake."

She hesitated, then whispered back, "I do. I believe you." Her hand lifted to run through his hair. He watched her eyes soften again. "Thank you for respecting my privacy. Not everyone in your position would."

"You say that like someone who's speaking from experience," he said, frowning.

She murmured, "That's right. You have no idea. Trust me, you don't want to know. Okay?"

He kissed her, not knowing what the hell to say.

When they broke apart, she tried to grin and said, "I'm really sorry I was such a bitch before. Can we please forget that part?"

"Sure. Yeah. Look, Julia . . ." He smoothed her hair back from her forehead. "The other thing you said before. I know this is just sex. I'm fine with that. I'm not looking for anything more, and neither are you. We're adults. We obviously enjoy each other. But like you said at the start: no strings, no ties. I won't ask you those heavy questions again when we're in bed. Okay?"

Her thin brows furrowed. "You said this was going to be one night. That statement implies . . . future encounters."

His mouth curved up and he let out a soft chuckle. "Tonight's been incredible. I'd be a fucking fool not to try to get you back in my bed again. And I'm not a fool." He nipped at her mouth playfully. "Come onnn," he wheedled. "Come on, Julesie. You know you wanna."

She groaned in mock frustration. "You're incorrigible."

"Notoriously so," he said, grinning. Dropping light kisses along her neck, his fingertips did a slow glide across her ass, stopping at the small of her back. "Come on. Admit it. We enjoy each other. Hell, we *more* than enjoy each other."

"Yes, we do." She laughed in spite of herself, then sighed. "But . . . my job . . ."

"Is secure," he assured her firmly, raising his head to look into her eyes.

"Seriously?"

"Seriously."

He watched as she considered his words, letting her fingers play with the scruff on his jaw. "No one can know about this," she finally said. "I mean . . . if we start sleeping together. Like, on a . . . I don't know, a regular basis?"

"Um, we already started sleeping together," he joked, cupping her breast. "Ooops." He pinched her nipple.

She squeaked and giggled in spite of herself, and his insides warmed at the sounds.

"I don't want gossip any more than you do, Red," Dane said. "I've got a reputation as a ladies' man? Fine, whatever, I don't care what people think. But more importantly, I've also got a reputation as a successful businessman, someone respectable, who's made a name for myself *apart* from my family legacy. I worked hard for that. *That* matters to me." His gaze sharpened and held hers. "I know you won't believe me, but I've never slept with someone who works for me before. Ever. You're the first. And likely the last. I don't ever mix business with pleasure."

"So why'd you break your rule for me?" Her voice and gaze had turned mischievous again, and whatever tension he'd still felt in her body melted away under his hands.

"Probably the same reason you broke your rule to sleep with me." He sucked on her bottom lip and released it with a popping sound, making her laugh. "Because we both really wanted to. Because we're like a house on fire when we're anywhere near each other." He grinned at the look of resigned humor on her face. He kissed her mouth, then moved to nibble the soft spot on her neck that usually elicited a sigh or a shudder. To his satisfaction, she did both. He licked her warm skin, blew on it, bit down. She whimpered and shifted beneath him. His blood started the slow burn again.

"Julia . . . you looked so good tonight, I couldn't think straight. Couldn't hold back anymore. All I could think about was having you. . . ." He kissed her mouth. ". . . being inside you . . ." Kissed her chin. ". . . making you scream for me." She gasped at that, and a helpless moan fluttered out of her. The sounds made his cock get hard yet again. His mouth and hands trailed along her soft skin, bringing more intoxicating shudders from her. "I wanted to watch your face when I made you come." She moaned at that and her eyes slipped closed. He felt her tremble and added in a husky whisper in her ear, "And God, it was even better than I thought it would be. *You* were."

"You are too." Her hands roved down his back, leaving delicious shivers in their wake as she let them rest on his ass. He felt his cock throb against her belly and she purred seductively, "Wanna watch me come again?"

"Hell yes," he said with a smile, and crushed his mouth to hers.

They kissed, caressed, stroked . . . until she flipped him onto his back. She eyed his thick erection, moved in to kiss him, and whispered against his lips, "I want something. . . ."

"Take it," he breathed raggedly. "Whatever you want, it's yours."

She smiled a broad, provocative smile. "Right answer." She kissed his lips again, then started on his neck, licking his throat, kissing her way down his chest . . . he realized her mouth was heading lower and lower and his whole body responded. Every nerve ending felt lit with fire, burning with fresh need. God, how she made him need. His eyes slipped closed and his fingers kneaded her shoulders as she traveled down.

Her tongue circled his navel, then her lips trailed down his belly as her nails scraped gently along his hips. His breath caught and he rocked against her, his hips needing to move. She teased him, taking her time . . . ran her tongue along the length of his shaft and flicked it at the head, making him groan helplessly . . . and then she took him into her warm, wet mouth. Another groan ripped from deep in his chest and his hands fisted in her hair. She took him in slowly at first, seeming to savor the feel of him, the taste of him. His mind went blank and his eyes slipped closed again. Then she moved faster, her mouth claiming him, owning him. With another groan, he willingly relinquished control. His hips rocked of their own volition, meeting her tantalizing rhythm as his hands got lost in her long, thick hair.

The incredible sensations engulfed him, sweeping him away . . . when he was close to exploding, he roughly moaned her name.

Her warm mouth released him. Still stroking him with one hand, she stretched across the bed to the nightstand and felt around for the strip of condoms there. Breathing hard, he reached up, grabbed them, and ripped one open. She took it from him and rolled it down over the hard length of him, then straddled him and lowered herself onto him, a slow, warm, wet descent. Again he groaned from deep in his chest as his mind spun out.

"Who's the moaner now?" she teased, her voice low and thick with passion.

"God, you're incredible," he panted. "Go, baby. Do it."

She smiled and began to ride him. Her lush hips rolled and swayed, drawing him in deeper. His fingers dug into her hips and he thrust up into her, hard and fast. He watched her face, flushed with desire. Her round, plump breasts bounced as she moved, hypnotizing him, stripping away the last shreds of his restraint. It only took about a dozen thrusts for him to explode, and he came with rough, deep groans, losing himself in her. His climax spurred hers on; her head fell back, her eyes squeezed shut, and she cried out, grinding into him as if her life depended on it. When she was done, she collapsed onto him in a boneless heap. His fingers laced through her hair, holding her to his chest as they both gasped for air.

"Holy fucking God," Dane finally sighed, still trying to catch his breath.

Julia smiled, but said nothing. Lazily she trailed her fingers down his torso to his belly and back up to his chest.

"That's it. I'm spent. I'm gonna pass out soon," he said, letting his eyes slip closed. He was beyond relaxed now, floating from the postcoital buzz and the feel of this incredible woman in his arms. All night, the sex had been mind-blowing, off the charts. She was so passionate, giving as good as she got . . . maybe even giving better. Jesus. There was definitely something to be said for the stereotype of experienced older women after all. Julia had just single-handedly proven it to be true, a one-woman wrecking crew. He hadn't gone three rounds in one night in some time, much less three rounds of sex like the ones they'd just had. The ways they'd pleased each other . . . he was surprised he could remember his name, much less speak.

But she shifted and slowly pulled away from him. "I really need a shower," she said. "Okay if I take a quick one here?"

"Of course," he said. "Just don't be offended that I'm not joining you yet. I'm a wreck. You destroyed me."

She laughed softly, dropped a light kiss on his lips, and rose from the bed. "Back in a few." He heard her flick on the light, heard the water start running. . . .

Something warm and bright was shining on his face. Lying on his belly, Dane groaned and slowly opened his eyes. Sunshine. It was morning; what time was it? He lifted his head to look at the clock on the nightstand: quarter after ten. What time had he fallen asleep? When had he—

Images of the night before flooded his brain. *Julia.* God, what a night. Smiling, he rolled over to kiss her awake.

But her side of the bed was empty.

The smile slid off his face and he sat up, listening.

There were no sounds in the suite. No sign of her being there at all. "Julia?" he called out. Nothing.

Uneasiness mixed with irritation, sparked a slow burn in his blood. He threw back the covers to prowl across the bedroom and canvas the suite. She wasn't in the bathroom. She wasn't out in the sitting room. No dress on the floor by the door. There was no evidence of her whatsoever . . . except for a sheet of hotel stationery on the desk. Swearing under his breath, he snatched it up and read:

> *See you tomorrow, Boss. Thank you for a very memorable night. It was fantastic.*

Dane didn't know whether to laugh or throw something. To his annoyance, he couldn't shake the feeling of . . . what the fuck, rejection? Was that it? Why? Because she hadn't stayed the night? She didn't have to. They'd agreed from the start, it would just be sex, and it had been. Okay, not *just* sex, because honestly, it'd been unbelievably hot, brain-melting jungle sex. Three times. Jesus, *three* epic, earth-shaking times . . .

But that was it. Right? No strings, no ties, the rule that they both lived by. They owed each other nothing.

Something struck him. For her to write "See you tomorrow" meant she'd gone in the night, slipping out in the dark when he was asleep, and hadn't stayed at all. Well. Okay. That was fine. Why not, she had to go home, all the way back to Long Island. . . .

So why did it bother him that she'd left without a word?

Mind spinning, he crushed the paper in his fist to a ball and tossed it into the wastebasket, then stalked to the bathroom to take a shower.

Chapter Nine

"Okay, honey, let's have it," Kelvin demanded as soon as the waiter walked away.

"Have what?" Julia asked, looking from him to Randi in confusion.

Kelvin narrowed his eyes at her. "You ask the two of us to meet you for dinner. Your two closest friends and most trusted confidants. On a Friday. At six, so we have plenty of time to talk before the show. You asked Randi to leave Stephen home so we have privacy." Kelvin leaned in. "Spill it, girl."

"You know me way too well," Julia said ruefully, reaching for her water glass.

"Damn right I do," Kelvin sniffed. "So stop stalling."

"Go on, honey," Randi said, always the quiet voice of reason. "Talk to us."

Not knowing how to phrase it well, or tactfully, Julia just blurted it out. "I slept with Dane last night."

Randi's mouth fell open. Kelvin's eyes flew wide as he let out something resembling a high-pitched girlish squeak. Coming from a six-foot-tall African-American man, it took everything Julia had not to giggle at the sound. It would have been funny if the situation wasn't serious.

Her gaze darted to him and she sputtered, "I'm sorry. I'm so sorry. I thought you should know right away. Now you do."

"Why?" Kelvin asked tersely. "Are we fired?"

"No! No, of course not," Julia said.

"Are you worried you *might* be?" Randi asked.

Julia sighed. "I don't know. It's always a possibility, isn't it?"

"Can't help wishing you'd thought of that before you jumped him," Kelvin said dryly.

"I know. I know." Julia let her head fall into her hands.

"I mean, he's beautiful," Kelvin went on. "He's seriously smokin'. I don't blame you. If he were gay, I'd be all over him. He looks like he'd be a great lay."

"He is," Julia confirmed, her voice muffled by her hands. "Holy crap, he *is*."

"Then I definitely wanna know more!" Randi demanded.

Julia gave them the short version of the story.

"I knew that man would cave first," Kelvin said. He looked at Randi and said, "Every time they're in the same room, it's like the damn smoke alarms are gonna go off from the heat between them."

"I felt that the night I met him," Randi said with a nod. "The way he looked at her. He totally wanted her. It was so obvious."

"Hooray for subtlety," Julia said. She sipped her water again.

"So now what?" Kelvin asked. "We're on notice?"

"No. *No,*" Julia insisted, shaking her head. "He swears that what happened between us has nothing to do with my job, that they're separate things. Reminded

me my contract is ironclad, and said he wouldn't fire
me regardless. He tried to reassure me. . . ." She
sighed. "You know me. I just don't trust anyone. Especially rich, charming, powerful men. But . . ." She
fidgeted with her fork, flipping it in circles on the
tabletop. "I think he's sincere. I hope this won't bite
me in the ass later, but I believe him. And I also believe
Tonio."

"Tonio?" Kelvin looked confused. "What does he
have to do with anything?"

"Who's Tonio?" Randi asked.

"Head bartender," Julia told her. "Works in the bar
and lounge. He's known Dane for a few years, he used
to work over in his midtown hotel before he came to
the Alexandra. I had dinner with him the other
night, and I asked him about Dane. Tonio's a good
boy from Brooklyn, no bullshit. He said Dane keeps
his word, that he's not a typical rich snob, that he's
generous and fair. So . . . I believe Tonio, and I believe Dane." She threw an apologetic look at Kelvin.
"I just thought you should know . . . just in case . . .
anything happens."

"Nothing's gonna happen, sweet pea," Kelvin said,
patting her hand. "Except you having mind-blowingly
hot sex with that gorgeous piece of man candy. I'm a
little jealous. But damn glad you're finally getting
some. Maybe you'll be less cranky now."

"Shut up, you," Julia laughed.

Randi giggled and squeezed her friend's hand.
"It'll be okay. Just . . . be careful."

"Aren't I always?" Julia asked.

"*Almost* always," Kelvin retorted. "Hello, you just
slept with the boss."

Julia groaned in defeat. "I *know*. I'm so stupid! So
goddamn stupid." She sighed again, thinking of Dane's

beautiful blue eyes, the feel of his hard body against hers, the naughty, dirty things he'd whispered in her ear while he . . . her stomach did a little flip. "But he's so . . ."

"Blindingly gorgeous, we know, sweetie," Kelvin said. He leaned in, dark eyes sparkling. "So? Give us the juicier details. *Three* times? Goddamn, girl, spill!"

Randi leaned in too, grinning. "I'm with him. Details. Three times in one night?" She shot her friend a look of admiration. "God bless you, girl. I don't think I've done that since college."

Kelvin raised his hand for a fist bump, which Julia gave him back with a laugh.

"My girl is BACK!" he exclaimed. "Hot damn!"

"But look," Julia said quickly, her voice lowering. "This stays between us. Only us. *No one* can know about this. Seriously."

"Who am I going to tell?" Randi said, shrugging.

"Not even Stephen," Julia said. "I'm sorry. But please."

"Okay," Randi said. "I don't like keeping secrets from him, but this isn't my secret, it's yours."

"You're not the one I'm worried about." Julia turned her eyes to her pianist. "Kel. You can't act like you know, babe. You can't let Dane even *think* you might know."

"Girl, I'm a vault," Kelvin sniffed. "You insult me."

Julia arched a brow in haughty challenge and growled knowingly, "Kelvin Jones, you bitch. Promise me."

"I'll be good!" he cried, throwing up his hands in surrender. The two women laughed.

Dane had sent her a short, casual text that afternoon, but didn't come to the show on Friday night—

the first one he'd missed since the lounge had opened. As far as Julia knew, he hadn't even come to the hotel at all that day. It made her curious, but she didn't speculate on it too much. It wasn't her business where he was. But the thought did go through her mind: Was he staying away because he'd gotten what he wanted? He'd had her, conquered her, and now he was gone?

She ran some errands on Saturday afternoon, trying to get them done quickly and stay out of the July heat. She did some quick grocery shopping and got an oil change for her car, picked up two bottles of wine, read three chapters of her latest book. But by the time she was on the train into the city at seven-fifteen that evening, she had the time to overthink, and she did. Irritated, she realized she was curious, and even slightly tense, as she wondered if Dane would show up that night.

The fact that it bothered her at all *really* bothered her. It was no-strings sex. They'd agreed on that. So he didn't need to call her the next day with platitudes or sweet talk that meant nothing. But for him to be so noticeably absent from the lounge once he'd finally gotten her into bed . . . it felt like he was rubbing her nose in the fact that she'd broken her own rule. He knew how nervous she'd been about crossing that line with her boss, mixing professional with personal. Yet it was the first time he hadn't shown up at her show since opening night. Was that merely a coincidence? She couldn't help but wonder if it was a subtle yet unmistakable message to her. And even if it was, she was being a petulant drama queen for wondering. Breaking her own rules. Again.

By the time she reached her dressing room, she was swallowing down bruised pride, and most of all, mad at herself. If it was no-strings sex, why did she feel like this? It made no sense. She was an idiot. She and Dane were just . . . what were they now?

"Hey, boss." Reaching over the bar, Tonio shook Dane's hand in greeting. "How's it goin'?"

"Great, Tonio. You?" Dane slid onto a barstool with a grin.

"It's all good. Getcha a drink?"

"Yes. Um . . . scotch."

"Be right back."

As Tonio walked away, Dane let his eyes canvas the scene. Almost ten on a Saturday night, and the place was packed. The bar was crowded and noisy, and every table in the lounge was taken. He smiled with deep satisfaction. Business was good.

"Entertainment here and ready?" Dane tried to make the question sound casual. Like he hadn't been able to stop thinking about his singer since he'd woken up Friday morning. Like he didn't keep flashing back on their hot night together, the way she'd looked, felt, sounded . . .

He realized Tonio had said something. "I'm sorry, what?"

Tonio repeated, "I said, yeah, they're here and ready."

Dane opened his mouth to respond, but took in the sudden frown on Tonio's face and followed his gaze. "Something up?"

Tonio's thick brows furrowed. "Not sure." He stared at a man standing alone by the booths a few seconds longer, then leaned in to speak in a low voice to Dane. "That guy along the wall, by himself? Dark hair with gray in it, shaggy looking. See him?"

"Navy shirt and jeans?" Dane offered.

"Yeah. He's been here for the last two weeks, hasn't missed one of their shows. Stays for both sets. Drinks nothing but ginger ale. Leaves as soon as Julia gets offstage for the night." Tonio pitched his voice even lower, so Dane had to lean in closer to hear. "Don't get me wrong, he hasn't done anything suspicious, but he just . . . he sets my gut hummin'. The way he looks at Julia the whole time she sings. I dunno. Bad vibe."

Dane's gut churned too. "I trust your instincts, Tonio. Keep an eye on him."

"Oh, I have been."

"Good man. You need any backup, you say the word." Dane looked Tonio in the eye. "That goes for this guy, or anyone else. Julia's beautiful, she's getting some attention in the press lately by being here . . . so if she gets any, uh, *admirers* that she dislikes? Handle it. Or tell me, and I'll handle it. But I trust you."

Tonio nodded curtly. "Done."

The audience started applauding, and Dane turned his head to see Julia and Kelvin get onstage to start their first set. "Good evening, ladies and gentlemen," she said, her rich voice a caress. Dane had a flash of that voice moaning in his ear, crying out his name, and got hard right then and there. He shifted carefully in his seat.

Kelvin started playing and Julia launched into an upbeat, swinging standard. With casual ease, Dane turned to look over the crowd . . . and at the guy Tonio had singled out. The man stood in the shadows, a perfect vantage point: he could see Julia, but Julia couldn't see him. His eyes were fixed on the redhead, just like Tonio had said. And, just like Tonio had said, something about the guy gave Dane the creeps.

His jaw tightened as something he couldn't really name surged through him. Anger? Protectiveness? Concern? Maybe all of the above.

He didn't want to make Julia nervous, so he wouldn't say anything. After all, it was likely nothing. The guy probably just thought Julia was hot, which she was, and liked her voice, and liked watching her perform. Hell, who didn't? She was magic up there.

Dane turned back to the bar and took a long swallow of his drink.

"You rocked it tonight, girl," Kelvin said from his sprawl on the couch.

"You rocked it tonight, babe," Julia replied from her couch. Their usual post-gig banter made them both grin.

"He's back tonight," Kelvin said.

Julia shrugged. "I know. I saw him sitting at the bar during the first set."

"Then at a table with two friends, it looked like, for the second set." Kelvin slanted her a look. "Stop sulking and go talk to him."

"I'm not sulking," she said.

"Really? Then your imitation of someone sulking is damn good."

She snorted and flopped back to lie down. "I'm an idiot sometimes. Sorry."

"I know. Don't sweat it."

Someone knocked on the door. They looked at each other.

"Five bucks says that's the boss," Kelvin said, his full lips curving wickedly.

"You're on," Julia said, sitting up. "I bet it's anyone *but* him." She got to her feet, crossed the dressing room in a few strides, and flung open the door. Dane stood there, looking damn fine in a cornflower blue button-down shirt under a dark gray suit. The very picture of casual sophistication, as usual.

"I'll just get my five from your wallet, sweetie," Kelvin said with a smug grin, standing.

"Hi." Dane's tone and smile were friendly. "You were great tonight. But you always are." He craned his head and added to Kelvin, "Both of you. Great sets."

"Thanks, Boss," Kelvin said as he rifled through Julia's bag. Pulling out a five-dollar bill, he shoved it into his pocket with another grin as he walked to the door. "If you two would excuse me, I'm going to go have something to eat before I head home." He glanced at Julia. "Should I order something for you?"

"You go ahead," she said. "Don't wait for me."

"Mm-hmm." Kelvin looked from one face to the other. "Okay then." He dropped a kiss on Julia's cheek and whispered, "Take it easy, girl!" before walking out.

Dane moved in past her. Annoyed, she closed the door behind him and stayed where she stood, hands on her hips.

"How are you?" he asked, amiable and light.

"Fine," she said. A wave of cool detachment had washed over her and she couldn't shake it.

He picked up on it, she could tell. His grin morphed into a slight frown. "You don't look fine. You look . . . well, pissed."

"I'm not."

He paused. "Yeah, that was convincing. What's up?"

"Nothing." She shrugged, chastising herself to knock it off. She had no right to be annoyed at him. She knew that. But then the words came rolling out of her mouth anyway. "You weren't here last night. I just thought that was interesting timing."

"What does that mean?" His frown deepened.

"If you were sending some kind of message, it was received. That's all." Her stomach tightened and she fought to keep her features neutral.

He stared at her with open confusion. "*What?* What are you talking about?"

She crossed to her makeup stand and grabbed her bottle of water. "You know what I'm talking about."

He threw his hands up as if in surrender. "Okay, I have *no* idea what I just walked into here. Obviously, I don't speak fluent Shay-ese. Enlighten me."

"You've been at every single show I've done since opening night," she said in a heated rush. "You didn't have to do that, but you did. Now I know why. It was a tactic, a ploy. Because as soon as you got me into bed, look at that! Nowhere to be seen."

He gaped at her openly, unable to hide his shock and consternation. "Are you fucking kidding me?"

She paused for a second. *Uh oh. Shit.* Cornered, she said, "Am I wrong?"

"Dead wrong!" he sputtered. "I wasn't trying to—I didn't not show up because—holy shit." He raked his hands through his hair, eyes flashing with anger. "I like you, Julia. But I don't owe you, or anyone else, any explanations for my whereabouts. Ever."

"I know that." She shot it back hotly, but she cringed inside. He had every right to spit at her like that, and she knew it. Mad at herself, she jerked the bottle cap open and downed some water.

A muscle jumped in his jaw. "I'll tell you where I was anyway, because you obviously need to hear it. So I'll tell you. *This time.*"

"No." She felt her face heat and winced. "Just forget it."

He ignored her. "I was out on Long Island last night. At my father's, at a family party. It was my nephew's birthday, and mine's next week, so we do a joint birthday dinner every year. That's where I was last night. I went out there yesterday morning so I could spend the day at the beach with my sister, then we had the party."

Julia felt the color drain from her face. *Oh crap.* "Dane—"

"I was tired, so I slept at my sister's," he continued, stepping toward her as he went on. His blue eyes glittered dangerously. "I slept late, had brunch with her, and got back to the city around three. Then I went to the gym—"

"Dane, stop."

"—I went to the gym"—his voice rose as he barreled on—"then took a shower and changed, had dinner, and got to the hotel around seven. I checked in with different people to see how things were going, and got here at ten." He was only inches away from her now, and his tension was palpable. She could feel heat coming off his body, but stood her ground as he stared at her. "I was looking forward to seeing you. This sucks."

She winced again but said, "I made assumptions and I was obviously wrong. I'm sorry."

"Damn right you did." His mouth tightened, and it was obvious he was taking pains to reel himself back to a calm place.

She said nothing. What else could she say now?

He searched her face, stretching out the moment. She almost squirmed under his searing gaze. "I've treated you with nothing but decency from the moment

I met you," he said. "Why are you always so quick to think the worst of me?"

Her stomach flipped and her heart sank a little.

"I know, you told me. You don't trust anyone." He shook his head slowly. "It was fun the other night. Really, really *hot,* and fun. And we were relaxed, in between rounds, you know? I thought that showed you that I . . ." His voice trailed off and he took a step back, his face darkening. "You know what? Forget it. My mistake."

"Wait. Just wait. Put yourself in my shoes for a minute," she said, maintaining her composure despite the way her stomach was desperately twisting. "You've been here every night. You wanted to sleep with me. You did. And then that happens to be the first night you don't come around. It felt like a message. A snub. Come on, what would *you* think?" She threw up her hands. "Sorry. That's where my mind went."

"I'd think maybe you had plans," he said, low and tight. "I'd think maybe you had a life outside this place. Which I do. A very full life. And I don't answer to anyone."

She stiffened at the rebuke. Her throat closed with embarrassment. Unable to speak, furious with herself for what she'd done, how she'd lost her cool and played into the jealous shrew stereotype, she turned her back to him. She leaned her hands against her makeup counter at the vanity, but kept her head high. Clearing her throat, she said, "Again. I'm sorry. I was out of line, and I was wrong about why you weren't here. I apologize. You can go now." Only then did her eyes fall away.

She hadn't heard him move, but his hands settled on her shoulders and turned her around. Her heart thumped as he looked into her eyes, searching, studying. Finally he said quietly, "I'm sorry too." He stroked her cheek with the backs of his fingers. "I just went off on you. Yes, you pissed me off, but I should've taken it down a notch."

She swallowed, her throat uncomfortably dry, as he continued, "So you thought I was . . . what, thumbing my nose at you? Blowing you off? No. No way. But now that you explained what was going through your head, I understand why you thought that. I might have." His hands slid slowly up and down her bare arms. She still wore her black sequined sheath dress, and his eyes roved over her body, apparently liking the view, before he lifted them to meet her gaze again. "Kind of like how I woke up to a note, instead of you, yesterday morning."

Now it was her turn to be confused. "What was wrong with that?"

He paused, then said coyly, "You could've at least kissed me good-bye."

Damn. Why did that make her feel awful? "You were passed out cold when I got out of the shower. I saw no need to wake you just to say good-bye. So I did what you'd suggested—I went and got a room of my own, here at the hotel. Passed right out. Slept 'til almost noon."

"Good for you. I slept like a rock. Bet you did too. It was a hell of a night." His eyes softened as they roamed over her face. "Okay, Julia. Truce. Yes?"

"Yes," she said. Relief washed through her and she tried to swallow down whatever it was that still had her heart thumping against her ribs. "I don't know what came over me. I'm an idiot."

"Far from it. You do still look tense, though." His blues took on a devilish glint. "Maybe I need to just kiss you hello and find a way to make you relax." He leaned in and brushed his lips against hers, slowly, teasing. "C'mere," he whispered as his hand cupped the back of her neck. He kissed her once, twice, then longer and deeper the third time. Long and deep enough to bring that tiny whimper of submission he'd come to adore. "You missed me, didn't you," he murmured in a taunt against her mouth. "I think you did, Red."

"In your dreams," she whispered back, but her arms snaked around his neck so she could tangle her hands in his hair to hold him close. She loved playing with his curls. They were soft and springy and adorable and sexy, all at the same time. "So what's your idea to make me relax? A massage in your spa?"

His eyes sparkled and his grin turned wicked. "Not even close." He untangled himself from the embrace to go to the door and flip the lock, then strode back to her.

She arched a brow. "Locking the door?"

"Don't want to be interrupted while I'm helping you relax. Relaxing is serious business." He took off his jacket and laid it over the back of her vanity chair, still grinning dangerously. "Come here, Red." He held out his hand.

She couldn't help feeling like this was making a deal with the devil, or something like it. But damn, he was so sexy. Why fight it? She slipped her hand into his.

He pulled her to one of the sofas and nudged her to sit down. Within seconds, he was next to her, kissing her, then easing her back to lie down and shifting to lie on top of her. They kissed hungrily, the fiery passion between them sparking in an instant. As the kisses deepened, making heat flood through her, her mind blurred as need filled her and sharpened.

"Relaxed yet?" he whispered against her lips.

"Nope. Keep trying, though," she teased. "I'm a tough nut to crack."

He chuckled. "Understatement of the year." Then he took her mouth in a possessive crush of a kiss.

As they kissed, she let her fingers slip through the longer curls at the back of his neck, returning his kisses with the same enthusiasm he exerted. Damn, he was so good at it. She could have kissed him forever. But when she whimpered into his mouth, he pulled his lips away to trail them sensually along her throat.

"Relaxed yet?" he murmured against her skin.

"Getting there," she said. Her fingers left his hair to trail gently down his broad back. "I don't know, though . . . you might have to work a little harder. I was pretty tense before."

He looked up at her, eyes dancing, as his low, sexy voice rumbled, "Challenge accepted."

Her stomach flipped with anticipation and her heart skittered as she wondered what he had in store for her. Something told her it would be delicious.

Later that night, Dane stared at the ceiling in the bedroom of his Tribeca apartment as his mind spun and whirled. He couldn't sleep, not with so many questions and thoughts in his head. Not with that gorgeous redhead consuming him.

He'd gotten Julia to relax, all right. He'd seduced her right there in her dressing room, and they'd both loved every second of it. After teasing her for a while, he'd simply hiked up her dress and gone down on her, shocking her at first. For about five seconds. But then the tigress in her enjoyed the ride. He could still feel her fingers fisting in his hair, holding his head as his mouth brought her to orgasm three glorious times. He could still hear her muffled moans, then how she'd shoved her own fist in her mouth to keep from screaming out her passion to anyone in the lounge who might hear. He'd been so aroused by her response that he was rock-hard and ready to explode. "I need you now," he'd told her roughly.

Still gasping for air, Julia had sat up, pulled him back up to the sofa, and opened his pants. As soon as the condom was on, she'd straddled him and ridden him until he came, groaning her name into her full breasts as he'd held her tightly against him.

But she wouldn't come up to his suite with him after. They'd lain together for a few minutes, catching their breath in content silence . . . then she'd slipped out of his arms and into the adjoining bathroom. He'd realized she was cleaning up and changing into her street clothes to head back to Long Island. Buttoning up his shirt, he'd joined her in the tiny bathroom. As he washed his hands and face, a silence had settled over them. He'd straightened to dry his face with the towel and marveled at her. She'd stood there in her lacy peach bra and panties like a goddamn Greek goddess, totally without self-consciousness. His eyes couldn't help but rest on the swell of her huge breasts, pushed up in the cups of the bra. He could have feasted on them for a week.

"Stay in my suite tonight," he'd said as he tucked his shirt into his pants.

"Not necessary, but thanks for the offer," she'd said.

He had been taken aback, but played it cool. "Any time. Standing offer, you know."

She'd smiled and looked away, back into the mirror to fix her hair. He had gone back out to the dressing room and drunk down a bottle of water as he'd waited for her to emerge.

"You can stay here," he'd said again as they had prepared to leave the dressing room. "At the hotel. It's two in the morning. Take a room. You must be tired. . . ."

"Thanks, but I'm pretty wired right now, actually," she'd said with a sultry smile. "Red-hot dressing room sex. Who'd have thunk it?"

He wasn't going to beg her to stay, for God's sake. She'd wanted to go, of course she could go. *No strings.* So he'd pulled her in and given her a long kiss instead. "At least let me call you a car. You need to get home safely. It's 2:00 A.M., Julia."

She'd cocked her head and considered. "You know what? That's actually a nice idea. Yes. That, I'll let you do. But I'll pay for it."

"No way. It's on me. I'm pulling rank." He'd winked, then held her face in his hands and kissed her once more. "Go get a drink at the bar. I'll stay here and make the call, then come out in a few minutes so we're not seen coming out of your dressing room together. A car'll be waiting outside, at the side door, in about ten minutes. Okay?"

"Sounds like a plan," she'd said with a playful grin. "Thanks, Boss."

Again, he'd stared at her. He loved looking at her. And while he'd gotten used to seeing her all dressed up and sexed up in fancy dresses onstage, right then she'd looked . . . adorable. In her simple pale yellow sundress and multicolored wedge sandals, with her hair pulled back in a ponytail, she'd kind of glowed. Her cheeks had still had a rosy flush that showed she'd very much enjoyed her time with him. God, he had too. He'd dropped one last kiss on her forehead and said, "Good night, beautiful. Sleep well."

Her hand had raised to touch his face for a second, and there had been something in her eyes . . . then it was gone as soon as he'd glimpsed it. She'd grinned, patted his cheek, and strode past him out the door without a look back. Sassy vixen, that woman.

But now, as he lay in bed in the dark, his mind was grinding away, not letting him sink into sleep.

First of all, it bothered him that she wouldn't stay the night with him. Not only that, but she very obviously wanted to leave. She'd left the last time too. He'd never seen a woman flee the scene as quickly as Julia did. In his experience, women always wanted to snuggle after, and talk . . . well, okay, fine. This was a woman who apparently didn't go for postcoital tenderness of any kind. He *liked* the postsex cuddling; she didn't. Or, if she did, she wasn't having it with him. It ate at him a little bit. Just a little bit. But that bothered him, because he didn't know why it ate at him.

Then there was the way she completely and willingly lost control during sex. It was mind-blowing. It was the only time he ever saw her allow herself to lose control, to surrender to her senses, to stop thinking, and just *feel*. And hot damn, did she. When he went down on her, she'd given in gladly. She let herself melt, let him take over, let herself drown in it . . . even now, he started getting aroused thinking of her. Julia lost in the throes of passion was the hottest goddamn thing he'd ever seen and heard.

He loved how she let all her inhibitions go, how

she really enjoyed it—and that she wanted him to enjoy it too. When Julia had sex, it wasn't a selfish act; she gave as good as she got, and it obviously turned her on to do so. It gave him a tiny window into the hot-blooded woman she tried to hold back most of the time, unless she was onstage. There was a raging fire burning under her cool, tough exterior, and it fascinated him. He wished she'd release that passion in places other than the stage or in bed. That she could loosen up across the board. That she could let herself be . . . lighter.

He enjoyed life. But she saw life as a fight, something to get through and survive day-to-day. Something or someone had obviously hurt her enough to make her feel that way. And that made him sad for her. He wanted her to have some fun once in a while, and hoped she was at least having fun with him.

What wasn't fun, however, was what she'd said when he first got to her dressing room that night. Ho-ly shit, Ms. Tough-As-Nails had thought he'd been playing her by purposely not coming to the lounge once he'd slept with her, like a proclamation of triumph over her or something. He hadn't expected that. He'd been floored by her attitude . . . which really, once he thought about it, wasn't about anger. That was a front. She'd been *hurt* by the perceived slight. He felt bad that she'd thought that of him, and been wounded by it. Even if she'd done it to herself, with him not lifting a finger, he felt guilty for it. Guilty enough that he'd snapped back at her, and he wasn't proud of that.

But there was one thing that bothered him the most, the little thing he'd seen that had surprised him and wouldn't let go . . . the more he thought about it, the more he realized it was making his wheels spin. He flipped onto his side, punched the pillow to fluff it up, and sighed as he stared toward the wide windows.

Dane had been with a lot of women. That went without saying. He'd had the pleasure of bedding women of all ages, from all walks of life. Julia was the oldest he'd been with, but only by two years. He'd been with women in their late thirties. He'd been with a few *very* sexy divorced women who were mothers. Hell, in his opinion, in bed they were the hottest of all. They were more comfortable in their own skin, knew what they were doing and what they wanted. Truth be told, he'd enjoyed his encounters with those ladies the most.

The first night he was with Julia, all their sex had taken place in the dark. Not because she was shy, but simply because they'd been too busy grabbing at each other to take time to turn on a light. But tonight, when he'd hiked her dress up in her dressing room, the lights were on. He could finally really look at her voluptuous body, take in and memorize her curves with his hungry eyes. And he knew what he'd seen. They were faint, the palest silver, but they were absolutely there on her lower abdomen: stretch marks. At some point in her life, Julia had been pregnant. And if she hadn't given birth, she had been far along enough in the pregnancy to leave stretch marks.

She'd never mentioned any children. She'd told him she was divorced, but that was the extent of her divulging any details about her past relationships. She was, or had been, a mother.

Now, Dane found himself wanting to ask her a hundred new questions that were none of his damn business. Curiosity gnawed at his insides. Because Julia interested him. He had grown to genuinely like her, on top of lusting for her constantly like a damn horny teenager. She was sharp, had a wicked wit, and was so damn smart. But the more he got to know Julia Shay, the more he realized there was so much about her he didn't know. And that she worked very hard to keep it that way.

He wanted to know why. What had happened? Where was her child? Had something horrible, un-thinkable, happened to the kid—was that the loss she'd talked about? Was that why she'd gotten a di-vorce?

And most of all . . . why did he care? That question burned hottest of all, searing and poking at him. Why did he want, almost need, to know what had hap-pened in her past? Why did he want to figure her out so badly that he was inches away from calling his private investigator to find out everything he could about Julia Shay?

He wouldn't, of course. He respected her too much for that. Besides, that wasn't who he was. Tempted as he was, he wouldn't have been able to live with him-self if she ever found out he'd done it, especially after he'd promised her he never would. No. That wasn't the way to go.

He sighed, flipped onto his other side, and closed his eyes to try to get some sleep.

Maybe one day, he'd find a way to get her to tell him all those things on her own.

Maybe he needed to figure out why the hell this was keeping him up at night. *No strings* meant he wasn't supposed to care. It was just fun, hot sex. Right?

Dane flipped questions in his mind for a long time before finally falling asleep.

Chapter Ten

Vaguely aware of her cell phone ringing, Julia roused from a deep sleep. Eyes still closed, she felt for it on her nightstand and answered the call without looking at the caller ID. "Hello?" Her voice was nothing but a gravelly whisper.

"Good morning, sunshine." Dane's jovial tone came over the line. "Did I wake you?"

"Yes," she said, rolling onto her back. She opened one eye to glance at the clock; it was 9:00 A.M. "It's Monday. Why are you calling?"

"Jeez, you're a grouch in the morning, huh?" He paused before adding, "I mean, I wouldn't know. You don't like to stay the night."

She didn't need the little reminder. But she couldn't help it, the corners of her mouth quirked up. She was glad he wasn't there to see it. "You woke me up. I haven't had coffee yet. I'd keep away from me until I do."

"Not a morning person, I take it," Dane said.

"No. I'm a night owl. Always have been." She yawned. "So, Boss, what can I do for you?"

He let out a wicked laugh at that. "Oh, I can think of plenty of things."

A shiver ran over her skin. His sensual voice, playful and sexy in her ear, affected her more than she could believe. "I'm sure you could."

"You know it. But that's not why I'm calling," he said. "You have any plans tomorrow afternoon?"

She thought for a few seconds. "No, not really. Why?"

"I was wondering if you'd spend the day with me."

Her eyes opened wide. She was fully awake now, even without coffee. "What?"

"What 'what.' You heard me," he teased. "I asked you to spend the afternoon with me."

"Yes. But . . . why?" she asked warily.

He laughed. "So I can kidnap and torture you in the basement of my father's mansion, of course. God, Red, you're always so suspicious."

"I am," she said. "So, why?"

"I'm coming out to Long Island for the day. Gonna take a ride out on the boat all afternoon and relax, then I'm meeting my sister and brother for dinner at seven." He paused. "I just thought it might be something nice to do, if you were available to join me for the boat ride. No strings, Julia."

Her mouth went dry at his earnest tone. She was pretty hard on him sometimes. He continued to be nice to her regardless, had even seemed to accept that this was who she was. Maybe he just liked a challenge. But it was time to give him some niceness back. With genuine warmth, she said, "That's nice of you. I haven't been on a boat in years . . . sure, I'd like to come. Thank you for asking."

He was quiet for a moment, and she figured she must have shocked him with her pleasant answer.

"You're welcome. Glad you'll join me. So . . . you live in Blue Harbor, right?"

"Yup." She knew he knew that. "My street address should be on the paychecks you sign."

He chuckled. "Right. Okay. I'll pick you up around ten-thirty. We'll have lunch on the boat, just hang out. I'll have you home around five, six at the latest. Sound good?"

"Sure." She rolled over onto her side to look out her window. Blue skies and hazy sunshine. "What am I wearing?"

"Casual. Whatever you'll be comfortable in on a boat. Shorts, sundress, whatever. Maybe sensible shoes, though, not those high wedge sandals you usually like to wear." His tone turned mischievous. "Which is a shame, since I love when you wear stilettos. Hmm. No panties would be nice. . . ."

She laughed. "You're incorrigible."

"I am!" he said proudly. "Lots of sunscreen, O Pale Redhead. The sun can be really strong, especially when it reflects off the water. And bring a swimsuit."

"Umm. Okay."

"Why the hesitation?" he asked. "I've seen you very naked, in varying interesting positions. Don't tell me you're shy to wear a bikini in front of me."

"I'm not shy," she said. "I don't own a bikini, so you're out of luck there. And . . . well, I can't swim. So if you're thinking of tossing me overboard, know that I'll sink like a stone."

"Really?" Dane said, surprised. "Huh. Well, okay. I won't toss you overboard, then. And I guess that means skinny-dipping in the Sound is out. You've foiled my best plan, but I guess the heads up was a good thing.

If my headliner drowned off my boat, that'd be *really* bad publicity."

She laughed again. "Okay, Charming. See you tomorrow."

"Great. It'll be fun. See you."

She ended the call and stared out the window. Flurries of excitement circled in her belly. And she was smiling. Like, the goofy smile of someone smitten. Ugh.

"Get a grip," she scolded herself, and launched out of bed, energized and ready to start her day. Coffee first, though. She had her priorities in order.

Deciding to treat herself, she threw on a blue cotton sundress and flip-flops and went a few blocks into the center of town, to the local coffee shop. She preferred frequenting that store over Starbucks; always a supporter of the little guy. The barista, who knew her, smiled when she walked in and made her an iced mocha latte, her usual. Julia also got a plump, delicious-looking blueberry muffin, and sat at one of the four tiny tables by the window to enjoy her breakfast.

Just after she'd taken her first bite, a young blond woman entered, holding the hand of a precious blond toddler. He couldn't have been more than two years old. Julia's enthusiasm for the day dried up and disappeared as she watched the little boy coo and babble at his mother. He tried to run toward the shelf of handmade mugs, but the woman scooped him up into her arms, smacked a kiss on his round, rosy cheek, and placed her order with the barista.

Julia's heart ached. The pain and longing suffused her bones.

"Mama!" the boy squeaked, and wrapped his little arms around the woman's neck. He blew raspberries onto her skin, and the woman and barista laughed together.

Tears stung Julia's eyes. She grabbed her things and rushed out of the shop.

As the town car drove through the small town of Blue Harbor, Dane stretched out in the backseat and looked out the window, enjoying the scenery. He'd always liked Blue Harbor. It was one of those cozy little North Shore communities tucked into the land but right on the Long Island Sound, with picturesque shops, cottages, and homes. It felt, to him, like something out of a Norman Rockwell painting—it had that kind of quaint, small-town charm.

When they got to the center of town, the charm of it enveloped him. Window boxes on storefronts and hanging buckets on lampposts spilled over with colorful flowers. A few people strolled slowly along the sidewalk—nothing like the rushing, vigorous strides of millions of Manhattanites. What had once been many old, weathered cottages in the center of town had been restored and turned into restaurants, boutiques, and galleries. It didn't surprise Dane that Julia would choose to live here. It was an enchanting village, slightly artsy, and scenic; but more than that, it was also quiet. The biggest things that happened here were the Art Show and Craft Fair in the spring, the Seafood Fest in the summer, and the Harvest Festival in October. The rest of the time, most of the time, it was so quiet it was almost sleepy. For someone so guarded, who cherished privacy and kept to herself,

Dane could understand the appeal of Blue Harbor for Julia.

When the driver pulled up to a large, charming three-story Victorian just past the town center, he was surprised to see Julia sitting on the top step of the wide wraparound porch, waiting for him. He surveyed the well-kept house—pale yellow paint, accented by white shutters and the white railing that lined the veranda, the neatly kept lawn and colorful flowers—and deduced that someone had taken great care to renovate the house. As the car stopped and he got out, she gave a small smile and rose from her rocking chair. From behind his sunglasses, Dane took her in and warmed inside. She looked so damn pretty. Dressed in a long tank-style maxi dress, a swirling mixture of all shades of blue, her hair down and blowing lightly in the breeze, she was delectable.

"Hi, Red." He smiled wide as he went up the steps to greet her. "You look gorgeous. Those blues are great on you."

"Thanks." She lifted the hem of the dress from her ankles to better show him her feet. "Followed your advice." She was wearing navy Converse. The funky sneakers made him smile wide.

"Jesus, those are cute." With a quick yank, he tugged her in for a kiss. He sipped from her lips, slow and easy. But her soft mouth opened under his, responding instantly, and it pulled him under. He deepened the kiss, letting his tongue tangle with hers. Every time he touched her, that spark was there, shooting warmth and want throughout his body.

"For someone who claims he doesn't have a shoe fetish," she remarked wryly, "you seem to react to my shoes a lot."

He cocked his head and considered that. "You

have a point. . . ." Flashing a grin, he shrugged.
"I think it's just where you're concerned, though.
Never been, like, a *thing* before. I wouldn't get too
worried about it."

"You don't worry me."

"Didn't think so. You're tough stuff." He glanced
around and said, "This house is nice. Looks good for
how old it must be."

"It's over eighty years old," she said. "My landlord
bought it and put a lot of money into the renovations.
He and his wife live on the ground floor. Their twenty-
three-year-old daughter now rents the apartment on
the top floor. I have the middle."

"How'd you find it?"

"Through a friend of Stephen's, Randi's husband.
I was lucky. It's a nice place, I feel safe here, and I'm
just beyond the center of town. I walk in every day."
She smiled and pulled away, leaning over to grab a
large yellow canvas bag. "Ready to go if you are."

"You're not going to invite me up to your apartment?" he asked in a light tone.

She blinked. "Um . . . I wasn't planning on it. I mean,
I'm here, I have my things." There was an awkward
pause. "Did you *want* to go up there? Need to use the
bathroom?"

Why it irked him that she didn't seem to want
him in her apartment, he couldn't say. But it did. He
swatted it out of his head and said, "No, I'm good.
Let's go."

"Well, this sure is different," Julia said as the driver
took them to the marina. "Seeing each other in the
light of day."

"And neither of us is flaming into ash as we're hit by the sunlight," Dane joked. "That's a good sign."

"I don't know," she said playfully. "You have a few vampire tendencies."

His brows raised and a slow smile spread across his face. "Such as?"

"You love to nibble on my neck," she said, getting hot just thinking about it. "And sometimes, you bite. . . ."

"It's not my fault you're so delicious." He leaned across the backseat and slipped an arm around her waist to pull her closer. With his free hand, he pushed her hair out of the way for access to the nape of her neck. As soon as his open mouth touched her skin, a shudder ran through her. She felt him smile against her skin as he murmured, "Mmm. Love that sweet spot."

"Where are we going, anyway?" she asked breathlessly.

"Kingston Point Marina," he said, the words muffled as he scraped his teeth along her neck.

Her breath caught from the feel of him. "I've never been in Kingston Point before." She felt . . . swoony. She hated that she felt swoony, even as her head fell back against the seat and her eyes closed.

"You're not missing much," he said, nibbling and licking now. She squirmed a little and felt heat spread through her like wildfire. "Bunch of pretentious snobs in that town." His hand slid over her breast, cupped it gently, and stroked his thumb over her nipple, drawing a feathery sigh from her. Then his hand dropped to her knee. "That's a long dress. Lot of fabric to hike up later. Gonna make me work for it a little, huh?"

She grinned. His deep, smooth voice was seductive,

and what he was doing to her neck should be illegal. Her hand tangled in his hair as she said, "Didn't want my dress blowing up in the wind, giving anyone a show."

He laughed softly at that. "Smart thinking. Too bad, though." He bit down with gentle heat on her skin and she drew a sharp intake of breath. "You're wet now, aren't you. Tell me."

God, when he spoke to her like that . . . "Yes," she whispered. "You bastard."

He laughed again, but wickedly this time. "You're a lusty woman, Red. I like that about you." His hand slid up the outside of her leg, over the dress. She twisted to get closer to him. "I should take you right here, right now," he half-whispered, half-growled.

"Don't you have any self-control?" she said, even as she wished he would follow his own suggestion.

"When it comes to you? Not much." His fingers traveled over her hip to squeeze her ass as he took her mouth with a slow, sumptuous kiss. She almost melted in his arms. But the car turned and the ride became slightly bumpy. She broke the kiss to look out the window and saw they were traveling up a gravelly path, the entrance to the marina. "We're here. Stop."

"Don't wanna stop," he grinned, kissing her again.

"I don't either, but . . ." She pushed him away gently. "Don't want gossip, Boss. Remember?"

His hands ran up and down her bare arms as he looked into her eyes. "And how am I supposed to hide this raging hard-on I have right now?"

She giggled. "You're resourceful. You'll think of something."

He flashed that killer grin and pulled away from her as the car slowed to a stop in front of the dock house. She watched as he ran his hands over his face and took a few deep breaths. "Okay. Think I can walk now."

She laughed again, she couldn't help it. As she pulled her big, dark sunglasses out of her bag, she said, "Hey. Dane."

He looked at her curiously. "Yeah?"

"Just so you know . . . wearing sneakers wasn't the only suggestion of yours I took." She gave him the most provocative smile in her arsenal.

He stared at her for a few seconds . . . then it hit him. His blue eyes flew wide. "You're not wearing any panties, are you," he choked out.

"Nope," she chirped, and stepped out of the car.

"*Damn.*" He got out on his side and shot her a look across the hood of the car as he growled, "You're evil. I've said it before: you're a vile, wicked temptress. How am I supposed to think about anything else now?"

She simply smiled again. He groaned and dropped his forehead to the hood in forfeit.

Ten minutes later, Dane reached for Julia's hand when they walked onto the slip. "The boat is down at the far end," he said casually.

She looked around with interest as they walked. Sunlight glistened off the calm blue water. The sound of seagulls screeching as they flew overhead traveled on the light breeze. The boats that bobbed up and down on the Sound varied in size, from small speed-boats to midsize sailboats to a few proud yachts. She also snuck looks at her date for the day. Dane wore a simple pale blue T-shirt and khaki shorts, but he still managed to make it look . . . well, wealthy. Dane Harrison could be the poster boy for casual, affluent sophistication. And easy charm. And raw sex appeal. And shameless seduction. She thought back to the steamy car ride over and felt a delicious flutter in her stomach.

He led her to the farthest dock at the very end of the pier. "Here we go."

Julia almost swallowed her tongue. The majestic, imposing yacht before them was the largest one in the marina. "You said we were going on a boat," she said.

He gave her a look. "Um . . . what do you think this is?"

"This isn't a *boat.*" She swiveled around and pointed back at one of the midsize sailboats. "*That* is a boat. This"—she whirled back to point at the yacht in front of them—"*This*—is a huge freaking mother of a ship!"

"It's a yacht," he said plainly, looking at her like she'd lost her mind.

"A big, fancy yacht like this is not just a *boat,*" she said, staring up at the gleaming white vessel.

Dane's mouth quirked. "It's not mine, you know," he said. "It's my father's. He lets me borrow it once in a while. I'll be sure to tell him you were impressed."

She gaped at him. He laughed and stepped in closer, hands circling her waist.

"Julia," he said, looking into her eyes. His voice lowered. "My family has a lot of money. You knew that."

"You said a *boat,*" she stammered weakly. She felt foolish. She didn't know why.

He smiled, kissed her, and said, "Come on board. It's a gorgeous day. Let's go enjoy it."

* * *

Julia couldn't get over the magnificence of the Harrison yacht. She'd never been on a boat like this in her life. The spacious cabins, carpeted dining room, polished brass and wood everywhere she looked, and enough room on board for a crowd of people. That someone like her was on a ship like this was crazy. She felt like she'd stepped into a movie or something.

"You like it?" Dane asked when he was done giving her a quick tour.

"It's unreal," she said. "Color me impressed."

He chuckled and led her out to the back deck. "This is my favorite spot on the boat. I sit out here, stare at the water, let my mind wander . . . sometimes I just fall asleep, it's so relaxing."

"You like being on the water," she said, more of an assessment than a question.

"Yeah. Always have." He put his sunglasses back on, she glanced at his profile, and thought he looked unbearably sexy. A soft breeze ruffled his dark curls as they leaned against the railing. "Maybe it's because I grew up here," he mused. "The main house is right on the Sound—like, it's practically part of our backyard. Went sailing and to the beach a lot as kids. . . ." He rubbed his scruffy jaw as he considered. "Or maybe it's a Long Island thing. I think, living so close to either the Sound or the ocean, it just becomes part of you in a way. Part of your life. Don't you? You grew up on the Island too, right?"

She nodded. She'd never heard him like this, and it intrigued her.

"Or, maybe it's just me." He shrugged and turned to her. "What about you? You can't swim. Does that mean you don't like the water at all?"

"I like *looking* at it," she clarified. "Being near the

Sound, on a beach, by a lake, that's all fine. Just don't drop me in it."

He smiled broadly and said, "Promise I won't. Even when you frustrate me."

Her brows arched. "Does that happen often?"

"What, you frustrating me? All the time." He winked, then looked up to the upper deck. "Ahoy there, Captain!"

"Hey, Dane, how've you been?" A cheerful-looking man in his sixties raised a hand in greeting. Julia thought his crisp white uniform looked pretty high-status.

"Just fine, Ray," Dane said, "just fine. You?"

"It's been a good summer so far. Can't complain." The captain nodded at Julia. "Afternoon, ma'am."

"Hi," she said, smiling.

"We're ready to go when you are, sir," Captain Ray said.

"Then let's do it," Dane replied with enthusiasm.

"Aye, sir." The captain straightened and added, "Enjoy the rest of your birthday. The chef made something special; your sister arranged it."

Julia's head turned sharply to stare at Dane. It was his *birthday*? What the hell? She'd had no idea.

"Ah, that Tess," Dane said, grinning up at the captain. "She's a clever one. Thank him for me in advance. I look forward to it."

"Lunch will be served at one, if that suits you."

Dane gently grasped Julia's wrist and turned it to glance at her watch. "That sounds fine."

"Then I'll get us going." The captain gave a jaunty salute and walked back to the helm.

Dane turned back to her as he said, "It's almost noon. You can wait an hour for lunch, right?"

"Sure," she said softly. His birthday. Goddamn.

His head cocked slightly to the side as he studied her, the way he did when he was trying to figure something out. "Why are you looking at me like that?"

"Like what?"

"I don't know. Like . . . I have something in my teeth. Or you're confused. Or I have two heads. You tell me."

"I didn't know today was your birthday," she said. *Keep it light.*

He shrugged. "I had mentioned to you that it was around this time. It's not a big deal. Thirty-six. So what?"

"That's right. I had forgotten. So . . . you asked me to spend your birthday with you." Something warm and fuzzy was threatening to envelop her insides. "That's . . . kind of . . . well, special for some people. Why'd you want to spend today with me?"

"Maybe I wanted to make sure I'd have mind-blowing sex on my birthday," he smirked, clearly teasing.

"Jackass," she quipped, smiling despite herself.

He reached up and tucked a stray lock of her hair behind her ear as he said quietly, "Maybe I like being with you, and wanted to spend some time with you. Outside of the hotel for once. How about that?"

She kept staring at him. The boat moved away from the dock and slowly headed out onto the water.

He smiled and murmured, "No strings, Julia. I promise." His fingers trailed down to caress her cheek. "I just enjoy you. So why not enjoy you today and make a day of it?"

Something was churning inside her. Half warning, half . . . ugh, something akin to tenderness. *Keep it light, dammit,* she told herself. But she couldn't help it. She was flattered. Touched. He wanted to be with her outside the hotel. Outside of bed.

She couldn't let herself think about that too much.

She inched closer and linked her arms around his neck. He smiled and slipped his arms around her waist. Looking deeply into his sparkling blue eyes, she moved in like she was going to kiss him, but dodged at the last second and ran her mouth along his unshaven jaw, up to his ear. "I'll make it a birthday you won't forget," she whispered in the most enticing tone she could muster, and she knew damn well it was pretty sexy. She dragged her tongue around the edge of his ear and bit the lobe, bringing a soft groan from him as she added, "I promise."

Chapter Eleven

Dane stretched out on the deck chair, closed his eyes, and let the sun beat down on his body. He was happy to wait for Julia out on deck while she changed into her swimsuit. So far, the afternoon had been an absolute pleasure. They'd made small talk over a drink or two as the boat had made its way out onto the Sound, first chatting about what types of songs she preferred to sing, then delving into a discussion about different types of music and artists they each liked or disliked. He realized her musical tastes were varied and eclectic, which both interested and impressed him. She didn't let the topics stray into anything too personal, and he didn't push.

At one, they went to the dining room for lunch. Tess had asked the chef to make paella, one of Dane's absolute favorite dishes, and it had been delicious. He and Julia talked about other random topics over the meal, like where he'd gone to college, business school, etcetera. She'd redirected the conversation to be about him, rather than her, more than once. Did she really think he hadn't noticed her subtle tactics? The chatter had been nice, though. She was definitely loosening up around him more, and he liked that.

Also, he liked how she was in awe of the magnificence of the yacht and trying to be cool about it. It was cute. He'd reined in his amusement at her obvious admiration throughout his quick tour of the vessel, but she'd seemed especially dazzled in the dining room. He guessed she hadn't been served many meals in such a fashion on a *boat*. All day, she'd done a damn good job of playing it cool, but he'd caught glimpses in her expressive eyes at various times—alternating between impressed, pleased, and sometimes wowed. It was interesting to him. Especially because he hadn't set out to try to impress her with the trappings of his family's wealth. It had never even occurred to him. He'd just wanted to spend the day with her, out on the boat.

He didn't know why. He didn't know what had possessed him to pick up the phone yesterday morning and invite her along. Maybe it was the scorching hot dream he'd had about her the night before, how he'd woken up with a throbbing erection and his mind filled with her . . . No. No, it was something more than that. He just wasn't exactly sure what.

He heard the distinctive sound of flip-flops moving across the deck, then stop next to him. Lifting a hand to shield his eyes from the sun, he watched as his beautiful red-haired guest lowered herself onto the deck chair beside him. His eyes roamed over her as she settled in. Her luscious body was tucked into a simple dark purple one-piece, deeply cut in the front and exposing a generous amount of cleavage. Her smooth, pale legs stretched out . . . and he briefly imagined them wrapped around his hips. "Goddamn, Red, your body was made for staring at."

"The cabin I changed in," she said, ignoring his comment, "is bigger and nicer than my dressing room at the hotel. You should try to do something about that, now that I have a basis for comparison."

He smirked as he put his sunglasses on. "I'll see what I can do."

She put on her wide sunglasses as well. "That sun is *hot*."

"So are you."

She let out a little snort. "Sweet talker."

"That is sweet, compared to what I'm thinking. I'm having some thoughts about peeling you out of that suit, and there's nothing sweet about them." He rose from his chair and stared down at her pale skin. "Did you sunscreen yourself within an inch of your life, I hope?"

"I did."

"Good. A complexion like that, you'll burn to a crisp otherwise."

"Might anyway," she said. "Half Irish plus half German equals no pigment."

"Heritage like that sure explains the strength and stubbornness. And the temper."

"You bet your ass." Julia smirked and added, "Irish dad was a cop. German-Jewish mother is a social worker. Yeah, I come from pretty strong stock."

Dane let that sink in. She'd never mentioned any of her family before now. A couple of drinks, good food, and the lull of the water must have relaxed her more than he'd realized. "Um . . . *was*? Your dad?"

"Yeah." She didn't move or look toward him. "Killed in the line of duty when I was ten. Robbery."

"I'm sorry," Dane said quietly.

"Thanks," was all she said.

He watched the breeze lightly lift and stir her hair,

and the way the sun played in it, bringing out streaks of copper. Beautiful. He sat back down on the deck chair and ventured, "Do you have any siblings?"

"Two sisters." Her voice became noticeably colder. "I'm the middle child."

He chuckled. "That explains a lot. I was the middle child for a few years myself."

"There's three of you, right?"

"Four, actually. Charles is two years older than me, Tess is two years younger. Then there's Pierce. He's four years younger than Tess."

"Was he an oops?" Julia asked.

Dane smirked and admitted, "Actually, he was."

"You don't talk about him. He wasn't at the hotel opening," Julia noted. "Right?"

"Right. He lives in England. Professional football player—soccer to you and me—loving life. He rarely comes back to the States anymore. He and I aren't too close."

"Ah." Julia leisurely stretched her arms over her head. "At least you like your siblings that are here."

"I more than like them. They're my best friends." Dane watched the slow rise and fall of her breasts as she breathed in the sea air, slightly hypnotized. "When you grow up in a situation like we did, you tend to band together tight with those who experienced it with you."

Julia turned her head to look at him. "A 'situation like we did'? What does that mean?"

Dane wondered how to explain without sounding obnoxious. "Well . . . when you grow up with money like our family has, the next generation of a family legacy—that means there are expectations put on you before you're even born." He crossed one ankle over the other and pillowed his hands under his head.

"Charles has it the hardest, if you ask me—firstborn son, gets the name, becomes heir to the crown—and all the bullshit that goes along with it. Tons of pressure to do what's expected of him, to be perfect, since he was a small child. Me, not so much."

"The heir and the spare," Julia half-joked.

"Exactly," Dane said. "Tess is the family's sweetheart. And then, there was Pierce, who was a troublesome kid and gave everyone hell. I cared about him, but he was so angry all the time, and a lot younger than me, so . . ." He shrugged. "Put all that together with our overbearing father and our wayward mother, and voila! The Harrisons sure put the 'fun' in 'dysfunction'."

Julia was quiet.

"Needless to say, Charles, Tess, and I trust each other the most. We can be ourselves when we're together, 100 percent." Dane shot her a sideways glance. "Make sense?"

"Absolutely," she said. "I'm glad you have each other. Must have made it a bit easier."

"Yes, it did. Still does sometimes." He heard footsteps approaching as he asked her, "You get along with your sisters?"

"No," Julia said. And that was it.

One of the two porters brought a tray with four cold bottles of water, as Dane had requested. "Anything else, Mr. Harrison?" he asked as he set them on the small table.

"No, that's it for now. Thanks." Dane waited until he'd left before grabbing a bottle and resting it against Julia's arm. She flinched from the cold and he laughed. "Want one, Red?"

"Not yet, thank you."

"You have to stay hydrated out here. Just saying."

He sat up to drink. He had more questions about her family, but didn't want to push. Whenever he pushed—about anything—she got edgy, then defensive. They were enjoying the day. His questions could wait. "So. You sure I can't persuade you to go for a swim with me?"

"Not happening. But you go ahead."

He hesitated, wondering if he should go in the water or not. "Don't wanna just leave you here . . . wouldn't exactly make me a gracious host."

"Oh, go swim," she scoffed.

With a short laugh, he rose from the deck chair. "Aren't you going to come watch me?" he teased, with the tone of a petulant child.

She looked up at him. "I didn't think you needed an audience." The corners of her mouth tugged up as she added, "Then again, who am I talking to. Dane Harrison, lover of the spotlight."

With dramatic exaggeration, he put a hand to his heart as if wounded. "You mean you don't want to see the water glistening off my body in the sunlight?" he joked. "Witness my godlike prowess in the water?"

She let her head drop back and said provocatively, "I'd rather watch your gorgeous body get naked in one of these cabins. And witness your godlike prowess in bed."

Lust kindled and flamed. He crouched down beside her. "You think I have godlike prowess in bed?"

She laughed, then said, "I plead the Fifth."

"Well, I think *you* have godlike prowess in bed. I'll tell you that outright."

"You tell that to all your women," she teased.

He took off her sunglasses, made sure her gaze locked with his, and said quietly, "No, I don't."

They stared at each other for a moment.

"I don't have a harem, or a steady string of women," he said. "And I'm not seeing anyone while I'm . . . with you. Whatever this is. I'm not sleeping with anyone else, or seeing anyone else right now. Just for the record. Okay?"

Julia's eyes went wide, but held his gaze with a steady cool. "You can, you know," she murmured. "If you want to. You don't owe me anything. No strings, remember?"

He gazed into her beautiful hazel eyes for a long beat before he found himself saying, "I know that. Maybe I don't want to right now."

"Okay," she whispered.

"You can do what you want, of course. Just letting you know that right now, that's where I'm at."

"I'm not in the habit of sleeping with more than one man at a time," she said. "Just for the record. Right now, you're it for me, too."

He nodded, not knowing why that filled him with a little burst of elation, but it did.

"Just because I said 'no strings'," she continued, still holding his gaze, "and that I like sex, doesn't mean I'm some slut who has a stable of my own, you know."

"I never thought that," he said. "I just meant—"

"I know what you meant," she cut in gently. Her eyes softened a bit. "We're good, Dane."

The sounds of the waves on the humid sea air filled in the silence as they looked at each other. Then he lowered from his crouch onto his knees at her side and pressed his lips to hers.

One of her arms slowly wrapped around his neck as he took the kiss deeper, and her other hand went to his chest. Her fingernails raked gently through the sparse hair there, circling his nipple. He nipped at her bottom lip in return.

"Is this where I get that mind-blowing birthday sex?" he asked.

She snickered. "Out here on deck? Your staff would be mortified."

"You think I care? You forget who you're dealing with, Red." He kissed her again as his hand cupped and squeezed her breast. Then he drew back just enough to peer into her eyes. "In fact, I dare you. I dare you to seduce me out here on the deck."

She held his gaze for a moment. Holy Mother of God, she was considering it.

"It *is* your birthday. . . ." she said.

Adrenaline shot through him and he kissed her again, with rising passion that was getting harder to hold back. Stroking her nipple through the swimsuit, he felt it pebble and heard her breath catch. "That's right. It is."

"But it lacks decorum," she said with mock horror. "Not very Harrison-like."

"I'm the good-time Harrison," he said with a grin. "People expect a stunt like that from me. I'd hate to disappoint."

She laughed softly and ran her hand down his chest, trailed her fingernails across his belly, and teased at the waistband. When he sucked in a breath, she smiled at the sound. His blood was heating and surging now, making his heart race and his mind cloud over. The thought of having her out in the open, with the sun beating down on them and the Sound's slight waves rocking them as they explored each other, had him almost mindless with lust. "Julia . . ." His voice was thick as he pushed her hair back from her face. "I want you out here. Now. I want you so much."

She stared at him for a long beat, then kissed him. "Okay. If you don't care if someone catches us, why should I?" she murmured against his lips. "I'll never have to see these people again, *you* will." Her eyes sparkled wickedly as her hand trailed down to palm his erection through his board shorts. He groaned with unbridled lust. "Come here, birthday boy."

He tangled his hand in her hair and held her to him, capturing her mouth with hungry kisses. She pulled him down to lie on top of her.

Dane quickly toweled his body dry after showering, wanting to get back to Julia as soon as possible. Images of her riding him on the deck—her fiery hair flying in the breeze as she hovered over him, incredible breasts bobbing slowly, her eyes closed and her head back as she ground into him—flooded his mind again. She'd not only taken his dare, she'd done it with gusto. After that, they'd managed to make it to one of the cabins. They'd fallen into a queen-size bed, laughing, kissing, touching. . . .

She'd crawled down the length of his body, leaving a trail of hot kisses, until she'd used that talented mouth to drive him wild and give him a birthday present he'd never forget. The feel of her lips, her tongue, so warm and wet . . . she'd owned him. He'd lost control, and she'd loved every minute of it.

His blood started heating up again just thinking about it.

He walked into the cabin and stopped at what he saw. Julia was asleep, her flaming red hair in stark contrast to the white sheets tangled around her. He'd never seen her asleep before. She looked so pretty . . . and so peaceful. When she was awake, he'd seen her in many different ways: fired up, singing, laughing, concentrating, pissed off, playful, sensual, even screaming out his name in the throes of passion . . . but never as calm and serene as she looked right then.

He hated to disturb her, so he slipped beneath the sheets as carefully as he could, then wrapped his arms around her to pull her close. She gave a sweet sigh and instinctively curled into his side, resting her hand on his stomach and her head on his chest.

Something inside him warmed, then melted. Quietly, almost unnoticeably at first. But the longer he held her, the more he enjoyed the feel of her in his arms. He played with her hair, twirling the thick, soft strands between his fingers as he watched the patterns the sunlight created on the walls. The boat barely rocked on the water, cutting across the Sound nice and steady. His eyes grew heavy and slipped closed. . . .

When he opened them again, he was disoriented for a minute, not sure where he was. The dappled sunlight in the room had changed angles. Time had gone wavy; how long had he been asleep? He lifted Julia's hand from his chest to peek at her watch and grimaced. It was a quarter to five. He'd been out for about an hour, and the yacht would be back at the marina fairly soon.

He stroked his hand along her smooth, naked back and kissed her temple. "Hey, beautiful," he whispered. "Wake up."

"Mmm . . ." she moaned softly and snuggled closer.

He breathed her in, a mixed scent of sunscreen on her skin, saltwater in her hair, and the faint hint of their sex. It was intoxicating. "Wake up, Red. Gotta go home soon."

"Huh?" She startled, lifting her head to blink and look at his face. "What . . . how long was I asleep?"

"Maybe an hour and a half," he guessed, still caressing her skin. "Guess I wore you out."

She snorted. "Last round, *I* did the hard work." Her head dropped to his chest again.

He was surprised she was letting him hold her. She usually didn't, not for more than a minute or two. It was nice. He savored it.

"How do you feel?" he asked softly. "Nice and relaxed, I hope? I sure am."

"Um . . . yeah, actually," she said, as if she were admitting a secret. "I'm very relaxed."

"It's okay to be cozy, you know," he said, only half-joking. "You don't have to be so . . . on guard all the time."

She stiffened ever so slightly, and his arm tightened around her.

"I mean . . . it's been a few weeks now," he murmured. "You're allowed to relax and enjoy the 'after' part. It doesn't mean I'm expecting anything from you. There can be no strings and still be . . . postsex cuddling."

"I'm not big on cuddling," she mumbled. "Haven't been with many cuddlers."

"Then let's just try it for a few minutes because it's nice," he said. "Consider it a birthday present."

"You mean doing you outside on the deck of your daddy's yacht wasn't a memorable birthday present?" she countered. "Or the oral I gave you that made you beg?"

"Well, yeah, those were . . . amazing. Damn." His hand lowered to pinch her ass and she squeaked.

"But hey, it's still my birthday. That's an all-day pass, as far as I'm concerned."

"You're so greedy," she joked. But she stayed in his arms and didn't push away. He exhaled.

"You look nice when you're sleeping," he told her.

"I do?" she asked, surprised. "Nice how?"

"Like . . . at peace," he said. "Sweet. Serene."

She snorted again. "Those are several words that don't describe me at all."

"Then that's a shame." Taking a deep breath, he decided to push after all. "Can I ask you a question?"

"Yes. Doesn't mean I'll answer it, though," she warned.

"Fair enough." Did he really want to do this? Yeah, why not. "I've just wondered . . . because you're so untrusting, so suspicious of anything I do or say to you that's nice . . . your ex-husband. He was awful to you, wasn't he?"

She went stiff as a board in his arms. He didn't let go.

"You don't have to tell me," he said quickly, regretting his words as soon as he'd said them. "I'm not asking for details. I just want to know . . . or, understand a little better . . . what happened to you that made you this way. Because, Julia . . ." He tipped up her chin to make her look at him. "I've seen you in a few rare, unguarded moments. You're actually, despite your best efforts to hide it from me, a really nice person, with softness. You seem to think that's a bad thing."

"I'm not a sad sack. Don't do that," she warned him.

"I'm just trying to figure out what makes you tick."

"Why do you need to know?"

"I don't *need* to. I'd *like* to."

She was quiet for a minute, playing with the hair

on his chest, and he waited. Then she said, "Yes, he was awful to me. He was nice at first, but soon after we got married, the good behavior ended, the mask fell off, and it turned horrible. I was so young when I met him, so open and trusting . . . took no time at all for him to sucker me, manipulate me . . ." Her voice trailed off.

"Was he abusive?" Dane asked quietly.

"Emotionally, yes," she said. "Physically, no."

"Abuse is abuse," Dane said. "And the emotional scars tend to run deeper."

They lay in silence. He could feel the tension in her body and caressed her smooth back with long, gentle strokes.

"Is this line of questioning over?" she asked. "I really, really don't like to talk about him, or anything that happened. The past is the past, and it should stay there."

"Still hurts that much?" he guessed.

She paused before admitting, "Some of it always will."

"I'm sorry to hear that." He pressed his lips to her forehead with the utmost tenderness, and felt her shudder slightly in response. "It's okay, Julia. It's okay."

She nodded against his chest. He wondered what she was thinking about, what memories were torturing her at the moment. He decided to let it go and not say another word.

But after a minute she said, "He wrecked my life. Meeting him was the worst thing that ever happened to me." Surprised that she was volunteering more information, he stayed silent to let her talk. He felt how rigid the muscles in her body had become, and kept rubbing her back in an effort to soothe her as she spoke. "We met in Boston, when I was still in college.

I was young and stupid. He was handsome, and oh so charming, and from a rich, well-connected family . . . a lot like you."

Ahh, there it was. "Then it's no wonder you were wary of me from the start," Dane said.

"Yeah. The similarities . . ." She swallowed hard, keeping her cheek to his chest so she wouldn't have to look him in the eye. "He swept me off my feet. Then he manipulated me, used me, lied to me, and eventually hurt me however he could. He was sick. He just wanted to feel powerful over someone. Then, he wanted to punish me for standing up to him. And he did." Another long pause before she whispered, "He took our son away from me."

Her voice was so sad, Dane had to close his eyes against the rush of pain he felt for her. He'd been right about that, at least: she had borne a child. She had a son. Things were somehow a little different now, knowing that.

"He took my son from me, he took *everything* away from me, and I had to rebuild my life from ashes." Her tone turned bitter. "At first, I had to go live with my mother. She and my older sister treated me like I was a pariah. They actually blamed me for everything, because Max made me out to be . . . whatever, they believed him, not me. And my teenage princess younger sister was mad that I was getting so much attention, even though it was negative attention, so she was just a mean brat. They were all angry at me, made it clear they thought less of me—like I'd had any control over the situation. *I* was the one who lost my son, my home, my bank account. . . ." She cleared her throat and shifted a bit beside him. "I took the first job I could so I could support myself and get the hell out of there. I ignored them the best I could, moved out after a year, and never looked back. I don't speak to any of them. I don't think they care. Too much damage."

Dane sighed and hugged her tightly, not knowing what to say. In response, she pulled away and sat up, pulling the sheets up over her breasts. He stared at her pale back, at her mane of red hair tangled and tumbling over her shoulders, and as much as he wanted to reach out and grasp her, he knew instinctively not to touch her right then. "Julia, I'm so sorry."

She nodded, but didn't turn back to him or say a word.

"Um . . . where's your son now?" he asked carefully.

"With his father." Her voice was a mixture of bitterness and resignation. "Max turned him against me. Poisoned him, filled his head with lies . . ." She cleared her throat again before admitting in a defeated whisper, "He doesn't speak to me. I've tried to call, e-mail . . . I still do on his birthday, holidays. He doesn't reply. His father did a thorough job of brainwashing him."

Dane closed his eyes and winced as a shaft of heartache lanced through him. "That's one of the worst things I've ever heard," he said softly.

"Isn't it?" She got up from the bed, leaving him with the heavy comforter as she wrapped the sheet around her, and went to one of the windows to look out at the water.

He watched her for a few minutes, giving her room. A lot more things made sense now. Her instant distrust of him, her defensive stance, her need for armor . . . and he still had no real idea of what she'd been through. The little she'd revealed to him was a nightmare, but he had no clue how deep the horrors went. He wanted to find this bastard ex-husband of hers and beat him senseless. Whatever he'd done to her, she was scarred for life, that was obvious. Max had broken her, her family had rejected her . . . thankfully she'd had the strength to rebuild, but *damn*.

She was so quiet now. His heart squeezed for her.

"Julia," he finally said. "Come back to bed."

She turned to look at him. Her expression was placid, yet haunted. Sunlight from outside backlit her, turning her hair into a ring of glowing fire around her face and shoulders. Sadness had etched a frown into her face and shadowed her eyes. He'd never seen her seem . . . fragile. Yes, she was still her strong self, but he saw the hint of fragility. It made him want to hold her for days.

"Thank you for telling me . . . any of it," he said. "I know you didn't want to."

She huffed out a resigned breath, and he watched her face tighten. "Why do you need to know anything about my past?" she asked tersely. "It's got nothing to do with us. I'm not your girlfriend. We're just sleeping together. No strings, remember? Why did you even ask? I hate talking about it. I don't want to again. Okay?"

He felt like she'd slapped him. But she wasn't wrong. That was their deal. She wasn't his girlfriend. In fact, he didn't have a label for her. She was his . . .

His breath stuck in his throat. Damn. He had no label for her, but he simply thought of her as his. She was *his*. When and how did *that* happen?

But right then, she was scrambling to get her armor back on. He got that. She was feeling vulnerable, regretting what she'd revealed, and needed both assurance and distance. This wasn't about him, it was about her. No more pushing today.

"No problem," he said softly, holding her eyes with his. "Understood. Now please come here."

She hesitated for a few seconds, but slowly crossed the cabin and got back into bed. He pulled her against him, kissed the top of her head, and held her close. Her arms snaked around his waist, and she let him hold her.

"Are you hungry?" he asked, trying to sound casual.

"I could snack," she said.

"I can have someone bring us some food here," he said. "We don't have to get out of bed yet. What would you like? Name it. Fruit? Chocolate? A sandwich?"

She kissed his shoulder and whispered, "Thank you, Dane."

His fingers slipped under her chin, raised it, and he looked into her eyes, searching. He saw so many things in her expressive, gorgeous eyes. The gold flecks seemed to glow in the sea of light brown, reflecting sadness, wariness, and some of the fiery strength he knew so well. He also saw such stark vulnerability there, it touched his heart.

He lowered his mouth to hers, brushing his lips gently against hers. He wanted to kiss away all the things that had hurt her, that made her look pained even now, that made her fight him and lash out and put on protective armor. He kissed her with all the tenderness he possessed. Then he swept her hair back from her forehead and said, "We'll be docking soon. I'd invite you to join my brother, my sister, and me for dinner, but something tells me you'd rather not."

"Maybe another time," she whispered. "But thanks."

"Okay." He kissed her again, long and slow. "You made my birthday fantastic. Thank you for coming out with me." His mouth took hers and he nibbled, played lazily against her lips. Her mouth opened for him and she touched her tongue to his, sparking new desire in him. They kissed and cuddled for a long time, just savoring the feel of each other, sealing something new between them without words. Slowly the kisses intensified and her hands tangled in his hair, then she raked her nails down his back, sending shivers through him. He cupped her breast, brushed his thumb over her nipple, and she pressed her body even closer. Then she nudged his hips with hers, his heartbeat stuttered, his blood raced, and their primal dance began again.

The ride from the marina to Julia's place was silent, in a pleasant and sleepy way. In relaxed contentment, Dane held Julia close the whole way back. Late afternoon sunlight slanted through the windows, tingeing everything with gold. One arm wrapped around her shoulders, holding her to his side, as he let her play with the fingers of his other hand. Her head on his shoulder, she traced his fingers with hers, light and languid and almost . . . affectionate. Something deep inside him warmed at that.

He found himself enjoying the moments of wordless intimacy more than he could believe. She felt good nestled into him, touching him delicately, warm and soft . . . he lifted his hand from her shoulder to play with the thick locks of her hair as the car moved smoothly along.

"This ranks up there with one of my best birthdays," he murmured, pressing a kiss to her forehead. "Thank you for that."

He felt her smile against his neck. "I'm so glad,"

she purred. "You're welcome. Thanks for inviting me. The boat's magnificent, the food was great, the weather was perfect. . . ."

"And the company was perfect," he said with satisfaction.

She tipped up her face to look at him. He could see a few freckles on her nose that the sun had brought out, and they made her seem younger, sweeter somehow. Adorable. He nuzzled her nose with his before kissing her, taking her mouth with slow, sumptuous sips until the car stopped in front of her home.

"Sure you don't want to join us for dinner?" he asked.

She shook her head. "That's a family thing. Enjoy your time with them. I had you to myself all day. It's their turn."

He looked deep into her eyes. She seemed so relaxed, floating in a sea of tranquility. At ease with him. He'd never seen her quite like this. It enchanted him, to the point he hated to let her go. Tangling his fingers in her hair, he kissed her a few more times before releasing her. The driver had already exited the car and pulled her bag from the trunk.

"Happy rest of your birthday, Dane," she said softly. Her hand lifted to ruffle his hair, then trail down to touch his cheek. "Thanks again, for everything today. It was really nice."

"Thank *you* again." He kissed her one last time. "I'll see you on Thursday night. Let me buy you a drink or two after your show?"

"Only if you promise to take me to bed after," she murmured provocatively.

His libido flickered to life in an instant, humming low in his belly. "That's a given, Red."

She smiled, dropped a quick kiss on his lips, and got out of the car.

Gazing out the window, he watched her smile and thank the driver as she took her bag from him, then walk up the path, up the steps, and disappear into the house.

Dane dropped his head back against the seat, tired but happy. He spent the ride to the restaurant with his eyes closed, mulling through images of the day, a besotted smile playing on his face.

Chapter Twelve

"To you, Dane." Charles raised his cup of sake in a toast, and his siblings did the same. "Happy Birthday. Many happy returns."

"Hope you have a wonderful year ahead," Tess said, smiling with affection.

"Thanks, kids." Dane grinned, and the three of them clinked their small clay cups and sipped.

"Ahh. Nice." Dane eased back in his chair. The waitress approached the table and took their orders. She'd only taken a few steps away when Dane said, "Bring on the sushi! I am starving."

"What'd you do all day, anyway?" Charles asked his brother.

"I went out on Dad's boat." Dane grinned as memories of Julia riding him mercilessly on the deck of the yacht flooded his brain. "Really good day."

"You went alone?" Tess asked.

"Nope," Charles guessed, his eyes narrowing on Dane. "Look at his face. Someone got lucky today. I'd bet the yacht on it."

Dane laughed out loud. "Well, Dad just lost his yacht, then. Busted."

Tess's big blue eyes widened. "You took a woman out on the boat?"

Dane nodded and reached for his drink.

"You've *never* taken a girl on the boat," Tess said in slight shock.

"Sure he has," Charles said, smirking. "Of course, it was *four* women, not just one. But that's our boy for you."

Tess's eyes nearly popped out of her head as she gaped at Dane. "Tell me he's kidding."

Dane just shrugged, unable to wipe the grin off his face.

"I was so pissed!" Charles said. "He invited me along, but since he didn't call until the last minute, I was stuck in a meeting. Poor Dane had to entertain all four women by himself."

"Something tells me that wasn't a problem," Tess said, trying to repress a smile and failing.

"Mmm. Good times," Dane said, sipping his sake. "Yup, you missed out that time, Charles. That was . . . memorable." His mouth quirked another grin. "But no, today, there was only one woman. Sorry to disappoint you."

Tess stared harder, scrutinizing her brother's features. "Someone special?"

"Tess is right, you've never taken just *one* woman on the boat to spend a day with her." Charles leaned in on his elbows. "Fess up."

Dane shrugged again, trying to keep it casual. "Julia Shay."

Tess's mouth dropped open as she gasped. Charles stared so hard, Dane thought his eyes would roll out of his skull.

"What?" Dane asked.

Tess stammered, "You said you weren't going to—"

"I know," Dane said.

"You've never crossed that line before," Charles said with a hard frown.

"I know," Dane said.

"You're . . . together?" Tess asked, almost a squeak.

"No," Dane said, even though a voice in his head whispered, *Bullshit.* "We're . . . just keeping each other company some nights."

"You're sleeping with your singer?" Charles hissed in a whisper. His incredulous disapproval was palpable. "She *works* for you. What the hell's the matter with you? Are you that reckless, or just insane?"

"Thanks, Chuckles," Dane said dryly. "Gee, none of that crossed my mind. Ever."

"You're seeing your employee," Charles repeated with disdain. "Unbelievable."

"I'm not seeing her," Dane corrected him. "I'm . . ." He leaned in to whisper. "It's just sex. We're only sleeping together. No strings. *She's* the one who set that ground rule. I was happy to agree."

"I'm sure you were," Charles replied.

Tess shot Charles a scathing look before asking Dane, "How long has this been going on?"

"Only a few weeks," Dane said. "And nobody knows. *Nobody.* And it needs to stay that way." He rubbed the back of his neck and blew out a breath.

"Of course," Tess said.

"You're an idiot," Charles said, grabbing his cup. He knocked the whole drink back.

"I know," Dane admitted. "But she's . . ." He shook his head in defeat. "I couldn't stay away from her. I literally couldn't. I've never been this attracted to a woman before. Seriously." He looked down at his little plastic soupspoon, picked it up, and started flicking it between his fingers.

Tess stared at her brother for a long minute. "You're not just sleeping with her. You like her. You want her."

"Of course I want her," Dane said. "She's the sexiest, most passionate woman I've ever met, and that's saying something. She's the first woman who's ever knocked me around like this."

"No," Tess said. "No, not just that. That's not what I meant, and you know it. You *like* her. Maybe even have real feelings for her."

Dane shook his head vehemently, but didn't speak.

"Dane doesn't play for keeps," Charles quipped. "He just plays. You know that, Tess."

"Shut up," Dane said to his brother, suddenly annoyed.

Charles arched a brow and sat back in his chair, pinning Dane with his eyes. "Struck a nerve, did I?" The corner of his mouth turned up. "Then Tess is right. And holy shit."

Dane looked from one sibling to the other. Fuck, Tess *was* right. He grabbed his own cup of sake and drained it. "No. We're just sleeping together. We enjoy each other. That's it. No strings, no ties, that's the deal. She made that very clear, and I'm fine with it."

"No, you're not," Tess murmured, watching him.

"Yes, I am," Dane insisted.

"I call bullshit," Charles said.

Dane huffed out a sigh of frustration. "You're both off course. You're making a bigger deal out of this than it is. Of course I like her, as a person. She's smart, and talented, and interesting. She keeps me on my toes, that's for damn sure. But that's not . . . it's not *that*."

"If you say so," Tess said, and busied herself with her chopsticks. She broke them apart and rubbed them together to take off the splinters.

Dane didn't know why there was a buzz in his stomach,

but there was. And it wasn't the sake. "She's . . . complicated," he said quietly. He stared at the center-piece on the table, the delicate white flowers in a tiny vase, and tapped the soupspoon on his leg. "She's been hurt in the past. Badly. I think she's afraid to get hurt again. So she keeps her armor on at all times."

"And you're not?" Tess said pointedly.

Dane frowned at her in confusion. "No. I'm noth-ing like that."

Charles barked out a laugh and said, "Yes, you are! Mister Never-Commit-To-A-Woman. Mister Fun-And-Games-Only."

Tess leaned in, speared him with her stare, and said, "You have a ton of friends, but your closest, most trusted friends are your siblings. You're thirty-six years old today. You've never had a relationship that lasted more than a month. There's a very good reason for that, don't you think?"

Dane scowled. "I just don't . . . I don't do commit-ment like that." Something started gnawing in his gut. "I don't get serious. It's not me."

"Bullshit," Charles said, pointing a finger at him. "You get fiercely serious in business. You refused to join Harrison Enterprises, worked damn hard to make your own name, and you've opened over twenty hotels across North America. Your work is important to you. You get serious. Just not with *people.*"

"That's right," Tess agreed. "Because, Dane, you're afraid of letting someone in." She covered his hand with her own, and her eyes and voice softened. "All of us are, sweetheart. Because we watched our parents destroy each other. We watched their marriage dete-riorate before our eyes. They tried to hurt each other as viciously as they could. And we had front row seats, and we were just kids." She rubbed his hand, looked at Charles, who was sitting as quietly as Dane was, then looked back to Dane. "They were our role models for relationships, and they were horrible at it. He only cared about Harrison Enterprises and us. He ignored her. She was lonely, so she started having affairs. He was furious, so he drove her out of our lives. She was self-absorbed, he was ferocious. It was a nightmare. And it affected us, all *four* of us. We're all single. It's not a coincidence."

"Charles got married," Dane pointed out, grasping at straws.

"Yeah, and it was a disaster," Charles retorted. "Marrying Vanessa was the worst mistake I ever made. You know that. *Everyone* knows that."

"And look at me," Tess said. "Burned badly, twice, and that was enough for me. I don't want to get that close to a man again, or get married. And Pierce? Plays the field, just like you."

"So all of us have issues when it comes to dating," Dane quipped. "Yay us."

"Apparently," Tess conceded. "You've done nothing *but* date. You *never* got serious. Because, deep down, you were afraid of getting hurt. And you don't even realize that." She smiled softly. "You were born gregarious, yes . . . but it's also a bit of a front, isn't it? You don't get close. You won't get serious. It's totally understandable, almost textbook, really. Then, on top of that, you watched Charles and Vanessa blow up, then me and Brady. . . ." She squeezed his hand and peered into his eyes. "Dane. I hate to tell you this, sweetheart, but it sounds like you and Julia are a lot more alike than you think. Maybe that's why you're so drawn to her. Not just because she's beautiful, or talented. But because . . . you recognize a kindred spirit. You wear armor too. It's just not as obvious."

"Tess is 100 percent right," Charles agreed, folding his arms over his chest. "As usual."

Dane could only stare at them as all the words sank in and took hold. Yes, Tess was right. Even Charles was right. He'd never gotten serious with a woman, and convinced himself it was simply because he hadn't met the right one, and was too busy having fun. What if he *had* met a possible love connection at some point, but never let her get close enough to find out?

He thought back on various women and situations, even friends through the years . . . no one had gotten close to his heart. Because he hadn't let them. None of it had been with conscious actions or thoughts, but yes, he'd kept people at a comfortable distance all his life, and very likely for all the reasons Tess had listed. Jesus. How hadn't he seen that before? How had he deceived himself so thoroughly? Self-preservation? Was that it?

He scrubbed his hands over his face. Tess was absolutely right, on every point. And maybe, just maybe, he was drawn to Julia so strongly not only for the almost tangible physical connection, but for what Tess had nailed on the head: because they were very much alike after all. Tough on the outside, tender on the inside, that was Julia—but was he any different? He just used his charm and his smile as his armor, whereas Julia's armor was akin to a warrior wearing a full chain-mail suit. Didn't matter. They were *both* hiding. It was mind-boggling to contemplate.

He reached across the table, grasped the small bottle of sake, and poured himself another cup. Charles watched him without a word, but the mixed look of curiosity and concern on his face wasn't lost on Dane.

"You okay?" Tess asked him.

"Sure." He nodded and downed half the cup. The warm liquid burned a sweet trail down his throat. "I'm fine. Just thinking."

"Dane," she said softly, still holding his other hand.

With affection, he squeezed her fingers. "You missed your calling, Tesstastic," he cracked wryly. "You should've been a therapist."

Julia checked her hair and makeup in the mirror one last time.

"I'm gonna go out there," Kelvin said from behind her, straightening his red-and-black striped tie. He met her eyes in the mirror. "I'll play a bit, just to warm them up, and you come on out when you're ready."

"I'm almost ready," she said. "Work your magic."

"Always. You too. It's a packed house for a Thursday. Let's do this." He put out his fist and she bumped it in return. "You look particularly gorgeous tonight, by the way. Whatever kind of monkey sex you're having with Dane, it's working for you." He put on his sassiest, most overexaggerated drag queen voice as he added, "You iz *glowin'*, sugarplum."

She laughed. "Shut up. I am not."

"Mm-hmm." He winked and left, closing the door behind him.

Julia sighed and looked at her reflection. Shit, he was right. She *was* glowing a little.

She hadn't seen Dane since Tuesday, but she hadn't been able to stop thinking of him since he'd dropped her off at her house with a long, sumptuous kiss and that devil-may-care smile. He'd texted her Wednesday morning and Thursday afternoon, just to

say hi. It made her smile the goofy, besotted smile of
an infatuated teenager. And every time she repri-
manded herself for doing so, every time she reminded
herself firmly *No strings!*, a little voice in the back
of her heart laughed and taunted her. *Yeah, right.
You wish.*

When she first met him, he'd reminded her of
Max, which set off big red flags and warning sirens.
Both men were rich and powerful, charming and gorgeous. But the similarities were superficial, they
ended there. The more she got to know Dane, the
more she knew there was a lot more to him than
being King of the Charmers and sex on a stick—and
holy crap, was he. In or out of bed, all he had to do
was look deeply into her eyes, and her blood heated
and sang.

Dane had real heart. She saw it in the way he inter-
acted with people, and she saw it in the way he treated
her. They were only sleeping together, he owed her
nothing. But he never treated her like an object, or a
slut, or anything other than . . . lovely, actually. Even
in his casual, smooth way, he wasn't slick, sleazy, or
dismissive. He was genuinely charming, and funny,
and sweet. He was outright tender at times. He'd
proved that on the yacht. She'd given him a peek
into her ugliness . . . and he hadn't rebuffed her, or
bolted, or made her feel less than him. He'd held her
close, dropped the questions, and ordered chocolate-
covered strawberries to the cabin.

She huffed out an exasperated breath. Goddammit,
she liked him more every day. *Shit.* It made her feel
both alive and off-balance. She had no anchor.

Suddenly gripped by a wave of loneliness and
yearning, she reached for her cell phone. Before she
could change her mind, she sent a short e-mail.

Hi Colin. Just thinking of you, as I do every day. I hope you've been enjoying your summer. My new job has been both demanding and amazing. If you ever find yourself in New York City, I'd love for you to come see me, and hear me sing. The lounge at this hotel is top-notch glamour, and Kelvin and I put on a really good show. Maybe you'd enjoy it. Never know.

Anyway . . . I love you. I miss you. Just wanted to say hi. Hope you're doing well, and are happy. I'm always here, Colin. I'll never stop loving you and hoping to hear from you. Never.

Take care.

Love,
Mom

Her eyes burned with tears. She sniffed them back forcefully, shoved her phone back into her bag, and stared at herself in the mirror. Time to drown her sorrows with song. She stood, smoothed out the hunter green cocktail dress, slipped her feet into the matching peep-toe stilettos, and headed for the stage.

Dane set down his drink to clap as the audience gave Julia and Kelvin a standing ovation. They'd finished their second set and kicked ass, as usual. Also as usual, she looked stunning. Her hair was up tonight, in some slick twisty bun on top of her head, sleek and glamorous. He wanted nothing more than to let down her hair with both hands, peel her out of that little green dress, and cover every inch of her delectable body with his mouth.

Across the crowd, she looked in his direction. A few times that night, she'd glanced his way, even tossed him a quick smile. Catching her gaze now, he gestured that he'd meet her back at her dressing room. She gave the slightest nod and turned her eyes back to the crowd for one last little bow. Kelvin stepped off the small stage and extended his hand to her. She took it, stepped down as well, and they both walked out.

The lights came up and a swinging Frank Sinatra song kicked in. The buzz of the crowd, both in the lounge and in the bar, was loud and pulsing with energy. Wanting to give Julia a few minutes to unwind, Dane sat back in his chair and thought about her. He really loved her voice. Every time she sang, she impressed him. He loved watching her perform, how she worked a room with ease. Three nights a week for over a month now, and he wasn't bored with their show. They changed up the set lists, they obviously had fun working together—Dane enjoyed it every time. Kelvin was as good as they came, there was no doubt. But Julia shone up there. Her talent and her presence were that electric.

He sipped what was left of his scotch and watched the crowd around him enjoy his hotel. Business was booming. He was going to have some incredible sex within the hour with an amazing woman. Life was good.

"Dane." Tonio was at his side, hunched over his shoulder. "Come with me."

The delicious high he'd enjoyed a few seconds before vanished, replaced by the feeling something was wrong from the tone of Tonio's voice. "What's up?" he asked, even as he rose from his chair.

"That guy, the one who always comes and stares at

Julia?" Tonio's dark eyes flashed. "I might be wrong, but I could swear I saw him head back to her dressing room."

A shiver ran through Dane's body, a nauseating adrenaline rush that had his nerves jangling. "Let's go."

The two men pushed through the crowd, trying to move quickly. When they got to the back hallway, Kelvin was rushing out, looking wild. "Oh, thank God," he said when he saw them. "I was just coming to call security or whatever you got here. Julia needs help."

Dane's blood rushed through his veins like liquid mercury. "Go, go!" he shouted at Tonio, pushing his shoulder. The three men jogged back up the short hall, and Tonio crashed the door open with his heavy hands.

The man Tonio had spotted, the shaggy-haired guy who'd been lurking for weeks, had Julia pinned up against the wall, his arms on either side of her, his face close to hers.

But even through his red haze of fury and burst of anxiety, Dane saw that Julia didn't look afraid. She looked angry, and actually, she was yelling in the guy's face to leave her alone.

Tonio got to him first. He took the guy by the back of his shirt and slammed him to the floor, face down. Dane went for Julia, but Kelvin grabbed her and pulled her away while Tonio grasped the man's shoulders, flipped him over, and held him to the carpet by holding his shoulders down and leaning on his chest with a heavy knee.

"I got you, baby," Kelvin cooed to his best friend, holding her close. "We're here."

Julia's breath came in hard gasps as she grasped him and held tight.

Dane watched Kelvin stroke her back to soothe her

and felt a pang. *Damn.* He knew they'd been friends for years, of course she'd go to Kelvin for comfort. But *he* wanted to be the one holding her. He wanted to rub her back and make her feel safe . . . she was *his* woman. That thought, combined with what he recognized as a pang of jealousy, shook his insides. He swatted them away. What he was feeling wasn't the top priority at the moment.

"Are you okay?" Dane asked her. His heart was still pounding in his ears.

She nodded and managed hoarsely, "He didn't hurt me, I'm fine."

Dane looked at her pale face, saw her hands shake as she clutched at Kelvin's jacket, and his blood surged with rage. Restraining the urge to kick the intruder in the ribs, instead he balled his fists, stood over the guy and shouted, "What the fuck are you doing here?"

"I just wanted to talk to her," the man wheezed. Tonio's knee was firmly on his chest. "I just wanted to apologize—to explain—she needs to know—"

"I don't want to hear a word out of your goddamn mouth!" Julia screamed wildly, pushing away from Kelvin. She tried to lunge at the guy, but Kelvin held her back. He braced his legs and locked his arms around her like bands of steel. "Let me go!" she cried, trying to break free. "He ruined my life, I want to punch his face in!"

Dane stared at her in shock for a second, then blinked and looked down at Tonio. "Call security, and the police. Get this guy out of here." He looked down at the guy and said, "The lady doesn't want to talk to you."

"But—"

"But nothing," Dane cut him off. "Because you didn't

hurt her, I'll let you out of here without needing a trip to the hospital. But if you ever set foot in *any* of my hotels, *ever* again, I'll have you arrested for trespassing so fast your head will spin. Got it?" He looked back at Julia, who was breathing heavily and as fired up as a warrior ready to go into battle. "You know this guy, I take it."

"Unfortunately," she bit out. She squirmed again. "Kel, let me go."

"Not a chance," Kelvin said, struggling to hold her.

"You know his full name?" Dane asked her. "So we can get a restraining order against him first thing in the morning?"

"Yes," she said, glaring down at him.

"Julia, please," the man croaked. His pale green eyes pleaded with her. "I'm sorry. I just wanted to tell you I'm so sorry. And it wasn't all my fault. You have to listen to me. I'm trying to tell you what happened, how—"

"Shut up!" she yelled, losing her composure at last. Panting, she struggled to break free of Kelvin's hold, absolutely feral. "I don't want to hear anything you have to say! I hate you! Don't ever come near me again, you hear me?" Her eyes spilled hot, furious tears as she continued to try to wiggle free. "Just let me hit him, Kel," she begged, her voice breaking. "Just once. Please. Please . . ."

"I wanna hit him too," Kelvin said against her cheek, holding on to her with all his might. "But no. No, baby. He's not worth it."

Dane's jaw set so tightly, his teeth ground together. Whatever this man had done to her, it had been bad enough for her to lose it this way. Her desperate fury and pain flooded him with anguish. "Is this your ex-husband?" he asked.

"No. God no," she spat. "But he's almost as bad."

"Julia, I'm sorry," the man said again. "You'll never know how sorry I am. I didn't know it was gonna go down like that, that he was gonna use it to—"

"Shut up, damn you!" she screeched, still trying to get loose.

"Stop it, Jules," Kelvin demanded as he restrained her. "Just stop now!"

"Get him out of here," Dane snapped to Tonio. "Before I let Kelvin set her free so she can tear him apart."

Without a word, Tonio rose, looking dangerous. His dark, flashing eyes and six-foot-three frame of hulky muscle had never seemed so intimidating. He gripped the guy by the front of his shirt, hauled him to his feet, and dragged him toward the door like a rag doll. "I got him, Boss," Tonio said. He slammed the guy against the wall once for good measure, hard, bringing a groan from the intruder. Over his shoulder, he told Dane, "You stay here. I got this. Security's on the other side of the door, being discreet. We'll just bring him outside. Police are on the way."

"Thank you, Tonio," Dane said, knowing he could trust him to handle the matter.

"You want him arrested?" Tonio asked.

Dane turned to look at Julia. "Do you?"

"No," she said, shooting daggers at the man with her eyes. "I just want him gone."

He pointed a finger at the man and warned in a scathing growl, "Never again. Don't you *ever* come near her again, or I'll make you *very* sorry you did. You'll answer to me, and the police—and Julia's good heart won't be there to save you."

The man only stared at Julia, as if no one else was there. "I'm sorry for everything," he told her raggedly.

His eyes conveyed pain, fear, sorrow, and . . . remorse. Dane saw it. It was real. The guy looked pathetic. *What the fuck?* he thought as Tonio dragged him out of the room and shut the door behind them with a bang.

Covering her face with her hands, Julia sagged to her knees, sobbing. Dane rushed to her as Kelvin tried to hold her up. The two of them lifted her to her feet and brought her to one of the couches. She crumbled against her best friend, slumping into his arms and crying into his chest.

"It's over, baby," Kelvin said, rocking her as he held her tight. "Shhh, it's over. He's gone. Liam's gone. You're fine. We're here."

Dane sat and watched Julia break down. She was shaken to the core, and he felt a bit shaky himself. Kelvin stroked her hair, her back, whispering words of comfort and trying to soothe her. He rested his chin on Julia's head and met Dane's eyes. They looked at each other, and while Dane knew Kelvin meant well, another twinge of jealousy burned through his chest. *Let go of her, dammit. Let me hold her.*

Dane had rarely felt so useless. His heart winced with every ragged sob that tore from her throat. Not knowing what to do, he went to her vanity table and got the box of tissues, bringing it back and setting it on the table nearby. He stared down at her for another minute, shoving his fists into his pockets. He wanted to *do* something. Her tears started to subside, but he was ready to pace the room out of frustration. "Should I leave and come back later?" he asked quietly.

"No," she said, her voice muffled in Kelvin's chest. She looked up at him. "Please don't go. I—I have to explain this to you."

"Not right now, you don't," Dane insisted.

"But—"

"You only have to tell me if you want to, Julia. Okay?"

"Okay. I do want to. I just . . ." Her eyes filled and she started to cry again. She let her head drop onto Kelvin's shoulder.

Dane stared at her heaving back as she cried. He hated feeling inept. Needing to do something, he pulled his cell phone out of his pocket and hit speed dial. "Yeah, it's me. You see where I am, yes? . . . Right. In the dressing room, though, not out front. Listen, I need a tray, three glasses of vodka and cranberry, two drinks for me . . . make it Macallan. The eighteen. And—" He glanced at Kelvin. "What do you drink?"

"An Absolut gimlet would be good right now," Kelvin said.

"And two Absolut gimlets," Dane said into the phone. "I also need food. Bring me some sandwiches, some cheese and crackers, you know . . . yeah. Yes. Chocolate too . . . uh-huh. Yeah, that works. Good . . . Right. As soon as possible. Okay, thanks." He ended the call and realized Kelvin was staring at him. "What?"

"Good move," Kelvin said with approval.

Dane nodded in acknowledgment. Tentatively, he reached out and touched Julia's back. He hated that she was so distressed, and he hated that he hadn't been able to console her yet even more. "Hey. It's okay, honey. You're safe now."

She lifted her head to look at him. Her makeup ran down her blotchy face, her eyes were puffy from crying, and she looked both wounded and drained. And so fragile it made his heart hurt.

"I'm sorry," she whispered, trying to calm herself.

"For what?" he demanded. "You didn't do anything

wrong! That guy had you trapped against the wall, for fuck's sake. He's lucky there were witnesses, or I wouldn't have just let Tonio beat him to a pulp, I would've done it myself."

She drew a shaky breath and her sobs ebbed. "Yeah, right."

"What, you don't think I could?" Dane challenged, trying to make her grin.

After another deep breath, she asked, "Have you ever even *been* in a fight, rich boy?" With a hint of a grin.

Atta girl. Show me your spunk. He grinned back. "Believe it or not, Red, I have. Guys didn't always take it well when I stole their women. Had a few fights in my twenties."

She hiccupped out a watery laugh. "Why doesn't that surprise me?"

Dane gave her a smile.

Kelvin grabbed a few tissues and handed them to her. "Mop your face, girl. You're a hot mess."

"Ugh, I bet I am." She took the tissues and wiped her eyes and cheeks.

As she sniffled and wiped, Dane made another phone call. "Tonio. Talk to me."

"Security escorted him out, no problems," Tonio said. "I may or may not have punched him once or twice before he left, though. Hard to say."

Dane chuckled under his breath. "You did good, Tonio. Real good. Thank you."

"Cops were outside and took his info. He wasn't arrested, but we can file a restraining order if Julia agrees to it." Tonio paused. "He said he was her ex-boyfriend."

Dane sighed. "How did I know you were going to say that? Okay. Thanks, man. I'll come find you in a bit." He ended the call and shoved the phone back into his inside jacket pocket. As he did so, Julia rose from the sofa, passed him, and walked to the vanity mirror.

"Ohh my God," she groaned as she caught her reflection. "Shit."

"Go clean up," Kelvin instructed. "We'll be right here. Go."

"Yes, Mom," Julia joked, but looked at Dane. "Um. You staying?"

He looked at her, unsure. "Do you want me to?"

Almost sheepishly, she nodded.

His heart lifted. "Then I'll be here," he said, a wave of something warm suffusing him. She *did* want him there. Suddenly, he felt a little less useless.

She went into the small bathroom and quietly closed the door behind her.

Dane turned to stare hard at Kelvin. Kelvin stared back at him, looking tired and pained.

"Tell me everything," Dane said in a low, tight voice. He speared the other man with his gaze. "Tell me what the fuck just happened in here. *Now.*"

Chapter Thirteen

"You should be asking her," Kelvin said. "Not me. I mean . . . it's *her* business."

"You're right," Dane agreed, "and believe me, I plan to."

Kelvin looked to the bathroom door, then back to him, and sighed. "She said she would tell you anyway, after all this, so . . . I'll tell you." Kelvin's dark eyes leveled on his boss. "But nothing I don't think she wouldn't say herself. It just spares her from having to tell it, and relive it."

"I admire your loyalty to her," Dane said.

Kelvin nodded, then reached to loosen his tie as he started to talk. "That piece of garbage was Liam McAllister. Her ex-boyfriend. Fucking scumbag."

Dane saw the ire in Kelvin's eyes and sat back to listen.

"I don't know what she's told you about her marriage to Mad Max," Kelvin said, "but as bad as the marriage was, the divorce was even worse. When she finally realized what an asshole he was and got up the nerve to ask for a divorce, he and his rich family wiped the floor with her." Kelvin pulled his tie out of his shirt collar and tossed it onto the table. "They didn't want some middle-class sexy bombshell singer raising their precious heir to the family throne."

Dane winced. Shit like that, he was all too familiar with. "How'd they do that?"

"We think his family knew the judge, or bribed him. Max didn't have to pay alimony, only child support, and that was minimal. She'd been a student at a music college when they met, for God's sake. Other than sing, even though she's smart as hell, what was she really qualified to do? She'd been at home with the baby. There was no reason for her not to get alimony. And, of course, she'd signed a prenup. She got almost nothing. She was broke." Kelvin made a disgusted face as he recalled it.

"What about the kid?" Dane asked.

"Max's number one weapon. He wanted ownership of that boy." Kelvin unbuttoned the top two buttons of his crisp white shirt. "He looked down on Jules, said she was 'nothing but a lowly lounge singer, shaking her ass for money.' So okay, it was great when he was getting laid, parading her around town like a trophy. But suddenly he was ashamed of her when she was the mother of his child, and she stopped being his doormat. Bastard."

Dane saw the animosity in Kelvin's eyes and hated to contemplate how bad things had been for Julia. With each new sentence, his stomach jolted and twisted.

Kelvin ran a hand over his dreads as he continued, "At first, they had joint custody, and she worked *two* office jobs. I wanted to move in with her to help with the rent and bills, but Max threatened her that if I did, he'd go back to court and say my living there was a bad influence on her son and get full custody.

You know . . . a gay black man? Living with his son? Oh hell no."

Dane scowled and let out a breath. "Sounds like a real prince."

"It gets worse." Kelvin's eyes flickered to the bathroom door again, then back to Dane. "After two years of that, she met someone. Seemed like a great guy. Liam. He promised her the sun, moon, and stars. She was so vulnerable, so desperate for love, and so damn tired, she fell for him, and all his promises. What he *didn't* tell her was that he was a recovering drug addict. Heroin. She had no idea. It all came out later."

Dane shifted in his seat. "Okay. So?"

"So after they'd been dating for about four months, and Julia thought things were peachy, suddenly Liam went back to using. Showed up at her apartment one day, high as a kite. And it was a Friday, so Max was there, to pick up Colin."

"Colin, huh," Dane repeated in a murmur. It was the first time he'd heard her son's name.

"Yup. And little Colin got to watch this heroin addict boyfriend of Mommy's throw up all over the floor, then pass out in his own vomit." Kelvin's face darkened. "Max lit into Jules, took the kid out . . . and never brought him back."

"What?" Dane felt sick. "He couldn't do that, not if they had joint custody."

"Not after that horror scene with Liam. You forget, Max came from money. Julia had no money, and no one in her corner but me and Randi. Her own mother and sisters bought that shit Max was selling, and Max used it against her in court. Said she was an unfit mother, her judgment was obviously for shit if she was dating a drug addict, much less letting him be around their son." Kelvin shook his head, his mouth twisting as he remembered. "The judge gave Mad Max full custody. Julia's rights got zapped down to supervised visitation, and no more child support, obviously. So, Max got what he wanted. A son to carry on the family name, and his 'lowlife slut ex-wife' out of the picture."

Dane's stomach churned violently and he scrubbed his hands over his face. He didn't know what to say. What was there to say? God. The injustice . . . that poor kid . . . Dane ached for the boy, and for Julia. He wanted to go get her, pull her into his arms, and hold her for a week.

Kelvin shrugged off his jacket, his usually jovial expression glowering now. "Max kept Julia away from Colin, and filled the kid's head with lies. The whole family did. They convinced him his mom didn't want him, that she only cared about her singing career. She wasn't even singing then! She hadn't in years! After a year, Max moved him back to Seattle, where his family lived, and kept Julia out of their son's life completely. The kid hasn't talked to her in a long time." Kelvin sighed, then leaned in and added in a whisper, "It almost destroyed her. That's her *baby*. Her only child. She loves him more than anything. But Max, and his lies, and his connections, shut her out of her son's life. She feels that guilt and that pain every damn day. Then her own family turned on her. She went through total hell. Can you blame her for that bitchy front she puts on?"

Dane closed his eyes and pinched the bridge of his nose. His head reeled from the story.

"And Liam? Max used Liam to nail the coffin shut," Kelvin said. "And that dumbass junkie disappeared after the custody trial, left her high and dry.

She thought he loved her, and she loved him. But almost from that first night, he just fucking vanished. Basically helped her lose her kid, and he never spoke to her again—until tonight."

"Jesus," Dane breathed. He ran his hands through his hair and flopped back against the sofa cushions, his mind whirring. "She must have flipped when he showed up." He slanted Kelvin a look. "What happened, how'd that go down? When Liam came back here tonight?"

"Someone knocked on the door, and she answered it. There he was. She was stunned speechless—which, I can tell you, rarely happens to Jules." Kelvin couldn't resist the flash of a smirk. "Liam barreled in, saying he needed to talk to her, to explain what happened. Right away I told her I'd go get security, and ran out to do that. That's when I bumped into you and Tonio."

"Good on ya." Dane rubbed his stubble-covered jaw and sighed. "I hate to tell you this . . . Liam's been here for weeks."

"What?" Kelvin's eyes bulged.

"Tonio noticed him a few weeks ago. He's been lurking. At every show. Stood in the back and watched." Dane shook his head in disgust. "Tonio had a bad vibe about him right away, so he's been keeping an eye on him. But the guy didn't do anything, so there was no reason he couldn't be here." He scowled and huffed out a breath in frustration. "Sonofabitch. I had no idea, obviously, or I never would've let the guy even set foot in my hotel."

"Of course," Kelvin said. "How could you know? Don't beat yourself up."

Dane swore under his breath and sat back again. He glanced at the still-closed bathroom door. "At least he didn't hurt her. I don't know what I would've done if . . ." His voice trailed off and he shook his head. Kelvin was staring at him. He shrugged. "Look, thanks for filling me in. I'm sure she'll hate my knowing any of it. I'll make sure she knows I all but forced it out of you so she won't be mad."

"No, you didn't force anything," Kelvin said dismissively. "Nobody forces me to do a damn thing." He half-grinned, but his eyes relayed a lethal promise that what he said was true. "Like I said before, I'm only telling you this because I know she will later. After this debacle tonight, she'll feel she owes you an explanation. I know how she thinks."

Dane shook his head and said quietly, "She owes me no such thing. I just . . . wow. Damn. I don't . . . I don't know what to say to her." He looked down at his hands. "God, it's all horrific."

Kelvin studied him for a minute. "You care about her."

Dane's eyes snapped up to meet his. "What?"

"Yup." Kelvin nodded. "You do. Okay. Good. You should."

"You know about us." Dane didn't ask it. He was merely seeking confirmation.

"Well *duh*." Kelvin rolled his eyes. "Look, you seem to be treating her right, so power to both of you. You're having fun? Cool. But you're lucky, you know. Don't you forget that. Because she's not only the sexiest thing walking, she's the most amazing woman in the world."

Dane grinned softly. "Yeah, she's all right. You are too."

Kelvin snorted. "Hey, Miss Thang," he called out toward the bathroom door, "you need me to call the cavalry, or are you all right in there? Did you fall in?"

"I'll be out in a minute, you bitch," Julia called back, sounding more like herself.

Dane chuckled, but said soberly to Kelvin, "Thank you. For telling me, and for before, and . . . just thanks."

"Thank *you*," Kelvin said. "That was a decent White-Knight-To-The-Rescue act y'all had going on."

Dane laughed. "Nah. Tonio was the muscle. I didn't do much. Between that, and now . . ." He looked down at his hands as he admitted ruefully, "I haven't felt so useless in a long time."

"What?" Kelvin slanted him a sideways look. "Dane, you did good tonight. You weren't useless. Trust me. She wanted you to stay, right?"

The bathroom door opened and both men turned to look. Julia's hair was brushed back and secured in a ponytail, her face scrubbed free of makeup and still a little blotchy from her crying jag. She'd wrapped herself in the luxuriously soft white robe Dane had bought for her to keep there. Beneath her drawn brows, her eyes were swollen, and filled with sadness.

And to him, she was heartbreakingly pretty. No, more than that. She was a breathtaking flame-haired warrior, as far as he was concerned. All she needed was a crossbow or a sword. His heart turned over at the sight of her.

Barefoot and quiet, she crossed the room and sat on the couch opposite them.

"You okay?" Dane asked, studying her face.

"Yeah." She tucked her feet beneath her. "I must look like a real glamour queen right now, huh?"

"Actually, you look beautiful," Dane said softly.

She blushed and her eyes slid down to examine her manicure. "Dane . . . I'm very sorry about what happened here tonight. Obviously, I'm mortified. And worse, I don't want any negative incidents harming the reputation of the hotel, or your name—"

"Stop right there." He held up a hand to silence her. "That didn't happen. We got him out of here quietly, no one noticed anything. There's no gossip, and even if there was? So what. You have nothing to apologize for, or to be embarrassed about. Nothing. You hearing me?"

She nodded and pressed her lips together, but her eyes stayed downcast.

He slid forward a drop on the sofa and commanded gently, "Look at me, Julia."

Slowly, her eyes flickered up to his face.

"You're amazing, you know that?" he said. "Most women, they have some nutjob pinning them up against a wall, they freeze from fear, start to panic, cry, yell for help. Which, of course, is understandable. Not you, though." Admiration made him grin. "You were shouting in his face to back off. Standing up to him. Fighting him. You're a fucking fighter. I have the utmost respect for that. For you." He hoped the sincerity in his voice was getting through to her. She looked so drained. "*He* attacked *you,* Julia. You have *nothing* to be embarrassed about. I'm just grateful we were all here to help you. It's over. He's gone. Okay?"

Her eyes bore into his. He held her gaze, willing her to relax, to breathe easier. To feel his sincerity, to know he cared, to recognize . . .

Kelvin grunted at her. "Snap out of it, Jules. Speak up. This is where you say, 'Yes, Boss, thanks for being so understanding and for even giving a shit at all.' I *know* that's what you were about to say."

She shot him a withering look. He merely arched a brow in challenge.

"I was getting there. I'm scattered right now." She

sighed and couldn't help but laugh begrudgingly as she looked back at Dane. "Thank you, Dane. For being so understanding . . . for being here at all. You and Tonio were a sight for sore eyes, I'll tell you."

"You don't have to thank me. But you're welcome." Dane chuckled and shook his head as he shot a look at Kelvin. "You're bad."

"Very bad," Kelvin said, grinning proudly. "Very, very bad. Which is good, 'cause she needs me to kick her ass."

With a laugh and a nod, she acknowledged, "That's true. And I'm very glad you've been doing it for twenty years."

"You better now, Princess?" Kelvin's voice softened.

"Much," she said. Her eyes darted from one man to the other, and she cleared her throat. "So. When I was in the bathroom. You were talking about me, I gather?"

"What makes you think we were talkin' 'bout you?" Kelvin said dismissively. "You just think you're the center of the universe, don't you?"

"You mean I'm not?" she joked back.

"Hell no," Kelvin said. "*I* am." He flashed her a wide smile, and she returned it.

Dane laughed as he watched them and marveled at their bond. "You two are awesome."

There was a knock on the door, and Dane sprung up to answer it. "Ahh, at last. Thanks, guys. Bring 'em in." He moved aside as two employees brought in the wide trays. "Let's eat, and drink. Drink a *lot*. Especially you, Red."

After an hour, Kelvin got to his feet. "This has been fabulous, but it's where I take my leave, I think."

"You don't have to go," Dane said.

"C'mon, Kel," Julia said. "Stay, hang out."

"You two aren't gonna touch each other as long as I'm in this room," Kelvin said. He shot a look at Dane. "And that girl needs some lovin'. The kind I can't give her."

"Jesus, Kelvin," Julia hissed, her cheeks coloring.

"Oh honey," Kelvin laughed. "You think he doesn't know I know?"

Dane grinned as he leaned back against the couch cushions. He stared across the table at Julia, who looked pissed off. She sat on the opposite couch, glaring at her best friend. Dane had to laugh. "Don't be mad at him, Red. He loves you."

"That's the only thing keeping me from strangling him right now," she said.

Dane smiled at her and stretched out his legs. Three drinks, some food, and some casual talk had helped her relax and regroup. She was fine now, even a little buzzed. He was relieved.

Kelvin leaned down to hug her tightly. They held each other for a long minute, murmuring things to each other Dane couldn't hear. Then Kelvin giggled, dropped a kiss on the top of her head, and turned to Dane with his hand extended. "Good night, Boss."

Dane rose to stand and shook his hand firmly. "You're a good man, Kelvin."

"Well, thanks. Back atcha." He half-grinned and said, "Take good care of her tonight, okay?"

"Will do," Dane assured him.

Julia watched the exchange between Dane and Kelvin in silent wonder. Whatever they'd discussed while she was putting herself back together in the bathroom, they'd bonded over it. Over her. It was interesting.

"Call you in the morning," Kelvin said to her over his shoulder as he breezed out, closing the door behind him.

Still standing, Dane moved across to sit beside her with a smile. "Ahhh. Alone at last." He wrapped an arm around her shoulders and edged closer.

She studied him in silence. Kelvin suggested some of what he'd told Dane earlier, which was more or less everything. Knowing what he knew now, did Dane still want her? Would he still find her desirable, or had her past tarnished her in his eyes? She tried to read him. He seemed the same, but who knew?

His smile slipped a little and he pulled his arm back. "You want me to go too?"

"No," she said. "No. I just, um . . . everything Kelvin told you is true, unfortunately. And I just . . ." Her voice lowered to a whisper. "I'm a little embarrassed. And I feel exposed, and I don't like it."

"Shhh." He leaned in and took her hands in his. "Julia . . . I hate what your ex-husband did to you. There's so many things wrong with it all, I don't know where to start. I'm so sorry you were hurt like that. That Max took your son away from you, and that he was a vicious control freak. He sounds despicable. I mean . . . I can't imagine what all that was like for you."

He rubbed her hands between his and dipped his head down to make sure he caught her eyes. "But that's on him, not on you. Same with what happened with Liam. On him, not on you. And . . . I just admire that you're still standing, much less made a good life for yourself after such tremendous setbacks. You're an incredible woman." He stared harder, as if compelling her to listen. "But it's okay to admit sometimes that it was too much to bear. Or that sometimes, you're still hurting. Especially when bad flashes from your past pop up out of nowhere and blindside you."

Her heart stuttered in her chest and she forced herself not to tear up.

"Tell you what," he said quietly. "Why don't you let me take you up to my suite? Have some down time in the dark. I won't . . . no sex tonight." His brilliant blue eyes seemed to blaze with compassion. "Just . . . comfort. Let me hold you. Stay over. Fall asleep with me, and let me make you feel safe. For both our sakes." He caressed her cheek as he revealed his feelings, "Truth is, I need a bit of that too. I keep seeing you up against the wall, cornered by that bastard, and I just . . ." A muscle in his jaw twitched and his mouth curved in a frustrated snarl. "I wanted to hurt him. I wanted to make him bleed. So now . . . I need to hold you. Because I'm just so damn glad we got here before that prick could do anything to you."

Her stomach pitched and her breath stuck in her throat. Jesus, what was he saying, what was he doing to her? *No strings, dammit, no strings . . . don't make me fall for you, Dane. Please. I can't handle that. . . .*

Her throat had closed from emotion, and she couldn't speak. As strong as her fear was, her desire to be comforted by him was even stronger. She was so tired. So she sniffled, tried to swallow back the lump in her throat, and nodded.

"Good." Dane stood and pulled her up with him. "Let's go upstairs." He leaned in and brushed his lips against hers so gently, so sweetly, that her bones melted and she thought she'd break into pieces right there on the spot. She felt a little dizzy and her heart pounded in her chest.

"Stop being so nice to me," she said raggedly.

"No." He caressed her cheek. "Sorry. In fact, tonight, I might even be *extra* nice to you. Deal with it."

Damn him. Damn him and his tenderness and his beautiful eyes and his gentle voice and his seeming to actually *care*. "Dane . . ." she said, fighting to keep sharp. "When we get upstairs. I want sex. I need it." *I need you.* "Make me forget for a while."

He stared at her, eyes blazing. Then he reached up with both hands to hold her face, kissed her softly, and whispered, "Whatever you want."

"I want to forget tonight happened," she whispered back. She pulled one of his hands down and pushed it into the open front of her robe, cupping his hand around her bare breast. The warmth of his hand against her skin felt like heaven. "Okay? Make me forget."

He stroked his thumb across her nipple and she sighed with pleasure.

"I'll make you forget your damn name," he promised, and took her mouth with his.

When they got to his suite, she went straight into the bedroom, silently stripped off her clothes, and got into his bed. He watched her almost cautiously, with that same look he'd had in his eyes all night. Concern. He was worried about her. Which implied caring, feeling . . . that look in his eyes made her uneasy, and she couldn't ignore it. She needed to concentrate on something else. Think about him, his face, his body, his sexy ways . . . yes, that was something better to focus on.

Without speaking, he also undressed, not rushing. As her eyes adjusted to the dim light, she let her eyes travel over his body as he revealed it to her, part by mouthwatering part. His broad shoulders, the taut muscles in his arms . . . his chest, lightly covered in hair, and the way his waist narrowed down into sinfully carved hips . . . his solid thighs, long legs . . . and his gorgeous cock, thick and standing at the ready for her. The sight of his hard-on, the evidence that he still wanted her after such a tumultuous night, made all her nerve endings tingle. Good Lord, he was handsome, astonishingly so. She loved his beautiful face, and she adored his beautiful body. She could admit that. Hell, she couldn't *deny* that.

Would she ever not enjoy looking at him, would she ever not get that rush of breathless desire? Just look at him like, eh, yeah, whatever? She couldn't imagine such a day would ever exist. He was physically flawless as far as she could tell. It wasn't fair. And the visceral response she had to him, every time, was heady and intoxicating. Dane's body was like a drug, and she was becoming addicted.

Addicted. Like a drug . . .

A flash of Liam's face burst through her mind. His face so close to hers, the desperate look in his eyes, his rank cigarette breath as he tried to kiss her. "God, Julesie. You look so good. Just one kiss, c'mon . . ."

She shivered.

Sliding beneath the covers, Dane reached for her and pulled her close. "You sure you're okay?" he asked quietly. He brushed her hair back from her eyes with careful fingertips, then trailed them down her cheek.

His kindness lanced her. The feathery gentle touch, his velvety and soothing tone of voice, the unmistakable worry in his gaze . . . her heart shook.

"I'm fine," she insisted. "And I'll be better once you throw me around a little. Don't be gentle."

His eyes held hers. "Funny . . . I think gentle is what you need right now."

"No. No, it's not," she said, almost desperately. Her heart bounced around in her chest.

"I beg to differ."

When he looked at her, he seemed to look into her. Oh, God, she *did* want him to hold her, to caress her, to tenderly make love to her, to make the ugliness go away, to make the smell of Liam's breath against her face disappear, to make her insides stop shaking from seeing him again and all the soul-crushing memories it had brought rushing back.

Dane sensed that. He knew what she needed even when she fought against it, and that flat out scared her. If she succumbed to his tenderness tonight, as vulnerable as she felt right then, she'd do something stupid like fall for him, or feel something she didn't want to feel.

Suddenly she realized that she was already fighting that—that she *did* feel something for him. And it was something big and encompassing, something beyond lust, or mild interest, or friendship. What she felt was a lot like affection, and adoration, and connection.

He was the one she wanted to comfort her tonight. He was the one who made her heart speed up every time she saw him. Every time he looked into her eyes, or touched her. Every time he gave her a wiseass remark or tried to coax a smile out of her. Oh God. It was too late. She'd fallen for him, hard. How could she have not realized it before? When had she gotten so good at lying to herself? And what was she *doing*?

Panic seized her, washing over her like a tidal wave. Her heart rate skyrocketed and she pushed away from him. "This is a bad idea," she blurted out, and tried to get out of bed.

"Oh no, you don't." Dane grasped her arm and turned her back to him. Quick as lightning, he slid one arm around her to hold her in place, and the other hand came up to cup her chin, forcing her to look at him. "Julia. Please, stop. Just stop. You don't have to run. You're safe here."

Her breath was coming in short, hard puffs and her eyes were wide with alarm. She looked completely freaked out. It made his heart squeeze in his chest.

"Shhh. Take a breath," he said in his most soothing tone, caressing her cheek with his thumb. "It's okay now. You're okay."

"No, I'm not," she said, her voice shaky. "I should go."

His insides churned. Damn Liam for showing up there tonight. Damn the both of them, him and Max. God, what they'd done to her. But Dane's hand tightened on her face, forcing her to look into his eyes. "Look at me, Julia. I'm not Liam. I'm not Max. They were despicable scumbags. You were alone. And you were vulnerable, at their mercy. You're not anymore. You never will be again, not to them, not to anyone." He stroked her face. She was trembling now, and it made his heart shudder and twist. "You're strong now, Julia. You have total control over your life. You're not at anyone's mercy. You know that."

His voice softened, and so did his touch. "And honey, I swear to you, I'm nothing like them. I respect you. I *like* you. I don't want anything from you but your company. I have no agenda. *You are safe with me.*"

Her eyes were wide on his, and her breathing had calmed. Carefully, he leaned in and dropped a feather-light kiss on her lips. "Let me hold you. Tonight, let me love you. Gently."

Tears welled in her eyes and she sniffed them back. Damn, she was always fighting.

"You don't have to be strong tonight, not now," he whispered. With the utmost tenderness, he kissed her forehead, her temple, her mouth. "Even if it's just for tonight, trust in me. Let me soothe you, care for you. Let yourself take it. Okay?"

She sniffled again, but a lone tear spilled over and ran down her cheek. He kissed it away.

With a shuddering breath, her arms slipped around his neck and she held on to him as if her life depended on it. She trembled in his arms, her breath warm against his throat as she clung to him. He felt her tears wet his skin. "Okay," she whispered.

Something inside him broke. Fell away, melted. Something like light replaced it. Brightness, warm and powerful. And caring. And protectiveness. And need. And . . .

Holy Mother of God, he loved her. He'd never been in love in his life, but he knew then, without a doubt, that he loved her. Nothing else could describe the overwhelming waves of what was crashing through him. She was it. He loved her.

He pulled back just enough to look into her eyes. Shining with tears, she looked back at him with such raw need, such fragile openness . . . the emotions swelled within him as he was consumed with wanting to make her feel his love, to make her feel safe and adored.

And he knew if he told her that, she'd run for the hills and never look back.

So he decided to do the next best thing, the only thing he could. He'd show her.

Caressing her body with light, feather-gentle strokes, he trailed his lips across her skin. He covered her face in kisses, tiny sweet ones, on her cheeks, her nose, her eyelids, her mouth, until her tears stopped. Slowly he continued along her throat, her shoulders, her chest . . .

Her fingers tangled in his hair as he worked his way down her body, covering her in tender kisses until she tugged at him to come back up. Looking into her eyes, he hovered over her and stared as he brushed her hair back from her forehead. Their gazes locked and held. Emotion rushed through him, quieter now but still powerful. He thought the words in his head, trying them on for size since he'd never said them to a woman before. *I love you. Love you* . . .

"I could look at you all day long," he said.

"It's nighttime," she pointed out.

"I could look at you all night long."

"Back atcha."

With her sassy little quips, he knew she was trying to hold on to the last shreds of her defenses. "You're a very beautiful woman, Julia," he murmured. He kissed her, long and slow. "And you taste good too."

A surprised giggle burst from her. "Yeah?"

"Mm-hmm." He dipped his head to sip from her lips some more. "God, yeah . . ." He deepened the kiss and she opened to him. Their arms entwined, their tongues tangled. They held each other close and kissed for a long time. With his mouth, with his hands, with his body, he tried to make her feel cherished, secure, even revered. Gradually, he felt her body ease at last, the trembling replaced by surer movements.

After a long, dreamy while, the kisses intensified, and then her hips nudged his.

"Make love to me," she whispered.

His heart skipped a beat. She'd never said anything so soft and so sweet to him before. Not like that. In answer, he cradled her head in his hands and kissed her deeply, with all the tenderness he possessed.

Chapter Fourteen

Golden rays of sunlight peeked in through the curtains, too bright on Julia's face. She moaned softly and rolled away from the light—into a warm, naked body. Her eyes snapped open. Her heart stopped for a second, then took off with a gallop. She'd stayed the night. Jesus, she'd slept there. She *never* stayed the night.

But even in her shock, she had to pause. While asleep, Dane looked like a Greek god, damn him. His long, dark lashes made her want to touch them. His chiseled jaw was covered in dark stubble, only making him even sexier to her. And his curls, those curls she absolutely adored . . . all tousled, calling to her fingers to come and play. She stared at him.

The rise and fall of his chest hypnotized and lulled her as she considered him. No man had ever made love to her as sweetly and attentively as he had last night. Her insides wobbled just thinking about it. He'd blown apart the last of her preconceived notions with might. Dane Harrison was no flighty playboy. He wasn't a player at all. He was decent, kind, and caring.

Sensitive and sweet. He'd been so good to her last night.

Last night . . . oh God, Liam . . .

She squeezed her eyes shut against the memory. Liam showing up, out of nowhere, after all this time . . . and at her job, for God's sake. She couldn't have been more shocked. Then, when he grabbed her and shoved her back against the wall, scared. Then, she'd totally lost it. In front of Dane. First screaming and trying to claw at Liam, then breaking down into tears like a weak fool. And he'd stayed. He should've gone running, dumped her on the spot. They were only sleeping together, after all—he didn't have to do a thing for her, much less stick around for that kind of garbage.

But no. What had he done? Stood up for her. Let her cry and fall apart. Asked for details so he could better understand. Ordered drinks and food and made sure she was all right. Hung out with her and Kelvin like they were all old friends. Took her up to his suite to comfort her, make love to her, and done so with a tenderness beyond anything she could have imagined. And then he'd held her. Held her close, and tight, with gentle softness in his eyes, his voice, his touch . . .

He'd been so gentle, so tender, that her heart had just thawed, tumbled, and split wide open. She'd never felt so adored; not just in how he touched her, but in how he spoke to her, looked at her. She saw true feeling in his stunning blue eyes, she sensed it. It had taken her breath away. And that was it. He'd looked right into her eyes as he slid deep inside her, touched her heart with that intense but affectionate stare, and she'd thought, clear as day, *I love you.*

She'd fallen asleep in his arms, with him stroking

her back and whispering honeyed words . . . "I've got you," he told her over and over as she drifted off to sleep. "I've got you."

How could she *not* love him after last night? And it was awful, just awful. Admitting to herself she loved him was the worst thing she'd done in a long, long time.

Her heart thumped against her ribs as panic started welling in her chest. *He'll never love you,* her mind screamed at her. *Get out now, while you can, you fool. He'll never choose someone like you.*

She pulled away from Dane, careful not to wake him. Her stomach flipped nauseously as her demons continued to torment her. *Come ON, Julia, get real! You're from another world. He's crazy rich, younger than you, drop-dead gorgeous. And one day, he'll want a child of his own. You're too old to give him children. You're a good time, "Red". You're for now. He'll never love you back. He was so nice to you last night because he felt sorry for you.*

No strings, remember? He agreed to that because that's what he wants. Go. NOW.

Shaking inside, she untangled herself from his arms and slipped out of bed. Her clothes were in a pile on the floor where she'd left them the night before, and she tiptoed to them. With trembling hands, she turned her back to him to pull on her panties, then her bra.

"Where you goin'?" came Dane's gravelly voice.

She whirled to face him. He was awake and watching her. Busted. "I . . . have to go," she mumbled, reaching for the pale blue cotton tank dress on the floor. She pulled it over her head and down over her body with quick, terse movements.

"No you don't," he said, his tone changing. "Come here."

"No. I have to leave." She looked around wildly.

Where was her bag? What had she done with her shoes? Her heart started to pound.

"Julia. Look at me."

She shook her head and continued to search. All she heard was roaring in her ears, the blood pulsing.

He threw back the covers and went to her, grasping her shoulders. "Look at me."

She did, hoping he couldn't see the swirl of raging emotions she was fighting. Hoping he couldn't see what she felt for him, bubbling deep and trying to break through. But his eyes were intense, searching her face for clues.

"Tell me why you have to go," he said.

"I just do," she stammered. Her mind blanked, and the rising panic was making it harder for her to breathe. Her heart felt stuck in her chest, and she rubbed at her sternum in an effort to relieve the pressure.

"What the—why are you shaking? Hey. Everything's okay." His velvety voice, intending to soothe, only made it worse. God, when he used that tone with her, her bones melted to goop. She adored it. She adored him. Ugh, she was in too deep. This wasn't supposed to happen. She wasn't supposed to care about him, much less fall in love with him.

"I—I need air. I have to go. Let me go." She shoved away from him and walked out to the sitting room. Her bag was on the coffee table, and she spotted her shoes by the door.

"Don't leave like this," he said with an edge, following her. "Please. Talk to me."

She glanced at him. Still naked, he was glorious to look at. Did he have to look so damn good when she was fighting off a panic attack? Fighting the frightening things she felt for him? Trying to make a clean getaway? "There's nothing to talk about," she bit out. She grabbed her bag and slung the strap over her shoulder.

"I think we have lots to talk about," he said, his voice clipped. "But you're running away. Even after last night. I thought—"

She turned on him and almost shouted, "I don't do sleepovers. I don't stay the night."

"Well, maybe you don't usually have nights like we had last night," he offered. "A night like that would wipe anyone out. I passed out pretty quickly too."

She shook her head and started for the exit. In two seconds, he had cut around her and stood in front of the door.

"You're going to keep me here?" she said tightly.

"No, of course not. But Julia . . ." He stared down at her, his bright blue eyes flashing. "Don't run away," he ground out. "You're better than that."

"Apparently I'm not," Julia said in a low growl. "Stop telling me what to do, what to feel, who I am. Stop trying to manage my life. Let me out."

Dane's mind raced. He knew a fight or flight when he saw one, and she was running for her life. She was anxious, shaky, and looked both mad as hell and scared to death at the same time. He wasn't trying to manage her life, for God's sake. But something told him that if he let her walk out the door now, their . . . relationship, arrangement, whatever the hell it was, would be over. And he cared about her too much to let her go. More than he'd realized.

But if that's how it came across to her, that he was trying to manage her . . . or even *control* her . . . hell, he never meant for it to seem like that. He was just trying to help her. He was a guy, he fixed things. That's what guys did. Or so he thought . . . Jesus, he didn't know which end was up right then.

Her flushed face, wild eyes, tight words, and need to escape told him several things. She was embarrassed about what had happened the night before with Liam—hell, that was obvious. She probably figured he thought less of her for being involved with someone like that, and for some of the things that had happened in her past, things she'd begrudgingly revealed to him.

But he didn't. He only thought *more* of her, for fighting back and making a life for herself despite taking so many horrible hits. He thought he'd made that clear to her last night. He'd done everything he could to make her feel cherished, cared for, and safe. He thought she'd finally relaxed enough to let him be there for her.

But not in the light of day, he supposed. He saw the panic in her eyes, and it made him want to punch the wall. "Julia, I'm not trying to manage your life. I'm not trying to tell you what to do."

"Yes you are," she countered.

"I'm not, really. If it came across like that, I'm sorry. Please, just listen to me. Okay?"

She didn't say yes or no, but she didn't move. Her eyes slid to his shoulder so she didn't have to make eye contact.

"I know we said no strings, but . . ." He stared her down. "Now . . . maybe . . . I'm seeing some strings here. I mean, I'm sorry, but anyone would have compassion for another person who went through what you did last night."

She gasped in what seemed to him like horror. Her eyes widened, and she staggered back a step. "You felt sorry for me," she whispered raggedly. "That was a pity fuck last night. Oh *God*."

"No! No, it wasn't. Don't you dare say things like that." He grasped her arms, but made sure to do so gently. "Julia, that bastard shook you up. He brought back terrible memories. I learned things I probably never would have if it hadn't been for that situation. Now you're regretting it. I get that. But you don't have to run out of here like a bat out of hell, you're safe with me. We're . . . I want you . . ." *To give me—us—a chance.* "I want you to feel safe with me. I'm feeling superprotective of you this morning."

She stopped wiggling under his hands and looked at him.

"I'm not asking a thing of you," he said. "Just . . . that you don't leave like this." His eyes bore into hers. "Last night—I'm talking about the part between us, *here*—that was . . . beautiful. Don't end a night like that with a move like this."

Her eyes went a little round at that. She drew a shaky breath and stayed silent, but didn't move to leave. Maybe he was getting through to her.

He relaxed his grip and rubbed her arms. "Stay a while. I'll order up some breakfast. Eat something. Then, if you want to go, you can go. I just . . ." Looking down at her, he realized he had no idea what was going through her head. The kinder he was to her, the more she bucked him. Sad frustration permeated him and he sighed in resignation. He was a fool; he wasn't going to undo years of emotional damage with one gorgeous night. What was he thinking? He released her arms. "You know what? I'm not begging here. You want to go? Go. Leave if you need to. But just know I'd've liked it if you said good-bye before you did, instead of slipping out without a word."

"You're right," she whispered mournfully. "I'm sorry."

"Thanks." *I love you. Just let me in.* He wanted to say it so much, but swallowed it. "I'm going to order up breakfast. I'm ordering for two. Then I'm going to take a fast shower. When I come out, if you're still here, I'd like for you to join me. Your call."

She didn't say anything, but looked into his eyes and gave a timid nod.

He quickly kissed her forehead, then strode away from her, went to the bathroom, and shut the door. Exhaling a deep sigh, he leaned back against the wall and squeezed his eyes shut.

Goddammit, she was hurting. Her usual self-confidence had been shaken, her shields hit, and she looked plain scared. He hated that for her. He hated the pain in her eyes. The doubt, mistrust, panic, and worst of all, a hint of self-loathing. After the day on his yacht, he thought he'd broken through her walls a little bit. Enough for her to relax around him, anyway. Not anymore. Last night's trip down memory lane had messed her up, and she was scrambling to both protect herself and shut him out. It was sadly obvious to him, and seeing all that in his strong, bold redhead filled him with anguish. He ached for her.

As for her comment about his trying to manage her life, it still bothered him. That wasn't what he'd been trying to do. Was it? He scrubbed a hand over his face. Since seeing Liam looming over her, Dane had felt a resounding need to protect her that had walloped him and wouldn't stop. Someone had threatened her, and every prehistoric male stereotype he-man instinct had kicked right in.

And then in bed, last night . . . she had drunk in his affection like someone who'd been dying of thirst.

She'd let him be gentle, shower her with tenderness . . . and he'd realized then, when he looked deep into her beautiful eyes as he slipped inside her, that he was totally head over heels in love with her. And, if he wasn't mistaken, as their eyes had locked as he moved inside her, he'd seen a hint of deeper feelings in her eyes too.

Now, she was trying to push him away. Neither of them was feeling sassy and playful, as they usually were together. She was scared and scattered, he was confused and fiercely protective. It was new territory, and he didn't know the landscape. All he knew was he cared. No, one other thing he knew: the more he showed her that, the more she'd push him away.

He'd have to play it cool. Keep his feelings hidden, not scare her off. For now, that was how he'd have to handle it, until she was acting and feeling more like herself again. Then . . . then maybe he could find a way to tell her how he really felt. In the meantime: damage control.

With a grunt of frustration, he turned and used the hotel phone on the wall to order room service, then stepped into the shower.

Ten minutes later, dressed in clothes he kept at the suite, he ventured into the sitting room. To his relief and delight, Julia sat on the sofa, staring across the room out the window, appearing calm and untroubled. Just looking at her, his heart did a quiet flip in his chest. "Hey."

Her eyes flicked to him. "Hey."

"You stayed."

"I was hungry. You promised me breakfast."

She wanted to play it cool and easy? Fine by him. He didn't care. She'd *stayed*. "I'm hungry too. It should be here any—" A knock on the door cut him off, and he grinned. "Minute." He went to the door, let the employee wheel in a covered tray, thanked him and slipped him some cash, and turned to Julia. "I didn't know what you wanted, so I ordered a couple of things. Hope you like something here. If not, just fake it and eat it anyway."

Julia watched as he lifted the silver domes to reveal mounds of scrambled eggs, whole wheat toast, a plate of mouthwatering strips of bacon, and a big bowl of cut fruit salad. Her stomach actually growled. "Looks fantastic to me," she said.

"Good. Coffee?" Before she could answer, he lifted a small silver pot and poured the steaming ambrosia into the two empty ceramic cups.

She rose from the couch and stood at his side. The owner of the hotel was serving *her*. Dane kept showing her over and over, in tiny ways, that contrary to her initial belief, he was no typical spoiled rich boy. That he was his own man, and a really good, decent one at that.

A quick scan of the tray, and she plucked two sugar packets from the tiny holder. "You tipped that guy."

"Huh?" Dane blinked, thrown by her random comment.

"The bellhop who brought the food. You tipped him."

"Of course."

She gave him a long look. "You own this hotel. You sign his paychecks."

"So?" Dane stirred some cream into his coffee. "He did me a service. I tipped him. That's what you do."

"That's what most people do, yeah. *You* don't have to."

"Bullshit." Dane snorted and slanted her a look. "I'm not an asshole. You tip people, period."

She had to smile. "You're decent, Boss. Very decent."

"Glad you noticed." His eyes sobered as he looked at her. "And if you noticed, why were you trying to bolt before?"

She winced. "I'm sorry about that. I just . . ." Her voice trailed off and her cheeks felt hot.

He shook his head hard, to cut her off. "Know what? Not now. It's fine." He waved a hand as if to dismiss the topic. "I'm sorry I brought it up. I'm glad you chose to stay. End of story." He reached into the bowl and plucked out a cube of honeydew, and popped it into his mouth. "Mmmm, it's perfect. Here, try." Still chewing, he took another piece and held it up to her.

Unable to resist his easy charm, she opened her mouth and let him feed it to her. The melon was sweet and juicy. "God, yeah. Delicious."

He stared at her mouth for a second, then leaned in for a quick kiss. His tongue swept over her lips, licking, tasting. "Yup," he murmured against her mouth. "Delicious."

She smiled and shook her head. "Sweet talker."

"Sometimes. Is it working?" He grinned, then pushed the tray closer to the couch and fixed her a plate, heaping on the eggs and bacon, arguing with her when she said no to the toast. Then he fixed himself a plate and sat beside her.

As they ate, he told her about the upcoming business trip he had to take. He was leaving on Sunday afternoon, going to check in on his hotels in Chicago and Detroit, and would be gone for about two weeks. He talked about the trip, the things he had to do in the hotels, and she let her eyes roam over him.

She didn't usually tell him, but she loved looking at him, listening to him, being near him. He was so easy to be with. And so handsome right then in a simple, clean white polo shirt and navy slacks. She admired how he was so comfortable in his own skin, so laid back in the way he sat, talked, moved . . . he had that aura of ease and natural charm that made people gravitate to him, want to be around him. God knows she wanted to be around him. And she'd almost left for good only minutes before. She was an idiot. A scared idiot.

She was glad he'd called her on her bullshit. She was glad she'd apologized, steeled herself up, and stayed. She'd done it for him, sucking up her fears, because she'd caught the betrayed look in his eyes when she'd headed for the door. It had made her insides unravel. He looked so hurt. . . .

God, she was such a bitch sometimes! Why? Why still, when he'd always been good to her? He hadn't been good to her last night out of pity. He'd done it because he was a seriously decent man, and he'd wanted to comfort her. To treat her with care and make her feel better. Which, truthfully, had been exactly what she'd needed. She'd loved every moment of it. She'd gone over the edge of the cliff and fallen in love with him last night. How could she not?

She had to stop punishing Dane for the sins of other men. It wasn't fair. To either of them. What he'd said was true: he wasn't Max, or Liam, and it wasn't fair to put him on their shelf. He deserved better.

She needed to cut back on the sharp quips, the running for the door, the standoffishness, and start reciprocating his goodness. It was the least she could do for him. She'd never tell him she had true feelings for him, much less that she loved him, but she could at least show it by being sweeter. The words would never be necessary if she did that. And she wanted to do that. She *liked* him. She really did.

He smiled at something she said and her heart
sighed. That smile. Like sunlight. *He* was like sunlight, bright and radiant and hard to look at without
feeling you had to shield your eyes. He was smart,
fun, kind, charming, considerate, smoking hot . . .
oh, yeah, she was crazy about him. Head over heels in
love, God help her.

But she could bury her true feelings for him. She
could, and she *should.* All she could do was enjoy the
ride while it lasted. Savor it while they were still involved, for however long that would be. Until he got
bored, or decided she wasn't right for him after all.

The thought of it ending made her heart wince.

But one thing he'd been right about: she was a
better person than how she'd been acting. Time to
start being that to him. Right now.

"Thank you for breakfast," she said softly. "And
thank you for last night. For coming in and handling
Liam, so I didn't have to. And for treating me with
such kindness, both during and after, up here. I . . .
I needed that, I admit it. You were right. And . . . you
were wonderful. I won't forget it. Thank you for that,
Dane. All of it."

His fork stopped halfway to his mouth and he
stared at her. As he lowered his hand to his plate, the
corner of his mouth turned up and his eyes sparkled.
"You're very welcome. I'm glad I helped. I'm glad
that you let me."

"Me too."

They gazed into each other's eyes. The air around
them was charged, thick with unsaid words and
sparks and that pull that always seemed to envelop
them when they were close. She wanted to crawl into
his lap, but didn't move a muscle.

He smiled at her and took the last bite of his eggs.

"So, I'll text you while I'm away. Should be two weeks at the least, three weeks at the most."

"Okay."

"Tonio will keep an eye out. You know. Just don't worry about anything, all right?"

She blinked. "I hadn't even thought of that yet. Yeah, all right. Thanks for that."

His eyes had softened, but they suddenly lit with wickedness. "Two or three weeks without you in my bed? Damn. I'll have to sustain myself by imagining how steamy hot it'll be when I come back." His grin turned devilish. "Mmmm yeah."

She laughed. "Sounds good."

"It does, right?" He tossed her a wink and reached for his coffee. "Try not to miss me too much while I'm gone."

She snorted and said, "I think I'll manage."

But a tiny pang hit her heart as she realized she *would* miss him. Damn. God, she was in so much trouble. So much for no strings.

Chapter Fifteen

The hotel didn't feel the same without Dane in it. Not that he was there every minute of every day anyway, but he had been there for some amount of time every day since before the opening. Not to mention that since then, he'd been there almost every Thursday, Friday, and Saturday night without fail. And had spent almost all of them over the past month or so with her.

It had only been a few days since he'd left for Chicago, but Julia felt the absence. It was strange; as if a light had dimmed, or the party had died down and gotten boring. She felt the lack of him.

She missed him.

She hated to admit it, but she missed him a lot.

And when he texted her, which was once or twice a day, they'd fall into a short but charming text exchange that had her smiling, all warm and fuzzy inside. It was a bittersweet feeling. And the depth of her growing feelings for him scared her to death.

On that Sunday afternoon, she was glad for the distraction of a barbecue dinner at Randi's house. She and Stephen and their kids were like family to her. They were certainly the closest thing she had to it since cutting ties with her own years ago. Thirteen-year-old Mike and ten-year-old Allison even called her Aunt Julia; they were the nephew and niece of her heart.

She helped Randi cut up and prepare food, hung out with the kids, and enjoyed a few glasses of vodka and lemonade. Later in the day, when the kids went to their rooms to get on their computers, she went and sat under the shade of the large oak in the corner of the backyard. The air had cooled a bit, and she just enjoyed the scenery around her as she tried not to think about Dane. She'd been doing way too much of that lately.

Randi emerged from the back screen door, a glass in her hand identical to Julia's. She walked across the grass and plunked herself down beside her best friend. "Hello there."

"Hiya."

"It's nice here in the shade. You're a smart cookie."

Julia smiled and clinked her glass to Randi's. They sipped.

"Having a nice time, I hope?" Randi stretched her legs out in front of her and crossed them at the ankles.

"I am. Thanks for inviting me over."

"My pleasure. Glad you're enjoying." Randi took another sip. "So, now we can really talk. Any news on Liam?"

"No." Julia felt a tiny chill whisper inside her and she swatted it away. "He's stayed away."

"Thank God."

"Yeah. He knows he got off easy, I don't think he'd push it and come back."

"He better not. I'll kill him myself," Randi muttered.

"Such a good best friend. Always volunteering to help bury the body."

"Absolutely." She clinked her glass to Julia's, and they sipped again. They sat together in content silence. The tranquil sound of birdsong floated on the warm evening air.

"I'm in love with Dane," Julia blurted out.

Randi burst out laughing. "Gee, no kidding. *Duh*."

"I'm that obvious?" Julia moaned.

"To me, you are. But I know you very well." Randi shook her head with a pitying look. "You poor thing. You're a mess, aren't you?"

"God, I am," Julia groaned with self-loathing. "It's awful. I think about him all the time. How did that *happen?*"

"Aww, honey." Randi put her arm around Julia's shoulders and squeezed. "You have good taste, at least."

"Yeah, well, how do I know?" Julia asked. "My judgment in men has always been lousy. Worse than lousy. Stupid and destructive." Her head dropped onto Randi's shoulder. "What if I'm wrong again?"

"You're not," Randi assured her. "Not this time. Seriously."

Julia huffed out a sigh. "He's kind of wonderful, isn't he?"

"More than kind of, honey. My goodness. You hit the jackpot this time." She squeezed her friend again as she added, "But so has he. *You* are the jackpot, Jules."

"He saw Liam. He knows about all that. . . ." Julia lifted her head to rest it against the trunk of the tree and stare up at the sky. She sighed again, a soft sound of resignation this time. "He knows about Max, and even a little about Colin. I . . . I don't know what he thinks of me now. Like, deep down."

"What do you care what he thinks of all that?" Randi asked.

Julia felt her face flush and she murmured, "What if now he thinks I'm . . . you know, trashy? Or thinks less of me, or that I—"

"Stop." Randi's voice was firm and steely. "Stop that. Right now."

Julia went silent, but her stare stayed out to the distance.

"I don't know Dane," Randi conceded. "But from what I saw, and everything you've told me, I don't think he'd be so quick to judge you like that. The only one who's carrying a grudge against you is *you*." She put a hand on Julia's arm, meant to soothe. "Sometimes I think you've come so far from those awful days . . . and then I realize you still beat yourself up for the things that happened, possibly every day. That breaks my heart." She squeezed and peered harder at her friend. "When are you going to forgive yourself, honey?"

"Never," Julia whispered, and hot tears spilled from her eyes without warning. She closed her eyes and let them fall. "How can I? I lost my son. I wasn't his mother, all these years."

"You weren't *allowed* to be," Randi reminded her. "You didn't abandon Colin, he was taken from you. You tried to fight. Max was a cruel, heartless bastard for what he did. One day, hopefully, Colin will wake up and see that."

"He won't even talk to me," Julia croaked. The sorrow she usually kept buried deep was bubbling now and threatening to overtake her. She wiped the tears from her cheeks with aggravated swipes. "He won't answer my e-mails, texts, nothing. It's like I don't exist. It kills me, Randi. It kills me. It's so unfair." She started to sob. "He doesn't know me, and I don't know him. I don't know my own son."

Randi pulled Julia into her arms, stroking her hair as she cried. "I know. It's horrible. It's so beyond awful, there are no words. But he's out there, and you're both alive, and as long as that's true, I'll never give up hope that you'll find your way back to each other. And you shouldn't either."

"I don't give up hope," Julia wailed. "But it's been so long already. . . ."

"I know." Randi held her, rubbed her back. "But Julia . . . you've made a good life for yourself despite that. Despite everything. And maybe now, with Dane, you can have something more in your life. It could be something really good. Does he know how you feel about him?"

Julia shook her head. "No. God, no. Mister 'Play It Fast And Loose'? No way."

"I think there's a lot more to him than that," Randi said, almost scolding. "And I think you know that there is, or you wouldn't have fallen in love with him."

"I don't do well with love," Julia ground out. She sniffed back her tears and wiped her face with her hands. "My track record is crap. I pick assholes. I get blind and stupid. I make mistakes. I desperately don't want to do that again."

"Honey. Listen to me." Randi took Julia's shaking hands in hers. "You have to forgive yourself for your past mistakes, and you have to forgive those that hurt you for what they did to you, or you're never going to fully move on." She squeezed her fingers. "Don't you get that?"

Julia stared at her lifelong best friend and asked in a quivery voice, "How am I supposed to forgive myself for not being a mother to my only child?"

"Because it wasn't your choice," Randi said staunchly. "You didn't give him up, or walk away from him. Max took him from you and kept him away from you. That is *not your fault.*"

Julia closed her eyes and drew a long breath to try to steady herself.

"When's the last time you tried to contact Colin?"

"Little over a week ago. I e-mailed him. No response, of course."

"Keep doing that. Don't give up. He's getting older. Old enough to think for himself. You never know when he might turn around and answer you."

Julia stared at her. "You think so?"

"With everything in my soul," Randi swore.

Julia shrugged, but mulled over the words. It was a thin thread to grasp, but she would. Randi was right; as long as they were both alive, there was always a chance. . . .

"Now, about Dane." Randi picked up the glass Julia had set down on the grass and put it back in her hand. "Drink that and listen to me some more."

"Yes, Mom," Julia joked feebly, but sipped her drink as instructed.

"List all the bad points about being involved with Dane," Randi said.

Julia snorted. "Um . . . well, to start, he's younger than me."

"Not by a lot."

"He just turned thirty-six. I'm forty-one. He's going to want kids one day."

"How do you know that? Has he told you that?"

"No, but—"

"He's loaded. He can adopt if he wants kids that bad. I'm crossing that off the list." Randi nodded firmly, as if to nullify that point. "Next."

"The money . . ."

"What about it? Like, he's a spoiled rich brat?"

"No." Julia was quick to shake her head at that. "No, actually, the total opposite. He's generous and considerate. I mean, he tips his waitstaff. His bartender, he treats him like an equal. He's good to everyone. He's so not what I expected. . . ."

Randi squinted at her. "Then what is it?"

Julia chewed on her lip before admitting, "It's a little intimidating. The money, the power he has . . . it reminds me of Max, and his family, and all of that."

"Max and his family are disgusting vultures," Randi spat out. "He was never decent to begin with. Dane is. That's got nothing to do with money, that's character. They're totally different. So that's on you, not on Dane. Get over it. Next."

Julia couldn't help but smirk. "You're fierce today."

"You need it. Next."

The smirk broadened into a smile. "Okay. He doesn't do relationships."

"You don't either."

"True, but I—"

"Don't want to risk being rejected since you actually want one with Dane," Randi finished for her. "You're the ballsiest woman I know. Get your balls out of your pocket and use them. Tell him how you feel, take a chance, or you'll never know."

Julia laughed in spite of herself.

"Look," Randi said, smiling back, "you don't 'do' relationships. He doesn't either. But hey, you're changing your mind. How do you know if you told him how you feel, he wouldn't also? You never know unless you try. Gotta put yourself out there."

Julia's smile twisted. "Why would he—"

"Want a relationship with you? Gee, I have no

idea." Randi rolled her eyes. "I mean, you're only mind-blowingly smart and talented, funny and sharp, stunningly beautiful, and already likely giving him the best sex of his life. Why would he want *you?* Seriously, I have no idea why he keeps coming back for more. Which, hello, in case you haven't noticed, he has been."

Julia scowled. Randi was right, and she knew it.

"You get up onstage several times a week and sing in front of people," Randi said. "That takes guts. You screamed in the face of a junkie who had you up against the wall. That takes guts. You walked away from your family because they didn't treat you right. That took tremendous guts." Randi's gaze narrowed. "You're brave, Julia. If you're brave enough to do all those things, you've got to be brave enough to tell Dane how you feel."

Julia took a deep breath and exhaled it slowly. "You make good points."

"I do. But don't listen to me," Randi said flippantly. She shrugged and waved her hands in the air in a dismissive gesture. "No, you keep doing what you're doing. It seems to be working for you. Right?" She arched a brow as if to punctuate the point.

"Shut up," Julia grumbled, then pulled Randi in for a hug.

Randi embraced her and held. "Please forgive yourself," she whispered into her ear. "Trust yourself. And trust Dane, too. Give it a shot."

"It's so hard to do all that," Julia whispered back.

"I know. But you've got to do it anyway." Randi swept a hand over her best friend's back. "You deserve to be happy. And at peace. It's long past time to give yourself peace."

* * *

Dane yawned as he closed the hotel door behind him. It had been a long day for a Sunday, but a good one. He'd been all over the hotel in the morning, met an old business friend for lunch, gone back to the hotel for a workout in their gym, then met up with two old college friends for dinner and drinks. He always had a good time in Chicago.

But now he was tired and ready to fall into a deep sleep. A glance at his phone told him it was almost midnight. It felt later than it was. He needed to go to bed.

He moved through the suite to the bedroom. The king-size bed, covered in a champagne-colored duvet and pillows, called to him like a siren's song. He let his clothes drop to the floor, placed his cell phone on the nightstand, and slipped beneath the covers. The coolness of the high-quality sheets caressed his naked body and he sighed in ecstasy. He finally relaxed, letting his body melt into the mattress. The only thing that would make the moment better would have been if Julia was beside him, also naked, and wrapped around him. Thinking of her naked brought a smile to his face, and he closed his eyes.

His cell phone pinged with a text message. He was tired, but too curious not to check. Opening his eyes, he rolled over and reached for the phone.

The text was from Julia. Thinking of you. Just saying hello. Hope you had a good day.

Something inside him kindled and warmed. She never texted him first. He always did. This was a first. And to say she was thinking of him? Bonus.

I was just thinking of you too, he texted back with a smile. Great minds …

Were you really? she responded. Tell the truth, Charming.

I really was! he wrote. I'm naked in bed. It's lonely here. You can figure out the rest.

LOL, she texted. And also: delicious image. Thanks for that.

He smiled and wrote, Nice to know you were thinking of me, Red. He paused, but then added, I miss you.

She didn't answer right away, and his stomach did a tiny twist. He'd pushed it. Too emotional. Too—

I miss you too, she sent back.

Wow. He stared at the words, stunned and softly delighted. When I get back, he wrote, I'm not letting you out of my bed for days. This is your warning.

Will I be fed at some point? she texted.

He laughed out loud. If you're a good girl, I'll consider it.

Oh, I'm good. Very, very good. Especially when I'm bad ...

Don't I know it. By the way, I'm hard now. Thanks a lot.

My work here is done. I'll let you go ...

He barked out a laugh. Wicked, wicked woman! I'll get you back for this.

I look forward to it, she wrote. Good night, Dane.

Good night, Julia. Talk soon.

Trying to ignore his hard-on, he scrolled back to read the chat again, smiling at her words. Then he put the phone back on the nightstand, closed his eyes, and conjured up deliciously naughty images of Julia as he fell asleep.

Chapter Sixteen

Julia entered the bar and lounge on Thursday evening, grateful to see it wasn't too crowded yet. As much as she loved a full house for her show, when she first got there, she preferred a more low-key atmosphere. Fewer people equaled less noise.

"Hi, guys." She waved to Tonio and the other two bartenders as she passed.

"Hi, Julia," Tonio answered. "Oh, hey, wait."

She stopped at the end of the bar as he looked for something behind the register underneath. He came up holding a white envelope and handed it to her over the smooth mahogany that separated them. "This came for you."

Julia didn't recognize the handwriting, or the return address. It had been addressed to her care of the hotel. She frowned at it, but thanked Tonio before heading back to the dressing room.

"Kelvin?" she called out as she closed the door behind her. No response; he wasn't in the bathroom, so he wasn't there at all. She dropped her duffel bag by the makeup table, then sat on one of the couches to open the letter.

It was several pages long, and handwritten. She glanced at the end to see who it was from. *Liam.*

The room was air conditioned, but that had nothing to do with the massive chill that skittered over her as she read the contents.

Dear Julia,

Please don't throw this out before you read it. I'm sorry I upset you when I came to see you at the hotel. I was just desperate for you to listen to me, and you wouldn't. So . . . I got angry. I never should have pushed you against the wall, I'm very sorry for that. But you really need to hear what I was trying to tell you. I know you won't see me or talk to me, so I figured this was the only way.

Hope you're still reading.

I should have told you this years ago but, among other reasons that I didn't earlier, you had left Boston and I had no idea how to find you. I eventually did thanks to the Internet. I saw the press release about you online and thought if I tried to approach you there, you would handle it better with it being in a public place. Obviously I was wrong. I had no idea how much you still hated me, though I don't blame you and totally understand why.

I've done three stints in rehab since I saw you last. I'm finally clean. I haven't used in over a year. So know that I'm dead sober and straight as I tell you this.

You were set up, Julia. Your ex-husband set you up.

He found me. He knew I was using. He thought I was your type. He paid me a lot of money, sent me your way, and had a plan. For me to seduce you, get you to trust me, and then do what I did (showing up high in front of him and your son) to help his case

*in court and make you lose full custody. He totally
set you up, and it worked. I am so, so sorry for my
part in that.*

Julia's hands shook so hard she almost dropped
the pages. She swallowed back bile past the lump in
her throat, trying to breathe as her stomach roiled
and her face flushed. But she kept reading.

*What Max didn't count on was my falling for
you. You're an incredible woman, Julia. Beautiful,
smart, sexy, fun—how could I not fall for you for
real? I did. Hard. And when I did, I tried to back
out of the deal. I stayed clean, and I tried to back out
on Max. I wanted to be with you for real. I didn't
want to help that scumbag succeed in taking your
son from you. But . . . I was an addict, Julia.
A junkie who couldn't turn away a fix. When I
threatened to expose him, Max found out who my
dealer was and had him pay me a visit. My dealer
had a "gift" for me. Max even paid for the drugs,
and said he would as long as I stuck to the original
plan. I loved you, but I needed heroin more. I don't
think you can understand, unless you've been an
addict yourself. Just try to understand: I couldn't
turn it down. And I will be forever sorry for that,
and for the pain I caused you.*

*I was so ashamed, so full of self-loathing, that I
couldn't bear to see you, knowing what I'd done and
helped set in motion. I knew once you found out the
truth about me, you would never believe me anyway.
You wouldn't believe how I'd come to genuinely care
for you, to love you. I had. I did. So I figured the best
thing I could do for you, since I'd helped to wreck
your life, was just to disappear. The coward's way*

*out, perhaps. But you didn't need to see me again.
That's why I vanished.*

*Just so you know, I spun into a deep drug spiral
immediately after. I used for several years, unable to
get away from the self-loathing. I was homeless for a
spell. I overdosed twice. It wasn't until after the
second OD that I finally started to try to pull myself
out of the hole. It was the hardest thing I've ever
done, but I did it. I'm clean now, and I'm living
with my brother and I have a decent job. Don't
worry, I live in Rhode Island, nowhere near you.
I'm sure you don't care. But I wanted you to know
that although I helped wreck your life, I wrecked my
own in the process. I didn't come away from that
unscathed, not by a long shot. Karma's a bitch,
right?*

*I wanted you to know the truth. I'm sorry it's
taken this long for me to find you, and to tell you.
I don't even know if you'll believe any of this is true.
But it is. You have to know this. Max set you up.
It was all his doing. He is a master manipulator of
the worst kind. You used to tell me he was. You had
no idea how right you were.*

*It seems you've gotten your life back on track. I
couldn't believe how amazing you were when I saw
you sing at the hotel. You are a true star. And still so
beautiful. I wish you success and luck. I hope you've
found happiness with someone else and have
goodness in your life. I hope you were able to still see
your son and forget about me.*

*I'm sure if you confront Max about this, he'll
deny it, of course. But everything I'm telling you is
the truth. I'll swear it on a stack of Bibles if you
want me to, Julia.*

You will never know how deeply sorry I am for hurting you. I won't ask for forgiveness, because I know I don't deserve it. But at least I know you finally heard this and know the truth, and that will have to suffice for me.

Liam

Julia dropped the letter, ran to the bathroom, and vomited violently into the toilet. When she finished, she burst into tears, the sobs tearing from her chest as she sank down onto the bathroom floor. Trembling, in a daze, in a flurry of sorrow and rage, she cried harder than she had since she'd lost her son in court. Her head spun at a hundred miles an hour as she tried to process Liam's words, and what they meant if they were true.

She didn't know how long she'd been lying there when there were warm hands on her arms, trying to lift her up.

"Julia." It was Dane. "Hey. Julia. Jesus, look at me, baby." He brushed her tangled hair away from her face to seek out her eyes. Staring down at her with open worry, he asked tersely, "What happened?"

"Please go away," she croaked between gasping sobs. She waved him off. "Leave me be."

"No way am I leaving you like this." He lifted her up to a sitting position. She felt like a rag doll, a puppet whose strings had been cut. "Can you stand?"

The tears wouldn't stop. Julia's mind was blank. She couldn't think, and she didn't care. She wanted to disappear.

* * *

Dane looked at her for a long moment, brows furrowed with concern. Whatever had happened, she was a total wreck. His insides coiled with worry. All he wanted to do was hold her, help her. . . .

Ignoring her request, he sat on the tiled floor with her. The small bathroom was narrow, but he managed to pull her into his arms. "I'm not leaving," he said against her hair as he stroked her back. "So just cry on me. I've got you."

She was too distraught to fight him. So she did what he said to do: she slumped in his embrace and cried brokenly onto his shoulder. He held her close, rubbed her back, said nothing, and let her cry. After a long while, her sobs began to ebb. Just when he was about to try to start her talking, he heard the dressing room door open and shut, and a few footsteps.

"What the hell?!" Kelvin looked down at them from the bathroom doorway.

"I don't know what happened," Dane told him. "I found her here, like this, about twenty minutes ago."

"Jesus Christ . . ." Sucking in a breath, Kelvin knelt down beside them. "Honey, what happened?"

"I . . . I can't," she managed. "I can't . . . perform . . ."

"Of course not," Dane said. "Kelvin, can you play all night without her? People get sick. Julia's sick tonight."

"Absolutely," Kelvin said. "Yeah, I'll play, don't worry." He reached out to caress Julia's hair. "Honey, please. You're scaring me. Did . . . someone hurt you?" He gasped as another thought occurred to him. "Liam didn't come back, did he?"

At that, she started to cry harder again. "Read the letter, Kel," she moaned.

"What letter?" Kelvin asked.

"On—on the couch," she sobbed.

"I'll go look," Kelvin said, rising to his feet. As he walked away, Dane's hands caressed her back, cradled her head, and didn't stop.

"Was it Liam?" Dane asked her. "Did he come back? Did he do this to you?"

"Kind of," she whispered.

Dane's blood rushed like molten lava, wondering how the hell that asshole had gotten past Tonio and security. When he got done with them . . .

Reading as he moved, Kelvin returned to the bathroom door with a few sheets of folded paper in his hands. As he read, his brows puckered at first. Dane watched as his face changed, morphing into a mask of horror. "Holy shit," he kept whispering as he read. "Holy fucking shit."

Dane was ready to jump out of his skin. "*What*? Tell me."

Kelvin held up a finger and kept reading. When he was done, he stared down at Julia, who had finally stopped crying and was down to sniffling. "I can't believe it," he breathed. "Do you believe him? Any of this?"

Julia nodded. She finally lifted her face from Dane's shoulder. Looking at her slammed Dane's chest like a physical blow. Mascara ringed her eyes, which were swollen and bloodshot. Her face was blotchy and wet with tears. It hurt his heart to see her this way.

"Why not?" she said to Kelvin, her voice raspy and rough from the crying jag. "It makes sense. He was an addict, he's clean now—he's working the program. You know, owning his mistakes, coming clean. Why else would he have come here at all? What would he have to gain?"

"Maybe he was hoping to get you back," Kelvin said. "Or, at least, back in bed."

"No." Julia shook her head hard. "No. From the minute he walked in that night, he said he had something important to tell me. He kept repeating it, over and over, but I didn't give him the chance to talk."

"If all he wanted to do was talk," Dane asked quietly, "why'd he have you up against the wall like that?"

"Because I pissed him off," Julia said. "He got frantic. I tried to leave, to walk out on him. He insisted I had to listen, so that was what he did to get me to stay."

"He's a douche bag," Kelvin seethed. "And I'm sorry, but I don't know if you should believe this."

Dane strove for calm as he said, "Would one of you please tell me what's going on here?"

Julia shifted off Dane's lap and tried to stand. Kelvin shot out a hand to help her rise. Dane got to his feet as well, and Kelvin handed him the letter as he pulled Julia out of the bathroom and over to the couch.

Dane watched them go, watched Kelvin put a protective arm around her and lower her to the couch, then grab the box of tissues and hand it to her. Then he started to read the letter.

When he was done, his heart was hammering against his ribs and he realized his teeth were clenched, his jaw was set so tightly. He leaned against the frame of the bathroom door and looked across the room at Julia. Jesus, what a story. He ached for her.

She was eerily silent now, sipping water from a bottle and staring off at nothing.

"I'm shot," she said quietly. "I have to go home."

"Are you sure about that?" Kelvin asked.

Dane crossed the room to sit on the coffee table to

face her. "Why don't you stay in my suite tonight? Just go upstairs and—"

"I need to be alone," she said. "I just . . . need to take this all in. Think."

Dane swallowed back the rejection. He knew she was a mess and let the sting go. "I'll get you your own room, then."

She shook her head. "I want to go *home*. I want to crawl into my own bed and be by myself, Dane."

A muscle jumped in his jaw, but he huffed out a shallow breath. *Don't manage my life* . . . her words from before echoed in his head. "Okay. I'll call you a car. You can't get on the trains like this. At least let me do that for you."

She finally nodded, and murmured, "That'd be great, actually. Thank you." Her head lifted and her eyes met his. She frowned in confusion, as if seeing him for the first time. "What are you doing here? I thought you weren't getting back until Saturday."

The corner of his mouth twisted ruefully. "I was done earlier than expected. I got back to New York a few hours ago. I wanted to surprise you."

She snorted. "Yeah. Well. Surprise." She twirled a finger in the air. "Woo hoo."

"Julia . . ." He took her hands in his, but she pulled them away.

"I appreciate what you both did here, I really do." She stood up and headed for the bathroom. "But I have to be alone right now. I'm sorry."

"You've got nothing to apologize for," Kelvin said.

Dane stared after her. She went to the bathroom sink and splashed water on her face.

"She's dying inside," Kelvin whispered sadly. "I'm going to kill them. Both of them. Max *and* Liam. My God . . ."

"It's unthinkable," Dane said. He kept his voice low. "When's the last time she saw her son?"

"Years," Kelvin said.

Dane was surprised. In his mind, he'd always thought Colin to be around ten or maybe twelve years old. But *years*? The kid had to be in his late teens. He'd never asked, and now wasn't the time. Julia needed comforting. Support. And Dane could already see she wasn't going to let him, or anyone, give it to her.

"You sure I can't get you a room?" he asked her.

"No thank you," she said. She ran her hands through her thick hair, pulling the tangled flames into a ponytail and securing it with an elastic band.

Dane's heart sank a little. He could feel her withdrawing from him. Only a few minutes before, she'd been clinging to him as if for her life as she cried. He'd held her close and tight and soothed her as best he could. Now, she barely would meet his eyes. Now, it was as if he was watching her put her armor back on, piece by piece. Swallowing hard, he exhaled long and slow, then pulled his phone out of his pocket and arranged for a car to take her home.

When he ended the call and put the phone back in his pocket, Kelvin got to his feet. Julia was still in the bathroom. "Can you stay with her, Boss? She's a little better now, and it's almost show time. I've got to get out there if you want me to—"

"Sure, I've got this. I'm here, you go. Thanks."

Kelvin looked down at him for a long beat. "You're a good man. But just so you know, when she gets upset, she withdraws. Goes inside herself, like a turtle. Needs to be alone to deal with things. It's not you."

"Thanks for the tip," Dane said. Somehow, knowing that still didn't make him feel any better. He wanted to hold her all night, make sure she felt safe, make sure she fell asleep in his arms and knew he was there for her. Turtle mode didn't work for him. But . . . right now, it wasn't about him. It was about her, and whatever she needed. He scrubbed a hand across the back of his neck.

"You, uh . . ." Kelvin gave a slow nod. "You were there for her tonight. Thanks for that."

"You don't have to thank me," Dane said.

He watched Kelvin go to the wardrobe closet and pull out one of his suits, then head to the bathroom. He and Julia exchanged a few words he couldn't hear, and Julia grasped her friend in a tight hug. Then she exited the bathroom and closed the door so Kelvin could change his clothes.

With a sigh, she went to the makeup table and sat down.

"Car'll be outside in ten minutes," Dane said to her back.

Finally, she met his eyes in the mirror. "Thank you for that."

"My pleasure."

She nodded absently, then said, "I'll be here tomorrow night. For work. I'll be fine, I'll do the show. I just can't now. I'm sorry."

"I know you can't. It's fine. We'll say you got food poisoning, whatever. You'll go on tomorrow." He stared at her, wanting to say something to comfort her and having no idea what. "That letter . . ."

"Please," she cut him off. "Not now. I'm so drained."

"I'm sure you are," he murmured. "I'm glad I found you."

She blushed and her eyes flickered away, down to her hands. She reached for her cosmetics bag.

"I wish you'd talk to me about it," he said quietly. "When you're ready."

She nodded but didn't say anything. She stared at herself in the mirror for a few seconds. Then she met his eyes again in the reflection and whispered, "I don't think I can see you for a while."

His heart plummeted. "What? Why not?"

"I just . . ." Her face flushed again. She shook her head and studied her nails. "I need space. I need to be alone for a while."

Dane stood and crossed the room in two long strides. He stood behind her, looked into the mirror, and said, "Don't do this."

Her eyes met his again. "I'm not right for you, Dane. We both know that."

"I know no such thing," he ground out. His mind spun as he tried to figure out her reasoning. "Why do you think you're not right for me?"

She only stared back at him in the mirror.

He gripped her shoulders and turned her around to face him. "I know you're hurting, and you want to be left alone. But I don't want to leave you alone to go crawl in a hole by yourself and get lost there."

"That's exactly what I need to do right now," she whispered hotly.

"I get that, but I just don't think—"

"I don't care what you think! This is what I need to do!" she cried. She shoved his hands from her shoulders and stood to face him. "Dammit, Dane, you don't always know what's best for me. Just back off!"

Kelvin burst out of the bathroom. "What's wrong?"

"Nothing," Dane said.

"Everything," Julia said. She grabbed her bag from the floor. "I have to go."

"Julia, wait—" Dane reached for her arm, but she shook off his hand. She left the room as quickly as she could. His heart thumped in his chest as his stomach roiled.

"What just happened?" Kelvin asked.

"I think she just dumped me," Dane answered, staring after her.

Chapter Seventeen

Julia stared across her bedroom, out the window, but not really seeing. Sunlight filtered in, streaming thick rays of bright morning gold into her room. The only sound was that of her air conditioner, humming from its perch in the other window. She curled up into a tighter ball beneath her pale yellow comforter and stared into the distance. As it had since she'd returned home, her body felt lifeless, but her mind kept spinning in endless circles.

She hadn't gotten out of bed since she'd hit it the night before, except to pee. She had no appetite. She had downed a few glasses of water, and that was it. Sleep had finally taken her around 3:00 A.M., but it had been a tortured, restless sleep. Since nine, she'd just been lying in bed, staring into space, thinking about everything. Going back down roads of memory she'd closed the gates to years ago.

It was all like something out of a bad movie, whether what Liam had written was true or not. It was mind-boggling. To think that Max would have gone to all that trouble, been so devious, underhanded, and scheming . . . not just to her, and to their son, but also to drag a heroin addict back under . . . Max was a true sociopath. And that was who had raised Colin all this time. It made her literally sick to think of that.

Colin. Her sweet boy. As an infant, they'd been inseparable. She had been his world, and vice versa. She'd always wondered what horrible, degrading lies Max had fed to their son to keep him so firmly away from her. Considering that broke her heart each time she wondered, and almost broke her spirit, even still. An innocent boy, used as a tool for a spoiled psycho of a man who wanted a trophy for his family. Who knew what kind of person Colin had become as a result?

And Liam. If everything he said was true, his life had been destroyed too. She had sympathy for him. She did. He'd been courageous to come and find her after all this time, and then to write that letter even after he'd been thrown out of the hotel. He hadn't had to tell her the truth. She never would have known, and he could have just gone on with his life. But he'd told her. And over the years, nearly killed himself to numb his self-loathing for his part in it. Yet another life wrecked by Max's hand.

Max. Damn him to hell. Thinking about him made her blood burn like volcanic lava. Max had to answer for his crimes somehow. She wished she had the power, the leverage, the evidence, anything . . . but she didn't, and she knew it. The feeling of powerlessness she'd suffered for so many years had returned and swallowed her whole. She couldn't get out of bed. She didn't even want to. If she hadn't promised Dane she'd show up for work that night, she likely would stay in bed for days.

Dane. She sighed for the hundredth time as she thought of him. How she'd been ready to let him in more. How they'd been growing closer, inch by inch, and how it scared her but thrilled her too. How she'd been planning, when he got back from his trip, to tell him how she felt. How she'd been . . . hopeful.

But not now. No way. He'd read that letter. He'd seen her in a ball on the bathroom floor. He'd held her as she cried and she'd needed that, needed him, more than she'd thought possible, but . . .

All those things combined—and the sad, pitying look on his face when he came to sit with her after reading the letter . . . she was horrified and humiliated. Now, to him, she must seem like not much fun anymore—and worse, weak and pathetic. A sniveling girl, not an empowered woman who stood on her own. A woman who'd been stupid enough to be set up . . . so she'd pushed him away last night. Shoved him away, before he had the chance to do it to her.

She didn't want to face him. Hell, she didn't want to face herself. That was the truth of it.

Her eyes slipped closed before the tears started again. She drifted in and out of sleep for a while, she wasn't really sure. A few hours, or a few minutes? The sunlight shifted position outside, and soon she knew it was past midday. She yanked the blanket up around her chin, then her mouth, almost concealing herself completely. She wished she could disappear, just vanish into thin air. The heartache was all-consuming.

The phone rang a few times. She ignored it. Finally, her stomach rumbled so hard that it hurt, and her hands and arms felt shaky from low blood sugar. She had to eat something. Slowly, she rose from bed, dismayed to realize she was light-headed from lack of food. Cursing herself for being an idiot, she dragged herself to the kitchen. She gulped down some orange juice straight from the carton to give her blood sugar a boost, then quickly made and ate a peanut butter and jelly sandwich. The phone rang again. She ignored it again.

Trying not to become consumed with hatred toward her ex-husband was the only thing that kept her from focusing all that hatred upon herself. Of course she was responsible for part of it; she'd made some bad choices. But Colin shouldn't have had to pay the price for that. Max was the one who had to pay for this horror show. And she had to reach Colin somehow; she had to do something.

As she put her plate in the sink, something started to bubble inside her, from a deep and dark place. She leaned against the counter and closed her eyes against it.

God, she hated him. She hated what that man had done to her life. To their son.

Red-hot rage seared through her like an electric current. But she stopped trying to swallow it, and finally welcomed it. Time to stop moping, get back up, and fight. When she was sad, she was paralyzed. When that ebbed and she got angry, she was revitalized. Now, she grew more than angry as she thought about it over and over, in different ways and scenarios. She was furious. She wanted to take an action, to strike back. But what could she do, really? "Think, Julia," she spat at herself. "Think!"

She started to pace her apartment, walking from room to room. When the urge hit her, she stopped in her tracks. She had nothing to lose.

She grabbed the cordless phone from the tiny table next to her couch, then went to comb through her old address book—still a paper book, with all the entries made in ink. Before she could think it through too much and possibly change her mind, she pounded in Max's phone number.

It rang once. Twice. Was it still a valid number? she suddenly wondered. She hadn't called his house in years. But on the third ring, a familiar male voice answered. "Hello?"

Her stomach twisted at the sound of his voice. "Max. It's Julia."

He paused for a second, then said, "What do you want?"

"A million things," she murmured. "But I wanted to tell you I just found out the truth. I know what you did."

He snorted. "Not too vague. Still a drama queen, nothing's changed. What the hell are you babbling about?"

"Liam told me everything," she said in a low voice, meant to cut like a blade.

Max was quiet for a long beat, then said, "You talking to that junkie again? After all these years? How wonderful. Was it a happy reunion?"

"There was no reunion," she ground out. She could feel her blood pounding at her temples. "He came to see me. To tell me what you did, because he's felt so guilty all this time for his part in it that he felt he had to. He told me how you set me up."

"You're talking nonsense," Max scoffed, but his voice wavered the tiniest bit.

"How you set me up," she repeated, with force this time. She felt her fire ignite and flame in her chest, and used that anger to spur her on. "How you paid him to work his way into my life so you could use him against me. How you paid for his drugs to keep him in line when he threatened to back out and tell me what you were up to. How you knowingly got him high and told him to come to my home that way so he could horrify our son. Our sweet, innocent, six-year-old son! He told me everything, Max, you filthy sociopathic bastard."

Silence floated over the line for a few seconds. Then, in a voice like the devil himself, Max snarled, "Prove it, you pathetic bitch."

"I will," she snapped back. "Believe me, I will. And then I'll find a way to get to Colin and expose you for the disgusting excuse for a human being that you are. He needs to know the truth. All of the truth, not just your twisted version of it. He needs to know just how deranged his father was, and apparently, still is."

"You stay away from him," Max warned. His voice was filled with fury now. He was done pretending. "You don't contact him, or I'll—"

"You'll what?" Julia laughed, a hollow, derisive sound. "You've already done the worst thing to me you could do. You took our son away from me, and kept him away from me, all these years." She knew she was almost shouting now, but she couldn't control herself. "I'll never get those years back! I have a son who doesn't know me. I have a son who I've always loved, and I might as well be dead to him, thanks to you and your manipulations. So don't you threaten me, Max. You don't scare me anymore." She forced herself to lock down her voice, sound more controlled. "If anyone should be scared now, it should be *you*. I'm not some powerless, naïve young girl anymore. I'm strong as can be, thanks to the hell you put me through. And now, one way or another, I'm going to make you pay for what you did."

"You listen to me, you goddamn slut," Max snarled ferociously. "You stay away from Colin, and you stay away from me. Liam's nothing but a lying junkie, and you're nothing but a tramp who lures men while you sing for your supper, one step shy of working the pole. I'm a pillar of the community. You're a trashy lounge act. No one will believe you. So if you try to stir this up—"

"Oh, I'll be more than stirring this up, Max. And people *will* believe me. Which is probably why you suddenly sound so . . . desperate." Julia tried to sound snide and calm, but her heart pounded wildly in her chest. "Consider this your only warning. When I bring this out, and prove what a disgusting, manipulative person you are to Colin—and the world—you'll be sorry you ever met me." She disconnected the call and stood there for a long moment, trying to catch her breath. Her words came back to her . . . and she laughed.

She had finally told him off. Her heart raced, her breathing came in short bursts, but . . . God, confronting that bastard had felt amazing! Empowering. She felt strong, like the woman she was now. The woman she'd worked so hard to become after all that misery. *That* woman was back on her feet.

Feeling energized, she went to take a shower and prepare for her trek into the city. She had a show to do that night, dammit.

As for Dane . . . she'd deal with Dane when she saw him. If he even wanted to see her at this point. After how she'd rebuffed him last night, she wouldn't blame him if he never wanted to talk to her again, much less them keep seeing each other. Maybe that would be for the best . . .

Her heart hissed at her. *No it wouldn't, idiot. You love him.*

She sighed as she stepped into the shower. She had no idea what he wanted now. Maybe she'd finally pushed him away hard enough that he'd stay away this time. The thought made her throat constrict and her chest tighten.

"Thanks for dinner," Tess said, smiling at her brother. "This was nice."

"My pleasure." Dane put a credit card inside the leather billfold and handed it to the waiter, who thanked him and walked away.

As soon as he did, Tess said flatly, "You're not yourself tonight." She stared across the table at him, scrutinizing without mercy. "What's wrong?"

"Nothing," Dane shrugged. Of course, he knew Tess knew. He'd been in a pissy mood all day. But he didn't want to get into why. Didn't want to talk about what had happened with Julia the night before. Or the fact that she'd been a total wreck, or the fact that he'd called her twice today and texted her and she hadn't returned any of his messages, or the fact that he couldn't stop thinking about her and it was making him crazy.

"I'm okay," he said.

Tess snorted. "No, you're not. All through dinner, I kept hoping you'd volunteer something, but you haven't. Talk to me."

He sighed and said, "I really don't want to talk about it, Tess. Please."

She narrowed her eyes at him, then switched gears. "Dinner was lovely. I'm glad you could meet me out. Now, let's go back to your hotel. I want to have a few drinks and see Julia's show tonight."

At the mention of Julia's name, he actually flinched. He tried to cover it by rising to his feet, but his sister knew him too well.

Standing along with him, Tess pounced. "You think

I didn't see that?" She leaned in and lowered her voice. "Talk to me, for Pete's sake. Did you two have a fight or something? You're obviously miserable, and it's obviously about her."

"Don't want to talk about it," he repeated. "Let it go, Tess. You want to see her sing, let's go. She goes on in less than an hour."

Tess sighed, but fixed him with a hard gaze and linked her arm through his. "Yes, I do. We're going to hear her sing, I'm going to buy you drinks, and I'm going to pry it out of you. Whatever it is."

"You can try," Dane smirked. "I'll take the drinks, though. Definitely that."

Forty-five minutes later, they were seated at a small table angled off the stage. The bar and lounge were packed with people happy to be out on a late August Friday night. Bouncy swing music played from the speakers in the bar, mingling with the sounds of talk and laughter. Dane and Tess soaked up the atmosphere, comfortable enough with each other not to have to make small talk, which he was grateful for. Even when their drinks arrived, which was his third of the night, he couldn't shake the tension that had gripped his insides since Julia had shaken off his hand the night before.

When the lounge's lights dimmed, an anticipatory hush fell over the small crowd. In the bar, the music switched off, leaving only the rumble of human sound, audible but not intrusive. Kelvin and Julia emerged from backstage to applause, and they both smiled in acknowledgment as they hit their marks.

Kelvin, as usual, wore a black suit and straight black tie over a crisp white button down. He preferred to keep it simple and wore the same outfit every night. Julia . . . damn, Dane couldn't take his eyes off her.

Smoking hot in a little black dress. Spaghetti straps over her pale exposed shoulders; he wanted to nibble on them. The neckline plunged to display her impressive cleavage, but not in a lewd way, and the fabric hugged her voluptuous curves until it stopped just below the knee. Sexy as hell, but with class. And just a bit of an edge . . . like captured fire. That was his woman.

His woman. He'd thought that as naturally as anything. She'd probably swear at him if she knew he thought of her that way. He studied her features, wondering how she was really doing. She seemed fine. No hint of her being a total wreck the night before. But she was a consummate professional, always; he admired and respected that.

"Thank you so much for coming out tonight," Julia said with a warm smile as her eyes skimmed over the audience. When she saw Dane, her face froze for a millisecond. He didn't know what to make of that. He looked right back at her, schooling his features into neutrality. Little shouts bounced around in his head. *Are you all right? What did you do all day? Why wouldn't you pick up the damn phone? You look gorgeous. I want to devour you. I've been worried about you. I want to strangle you for your stubbornness. I love you. Please don't shut me out.*

He wasn't even aware that Kelvin had started playing, but suddenly Julia was singing, and her gaze locked with his as the words flowed from her mouth.

"I need to go now, and you need to let me . . . I think it's time to go, my baby . . ."

Dane sat transfixed. The spotlight caught in her hair, bringing out glimmers of copper and gold in that fiery mane. Her voice was hypnotic, beautiful . . . and she was all but serenading him, hurling those lyrics his way as her soulful eyes pinned him. His breath came slowly; it was like the air had changed or time had slowed. All he could see was her, and all he wanted to do was hold her close.

But as he listened to the lyrics, filled with yearning and regret about how some things just can't be, his jaw and gut tightened. If the song was any indication, if it was aimed purposely at him . . . wasn't it?

As the song ended and the audience applauded, Julia's eyes held his for a meaningful beat, then slipped from his, back out to the crowd. He grabbed his drink and gulped back a hard swallow.

Tess put her hand on his arm. He turned his head to face her. His sister's big blue eyes were filled with sympathy.

"Don't look at me like that," he warned.

"She loves you," Tess said softly. "It's written all over her."

"Really? Because what I just saw was her singing me good-bye," he bit out.

Tess pressed her lips together, then sighed. "I don't care what she sang. I saw the way she looked at you. That is a woman in love if I ever saw one."

Dane's heart skipped a beat. It startled him, how much he wanted to believe his sister. She was rarely wrong when it came to reading him, but she didn't know Julia. "I don't think so," he grumbled.

Tess leaned in and whispered into his ear, "That's because you're so in love with her you can't see clearly. You can always read women! No one knows how to read women like you do. But you can't read *her*? There's a very good reason for that. No objectivity. You're emotionally invested, and that clouds what you see."

He scowled and pulled back, shaking his head.

"I'm not wrong," Tess said, and sipped her ice water with a bit of a smirk.

Dane felt . . . off-kilter. He wasn't easily thrown, rarely got confused like this—about anything. But least of all over a woman. He didn't like it one bit. He knocked back the rest of his scotch in two gulps, then raised his hand to catch a waitress's eye.

Julia sank back against the cushions of the sofa, exhaling deeply as she kicked off her shoes. When she'd first spotted Dane in the audience with his sister, her heart had stopped for a second. He was there. He wasn't just going away quietly, that's what his being there was messaging to her. But she looked at him, so handsome, so sure . . . and at his sister, so regal she almost seemed like royalty . . . and knew she'd never measure up.

She sighed. They were from different worlds. She'd been right to push him away. Before she loved him even more, before they could really hurt each other . . . oh God, she loved him. She really loved him. Just looking at him made her heart ache and throb and pound.

"Earth to Miss Thang," Kelvin said.

Julia blinked and looked up. Kelvin was standing over her, holding a large white plate. "Eat, missy." He set the ceramic platter covered with various kinds of cheese and crackers on the table, then sat beside her. "He came tonight."

"I saw," she said, shifting to reach for some food.

"He's here because he wants to see you," Kelvin said.

"Thank you, Captain Obvious."

"You gonna talk to him?"

She felt her face heat and mumbled, "Probably not," before jamming a round cracker into her mouth.

Kelvin shook his head, making his dreadlocks sway. "You're being stupid."

"Thanks."

"And unfair. And stubborn. And maybe even childish. And definitely selfish."

Julia glared at him. "Back off, Kel."

"Hell no." Kelvin met her eyes and didn't flinch. "I saw his face last night. He was in pain for your pain. He *cares* about you. This isn't just hot fun anymore, for either of you. He cares. You care."

Her mouth full, she shook her head violently.

"You can deny it all you want, but I know what I saw last night. You needed someone, and he was *there*. On his own, because he wanted to be." Kelvin speared her with a look, but softened his voice. "You push him away, you'll regret it for the rest of your life. Don't you have enough regrets already, sweetie?"

She wanted to shoot back a wiseass remark, but there was one problem. Kelvin was absolutely right. She grabbed another square cube of cheddar and popped it into her mouth, unable to meet his eyes.

"Okay," Kelvin sighed. "Tonight's lecture is over. You've been beat up enough this week. So I'm gonna let this go for now. But *only* for now. I'm onto you, woman." He made a *V* with his long fingers and aimed them at his own eyes, then hers. "I'm watching you. Too bad if ya don't like it."

At his exaggerated gesture, she couldn't help it— a giggle slipped out. She shook her head. "You're an ass."

"You're a bigger one."

"You're probably right."

There was a soft knock on the door, and the friends glanced at each other.

"Ms. Shay?" came a female voice. "It's Tess Harrison. I was wondering if I could talk to you for just a few minutes?"

Julia's eyes widened as she looked at Kelvin and whispered frantically, "Why does she want to talk to me?"

"Only one way to find out." He rose from the couch and went to open the door. "Hi. I'm Kelvin Jones."

"I know." Tess smiled and held out a hand. "I really enjoyed your playing tonight. What talent! You're fantastic. It's such a pleasure to meet you."

"Why thanks." He shook her hand and ushered her into the dressing room.

Julia was on her feet, trying to squelch the sudden unease threatening to close her throat. "Hello."

"Hi. I just wanted to . . . um . . ." Tess swept her long, impressive mane of dark curls back from her shoulders. She was dressed in a deep blue pantsuit and heels, and it hit Julia that she'd never realized how tall Tess was. She was looking up at her, like she had to with Kelvin or Dane. Tess's legs went up to her neck; with the shoes, she was probably six feet tall. "I know this is your break in between sets, and I don't want to take up your time. Just a few minutes?"

God, she was so polite, so refined. Julia almost felt like she should curtsy or something. But she nodded and said, "Of course."

"Why don't I let you two have some privacy?" Kelvin gave a little nod to Tess. "Lovely meeting you, Ms. Harrison."

"Please, call me Tess," she smiled. "Lovely meeting you, too."

Kelvin closed the door behind him, leaving the two women facing each other in silence. Julia wondered what Tess wanted to say. She had an uneasy feeling it wouldn't be anything good.

Chapter Eighteen

"I won't take up much of your time," Tess promised. "Can we sit?"

"Of course." Julia sat on one sofa, smoothing out her dress as Tess sat on the sofa across from her. The coffee table was something of a buffer between them.

Tess launched right in. "If my brother knew I was back here, he'd be really pissed. I told him I was going to the ladies' room. But I wanted to see you."

Julia worked to keep her features neutral, though her insides hummed with soft anxiety.

"First of all, I just have to say—you have an incredible voice," Tess said. "You're wonderful. Listening to you and watching you sing is such a pleasure."

"Thank you," Julia said.

"You own your audience," Tess continued. "You know how to work a room. Your presence is powerful, electric." Her bright blue eyes held Julia's. "But you know that. You're that good. That's why Dane hired you. Out of all the singers he saw, the only one he knew who had star quality was you."

Julia nodded, keeping quiet, waiting to see where Tess was going.

"I know you and he are together."

Julia simply nodded again. *He'd told her.*

"I hope that doesn't bother you," Tess added.

"Not at all," Julia said. "I know you and he are very close. It doesn't surprise me that he'd confide in you."

Tess nodded at that and crossed her impossibly long legs. "He's not just one of my big brothers, he's one of my best friends. I know him so well. Sometimes, better than he knows himself. For instance . . . I knew he had feelings for you even before he did."

Julia's heart skipped a beat.

"He does, you know. I mean, I don't know how you can't see it." Tess's gaze was both gentle yet unrelenting. "But I know a kindred soul when I see one, so I thought maybe you needed to hear that from an outside party."

Kindred soul? Julia's brows puckered. "I'm sorry, you just lost me."

"A woman who's been through hell." Tess's voice was quiet, but the words pelted like stones. "I've had my heart torn out and shredded. I've had my share of trust issues with men. I know someone who's strong on the outside because she *has* to be." Her gaze didn't waver. "I know that's forward, but tell me I'm wrong, and I'll go now."

Julia's mouth was dry. The regal, elegant Tess Harrison had had her heart shredded? Related to *her?* She cleared her throat and murmured, "You're not wrong."

Tess nodded slowly. "That's unfortunate. But I didn't think I was wrong." She cocked her head to study Julia, a familiar gesture—Dane often did the same thing. "I don't know what happened last night between you two, but Dane's way off his game tonight. He's upset. He's confused. He's hurting. You're not the only one."

Julia sucked in a breath. On the one hand, it was none of Tess's business. On the other, hearing this was more than interesting . . . it was . . . affirming, in a way.

"I'm not trying to interfere," Tess continued. "What goes on between you and Dane is not my business. I just . . ." She pursed her lips, searching for words. "I just want to help, and I don't know how."

Oh my God. Julia's insides liquefied. Tess wasn't there to berate her. She was being kind. "Why do you want to help me?" she managed.

"Don't you know?" Tess smiled softly. "Because my brother cares about you. And I care about him. So if you two need a third party to kind of . . . give you a push . . . I'm jumping in to do that. But I don't want to overstep. I'm sorry if I am." Tess blinked, and a quick laugh slipped out. "No, you know what? That's not true. I'm not sorry."

Julia couldn't help but laugh too. Warmth slid through her. "I like you."

"Oh, good." Tess's smile broadened, and Julia marveled at her. She was as stunningly gorgeous as her brother. Those Harrisons had some magic gene pool. "I guess all I'm trying to say is . . . his feelings for you are genuine. What he doesn't say, I can see as plain as day." Tess's mouth twisted for a second. "I know his reputation with women . . . I understand why you'd be doubtful . . . but I'm telling you, I've never seen him like this over a woman. He's *never* cared before. He cares about you. That means something. Hopefully, it means something to *you*, too."

Julia stared, hoping her outsides seemed cool and not as chaotic as her insides.

"Okay." Tess suddenly got to her feet. "I've interfered enough. I'm going now, before my darling brother thinks I fell into a toilet and sends a search party after me."

A surprised laugh burst from Julia as she stood.

Tess grinned, but said, "Will you think about what I said? Just consider it."

"Consider what?"

"That his feelings for you are real. And then, what you're going to do about that. If you're going to let him in . . ." Tess's gaze held. ". . . or let him go. Because if he loves you, and you don't love him, it's not fair for you to stay undecided and string him along. Let him in close, or end it. For both your sakes."

Julia froze, stunned speechless. Her skin prickled with a chill.

"Yeah, *that* was totally interfering," Tess muttered to herself. "Well. I'll see myself out. Thank you for listening to what I had to say." She gave a small smile. "For what it's worth, I hope it works out. You're the only woman I've ever seen keep him on his toes like this. It's good for him. *You're* good for him. And he'd be good for you, too. He's one of the best men I know." Turning away, she crossed the dressing room in a few long strides, closing the door behind her.

Julia sank to the sofa to think over everything Tess had dropped in her lap.

"Where were you?" Dane asked when Tess retook her seat beside him. "I was getting ready to send out a search party."

Tess laughed out loud, thinking of what she'd said to Julia only minutes before. Did she know her brother or what? "I'm fine."

"Good. Listen . . ." Dane scrubbed a hand over his face. "I'm drunk. I don't like to be drunk in my own hotel. And Julia won't talk to me tonight, that's pretty clear."

"Dane—"

"I know this is ungentlemanly of me, but I want to leave. Julia wants space, I'm going to respect that and give it to her. But I can't take looking at her up there. . . ." He shook his head and hissed out a frustrated sigh. "I'm spent. I'm sorry to abandon you, Tess, but I gotta get out of here."

Tess looked her brother over. Her heart winced for him; he was unhappy. And maybe it would be good to let Julia think over the things she'd said before facing Dane, especially if he was drunk and upset. "Let's go." She grabbed her clutch and stood.

"What?" Dane got to his feet. "You can stay, you were enjoying the show—"

"I was. But I caught one set. We don't need to stay for the second. It's after midnight, I'm tired. Let's go." She smiled for punctuation. "Come on."

With a grateful grin, he put his arm around her shoulders and they walked out of the lounge. He didn't look back.

Julia and Kelvin got back onstage to kick off their second set. She smiled brightly at the audience as they applauded and thanked them for staying, then glanced over to where Dane and Tess were sitting. The table was empty, and a waitress was clearing their empty glasses.

Julia's stomach dropped. A rush of wild emotion rose up in her throat and she swallowed it down. She didn't have even two seconds to let Dane's sudden departure or lack of good-bye affect her. She had a show to do. Later, in private, she'd let herself speculate what his leaving without a word to her meant.

On Saturday evening, Julia got to the hotel a half hour earlier than usual. Instead of entering through the bar as she always did, she went through the smoky glass doors at the main entrance and headed to the main reception desk.

"Hi, Julia," said Mina, the evening shift manager. "You need anything?"

"No, thanks," Julia smiled back. "I was just wondering if Mr. Harrison's been here at all today?"

Mina's brows scrunched. "I haven't seen him at all, but I came in at four. Let me check for you." She picked up the house phone and made a quick call. As she replaced it in the cradle, she shook her head. "No, he hasn't been in at all today. Do you want to leave a message of some kind? I'll make sure it gets to him."

"No, no, that's fine. It's nothing urgent. Thanks though." Julia walked away from the desk, through the magnificently stylish lobby toward the back, where the bar and lounge were. Her instincts were screaming at her that she'd screwed up, that he was giving her space not only because she'd asked for it, but because he wanted to. He hadn't called or texted since yesterday afternoon. The silence was deafening.

She pushed open the door to the bar and relished the dimmer lights, the cooler air, and the relative quiet. The bar didn't usually start really filling up until after seven. She'd been hoping to catch Dane and try to talk to him, but it looked like that wasn't going to happen. She entered her dressing room, dropped her bag on the floor by the vanity, and sat on the sofa. Then, with a heavy sigh, she lay down and stretched out. Closing her eyes, she tried to breathe deep, slow breaths and meditate to calm her jittery nerves.

She'd messed up and she knew it. Dane had held her as she cried in a heap on a bathroom floor, and she'd shown her gratitude by pushing him away? She had to break this pattern. It was destructive, and she wasn't only hurting herself, but Dane, too. She'd seen the flash in his eyes. When she'd rebuffed him, he looked pained. And that wasn't fair. She knew deep down that he genuinely cared about her. If she'd doubted it before, she couldn't after Thursday night. Not after he'd scraped her off the tiled floor and into his arms, holding her tight and whispering sweetness as he tried to soothe her . . . that wasn't an act. Those were all the actions of someone who cared.

Her eyes opened to stare up at the ceiling. The next time she saw Dane, she had to try to fix things, and to apologize. To just talk honestly to him. Not with flirtatious banter, not with the distraction of sex, but a scary, open discussion. She had to, before she lost him. And one of the only things she was sure of was that she didn't want to lose him. She just hoped it wasn't already too late.

Later that night, Dane entered the bar and lounge at five minutes to ten. He hadn't been able to stop thinking about Julia all day, but hadn't called or texted her. She wanted space, he'd give it to her. But he couldn't stay away.

He loved her too much.

He was tired of the games. The holding back, the push and pull. He loved her, and tonight, he'd tell her that. After trying to drink her away last night without success, then thinking about her all damn day, he couldn't see the point in not telling her anymore. Maybe it would change things for the better. Maybe she'd bolt. He wasn't sure. But he'd swallow his pride, take a deep breath, and just tell her how he felt. And also tell her that she had to stop pushing him away. And that he wanted to be with her, only her. That he'd never felt this way about anyone before.

After the show.

He sat at the bar, not taking a table in the lounge, keeping his distance so he wouldn't distract her. And, he could admit to himself, so he could watch her from afar, free to stare at her as much as he wanted.

Tonio came to his side and they shook hands. "How's it goin', Boss?"

"Going just fine. You, sir?"

"Same." Tonio waved over a bartender to take Dane's drink order.

"Sit with me," Dane said.

Tonio quirked a brow, but a pleased grin spread over his face. "Okay, but you know I don't drink on the job." He maneuvered his huge frame on the barstool next to him.

After the bartender moved away, Tonio asked in a teasing tone, "Why are you sitting back here tonight? Slumming?"

Dane laughed. "No one slums in my hotels."

Tonio laughed back. "True." He edged closer. "Just saying . . . that Liam never came back. Haven't seen him; no one has. Think he's gone for good."

Dane gave a nod of acknowledgment.

The bartender set a dark beer in front of Dane and a ginger ale in front of Tonio.

"Labor Day next weekend already," Tonio said after a swallow of soda. "Can you believe it? Where'd the summer go?"

"No idea," Dane replied. He picked up his beer and sipped. "I'll be gone most of September. Trips to my other hotels." He slanted his head bartender a look. "Keep an eye on her while I'm gone, okay?"

"You don't have to ask," Tonio said quietly. "Of course I will."

The sound of applause traveled back from the lounge area as Julia and Kelvin stepped onstage. Dane's insides warmed and his heart gave a little squeeze at the sight of her. Tonight she wore a strapless dark purple gown that displayed her creamy skin up top, but floated all the way down to her ankles. Her hair was up in some twisty bun, sleek and sophisticated. Dane had a flash of taking the pins out and running his fingers through all that soft, thick red hair as he kissed her. They hadn't slept together in a few weeks now; he missed her. He wanted her. His body tightened and jumped to life just looking at her. With a wry grin, he shook his head at himself. Even when he wanted to shake her for her stubbornness, he still longed for her. Amazing, the power she had over him. The pull he felt whenever he saw her. His woman. *His,* dammit.

Kelvin started to play, Julia started to sing, and Dane sat back and enjoyed it.

When the set was over, Dane decided to go talk to her on her break. He couldn't wait until after the second set. Just to ask if she'd see him after the whole show was over, so they'd have time to talk at length. He shifted off his stool and made his way through the crowd, trying to ignore the knot of tension in his chest.

She had to hear him out. He had to tell her how he felt. He couldn't hold it back anymore, and the more he'd thought about it all day, the more he'd realized he didn't want to. He wanted her to know he loved her . . . that he wanted to build something with her, that the no-strings rule had been broken and discarded long ago. That he cared. His heart thumped in his ribs as he approached the back of the lounge.

As he got to the hallway that led to the dressing room, most of the noise of the crowd became muffled. The quiet of the hallway was almost strange. But he'd only taken two steps when he saw a dark-haired man in a light blue button down and jeans standing in front of the dressing room door. Not doing anything . . . just standing there, staring at the door.

Alarms went off in Dane's head. Another admirer? Or another admirer intending to harm Julia, like Liam? With stealth, he moved to stand right behind the man and said in a hard tone, "Do you have business here?"

The man jumped in surprise and whirled around to face Dane. It wasn't a man; it was a very young man. A kid. Maybe twenty-one, if that. His eyes flew wide, as if caught doing something he shouldn't have. "I—well, not exactly." His voice wavered a bit. "I was— I wanted to talk to Julia Shay."

"Do you have an appointment with her?" Dane asked. He had two or three inches on the stranger, and stared him down with the steeliest glare he could muster.

"No."

"Then you need to make one. She doesn't receive surprise visits."

"How do you know?" the young man challenged.

Dane's jaw tightened. "Because I'm her boss. You can send her a message through me, if you like."

"I just wanted to talk to her," the guy said. "And I really do think she'd want to talk to me."

"You do, huh?" Dane eyed the kid. He could take him easily if he had to. "Does she even know you?"

The young man's expression turned strange. Something like discomfort swept across his features. "Yes . . . well . . . not exactly, but yes."

"I see." Dane didn't like it. Something was off. His gut was humming like crazy. "Tell you what. Leave me your information, and I'll make sure she gets it. And then you can leave."

"Since when is a boss so involved in his employee's personal life?" the young man asked with a surly edge.

"Since the safety of all my employees is my responsibility," Dane ground out. "Now give me your message, or leave. I don't want you bothering her, she still has another set to do."

The door to the dressing room opened and Kelvin stood there. "Thought I heard voices. What's going on?"

The younger man turned and tried to walk into the dressing room.

Quick as a flash, Dane grabbed him by the arms and slammed his back against the wall. "What do you think you're doing?" he shouted in his face. The young man struggled, but Dane was stronger. He locked one arm across the man's chest to hold him in place, slamming him again as he did so.

"Should I call security?" Kelvin asked, looking alarmed but ready to assist.

"Absolutely," Dane growled, not taking his eyes off the young man's face.

"I don't want to hurt her!" the man cried. "I just want to talk to her!"

"Heard that one before," Dane rumbled, holding him hard against the wall.

Julia appeared in the doorway. "What's going on?" she asked. Then she looked at the younger man and gasped loudly. Her features froze in shock. "No . . . it can't be."

"Mom?" the young man pleaded. "Mom, it's me. Get this guy off me!"

Dane froze. *Mom?*

"Dane, let him go!" Julia yelled. "That's my son!"

Dane looked into the kid's eyes, wide with fright. Hazel, with gold flecks. Christ, he had her eyes. He released him and took two steps back, trying to calm himself.

"What the hell were you doing?" Julia demanded of Dane.

"I thought I was protecting you," he snapped, unable to take his eyes off the young man. He'd thought her son was maybe in his late teens. This was a grown man. God, how young had she been when she'd had him? And what was he doing here now, after all this time? Did she know he was coming? Questions raced through Dane's mind, but when he looked at Julia, he saw incredulous fury. *Ah shit.*

She turned her back to him and faced her son. She looked at him for a long beat and murmured tremulously, "Colin? It's really you?"

"Yeah. It's me." He stared back at her. "You knew what I looked like. How?"

"Once in a while, I sneak peeks at your Facebook page to keep up on you," she blurted out. "I mean, I can't see details . . . but at least I can see some pictures . . ."

Dane's heart winced at the vulnerable note in her voice. He and Kelvin watched silently as she wrung her hands, obviously not knowing what to do. "Why are you here?" she asked. "I'm so happy to see you, but I'm just . . . I'm in shock, I'm sorry."

"I'm sure," Colin said, genuine regret in his tone. "You, uh . . . you called Dad yesterday."

"I did," she said, nodding. "He actually told you I called?"

"No . . ." Colin glanced at the two men not leaving Julia's side and swallowed hard before looking back to her. "He doesn't even know I'm here."

"Why? What happened?" Julia asked.

"When you called, it rang a few times but he wasn't picking up the phone, so I did. At the same time he did." Colin's face contorted with something between sadness and rage. "I didn't hang up when I realized it was you. I was curious. I wanted to know why you called him. And I heard the whole conversation. Everything, Mom. Everything you said."

Julia gasped and clapped her hands over her mouth.

"When Dad hung up, I confronted him," Colin said. "We had a huge fight . . . but he admitted parts of it were true. Enough for me to know what you'd said was more than likely the complete truth. And I started wondering what else Dad's lied to me about over the years, about you. You sounded so . . . and I just . . ." He raked his hands through his wavy reddish-brown hair. "I had to see you. You texted me and said maybe I should come see you sing some time. So I looked you up on the Internet and found you. I flew here this afternoon. I'm staying here, at the hotel."

"Oh wow," Kelvin murmured, leaning against the doorframe for support.

"You've been *here?*" Julia almost squeaked. "For hours?"

"Yeah. I went out, walked around, got some dinner. And I've been waiting for your show." Colin's mouth twisted in a combination of sheepishness and regret. His eyes bore into hers. "I wanted to talk to you. I have so many questions. . . ."

From behind her, Dane could see Julia's whole body was trembling. He reached out and gently placed his hands on her shoulders.

She shook them off and turned to him, her eyes wet with unshed tears. "You had him up against the wall?" Her accusatory tone felt like a slap. "Why didn't you just ask him who he was? He might have left, and I never would've seen him! My God, Dane, what were you thinking?"

Stunned, Dane blurted out, "After what happened with Liam, I wasn't taking any chances. I was trying to—"

"But you could have hurt him!" she said, wide-eyed.

"I wasn't trying to hurt him," Dane ground out. "I thought I was protecting you. Why aren't you hearing me?" His heart pounded as his blood surged. He grasped immediately that Julia was too emotional right then, that there'd be no reasoning with her. He wanted to be there for her, but clearly, she wasn't going to let him. Yet again.

Something snapped inside. The blood rushed red hot throughout his body. "Julia, I'm thrilled for you that your son's finally come to see you. But I didn't know who he was. I just saw some strange guy at your door, and I was trying to protect you. To *help* you.

And as usual, you're just defensive and shoving me away."

Her eyes went wide and she paled. She opened her mouth to speak, but he cut her off, holding up a hand in a harsh halting gesture. "You know what? You obviously don't want anything real from me, and I'm done trying to give it, only to be pushed off. You want me away from you? I'm gone. You finally got your way, Red. There you go. I'm done." Before he said anything else he regretted, Dane turned and stormed down the hallway, through the lounge, through the bar, and slammed open the doors, getting out of the hotel altogether.

He had no idea what had just happened. His head was spinning, his heart pounded against his ribs, and his blood roared in his ears. All he knew was he was angry and miserable. Hurt. Adrenaline streaming through him, he stepped into the street and hailed a taxi. He had to get the hell away from there.

Chapter Nineteen

Julia couldn't believe she was sitting on a sofa next to her son. That he was *there*. It was too much to fathom, she couldn't wrap her head around it. Even as they chatted briefly, she couldn't stop staring at him. He'd grown into a sweet, well-spoken, handsome young man. Her baby was a twenty-one-year-old man. It was surreal.

"I don't want to leave," she said with regret after ten minutes, "but I have to go back out and do the second set."

"I understand," Colin replied. He moved to stand.

"Would you stay?" she blurted out. "Please? Like, through the show?"

He smiled softly as he nodded. "Yeah, sure. I like hearing you sing. You're really good. I'm, like, in awe of you up there. Honestly. You're . . . impressive."

Julia's eyes burned with tears, and she sniffed them back. "Thank you so much."

"You're welcome."

They both got to their feet and stood awkwardly for a moment. She clasped her fingers in front of her to keep from reaching out and touching him.

"After the show," she said, "why don't you come back here, and we can sit and talk. I'll make sure there's some food, you can order whatever you like, and they'll bring it back here to us. We'll have privacy, and we can relax. Would that be okay?"

"That sounds good," he said.

"Oh, great," she said on a relieved gust of breath.

They looked at each other for a long beat.

"Can I hug you?" she asked in a small voice.

He looked startled for a second, then nodded and half-smiled. "Sure."

She moved in slowly and put her arms around him. The feel of her son in her arms made her heart swell and almost burst wide open. Her eyes slipped closed and she savored the moment. When she felt his arms come up and return her embrace, she couldn't stop the tears that slipped out. "I love you, Colin," she whispered. "I've always loved you, and I've missed you so much. Thank you for coming to see me. This means the world to me."

"I wish I'd known," he said into her hair. "I wish . . . I should've . . ."

She pulled back, sniffed hard to stem her tears, and held his face in her hands as she looked into his eyes. "No. Don't. None of this is your fault. We are going to talk, you'll ask me whatever you want, and I'll answer you honestly. I promise you that. If you're willing to listen, I'll tell you whatever you want to know. At least, from my side. Okay?"

He nodded, and his eyes looked wet too. "Yeah, Mom. Yeah. Okay."

Mom. Her heart ballooned again. She smiled at him, then released him and walked to the vanity table and mirror. "I've got about a minute to fix my face now. Please excuse me, I don't mean to be rude."

"You're not, not at all," Colin said. "I'll go back out front."

"Take a table closer to the stage," she said, looking at him in the reflection. "Or, don't. Sit wherever you want. Whatever makes you comfortable."

"All right." He gave her a small, crooked smile and moved toward the door. But he stopped and turned back to her. "Can I ask you one question now?"

She stopped cold, her mascara wand in her hand. "Yes, anything."

"Your boss . . ." Colin scowled, then shrugged. "He likes you, right? Like . . . you two are more than friends?"

Her breath stuck in her chest. But she managed to say in a calm tone, "Yes. Does that bother you?"

"No." He shrugged again. "It's not my business. I was just wondering . . . well, if you're . . . dating, or whatever . . . he was pretty pissed off when he left. Are you okay?"

Her heart grew about ten sizes as she gazed at her son. "I'm fine. Don't you worry about me. I'm made of steel."

He nodded and said, "Awesome. Okay . . . well . . . I'll see you out there."

"Great. Enjoy the second set," she said with a bright smile.

As soon as the door closed behind him, she drew a long, deep breath and exhaled it slowly. She dropped the mascara wand onto the table. Her hands were shaking so much, she didn't know how she was going to touch up her smudged eyes. Jesus. The surprise of a lifetime. Her son was there. They were going to talk after the show, hang out in her dressing room like two adult acquaintances would . . . it was truly unbelievable.

But Dane . . . she winced as she thought of him. *You want me away from you? I'm gone. You finally got your way, Red. There you go. I'm done.* She'd never seen him like that, so hurt and angry and fed up all at the same time. Oh God . . . she'd been thrown off balance, and taken it out on him. Not fair. Not good. He was gone. How was she ever going to fix things with him now?

When Tess pulled up to her house after midnight, she noticed some of the lights in her home were on. Her heart gave a jolt. She hadn't left on the lights in the house, or in the backyard. With her heart pounding, she cut the ignition and got out of the car.

Music was playing. Softly, but she could hear it, coming from the backyard.

A burglar wouldn't bother playing music while he ransacked the house. It had to be a friendly intruder. That realization had her breathing a little easier.

She could only think of three people who would show up at her house unannounced and make themselves at home. One was in England. One was at his own home; she knew this because she'd just spent a long, lovely evening at Charles's house, having dinner and watching a movie with him and his three children. That left the third brother. She hoped she was right as she walked around the back of the house, reaching into her bag for her pepper spray. Clutching it in her hand, she edged around the hedges, stealthy as a cat. She could hear the music better now. The Dave Matthews Band. She instantly relaxed. It was Dane, all right.

Straightening, she strolled around the garden and the pool to see a man in the shadows, sprawled over a lounge chair. One arm hung over the side, holding a glass bottle. The other hand held a glass.

"Breaking and entering?" she teased, trying for levity as she sat down beside him. She could smell the alcohol and wondered how many drinks he'd had. "That's a new one for you, isn't it?"

"S'not breaking and entering," he said, slurring his words just enough to let her know he was wasted already. "I have a key. You gave me a key, remember?" He waved the bottle in the air, gesticulating as he spoke. She saw now that it was his favorite brand of scotch, and it was half empty.

"You are shitfaced," she said.

"You are correct," he replied jauntily, rising his glass in a toast to her.

"What happened?" She sat back in her chair. "Wait, before you tell me—where's my dog?"

"She's *fine*," Dane said, waving the hand that held the glass. A bit of liquid sloshed over the rim and onto the cement. "She came out, had a pee, or a poop, or whate'er she does over in that bush she loves, and went back inside. I gave her a treat, and I think she's sleepin' now. She's quiet, so yeah, she's sleepin'."

"I'm going to go check on her," Tess said, rising. "I'll be right back. Don't go near the pool, you'll probably drown."

"I won't, Tesstastic," he said, crossing his glass over his heart with a mock somber nod and a boyish grin. "Promise."

She snorted and went into the house through the back sliding-glass doors.

Dane tipped his head back to look up at the night sky. He could make out a few stars, but knew he'd see a ton more if he turned out all the lights in Tess's yard and the house. From all around, the chirping of crickets was loud and sweet. Tess had once called the sound of them the "ultimate summer symphony", and that had always stayed with him. He listened to the symphony, looked out at the stars, took another sip of scotch, and ran the scene with Julia over in his head for the hundredth time.

He'd been too impatient, too short with her . . . damn, he rarely lost his temper like that. But he'd been totally on edge—not knowing who the kid was, being nervous for Julia's safety once again. His eyes slipped closed as he recalled the look on her face when she'd realized it was her son. How the color had drained from her cheeks and her eyes went wide. The mixture of disbelief and hope had been so tangible he could feel it, and it had lanced his heart. But when he'd reached out to her, she'd literally shaken him off. He was so damn tired of her pushing him away. He'd treated her well, showed her he cared . . . what would it take for her to see that and pull him *in* instead?

A rueful sigh streamed from his lips as he stared at the heavens. Slamming her long-lost son against a wall was certainly not the way to do it. That was clear. Shit.

The back door slid open and closed. Tess sat beside him again, a tall glass of water in each hand. She set them down on the small table between them. "Lookie here, big brother. Ice water. One for me, one for you. Unless you want to be in some big-time pain in the morning, I suggest you switch that scotch for this right now."

"I thought I was supposed to take care of you," he said with a wry half grin.

"I know you think that. It's cute." Tess leaned back to cross one long leg over the other. "But we're a team.

When I need you, you're there. When you need me . . ."
Her eyes held his. "I'm here. Talk to me, honey.
Whatever's going on, just tell me. Unload."

Dane leaned back in his seat as he took one last sip
of his scotch. He leaned over and set the bottle and
nearly empty glass on the table, picking up the water.
He took a long swallow of that. Then, without any
real conscious thought, he started talking. He told
Tess everything. All about how he and Julia had a
"no-strings" rule that had somehow, sometime, fallen
by the wayside for him. He told her what he knew of
Julia's past, the run-in with Liam a few weeks before,
the letter she'd received from him, how she'd pushed
him away again, the surprise visit from her grown
son . . . all of it. Tess listened to everything in easy
silence, absorbing the information as she let him
ramble on. He was grateful for that, because once
he started talking, he couldn't seem to stop.

When he was done, she said softly, "Wow. Okay.
That's . . . a lot."

He nodded and let his head fall back to stare up at
the stars again.

"And I'm glad you got all that out, because you obviously needed to. But there's one crucial part you
didn't touch on. Honey . . . how do you *feel?*" She
reached across to touch her brother's forearm. "I
heard your frustration, I heard how concerned you
are for her. I heard the *events.* But talk about how you
feel, you big dopey man. Because you need to get that
out too."

Dane felt his jaw and chest tighten at the same
time. He set down his glass on the table and scrubbed
his hands over his face. "What do you want me to say?"

"Whatever it is that's got your stomach in knots,"
Tess said. "Whatever you're feeling or thinking.

Besides all that other stuff." She offered a small, sad twist of a smile. "Poor baby. You're so in love with her."

He hissed out a puff of air, a sound of self-loathing. "Am I that obvious?"

"To me, you are. I've never seen you like this over a woman before. They've never gotten close, or in deep enough. It's different this time. Julia's in there deep."

"Yes, she is," he ground out. He huffed out another aggravated sigh. "I had to go and fall for the only woman I've ever met who doesn't want any kind of serious relationship. Who doesn't want me too close. If at all. How's that for irony?"

"God's got a sense of humor sometimes, that's for sure," Tess said wryly. "Oh, honey. Just tell her."

"Tell her what?" Dane blinked at her in confusion.

"That you love her!" Tess almost laughed. "That you're crazy in love with her, that you're hurting for her because she's hurting, that you want to be there for her, and support her, and fight at her side, and help her heal. And whatever else is inside you that's eating away at you. Tell her. Hasn't it occurred to you that it may bridge this gap between you? If she knew how you felt about her?"

"If she knew how I felt about her," Dane said evenly, "she'd run like hell and never look back."

"You really think that?" Tess shook her head. "God, men are so dumb sometimes. No, *you* are so dumb sometimes."

"Thanks. Thanks a lot."

"Dane . . ." Tess paused, obviously searching for the right words. He waited patiently for his sister to speak. "From what you just told me, there are some very legitimate reasons that she's so untrusting, afraid to let you get close. She thought these men loved her, and believed in or depended on them. And they betrayed her in the worst ways. Right?"

He nodded glumly.

"And you just told me it happened to her not once, but twice. *And* she lost her son over it. I can't imagine what that was like for her. Any woman who had her child taken from her in that way . . . after having trusted the men she loved that way . . . I'm sure it wrecked her." Tess shook her head in sympathy.

Dane slumped back in his chair. "I've thought about that. I have."

"I'm sure you have."

"I *have*, Tess," he repeated emphatically. "Seriously. And when I start to really think about what she went through . . ." His eyes went to the stars again. "It kills me." In the darkness, the twinkling stars seemed to glitter right at him. "I love her. And . . . I don't know what to do with that."

"I'm sure you don't," Tess said gently. "So now here you are, when from the start your agreement was 'no strings'. Now you're trying to move beyond that. To push into new territory. I'm sure she's thrown by that. And . . . let's face it, Golden Boy, you have a bit of a reputation with women. If you want her to trust you, after what she's experienced, you need to show her she's the *only* woman for you."

"She is," Dane burst out. He blinked, realizing the force of his feelings as the words came flying out. "She's the only woman I want. I've never met anyone like her, and I don't think I ever will. She's . . . special. Unique. Incredible. Even when she makes me crazy, I still want to be with her."

"Then tell her that. Make her see that. Shock her with the depth of your love for her like you just did to me," Tess emphasized. "Then, hopefully, she'll stop testing you and she'll believe you."

It finally hit Dane like a physical blow, taking his breath away for a few seconds. Jesus, he *was* dumb. "So *that's* what she's doing? Testing me?"

"She may not be doing it consciously, but it sure seems that way to me," Tess said. "And added bonus—you're her boss. Knowing you like I do, I'd bet you don't ever throw that around, but it doesn't make it any less true."

He groaned as he realized the veracity of that.

"If she likes you even a little bit, the parallel between you and her ex probably hits too close to home. The power, the money . . . and it must scare her to death."

He shook his head at that. "Very little scares Julia Shay. She's strong as hell."

Tess gaped, openmouthed. "How can you be so obtuse?"

"*What?*"

"Just because someone is strong doesn't mean they don't get scared," she said incredulously. "I'd bet this bottle of scotch, if you hadn't already polished off most of it, that you scare the hell out of her. Because you're being nice, and you're obviously genuinely interested—which means you want more than her body and the sex." She shook her head. "Hey, you were easy to dismiss when you were just her bed buddy. But now, you seem to *like* her. To *care*." Tess saw Dane's mouth clamp shut as he listened, so she went on. "You actually tried to *be there* for her. You protected her. The night Liam came to see her, and the other night too. You're honorable. She's not used to men being honorable with her, much less caring about her and how she feels. She's convinced herself she doesn't want that, or need that. Which is bull. Everyone wants and needs to feel cared about." Tess smirked. "I'd bet she has no *idea* what to do with that, just as much as you don't."

He stared at his sister for another moment, then out to the distance. He heard the sweet song of the crickets, along with the pounding of his own heartbeat in his ears. With a heady rush, something washed over him, through him . . . it felt as if the blood slowed its flow through his body and his brain actually hummed. He knew the scotch was partly to blame, but it was mostly that all the words sank in and took hold. Tess was right, on all of it, as usual. It was an interesting insight: for two strong people, he and Julia were both scared shitless.

So what should they do about it? Were he and Julia at an impasse? Or was this salvageable? More than that, did he *want* to salvage it? "So . . . do I try again?" He looked at his sister. "Tell her what I want, ask her flat out what she wants, give her a chance, and see what she does with it? Because I've gotta admit . . ." His eyes flickered down to his shoes. "I'm really tired of being pushed away. Tonight, I just . . . I lost it. Because I don't want to do this anymore, this push-pull thing."

"If you love her, yeah, trying again sounds like a good idea." Tess squeezed his hand and murmured, "But if you don't, let her go. Walk away now, before either of you gets hurt any more than you already are. I hate seeing you like this, I can't lie."

Dane sighed, turning her words over in his head.

"She hasn't made it easy for you, has she," Tess surmised.

"Fuck no," he muttered with a caustic laugh.

"But truthfully? I think a part of you likes that. She keeps you on your toes. She makes you work for it. Women have always fallen at your feet, but not her. It's begrudging respect. Right?"

He couldn't hold back a small grin. "Maybe."

She squeezed his fingers before pulling her hand back. "Hey, I could be wrong about all of this. Maybe she keeps pushing you away because she just doesn't like you." A teasing glint shone in her eyes. "You think she doesn't like you?"

Dane recalled the look in Julia's eyes when he'd tended to her, gently and sweetly made love to her . . . the way the silence settled over them as he moved inside her and the air stilled and their eyes locked . . . "No. I know she likes me. Maybe a lot more than she counted on."

"Just like you," Tess pointed out. "You need to talk to her. Maybe in a few days. Give yourself time to cool off, and give her time to be with her son. Definitely when you're not reeking of scotch, like you are right now."

He laughed. "Am I?"

"Either that, or the Sound is made of whisky, and the breeze blowing off it is carrying that scent to my backyard." She rose to her feet. "Come on. Let's go inside. We've got to sober you up a little before you fall into bed."

He laughed, then wobbled to his feet. "Whoa. You're not wrong."

"When it comes to my family, I rarely am," she said. "Lucky for you guys."

He leaned down to kiss her forehead and murmur, "Thanks, Tess. Seriously. Thank you."

"Anytime." She slipped her arm through his and gave him half a hug. "At least if you were finally going to fall in love, you picked someone smart and sassy. She'll keep you in line if you end up together. I like that."

He gave a short laugh. "Glad you think so much of me."

"Shut up," she teased. "I think the world of you, and you know it."

"For which I'm eternally grateful." They took a few steps toward the house, but he stopped, frowning, hesitant. "Tess?"

"Yeah?"

"What if she doesn't . . . ." His voice trailed off and he stared into the distance. The symphony of crickets swelled beautifully around them. "I just wanna be with her, for Christ's sake."

"Tell her that." Tess rubbed his shoulder. "You, Dane Harrison, are a go-getter. When you really want something, you go after it with everything you've got. I love that about you. Not to mention you're easily the most charming and persuasive man I've ever known." She gave him a smile. "Just lay it all out there. And if she pushes you away again, you have your answer. Which, by the way, would make her a first-class moron. Who in their right mind would push away a guy like you?"

"Thanks, Tesstastic." He pulled her toward the house again. "More water. And I'm going to play with

Bubbles to amuse myself instead of passing out right away."

She laughed. "Sure, harass my dog for your drunken pleasure."

"At least Bubbles is always happy to have me around," he muttered.

Chapter Twenty

Julia stared at her reflection as she braided her damp hair. When it was done, she stretched her arms over her head and yawned lazily. A glance at the clock told her it was one-thirty already. She'd slept until one. She and Colin had stayed up until after four in the morning, talking, getting to know each other, and clearing the truths from the lies he'd been fed all his life. It had been an extraordinary experience. Sitting and talking with her grown son . . . wow, was he a sweet young man. Polite, articulate, quick-witted, and smart. Someone to be proud of. He had one semester of college left, then would graduate from Stanford University in December with an engineering degree. He'd asked her to be at his graduation, promising that Max could and would do nothing to stop it, or to get at her, if she wanted to be there. She'd been so touched that she'd started to cry as she blubbered how she wouldn't miss it for the world.

They'd both shed tears last night at various points. So much damage had been done. So many hurtful lies, time wasted, years stolen from them . . . the only thing that made it bearable was that they'd finally talked, and by the end of the night, they both wanted to have a relationship from then on. To start anew. To be in each other's lives. The thought of it made her heart swell. Even if he was an adult now, to get to be Colin's mother again . . . it was more than she'd ever dared to dream about.

But at the end of the night, she'd been too tired to make the trip back to Long Island, so she'd taken a room at the hotel, as Dane had often told her to do.

Dane. She sighed and sank onto the bed. The joy of reuniting with her son had been smudged by how she'd hurt him. She hadn't been able to stop thinking of him. Every time she recalled the flash of pain in his eyes before he'd stormed off, replayed the scorn in his words, her insides seized with shame and she cringed. He'd tried to protect her, had been worried for her, and what had she done to repay him for his kindness? Rebuffed him so coldly that she might as well have spit in his face.

What the hell had she been thinking? Her eyes shut as she shuddered for the hundredth time.

Truthfully, she hadn't been thinking. She'd been shocked, and thrown off balance, and a bit scared—scared that Dane's actions would drive Colin out of the hallway before she ever got a chance to talk to him. And she'd taken it out on Dane.

She had to fix things.

Her cell phone rang on the nightstand. She'd chosen the ringtone of Dave Brubeck's "Take Five" only for her favorite pianist, so she didn't have to check the caller ID. "Hey, Kel."

"Hey yourself," came Kelvin's voice. "Tell me everything."

She lay back on the bed and exhaled a deep breath before launching into the tale. "Colin stayed in my dressing room and talked with me until a quarter after four. He had a million questions. Long story short, for now? It's pretty much what I've always thought: Max filled his head with lies about me. Told him I was too focused on my singing career to be a mom, that I always put myself first, so Max had to sweep in and take care of him all by himself. Painted himself out to be a hero and me to be a selfish bitch who willingly abandoned her son."

Kelvin let fly a string of curses.

"I know. I know." Her stomach tensed just thinking about the vile things Colin had told her. "But hey, he's here. I think—I *hope*—he believed me as I dismantled Max's lies one by one. I didn't bash his father; I just told him the truth. And I told him he could ask you or Randi for verification on anything if he wanted to."

"Oh, I'd give that boy an earful," Kelvin promised.

Julia smiled. "I bet you would."

"My God, Jules . . . you must be so relieved. And *happy*."

She chewed on her lip for a moment as she considered. "I am. I really am. But there's a piece of me afraid to believe it, you know? That he's *here*. That he came to find me, that we're going to talk regularly now, that we can have a relationship of some kind. It's . . ." Her throat thickened and she swallowed back the lump there. "It's overwhelming. It's all I've ever wanted. A chance to explain what really happened, and have him believe me. And mostly, just to have him back in my life."

"And now you have it, sweetheart," Kelvin cooed. "God, I'm so happy for you. Let yourself believe it. It happened, it's real."

"He's probably still sleeping," Julia said. "I got a

room just down the hall from him. We're going to have dinner together at seven. Isn't that wonderful?"

"It is."

She smiled to herself with soft pride. "He's such a great guy, Kel."

"Of course. He's got your DNA in him. Max couldn't flush *all* of that out of him."

"I'm sure if there was a way, he would have." Julia sighed. "You know that Colin is afraid to go back there, to see him? He's half scared, half furious. He said half of him wants to get in his dad's face and blast him on all of it, and the other half just doesn't even want to deal with it. I don't blame him. Max can be scary when he's angry . . . Julia sighed again. "I don't know what to do."

"You need to step back and do nothing," Kelvin cautioned. "Let him choose what happens next, and don't try to sway him at all. You just let him know you're here, that you'll support him in whatever he decides to do, and then just step back. 'Cause my bet is Max will push, threaten, make demands, like he always did—and Colin will quickly see who really wants him to be his own man."

"Good call, Mr. Jones," Julia said. "I think you're right."

"Good. While you're actually listening to my pearls of wisdom, hear this," Kelvin warned. "I wasn't gonna get into it with you in front of your son, but *damn*, you were a raging bitch to Dane last night."

She cringed. "I know."

"He was just trying to—"

"I know."

"And you were so—"

"I know!"

"Well, what are you going to do about it?" Kelvin

demanded. "Julia Shay. When are you gonna get your head out of your ass and see that man's the best thing that's happened to you in a long time? That he cares about you? That man has *feelings* for you, Princess, and you stomped all over 'em in your stilettos."

"Stop," she moaned. "I know. You're right. I suck. Guilty as charged. This one's all on me. I really messed up, and I have to be the one to fix it."

"Agreed. So, then? What are you gonna do about it?" Kelvin repeated. "I don't hear a plan of action. All I hear is you flogging yourself, as usual. Knock it off."

"You are one fierce bitch today," Julia remarked.

"If I was *there,* I'd be smacking you upside your sorry red head," he replied. "You're lucky. Now. It's a Sunday afternoon. Where would our favorite hottie hotel owner be? At the beach? At his apartment?"

"I have no idea."

"You don't—have you even *tried* to call him or text him yet?"

She shifted uneasily on the mattress. "Well . . . no. I figured he's so mad at me, I should give him some space."

"That's the dumbest thing I've heard today!" Kelvin cried. "Dane doesn't need *space.* He needs to know you didn't mean to be so thick and that you're sorry and that you love him! Damn, woman, do I have to tell you everything?"

Even as her stomach churned, Julia couldn't help but chuckle softly.

"You need to talk to him face-to-face, Jules. You need to go find him in person and beg forgiveness. But." He paused. "Only if you want something real with him. Like, a relationship. Because he quite clearly wants more. If you don't, he just gave you the perfect out, and it'll be over. You can have a clean break, leave it as it is."

"No. I don't want it to be over. I . . ." She swallowed hard. Her mouth was dry and her heart started to thump in heavier beats. "Kel, I don't know if he'll still want me. And if he doesn't want to work it out, I couldn't take that rejection. Not now. Not after . . ." Her voice trailed off as she closed her eyes against new tears.

"Not after what?"

"Not after I realized how much I love him. I've just been scared. . . ." She wanted to kick herself. "I've been such an idiot," she whispered hotly. Her throat closed up and she sniffed back the tears that threatened. "Oh God, Kelvin . . . I want to be with him. I love him. I've been so afraid that he was going to hurt me, that I hurt him first. More than once. I didn't mean to. I didn't . . . God, I don't blame him for walking away."

"Then go get him back. While you still can."

"*If* I still can . . ." She drew a quivery breath, then reached for a tissue from the nightstand and dabbed at her eyes.

"Answer me something," Kelvin said. "You really want something with him?"

"I do," she said. "I love him. He's wonderful."

"Then you have to really go for it. Swallow your fears, swallow your pride, and go tell him everything you just told me."

"You make it sound so easy," she said.

"It is, Jules." It was Kelvin's turn to sigh. "Honey . . . you deserve him, you know. And you deserve to be happy. Don't you know that yet?"

"Yeah," she whispered back. "I didn't know that for a long time. And with him, not at first. I've been too busy beating myself up, and protecting myself, to see what was right in front of me. I know he cares about me. He might even have feelings for me too. That scared me a few weeks ago. Not anymore. I have to just get over it already. Dane's never been anything but good to me. He's never given me any reason to doubt him."

"Finally, she gets it." Kelvin sounded relieved. "Honey . . . I've had many boyfriends. They've been fabulous. We had fun, I adored them, the sex was great. . . ." He paused, and his voice got hushed as he said, "And I'd give anything for any of them to have ever looked at me the way I've seen Dane look at you. He's head over heels for you, Julia."

Her breath stuck in her chest. Stunned speechless, she stilled.

"I wouldn't encourage you to go after him if I thought he didn't give a shit about you," Kelvin said. "I know he does. And *I* know you love him, but you need to let *him* know that. Now. Yesterday. Last week."

A quick, wry laugh bubbled from her.

"Okay. Go find that man and lay it all out there. This is not the time for holding back, you hear me?"

"I hear you." Julia sat up on the bed. New resolve and determination flowed through her like liquid, something powerful, infusing her with strength and fire. "I don't want to lose him, Kelvin. I have to tell him."

"Thatta girl."

"But . . ." A last burst of fear skittered through her. "What if it's too late? What if I really blew it?"

"Only one way to find out."

"Right." Julia rose from the bed and went across the room to her tote bag. "Kelvin Jones, you are the best friend in the world."

"You're right. I am. Lucky you."

She laughed. "I love you."

"I love you too," he said. "I'm glad I could help. And I'm so glad it went well with Colin."

"Why don't you come out with us tomorrow night?" she asked.

"I'd love to, but I'll leave it at maybe," Kelvin said. "I'm hoping tomorrow night you're going to be too busy having dinner with Dane to have time for me."

She huffed out a nervous breath and said, "I'll get back to you on that."

She hadn't been able to reach Dane. He was unreachable. He was avoiding her.

Julia had sent three texts and left a voice mail, with no response. She couldn't even be mad at him for it. He'd never shut her out like this before. Whether he was doing it to give her a taste of her own medicine, or because he was really done with her, she didn't know. All she knew was she hated it.

At least dinner with Colin was delightful. They went to a small Italian restaurant on the Upper East Side that Dane had taken her to a few weeks earlier. The food was fantastic, and the moments of awkwardness between them were noticeably fewer than only the night before. They were already moving into a good groove, feeling more comfortable with each other. Conversation didn't stop; she asked him about his friends, high school, college, his courses there, did he have any girlfriends, where did he want to live when he finished school, a million things. He answered all her questions, seemingly fascinated and touched by her interest in him. She worked hard not to seem overeager and kept it cool.

When they got back to the hotel, they'd parted ways. She needed to go home. He decided he'd spend Monday walking around the city, maybe the Village, maybe go to a museum, whatever hit him when he woke up in the morning. They made plans to have dinner again on Monday night, with Kelvin and Randi joining them, and he'd decide how much longer he'd stay in New York.

It was like a dream come true.

But on the train ride home, the raw ache in her heart floated back to the surface. Dane wasn't answering her messages. Would he ever talk to her again, or was he just done with her? She'd gotten back to her apartment with her insides swirling, almost nauseous. Even after a fourth text to Dane around midnight, he clearly wasn't responding. Crawling into bed with her eyes stinging, she ruefully thought that maybe the universe wasn't done toying with her after all: she had gained back her son, but it seemed she'd lost the man she loved.

She barely slept all night. Early Monday morning, Julia opened her heavy eyes and stared at the ceiling again. Had she even slept at all? she wondered. Barely. Between the tossing and turning, her brain unable to stop grinding, and her heart just aching, who could sleep?

She wasn't even hungry. She lay in bed for a while and watched the sunlight filter through her curtains, making patterns on the walls, and felt absolutely miserable.

At eight o'clock, her phone pinged with a text message. Her heart stopped for a second and stuck in her chest before taking off with a wild gallop. *Please,* she thought. *Please be Dane.* She reached for the phone and looked.

It wasn't a text from Dane, but from his sister. Taken aback, Julia read:

> Hi Julia. It's Tess Harrison. I got your cell number from Dane's phone. He's here, at my house. He's been sulking since Saturday night. I think you two need to talk. If you want to make the trip, it's One Coventry Drive, in Kingston Point. Not the big mansion, the guesthouse behind it. He'll be here until Tuesday evening.
>
> Fix this, Julia. You can, if you really want to. Don't let his petulant silence fool you into thinking otherwise. He's hurt, but he wants you. Ball's in your court.

Julia flung back the covers and practically ran to the shower.

Dane had spent the first half of Sunday nursing a hangover, and the second half up at the main house, spending time with his whole family: Tess, his father, his brother, and his two nephews and niece. He loved Charles's kids because they were his blood, and really, they were kind of sweet, separately. One-on-one. But they were really young, and motherless, and Charles often spoiled them out of guilt. So, when all three children were together, they often turned quickly into a loud, bickering mess that resembled a minia-ture version of the Wall Street floor. At the end of the evening, by the time Dane had walked across the enormous back lawn to Tess's house, it had felt like a sweet escape.

He'd gotten Julia's messages. He wanted to answer them. He didn't mean to play games. But he just couldn't yet. He wasn't sure what to say, or how to go about it. Yes, Julia's texts and voice mail seemed heartfelt and appropriately repentant. But . . . he was still hurt. Tess had accused him of pouting. Maybe a little. He went to sleep much earlier than usual, intending to text Julia on Monday.

It was gorgeous out when he woke up, and he felt much better, all traces of the hangover finally gone. He realized with a rueful twist that he was thirty-six now—yes, closer to forty—and these days, the effects of a hangover hit him harder and longer than they used to. That made him cranky. So he went up to the main house to work out in the gym there, which he knew his father kept in top shape solely for Tess's benefit. After a good workout, he walked back across the grass, letting the sunshine bake dry the sweat on his skin as the salty scent of the Sound floated on the air.

Tess sat at her kitchen nook, Bubbles in her lap and her laptop open on the table.

"I wondered where you went," she said. "Good morning."

"Morning, Tesstastic." He took the orange juice from the fridge and poured himself a short glass. "I was in the gym. Now I'm going to jump in your pool for a while. Want to join me?"

"Thanks, but no. Maybe later. Getting through a bit of work here."

"Gotcha. What are your plans today?"

"Don't have any," she said. "Work's so slow this week, with Labor Day weekend a few days away, I won't go in. But I'll do something from here. Might get some reading done later on. You?"

"I'm going to be a lazy ass and hang out by your pool most of the day," he said, grinning. "Probably watch a movie later. I'm just going to relax. The world won't fall apart without me for a day. I'm playing the boss card. I'll go home tomorrow, like I'd planned. But hooky today."

"Good for you," she said. She ran her hand along her dog's soft white fur. "Hey, want to do a lobster dinner down by the water? Maybe over in Blue Harbor, or Port Richard?"

Blue Harbor. Julia. Dane sighed inwardly. He hadn't thought of her for all of two minutes, and boom, she was back on his mind. "Port Richard sounds good. I'm in."

He didn't bother to shower, just changed into the swimsuit that he kept in one of Tess's guest rooms and headed straight to the pool.

The sky was bright with sunshine as he swam a few laps. He leaned idly against the wall and watched a few white puffs of cloud creep slowly along the brilliant blue sky.

He missed her.

When he went back inside, he'd text her back. Or maybe call. Yeah . . . he'd call her. He missed the sound of her voice. He missed her throaty laugh, and the way her voice lilted with humor when she bantered with him, and the way her voice got rough and hot when she moaned beneath him. . . .

Emerging from the pool, he shook off some of the water before drying off with a colorful towel. He angled one of the deck chairs toward the sun and lay on it, closing his eyes as the sun beat down on his skin. When his swim trunks were dry, he'd go in and text Julia back. He didn't know what he'd say, but he'd answer her. . . .

He realized he must have drifted off when the sound of the sliding glass doors closing startled him. He heard soft footsteps slowly cross the deck. But he didn't bother opening his eyes as he said, "Please tell me you brought me a nice, cold drink, Tesstastic."

"No. I just brought me."

The voice made his eyes snap open, and he put a hand over them to shield them from the sun. It wasn't his sister standing there. It was Julia.

Chapter Twenty-One

Julia exited Tess's house through the sliding glass doors, not knowing what to expect, but prepared for anything. She was here for a single purpose, and she wouldn't go until she'd given it her all. So she ignored the way her heart pounded against her ribs as she made her way across the back deck. The wood, stained and polished, shone under the gleaming sun. Her favorite smells of summer assaulted her: salty air off the Sound, freshly cut grass, even the faintest hint of chlorine from the pool.

And there he was, sprawled out like a Greek god in repose. Dane was stretched out on a lounge chair with his eyes closed, apparently asleep. The tingles that usually started whenever she saw him wasted no time, shooting through her mercilessly as her eyes caressed him. He was so flipping gorgeous . . . the low burn in her belly reminded her it had been a few weeks since they'd had sex. It was amazing how her body instantly, undeniably responded to his. Just looking at his half-naked body made her ache. It took serious restraint to keep from straddling him to wake him up.

A wicked grin lifted her lips. She could do that. Take him by surprise.

No, this wasn't the time for sex. But the image flashed in her mind: straddling him, securing her legs around his hips, scraping her teeth along his chest before kissing her way up to his gorgeous mouth, and looking into those beautiful blue eyes as she whispered to him, "I love you. I'm sorry for being an ass. Please forgive me. Let's just love each other. . . ."

But he surprised her instead. Without opening his eyes or moving, he spoke. "Please tell me you brought me a nice, cold drink, Tesstastic."

She hesitated for a second. Then she drew a deep breath, gathered up her courage, and said quietly, "No. I just brought me."

His eyes flew open. He lifted a hand to shade them from the sun and stared at her. "Well. This is . . . unexpected."

"I bet."

"What are you doing here?"

"I came to see you, obviously," she said, fighting to keep her tone calm, not quivery. It was suddenly a little hard to breathe.

He stared for another long beat before asking, "How'd you even know I was here?"

"Heh. Well . . . a little birdie told me."

His lips curved. "A little birdie with long, dark curly hair who lives here, perhaps?"

"Perhaps." She smiled back, a small smile, as their eyes met. "I'd like to talk."

He nodded, then gestured toward the nearby table. It had a huge, blue-and-white striped umbrella sticking up from the middle that shaded it from the sun, and six cushioned white chairs around it. "Your skin will burn out here in five minutes flat. Why don't we move over there?"

"Thanks . . . that'd be better, you're right." She swallowed hard and drew another deep breath to try to calm her racing heart as they took seats across from each other at the white, rectangular table. The sound of Tess's dog barking resounded from within the house. Dane watched her as she smoothed her turquoise cotton sundress beneath her and got comfortable.

"Want a drink?" he asked. "I'm thinking a pitcher of ice water would so hit the spot right now."

"Agreed," she said. "But I want to say what I came to say."

His eyes held hers. "Before you lose your nerve?"

"While I still have your interest."

The corner of his mouth curved up wryly. "Julia, you always have my interest."

Something about the way he said that, and the way he looked at her, gave her hope. He didn't seem angry at her, and up until that moment, she hadn't been sure if he still was or not. Buoyed by that realization, she said, "I don't know where to start."

"Say whatever jumps to mind," he suggested.

"Okay," she said. "I love you."

The grin, meant to cajole and charm, slid off his face. His features stilled and his eyes went soft. "Well. That's a damn good start."

She bit down on her lip, then let out a short nervous chuckle.

"Say it again, please?" he murmured.

Her heart melted into a puddle of warmth and light. She locked her gaze with his and said, "I love you, Dane. I'm very much in love with you."

"Cool. I wouldn't want to be the only one." He grinned an easy, captivating grin.

She blinked at him. "What?"

"I'm totally in love with you, too," he said. "Like, crazy in love with you."

Her heart stuttered before taking off with a rapid pound. "You'd have to be, since I drive you crazy," she cracked.

He laughed, his eyes sparkling. "You do! You really do. But I love you anyway. So go on, I'm listening." He reached across the table and took her hand, intertwining their fingers. The touch sent a jolt of warmth rushing up her arm, and she stared at him. "I mean, you came all this way . . . I'm thinking you have more to say than that?"

He loved her too. He loved her, he was smiling at her, he was sitting there looking all delicious and holding her hand, waiting patiently to hear her out. God, this was better than she'd dared to hope. She'd told him she loved him, and the king of the ladies' men wasn't running away. In spite of everything, in fact, it seemed he was running toward her. Astonishment froze her brain for a minute, then the words came out in a rush.

"I'm so sorry for the other night," she said. "I was an unbelievable bitch, I was rude, I was thoughtless. But that's the thing, I wasn't thinking. I was in shock."

"I know."

"I had *no* idea Colin was coming. And then holy crap, there he is, standing there!"

"I figured that out."

"And then when I saw you roughing him up— which I totally understand why you were, but I didn't then—I was just so scared he'd leave. And I desperately didn't want him to leave."

Dane nodded. "I understand that."

"Thank you. But that didn't make it all right that I took out my fear on you. I treated you horribly, and hurt your feelings, and made you angry, and I'm very sorry."

He nodded again and gazed at her, his eyes filled with kindness. His long fingers caressed hers as he held them.

"I'm sorry for a lot of things," she went on. "I'm sorry for pushing you away every time you tried to care for me, support me . . . it's just that the truth is, that scared me too. Because I was falling for you, and I was trying really hard to deny that, and it's hard to deny that when you were being wonderful all the time, you know?"

"Hmm. Sorry about that. I'll try to suck more."

His mouth twitched and the corners of his eyes crinkled. He was suppressing a laugh, she could see it. It made her heart squeeze. God, she loved him. Until that second, she hadn't even realized how much. It was overwhelming.

"No, you don't have to suck. I love that you're wonderful." She fidgeted with the edge of the table. "I know you know this, but I'm going to say it. The men I loved, who let me down and hurt me . . . they left me damaged. Are you really okay with that?"

His voice pitched low and somber. "I know you were. I don't care."

"You sure? Because you could find a younger model with less baggage with a snap of your fingers."

His gaze held steady. "I like older women. Better in bed. Better at life."

"True. Unless they're broken like me."

"How does that song go? You're not broken, just bent." He leaned in and tightened his grip on her hand. "I know the feelings you have scare you. And maybe you *were* broken, or damaged. But you're not anymore. You're strong. So leave all that crap behind for good. And move forward . . . with me." His eyes burned into hers.

Her breath caught and she actually felt physically lighter. He really did want her too. "You've been so understanding. Patient. Kind. You've been what I needed. What I secretly wanted. And the fact that it came to me made me want to fight it, to run. But I don't want to fight it anymore." Her eyes stung with tears and she squeezed his hand in hers. "I don't want to run anymore. I love you. I want to be with you, and I want to . . . well . . ." She sniffled. "I don't know what you want. But I just needed to say I'm sorry for how I've been."

"Thank you for that apology," he said gently. The grin returned. "I know that was really hard for you. I'm humbled. Seriously."

"You know what?" She laughed at herself. "I can sing in front of a room of hundreds of people, but I've never been so nervous in my whole life as I was when I rang the doorbell here today."

His grin widened into a smile. "I'm not that scary, am I? I know Tess isn't."

"Of course not," she said with a snort. "But coming here today was. I had so much at stake. I really screwed up and I knew it. *You* didn't give me the okay to come here; Tess let me know you were here. I didn't know if you'd even talk to me. You haven't returned my texts. I took a chance. I had to try."

"I was licking my wounds," he admitted. "But that's done. I was going to call you today. Soon, actually. You saved me a call. A call to try to work things out."

"You were?" She blinked. "What were you going to say?"

"That I'm sorry I blew up at you like that. I was on edge, frustrated, and then when you were so . . ." He shook his head and interlaced his fingers with hers. His skin felt so warm, his touch assuring. "I acted like a petulant child. I was hurt that you were pushing me away again, and I lashed out. I'm sorry for that."

"Thank you," she murmured. "But I understand. I pushed you to that point."

"Doesn't make it okay. So I apologize." He squeezed her hand again, a reaffirmation of his words. "And I was going to make sure you were all right." His thumb caressed the back of her hand. "How'd it go with your son? Did you get to talk with him?"

Warmth and delight surged through her. "Yes, I did. He's wonderful. I'll tell you about that later, all right?"

"Sure. I'm happy for you, Julia. Really." He grinned, and his eyes relayed genuine affection. "Can't imagine what that was like for you . . . okay, tell me later. Back to us." His grin faded and his expression turned serious. "What do you want for us?"

"Well, I, um . . ." She licked her lips, suddenly dry from nerves. "I'd like to try it a different way now. Or, more accurately, with me not being so closed off and defensive. With us being together . . . like, a real couple. I mean . . . I love you, Dane. I don't want to be with anyone else, and I don't want you to be with anyone else." Her stomach twisted nauseously. "I'm rambling and groveling here. Say something, cut me off, will you?"

His grin almost a smirk, he stared into her eyes for a few long beats, then rose from his chair and moved around to her. "Stand up, please."

She did, meeting his intent gaze.

His hands came up to cup her face tenderly. "I love you, Julia. I'll never hurt you on purpose, but I'm human. What I can promise is that I'll never knowingly, willingly do anything to cause you pain. I'll never lie to you. We'll be partners. I'll treat you with the respect and affection you deserve, and nothing less."

A light breeze blew, shifting a lock of her hair into her eyes. He caught it quickly and brushed it back, tucking it behind her ear. "I know now I kind of pushed at you to trust me. Because I trusted you, and wanted that in return, and it frustrated me that I wasn't getting it. So I may have been a little . . . well, pushy." His lips twitched in a flash grin. "I'm used to getting what I want. And fixing things. Maybe even *managing* them, as you pointed out. But you pushed back. Rightfully so. You don't give me an extra inch. I love that. I *need* that." His gaze softened. "I need *you*, Julia."

Her breath hitched and stuck in her throat. If he hadn't been holding her, she might have actually swooned.

He smiled and continued in the same warm tone, "I want us to be together too. You're the only woman I want. I've never met anyone like you, and I never will. You're smart, talented, passionate . . . so beautiful, so damn sexy . . . and strong. And, on top of all that, you call me on my bullshit." His smile widened and his hands caressed her face again. "Julia, I think you're amazing. I want you all to myself. So, if you can find it in yourself to trust me, truly and completely? We really can have it all. I believe that."

Her heart fluttered wildly in her chest, but her hands lifted to hold his wrists as she met his direct gaze. "I do trust you completely, Dane. If I didn't, I wouldn't be here right now."

"I hoped so. . . ." His expression sobered as he caressed her cheeks with the pads of his thumbs. "That you trust me means the world to me. Because I know that's harder for you than anything else. I trust you, too, of course, but I always have."

She looked deeper into his eyes. Something cold and hard inside her melted away, and what replaced it felt something like freedom. She never thought tying herself to someone again could make her feel free, but it did. So she swallowed hard and said, "I want everything, with you."

His smile returned. "Then that's what we'll have. Everything. Together." He lowered his head, brushed his lips tenderly across hers, and whispered, "I love you."

Finally relaxing, she let herself lean into him and smiled back. "I love you too."

"That's all we need. So it's you and me now, Red. We got this." His smile was like the sun. "You and me. Everything."

"Everything," she whispered back, and pulled his head down to hers to kiss him deeply. As his arms banded around her and his mouth consumed hers, she felt as if her entire core filled with light. With hope, and optimism, and trust, and deep love.

Love the Harrisons?
Then keep reading for a
sneak peek at

SOMEONE LIKE YOU.

Available in May 2016
from Zebra Shout.

As the boys sucked down Capri Sun pouches and ate orange slices, Abby tried to explain to them what they needed to do to improve in the second half. She knew they wouldn't win; but at least if they weren't shut out by an embarrassing number of goals, it wouldn't be too hard on the kids' self-esteem or morale.

But it was like herding cats. Some of the boys listened, but the rest were either more interested in the peeled slices of orange they were eating or playing around with the ball behind her. Sure, eight-year-old boys had energy to spare. But she'd tried so hard to come up with strategies, good plays . . . this group just didn't respond. The basics were all she'd gotten from them. She didn't know if they weren't capable of achieving what she was trying to teach them, or if she was just the world's lousiest soccer coach.

I never should've signed up to do this, she thought miserably.

A few of the kids' parents came over, either to say hi to their sons or to ask her questions about upcoming practices. Feeling inadequate, she held her clipboard against her chest and tried to smile as she spoke.

Mr. Morales seemed to be more interested in something behind her than what she was saying to him. Hearing more noise from the boys, she turned around. A tall guy was approaching her team, dribbling what looked like one of their soccer balls between his feet. With nimble agility, he lobbed it back and forth, then started tapping it into the air, ankle to knee to other ankle to other knee and back again. He made it look effortless. Even she had to admit it was a cool trick. The boys all responded with excitement and awe, instantly crowding around him in a circle and demanding to know how he did that.

From behind her sunglasses, Abby did a quick once-over. The guy was about her age, with tousled dark hair, dark sunglasses, and a scruffy jaw that could have used a shave. He wore a sleeveless blue T-shirt that exposed nicely muscled arms . . . but along his right arm, there were more tattoos than unmarked skin. A few were on his left arm, too, but weren't almost a total sleeve like his right arm. Scanning the rest of his lean, taut frame, below his knee-length mesh shorts she spotted another large tattoo on his left calf, and something around his right ankle. Whoa . . . *great* legs. Muscles like rocks in his calves and what glimpses she could see of his upper legs as he maneuvered the ball.

Abby scowled. Okay, the guy had a fantastic body, and his tricks with the ball were impressive, but who was he, and what was he doing there? She'd let a grown man, a stranger, approach her kids. She could only imagine the complaints some parents might make, and she wouldn't blame them. Excusing herself to Mr. Morales, she quickly got closer to the group of her players gathered around the stranger. Now that she was a little closer, she realized he was really good looking. *Whoa.* But still, hot or not, he was a stranger. "Excuse me," she said sharply, in her best teacher voice. "Do you know one of these boys?"

The hot stranger stopped, catching the ball and holding it in his hand as he looked her way. "Um . . . no."

Something roiled in her chest. "Then what are you doing here?"

"I just—" he started to say.

"If you don't know any of these kids, it's highly inappropriate for you to just wander over here, don't you think?"

He froze, seeming to grasp what she meant. With a quick sweep of his free hand, he removed his sunglasses to earnestly stare at her with the bluest eyes she'd ever seen. "Wait, I'm no creep. Slow down."

"Then what—"

"They were fooling around and kicked this ball all the way across the field," he explained quickly. "I was just bringing it back to them."

Abby heard the murmurs of the three dads behind her and cringed. They must've been discussing her competence, or lack thereof, to keep their children safe. "Well," she said in a clipped tone, "thank you. You did. You can go now."

"Does he have to go, Coach?" young Andy asked.

"Yeah, Aunt Abby," Dylan piped up. "Didja see what he could do? He's awesome!"

"Look, boys," she said as sternly as she could, "we

don't know this man. You're not supposed to talk to strangers, right?"

The boys all looked at the ground and mumbled their assent.

Mr. Morales and Mr. Esdon, two of the kids' fathers, were suddenly standing on either side of her. She looked from one to the other and said, "I appreciate the show of support, but I'm sure he'll just leave on his own now."

"Don't go yet!" Mr. Morales said to the man. He and the stranger looked each other up and down. "I know this sounds crazy . . . but by any chance, are you Pierce Harrison? From the Spurs? Because you sure look like him, and you definitely know how to handle that ball."

The man's bright blue eyes narrowed, suddenly wary as he said, "And if I am?"

"Then can I have your autograph?" Mr. Morales smiled, obviously starstruck. "I mean, Premier League! You're a great player!"

"Thank you . . . but I'm not anymore," the man said flatly. He put his sunglasses back on. "I left the league, I'm out."

"Yeah, I know. But still. You were always great to watch." Mr. Morales stepped right up to him and held out a hand. The stranger finally cracked a grin and shook it.

At that, all the boys started to yelp and surrounded him like a pack of puppies.

"What the hell . . . ?" Abby said under her breath.

"It's okay, Ms. McCord," Mr. Esdon said. "The minute he took off his sunglasses, Diego recog-

nized him. Look." He held up his cell phone for
Abby to see.

She peered at it and felt a gut punch of embarrassment. There was the hot stranger, in a soccer
uniform—no, football, if he'd been in the Barclays
Premier League in England, as it said in the caption.
Looking back over at him, she suddenly saw he was
every bit the professional star athlete, flashing a
megawatt smile as the kids posed with him for pictures. The parents with their cell phones were like a
swarm of paparazzi. It had become an instant mob
scene.

"What the hell would a European soccer star be
doing in Edgewater?" she asked.

"Well," Mr. Esdon said, "he played in England, but
he's originally from here. He grew up on Long Island.
Maybe he came home for a family visit or something.
Excuse me, won't you?" He quickly made his way over
to the growing crowd of parents and kids. The other
team had noticed the commotion, and someone
must've spread the word that a famous soccer player
was there, because Pierce was at the center of a small
crowd now. The entire field had all but cleared to see
this man up close, except for a few random spectators
who didn't seem to care and stayed in their lawn
chairs.

Abby felt ridiculous. First she'd let a stranger near
her boys, then she'd spoken harshly to someone who
turned out to be famous, practically accusing him of
trying to kidnap or harm one of her players. Great.
Just great. She didn't follow English football, how the
hell should she have known? Huffing out a frustrated

sigh, she crossed her arms over her chest, hugging the clipboard to herself.

Pierce Harrison, huh? She'd have to google him when she got home. But while he was busy chatting amiably with the small crowd, signing autographs, and posing for pictures, she studied him. Her initial brief assessment had been right: he was drop-dead gorgeous. She wasn't blind, and she wasn't dead inside. Something about him made her insides buzz with heady warmth. But all those tattoos . . . his scruffy jaw . . . the way he glanced over at her twice with a hint of a smirk, brazen and cocky . . . he radiated danger. This was a very bad boy, she could tell.

So not her type.

Then again, did she even have a type anymore? Nowadays, she was practically a monk, by her own doing. Better off that way . . . don't get involved with men, and they can't lie to you and end up breaking your heart. . . .

With a disgusted grunt at her thoughts, she turned away, dropping her clipboard to the ground and reaching for her water bottle instead. A few sips in, someone tapped her on the shoulder. "Coach?"

Abby whirled around. It was Pierce Harrison. He was taller than she'd realized, had to be six-one or six-two. He had the tight, leanly muscled frame of a soccer player, which appealed to her more than she wanted to admit. His wavy dark hair was tousled, but gelled just a little in the front, begging to be played with. And that face . . . God, what beautiful features. Those *eyes*. Such a brilliant marine blue, fringed with long, dark lashes. Roman nose, great cheekbones, and a strong, square jaw covered in dark stubble, which only seemed to draw her gaze to his mouth.

His full, sensual lips widened in a smile that revealed what seemed to be perfect teeth.

Jesus, this guy was too gorgeous. He probably ate women like her for breakfast.

She found herself speechless.

Luckily for her, he spoke. "I wanted to apologize." He sounded sincere.

"For what?" she managed to say.

"For making you think even for a second that I was some pervert coming over here to snatch up one of your players." The smile turned a bit wicked. "That is what you thought, right?"

She felt herself blush furiously and cursed inside her head. "I . . . well, yeah. Wouldn't you? I mean—"

"Yeah, I would. I understand," he said, the grin not leaving his face. "You were right to be concerned and protective. If some strange guy approached my nephews, I'd get in his face too. You did the right thing."

"Oh." Why did this make her feel worse, not better? God, she felt off-kilter. She took off her sunglasses so she could look him in the eye in an attempt at seeming in control. Because she certainly didn't feel in control at the moment. Something about him, his very presence, was turning her into mush. Talk about natural sex appeal. Her girly parts were doing a primal dance she had rarely experienced. *Get a grip, Abby!*

"I'm also sorry I turned your soccer game into a circus." Pierce said, gesturing toward the people behind him with a flick of his chin. They were starting to disperse now, and the referee blew his whistle to signify the second half would start in a minute.

"That's not your fault. I'm sure you get that a lot."

"In England, yeah, sometimes. But not here."

"Well, these are soccer players, so . . . anyway. I'm sorry I didn't recognize you," she said. "I have to admit, I'm a little embarrassed."

"God, don't be. I'm not famous here. At least, I didn't think I was. That one dad who recognized me? Apparently watches European football religiously." Pierce's grin finally faltered. "I left the sport. Two months ago. I'm not playing anymore, I'm officially retired. I'm just here visiting my family, over in Kingston Point."

Abby nodded, but thought, *Kingston Point*? If he has family there, they must be disgustingly wealthy. Her whole house could fit into any one of those tremendous Kingston Point mansions. It may have been only ten minutes away from Edgewater, but it was a totally different world. "Well, I hope you enjoy your visit."

Looking like he wanted to explain further, he said, "I'm here—at the park, I mean—because I went for a run, then I'm meeting a friend here. His daughter plays at noon, the next game. He lives in Edgewater. Old friend from high school. Private school, not Edgewater High. So . . ." Pierce shrugged. "I don't know why I felt compelled to tell you that. I guess I just wanted to assure you I'm not some creepy guy."

"No explanations necessary. It's a public park. But I appreciate it." Abby wondered who the dad was and if she knew him, but before she could ask, the ref blew his whistle again. She shot a glance over at her team, who were now standing together, waiting for her directions. "I have to go, sorry. Nice to meet you."

"Nice to meet you, too." Pierce gazed down at her, and she felt a little jolt from the intensity of his stare. "What's your name, Coach? Didn't catch it."

"Abby." She held out her hand. "Abby McCord."

"A pleasure to meet you, Abby." His fingers wrapped around hers and the firm handshake sent a rush through her, a strange jolt of sensation. She pulled her hand back quickly, met his eyes one last time, then hurried over to her players.

As they ran onto the field to start the second half, Pierce Harrison didn't leave. She watched out of the corner of her eye as he strolled over to the far corner of the field and sat himself down on the grass. It seemed he was going to watch the rest of the game as he waited for his friend to arrive.

Abby didn't know why that both unnerved and delighted her, but it did.

Books by Bestselling Author
Fern Michaels

___The Jury	0-8217-7878-1	$6.99US/$9.99CAN
___Sweet Revenge	0-8217-7879-X	$6.99US/$9.99CAN
___Lethal Justice	0-8217-7880-3	$6.99US/$9.99CAN
___Free Fall	0-8217-7881-1	$6.99US/$9.99CAN
___Fool Me Once	0-8217-8071-9	$7.99US/$10.99CAN
___Vegas Rich	0-8217-8112-X	$7.99US/$10.99CAN
___Hide and Seek	1-4201-0184-6	$6.99US/$9.99CAN
___Hokus Pokus	1-4201-0185-4	$6.99US/$9.99CAN
___Fast Track	1-4201-0186-2	$6.99US/$9.99CAN
___Collateral Damage	1-4201-0187-0	$6.99US/$9.99CAN
___Final Justice	1-4201-0188-9	$6.99US/$9.99CAN
___Up Close and Personal	0-8217-7956-7	$7.99US/$9.99CAN
___Under the Radar	1-4201-0683-X	$6.99US/$9.99CAN
___Razor Sharp	1-4201-0684-8	$7.99US/$10.99CAN
___Yesterday	1-4201-1494-8	$5.99US/$6.99CAN
___Vanishing Act	1-4201-0685-6	$7.99US/$10.99CAN
___Sara's Song	1-4201-1493-X	$5.99US/$6.99CAN
___Deadly Deals	1-4201-0686-4	$7.99US/$10.99CAN
___Game Over	1-4201-0687-2	$7.99US/$10.99CAN
___Sins of Omission	1-4201-1153-1	$7.99US/$10.99CAN
___Sins of the Flesh	1-4201-1154-X	$7.99US/$10.99CAN
___Cross Roads	1-4201-1192-2	$7.99US/$10.99CAN

Available Wherever Books Are Sold!
Check out our website at **www.kensingtonbooks.com**

More by Bestselling Author
Hannah Howell